CINDERS OF YESTERDAY

LEGACY OF SHADOWS
BOOK 1

JEN KARNER

Robot Dinosaur Press
robotdinosaurpress.com

PRAISE FOR CINDERS OF YESTERDAY

"Smooth as a knife's edge and just as sharp, an exciting and sapphic new entry into the paranormal genre with plenty of scary monsters to go around."

— LADZ, AUTHOR OF THE FEALTY OF MONSTERS

"Hot-blooded and heartfelt, CINDERS OF YESTERDAY lives at the fiery crossroads where magic and trauma collide, the sweetest sapphic romance simmers, and a haunting villain awaits. An ass-kicking debut for fans of Supernatural and Buffy!"

— ANN FRAISTAT, BESTSELLING AUTHOR OF A PLACE FOR VANISHING AND WHAT WE HARVEST

"CINDERS OF YESTERDAY promises sapphic yearning, badass female characters, and epic battles all wrapped in a spooky packaging perfect for fans of Supernatural, Buffy, and Charmed and it delivers!"

— LOU WILHAM, AUTHOR OF THE HEX NEXT DOOR

CINDERS OF YESTERDAY is a riveting urban fantasy with paranormal elements, featuring a sapphic romance and two deeply sympathetic heroines living with magic (and its perils) on a daily basis. Karner doesn't shy away from using curses and dark magic as an apt metaphor for generational trauma—the layers of meaning are deep in this novel. The plot, world-building, and magic system are fully dimensional and immaculately rendered. I savored every word.

— PAULETTE KENNEDY, BESTSELLING AUTHOR OF
THE WITCH OF TIN MOUNTAIN, AND THE DEVIL
AND MRS.DAVENPORT

This book is for everyone who loves complicated, Dean Winchester-esque disaster lesbians and the investigative, monster-of-the-week parts of SUPERNATURAL—Destiel for sapphics. At times horrifying and heartwarming, CINDERS OF YESTERDAY is a crisp and sharply written paranormal fantasy with clever characters and visceral, precise action and imagery.

— MORGAN DANTE, AUTHOR OF PROVIDENCE
GIRLS

CINDERS OF YESTERDAY

JEN KARNER

Legacy of Shadows #1

Book Cover by Therese

Editing by Heather McCorkle

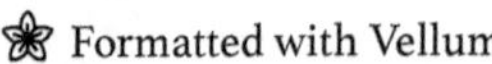 Formatted with Vellum

For everyone who thought they'd never survive.
You made it.

1

DANI

For some people, comfort came from a hot cup of coffee and a warm blanket wrapped tight against the cold. For the hunter, it had always been adrenaline, the thrill of a fight, a blade in her hand, and a smile that promised death to the wicked.

Anyone else would have turned back two miles ago when the sun still hung low in the sky and they could see the trails ahead clearly. In the misty rain and fading light the deep furrows in the ground were almost invisible, almost. Dani stopped at a tree torn in half and looked for tracks. For months a monster had been slicing its way through hikers, and she was here to stop it.

Exhilaration pulsed through her. She hadn't felt this alive in a long time, not since Alabama and the fire and everything that followed. She was doing her job, not looking back over her shoulder for signs she was being followed.

Most hunters didn't tussle with the talented, humans with unique abilities and internal reservoirs of power and magic. The problem being that when they went bad, they turned into something else and evolved into monsters. Like the one that had murdered her partner, Graham, in front of her.

She'd needed a run-of-the-mill job, and tracking down a talented gone wrong was right up her alley. Dani chuckled darkly. Hunting a monster in the rainy woods—totally normal way to decompress from too much stress.

An inhuman screech cracked through the air, and she stopped short. Dani looked like Mortimer's type: young, dark haired, and alone. Then again, the shotgun probably ruined the look. She licked at her lips, trying not to let the grin threatening at the edge of her mouth take over. He wanted her alone and afraid, and off the beaten path in the woods. She'd give him that to look him in the eye and be sure everything that had been human in him had burned away. Then she could blow him away and leave his bones for whatever animals were living up here. Talented this far gone had a habit of more less dissolving when you killed them, proving they were more monster than human.

As she slinked through the trees, her thoughts drifted to the monster who had ripped the life from Graham. Spectre. He was as old and as nasty as they came. Far as she could tell, far as every hunter she knew could tell, Spectre's ass just couldn't be killed. But Mortimer? Him, she could put down, keep someone else from feeling what she endured each morning when she woke up and her partner was still dead.

"Little girl get lost?" a hoarse voice croaked from behind her.

Dani stopped in her tracks. Every muscle quivered, the moment between action and inaction. The rain coated her skin in a cool blanket. She counted her heartbeats. One. She held the shotgun steady in her hands, and she shifted her weight to her back foot. Two. She pivoted, swinging the barrel up so she could look right down the sight. Three. Stock braced against her shoulder, she looked into the dark eyes of Mortimer Byrant as he growled at her. Where irises should have been, only dark pools of cold fire remained. There was nothing human left inside them. Her finger curled over the trigger, and she bared her teeth in a vicious smile.

"Oh, sugar. I'm not lost."

The modified shotgun with its riot magazine of ten rounds kicked like a mule. She racked it as his chest exploded in a spray of crimson.

He snarled as the impact threw him back. One of his clenched fists transformed into a deadly blade of bone as he lurched back to his feet. He charged at her, but Dani was waiting. She fired again, racking another round into the chamber as he was thrown backwards again.

Dani stepped forward with every shot as the slugs tore his body apart and forced him back, step by step. That was the way she wanted it—keep him at a distance, far enough away he couldn't touch her, close enough that each slug tore him more to pieces. Five rounds in and he hit the dirt. Six and the light went out of his eyes. But some lessons got learned early. You always kill them a little bit more. She kept firing until the shotgun clicked empty and nothing remained but a mass of flesh and bone sinking into the mud.

The thing that had been his arm, or a weapon, or both, didn't shift back as he died. Happened that way sometimes if a talented was corrupted enough. Dani smiled, a predator's smile, more to warn things off than to invite them in. It took a few minutes, but as his body cooled, the power inside him ate away at the flesh. She spat on the ground next to it as it smoked away, leaving a bed of grey ash.

Trekking back down the path took forever, the dark and the rain combining to make a treacherous hike back to the truck. She ducked inside and settled the shotgun onto the rack behind the empty passenger seat. Graham's seat. Memories of his eyes going dark surrounded by fire washed over her, and she forced them away. While killing Mortimer had felt good, it hadn't been enough. Each monster she felled only reminded her of the one she couldn't kill, the one whose blood she ached for. She couldn't will Graham alive again, or erase his murder, but she could hunt down the son of a bitch that had done the deed.

She had to stop filling the void with the death of other monsters. It was time to stop running from Spectre.

But how do I kill a necromancer? Dani had worked every lead, talked to anyone who claimed to have any information, everyone, except for the one man she needed to speak to. A single name kept coming back up who might have details on something to help. Just so happened it was the same person she didn't want to face.

Joe's Grill, the last hunter hub she hadn't checked in with, was three hundred miles away, and his name the final one on her list. At least she hadn't done so since before Alabama when Spectre had murdered Graham in front of Dani's eyes while she was helpless to do anything. But there were no more options. He might have the intel on Spectre she needed, like how to kill him for good.

She had to talk to Joe.

It was time to go home.

2

DANI

With the engine cooling after a four-hour drive and last night's hunt still vivid in her mind, Dani couldn't seem to make herself get out of the truck. She should have known no matter how far she ran, she would always end up back here, where it all started, before Spectre, or losing Graham, or wraiths watching her from the shadows.

Joe's Grill didn't look like much, but he swore he liked it that way. It was a squat two-story building stained by rain and time, with peeling green paint. The parking lot was a wide expanse of cracked pavement that only accented the sign which never wanted to stay lit, no matter how many times they replaced the bulbs.

She'd been avoiding coming back. Somehow, walking through that door and talking to Joe about what had happened meant admitting Graham was really gone, and she didn't know if she was ready. More so, she didn't know if she would ever be fit to walk into the Grill without the most important person in her world pushing her along.

The minute she walked in solo there'd be questions from whoever was in town because there were always questions. Word spread fast among hunters, gossipy things they were. They'd want details on what happened. Dani didn't owe anyone but Joe an explanation, and the questions she knew he had waiting for her were terrifying. Graham was the brains, and she was the muscle. It was her job to protect him, the most important job she'd ever had, and she'd fucked it up. Now he was gone, and she didn't know how to look Joe in the eye and say that.

If there'd been any other way...another hunter, a talented she could ask? Hell, she would've pulled out a spirit board and spoken to the dead if she thought it would help. But Joe was the only one. He was the most connected person on the East Coast, maybe in the whole damned country. He took in strays like Graham and Dani and added them to a network of informants and hunters, trained them in this life. Facing a firing squad sounded easier than admitting to him she had let Graham die.

Her fingers tapped out a staccato beat on the steering wheel. Inside the truck there were plenty of wards that kept her safe. She took a deep breath and cracked the door, sliding onto the pavement. She crossed the parking lot and wished it didn't feel haunted here. Months of avoiding anything that reminded her of him, and now she was in a place where he lingered everywhere. A ghost she couldn't hunt.

Being outside raised the hackles at the back of her neck, and Dani fought the urge to look over her shoulder. Nobody followed her, not this time. She grabbed at the amulets under her tank top, glad for the bruja in New Orleans who had been willing to trade some powerful mojo for taking care of a few spirits. Anything and everything to protect herself from Spectre and his pets.

Walking inside, memories crashed over her in a wave that stole her breath. It made it bittersweet, hard to swallow the pain and still taste the pleasure.

Joe's was somewhere between a saloon, a restaurant, and a halfway house. It was dimly lit, with a dining room, bar, and full kitchen. A dozen scarred wooden tables with mismatched chairs that had no real homes sat to the right. On the left was a pair of thread-bare pool tables and a spot where hunters, who needed to crash or hide, could catch a few Zs. It smelled like alcohol and cooking grease, gun oil, smoke, and leather.

She sighed and her breath trembled in her chest. It was so easy to look at any part of this room and see Graham. At the pool tables, he was teaching her how to hustle before she was legal to drink; at the tables, running down jobs and figuring out what was worth their time; and at the bar where Dani met him so many years ago.

Her chest ached, and she had to blink to keep tears from spilling over. Hunters didn't cry, not where anybody could see anyhow. She fisted her hands inside the pockets of her leather jacket and decided to pretend that being here didn't rip her heart apart.

"Dani!" Joe's voice boomed from behind the bar, and it pulled her from dark thoughts.

She forced a smile, even if she didn't want to, because it was Joe. At six-foot-four, he looked like a grizzly bear, with short hair and broad features. His hard expression made it appear as though he might tear your head off, but he was more of a father than anyone else in this screwed-up world. Joe's whole face lit up at the sight of her, and she almost started crying after all.

"Aww, Firecracker." Joe clucked at her and came around the bar to wrap her in a vise-tight hug. She leaned into the embrace before sniffling and pulling back.

"Hey, Joe." Her voice cracked, going high and weak for a moment before recovering. She wiped at her eyes with a small sigh and shook her head.

"Come take a seat, darlin'. You're too skinny again."

"Well, some bacon cheese fries wouldn't be out of the question." She smiled and followed him back to the bar. Joe slid her a beer. Questions swirled in his eyes, and she knew he deserved answers, but Dani wasn't sure she had the ones he was looking for.

"Already put the order in. Saw ya pull up in that old junker—"

"Delilah is not a junker—"

"And figured it was only a matter of time until you made it in." He smiled, warm and sympathetic. "Shouldn't have taken you this long to come see me, huh?"

Dani let out a stalled breath and shuddered. She had been ready for the blame and the anger, and now there was neither. The weight in her chest broke up just a little. Not enough to fade away, but it made breathing easier. So instead of answering, she sipped at her beer and attempted to concentrate on why she was here and on the fact that Joe was right. Graham would have kicked her ass if he'd been alive, or tried to anyway.

"It wasn't on purpose." She swallowed and looked at Joe, unsure of what to say.

"Hey. I noticed." He cocked his head. "Just don't make it a habit, yeah? I don't adopt strays for my health, ya know?" He winked, and Dani shook her head.

"I'll try. Hell, I wouldn't even be here, but you're my last best hope."

"Stroking my ego will only get you everything." Joe grinned.

"You said you found something? Because nobody else has jack shit." Dani took another long drink from her beer. She watched him, trying to read every shift of expression for any information.

His smile faded, turning grim, determined. From under the bar he pulled out a bin filled with folders. He rifled through them before pulling one out and dropping the box out of sight. Joe looked at the folder and then shifted his gaze back to Dani.

"You're sure about this?"

"He killed Graham." Dani could hear the way her voice went flat and cold, hard as iron. "We don't let him live."

"Good." Joe nodded and slid the folder across the bar with two fingers.

Behind him a bell chimed from the kitchen, and he turned to grab Dani's order, leaving her alone with the best information she was likely to get. She stared at the file. If she opened it, there would be no turning back. Either it'd have what she needed, or she'd spend the rest of her life playing trial and error with a monster that wouldn't stay dead.

Talented were human, mostly. But some of them went bad, and when they did, everyone suffered. Spectre was proof enough of that, staring her in the face. He was a necromancer who might as well have been the bogeyman in the damn flesh, so far as the hunting community was concerned. He'd murdered Graham and laughed while he did it. He deserved to die in the most permanent sense.

Good thing she killed things like him, professionally.

Her stomach growled as Joe slid a heaping plate of food in front of her. She pushed the folder to the side to focus on lunch. Grease-soaked fries, cheese so hot it burned her mouth, and chunks of real bacon was the perfect remedy for too many hours behind the wheel. She cleared half the plate before stopping to take a drink, the angry edge of hunger sated.

"Spectre isn't your run-of-the-mill talented," Joe said with a lingering look. "He's old, and he's nasty. Bastard don't like stayin' dead."

"Is it because he's a necromancer?" she asked.

"Doubtful. Even powerful talented stay down when you put 'em there—provided you do the job right the first time." He tapped the bar counter with two fingers. "But he's worked some kind of mojo, keeps him safe. Nobody's managed to keep him dead."

"So I've seen." Dani clucked her tongue and finished her fries before pushing the plate to the side. "Same shit I heard from everybody else." She waited a beat. "More or less."

"Time was, there were weapons capable of handling things like him." Joe wiped at the scarred counter with a rag, keeping an eye on her as he did.

"I'm listening."

"Old weapons. Older 'n pretty much anything but lore these days. Called veilblades. Nobody's seen one in...a long time. But rumor is, there's one up in Maryland."

"Rumor?" Dani opened the folder and scanned the details as Joe spoke.

"You gotta understand, Firecracker, we're dealing with rumors. And you—"

"Know how hunters talk." She finished his sentence for him with a smile. "Yeah, but you're the one who taught me most every rumor started with a seed of truth, right?" She cocked an eyebrow. "Nobody has anything concrete. Fucking everybody has heard of Spectre, but he might as well be Valkyrie."

"Valkyrie is no joke." Joe's eyes slid away, and Dani filed away the "tell" for later.

"Okay, sure. But there isn't a trail. No real name, no hometown, no associates. It's like he's made of smoke and mirrors. Just...a nightmare for baby hunters." She finished her beer with a scowl. "Except he's real."

"Way back when, there was a well-known family of hunters up in Dawson," Joe said. "Capable of taking out nastier things than most of the hunters working these days."

"Back when?"

"It's been years since anybody caught up with 'em. They worked outta Dawson for a long time, and then overnight, they were gone." He shrugged and his gaze slid away from hers for the second time in as many minutes.

"Dawson...the name sounds familiar but..."

"It's a little spot, up on Catoctin Mountain."

"And what? You think this veilblade is still up there?" Dani raised an eyebrow.

"Maybe. Veilblades are old as legend and just as powerful. The hunters up there had at least one, maybe two. And after the family disappeared...well those blades aren't the sort of weapon that disappears without a trace." His eyes slide away from Dani's again, as though keeping something from her.

"Why did they matter so much?"

"I've only got tidbits to go on."

"So share with the class." Dani gestured widely.

"You know the stories about the first hunters, right? Bladesingers, able to cut through wraiths like they were smoke and shadows. A blade for each of 'em. The Black family had a pedigree in hunting when they were still around."

"And they up and poofed?"

Dani shifted in her seat and leaned forward, hungry for more information. Growing up without family, without anybody until she was a teenager, made hunting different for her than for other lifers. They'd been raised in the life, or trained by family like it was a legacy they needed to uphold. For her it wasn't any of that, it just felt right. Down to the marrow of her bones she was a hunter, so hearing about a family that shared her last name and had a way with hunting wasn't easy. She didn't want to think about it, especially not if they were all gone.

"Like I said, they disappeared overnight. Nobody knew what went down, but sentinels locked the place down." Joe tossed the rag under the counter and avoided her eyes.

Dani blinked and sat back, rubbing a hand over her face. Wasn't this what she'd wanted? What she'd been asking and hoping and praying for? Something that might help her take Spectre down and keep him there. But things were getting complicated fast.

She'd left Graham dead and staring at her from the ground of a dirty warehouse in Alabama, but Spectre had followed her, chased her across eight months and twelve states. Only quick thinking and every spell and precaution in the book had kept her alive.

Sentinels elevated this to a whole new level though. There was a magical ecosystem in the world, three basic branches that tried to avoid each other. Hunters handled the rogue elements. Talented and casters could enjoy their lives without worrying about having their face blown off, so long as they didn't screw up. And sentinels kept the peace and protected the land. They made sure that the supernatural didn't spill over into the normal world and tried to keep regular people from sticking their nose in where it didn't belong.

"Do you know the sentinels up there? Any of the talented? Anybody?" Dani insinuated the real question under her words. Can we trust these rumors if they involve sentinels? No way was she crossing one if she didn't have to.

"Yeah, yeah I do." Joe cracked open a second beer and drained half in a single long swallow. "I knew the hunters back then. Ben." He tipped the bottle in his hand, staring at the label as though it would explain something to him. "And the Lockgrove family."

"As in Ephraim 'I own half of the antique relics on the market' Lockgrove?" Dani's jaw dropped. "You've been holding out on me."

"Don't get so excited. Ephraim handed over the biz to his son, who is...not the man his father is."

"So we can trust this rumor then. It isn't just bullshit from the road."

"It isn't just BS from the road," Joe said.

"So the hunters. They never...came back?"

"Only one of 'em. In a body bag. Blade never showed up either, and after they went down, Spectre got bolder. More active than he'd been in a long time."

"So Dawson is my best shot."

"Darlin, I think it might be the only shot."

"Guess that settles it then, huh? Maryland here I come."

3

EMILIE

The shadow of the Lockgrove house loomed above Emilie, hiding her from the sun. Built the first time in the mid-1800s, the manor survived calamity after calamity, just like the family. Her breath stabbed at her chest, stealing all rationality and thrusting her mind into a whirlpool of death and tragedy. Murder, mayhem, and fire. Like the one that killed Mama ten years ago when Emilie ran as fast and as far away as she could.

In the afternoon light, the house didn't resemble the nightmare blaze she remembered from her adolescence. Exquisite wood turned into a skeleton, fingers of flame reaching out of windows to a red horizon. She looked up to the second floor where Mama stood in the window—and clamped her eyes shut. Mama wasn't there. She was dead and in the ground. Emilie had watched them lower her into the dirt.

Dad wanted her to stay away, but he had stopped answering his phone, and Grandpa was sick, or might be. Her last therapist had tried fruitlessly for months to get her to come back, saying it would help her deal with all the "buried trauma," but standing here, Emilie wasn't so sure. She got it in theory, confronting old demons so she could move on with her life, but it seemed easier said than done.

Lizzy's last letter burned like a brand in her pocket, and it had been the straw that broke the camel's back.

Her fingers twitched, and Emilie nearly pulled the envelope out again to look at it, as though it would have changed since the last time she'd pored over it.

If you're ready to know what happened, I'll tell. But only if you come visit in person. That's the deal. Those simple words in Lizzy's messy scrawl had knocked the air out of her lungs and convinced her that it was time to face the past.

Something in her stomach unfurled, and the ground dropped out from underneath her. Static roared in her ears for a moment, fading to a quiet crackling noise that echoed through her bones. Deep breaths. She needed to breathe if she didn't want to hyperventilate. She'd managed to keep her cool for the whole drive up here, and she didn't want to crash and burn now.

Instead of giving in to the spiral, Emilie curled her nails into the palms of her hand and focused on the pain. Tension still thrummed inside her, a steady hum that kept her on edge, but any excess anxiety faded until only the normal thrashing of the beast that lived under her breastbone remained.

She wrapped her hands around the spikes of the wrought-iron fence that demarcated the front yard and let her gaze settle on the windows. The feel of metal sank into her skin, cold and rough against her palms, but it kept her steady. This time when her eyes drifted up to the second floor, Mama's silhouette wasn't waiting for her. No half-cocked memories of fire or death either, just glare bouncing off the glass and a cool October breeze.

That was the whole point of her return: face the house where Mama died. Find the truth behind the night she still couldn't remember. Then move beyond it and leave the past, ten years ago, where it belonged. She was twenty-seven, not a frightened teenager but a woman who wasn't afraid, who knew how to take life's curveballs and keep on going.

She let out a breath, the air whooshing out of her lungs in a rush. It was now or never. Emilie picked up her bags and trooped up to the door. Grandpa had offered space at his place, but she had promised herself years ago that when she finally got up the courage to return, no doing it halfway. Either she came home and walked through that house, or she never went back to Dawson.

Her phone vibrated in her pocket, and she fished it out with a frown. She unlocked the screen, swiping past a photo of her and Grandpa at the beach last summer.

A new message from Grandpa waited for her. "Are you driving in or taking the train? I can pick you up from the station if you need me to."

Her fingers hovered over the keyboard for a second, and she frowned before firing off a response, telling him she'd already arrived. She let herself in after a long moment and dropped her things by the narrow stairs with a shudder.

The house was immaculate. Wooden floors gleamed with polish, bright patterned rugs settled under antique sofas and end tables. She recalled a few items from childhood: the couch Dad had only pretended to like for Mama, a weird side table that everyone was forever running into. However, Dad had replaced most of the furniture with pieces that echoed Mama's taste.

On the mantle were family photos in the same place Mama always kept them. Seeing the little shards of her made tears prick at the corners of Emilie's eyes. Mama's presence felt hollow, Dad's tribute to the woman who'd lived and died here.

Emilie hastened out of the sitting room and wandered through the house. It was quiet as a tomb, and the air tasted stale. Not surprising. Dad traveled so much for work, and Liz hadn't lived here in almost as long as Emilie. But the feeling that someone else lingered in the shadows persisted, taunting her. They moved at the edge of her vision, and static buzzed in her ears again.

It must have been her mind playing tricks on her. Memories haunted every floorboard, and it was bound to bring up tangled feelings. But wasn't that was the point of coming back? To make her brain give up the secrets it had locked away from her?

Emilie'd had plenty of years to process the worst night of her life.

Mama dead, her sister Lizzie screaming, these weren't the makings of good dreams. Therapy became mandatory when she woke up from a house fire and there were wide blank spaces where her memories ought to have been, not enough to make life impossible, just enough to complicate everything. The big things? The fire, Mama's death, why Lizzie had to be locked up? None of that was anywhere to be found. Processing something she didn't remember? Not what anyone would call easy.

Over time, many of her memories returned, but others remained locked away. Flashes came when she rediscovered a favorite food or movie, smells and textures and tastes alike, all triggering things her mind had locked up. But the night of the fire? All she had access to were smears of color, a child's watercolor rendition of the worst moments of her life.

Emilie peered into empty rooms, trying to identify clues to where Dad might be this time. His office was closed, and she paused, pressing one hand against the worn wood of his door. Although she was sure he wasn't home, and the office was where she was most likely to find out where he'd gone, opening it up seemed like an intrusion. Better to wait. Grandpa would know, and he'd be here soon enough.

Somewhere upstairs, something creaked, the sound of someone walking down the hallway past the bedrooms.

"Dad?" Her voice echoed through the empty house, bouncing back toward her.

When nobody answered, she crossed to the stairs and peered up to the dark second floor. Static buzzed in her ears, and a whisper emanated from inside of it, amplified when she grabbed the banister.

"You have to listen close if you want to hear them..." someone whispered softly. Emilie shook her head to banish the words. Her mind was playing tricks on her again, and somebody was on the second floor. She took the steps two at a time to the landing, half expecting to find Dad hiding in one of the rooms, but there was nobody here and all the doors were closed.

Restored or not, this house had always creaked. The rain echoed all over during a storm, and on a blustery day it swayed in the wind. The only good thing was that on a cool, quiet afternoon, like today, it stood silent. Unless someone was moving around.

The door at the far end of the hallway popped ajar at the thought. She watched as it groaned open a quarter of the way and then stopped. Mama's workroom. It had to be that room because nothing was ever, ever simple, not for Emilie and not in this house. The door had never latched right, always popping open. Dad never did fix it. She stood at the top of the stairs and kept her eyes pinned on it, waiting a moment for someone to open it and breeze onto the landing. Nothing came but a silence that grew thicker with each passing second.

"Dad?" She licked her lips and moved close enough that she could see inside. Smoke and flame and screams echoed through her head as she shoved the door open. It slammed against the far wall. Nobody waited inside.

One step, and then another, and she crossed the threshold. A sharp pop cracked at the base of her skull, and something unspooled in her stomach.

Emilie blinked and flames enveloped her. Heat cracked the air around her, and panic expanded through every atom of her body. The wallpaper burned away to a crisp as her hands scrabbled against the floor for purchase because this couldn't be real. Something popped in the flames and drew her eyes upwards. Up in one corner the shadows were thicker, and a pair of dark eyes watched her. Emilie clamped her hands over her ears and collapsed to the floor with a scream.

"No. Nonononono. Not real. THIS ISN'T REAL!"

When she looked up, the fire and the monster in the shadows were gone. It was just an empty room with sheet-covered furniture. Fragments of memory assaulted her without any way to put them in order, Mama's high-pitched scream echoing around her. This was where she'd died. Splinters gouged under her nails as she dug her fingers into the wood floor, bringing herself back to the here and now.

"Steady, my darling..." A voice washed over her, a quiet whisper that curled around her shoulders like a comfortable stole.

Emilie would have recognized it anywhere. She'd spent years trying to remember the way each syllable of Mama's voice sounded, desperate to hold on to every wisp left to her after the fire took so many of her memories.

She raised her gaze, afraid that coming back to this house had made her snap. Her breath stalled in her chest. Mama, or a shade, a delusion, a wish of her, stood at the window. Catherine Lockgrove smiled, long dark hair flowing around her in a phantom breeze. She reached for Emilie and a beam of sunlight pierced through her.

"Mama?" The words tumbled from Emilie's lips as someone pounded on the front door downstairs. She looked to the hallway for a moment, and when she turned back, nothing of her mama remained. Her lip trembled, a sharp bolt of grief stabbing her before fading to the usual dull ache.

She got to her feet and shuffled down the stairs. Her head felt too full. She stumbled to the front door and flung it open with a grimace. Grandpa stood in the doorway with a sly twist to lips that nestled between a strong jaw and straight nose. His sun-bleached, white-blonde hair—the same as Emilie's—had become a little whiter than blond, and his pale grey-blue eyes, which Emilie shared with him as well, a little paler with age. Was his slim frame even slimmer? She couldn't quite tell, but it worried at her.

The way he slouched in a pair of nice slacks and a comfortable sweater pushed up to his elbows, he looked harmless enough, but she knew looks could be deceiving. He was a lion in sheep's clothing, her fiercest defender, and had been the owner of Lockgrove Antiques for decades. She adored him, and he acted like more of a parent than her dad did, visiting her and staying an active part of her life as it twisted and turned. Now in his seventies, she could see the years weighing on him, leaving him wan and drawn. She didn't want to consider what her life would look like without him in it.

"Don't you have a key?" Emilie closed the door behind him and followed him through the house into the kitchen.

"I do. But I promised Phillip I'd knock."

Emilie frowned at the back of his head as he moved around the kitchen. "Dad isn't here. I don't think he's been here in a few days. Is he on another work trip?"

Ephraim paused and tapped one foot, and started up a pot of coffee. "You must be right. I can't keep track of when he's home and when he's gone anymore."

"Well, if Dad's not gonna be around, that'll make this visit at least a little less stressful."

Neither of them said anything. Emilie pulled two coffee mugs out of the cabinet as the coffee brewed, before sitting down at the table. That way at least Grandpa couldn't see how antsy she was after upstairs. After a few minutes, he poured them each a cup of coffee and sat down across from her. Few things in the world were made worse by caffeine.

"I wanted time alone. Here. With the house." Emilie took a sip of her drink and let herself sink into the taste and heat for a moment, eye slipping closed.

"You look like you saw a ghost."

"Maybe." Emilie reopened her eyes and met his gaze. "Okay fine, no. This place was just messing with me. My brain showing me what it thinks I want to see."

"Isn't that why you came back?"

Emilie bit the inside of her cheek. She didn't know what to say. He wasn't wrong, but he hadn't seen what she had upstairs either. Telling Grandpa should have been easy. He'd been her foundation since the fire burned her life to ashes. What if he pulled away? What if it made him think she was as crazy as Mama had been?

"You saw something."

"Maybe. I don't know." Emilie pushed her cup to the side and curled her legs up into the chair. She chose her words carefully. "I heard Mama's scream and..." She shook her head. "And then right before you got here I swear I saw her."

"In that room?"

"Yeah. Something about it..."

"If all of this is too much, Emilie..."

"It's not." She pressed her lips into a firm line. "It's time, past time, and we both know it." Emilie reached out for her mug and took another sip. Grandpa didn't say anything either for a long minute. This was a years-old argument between her and Dad about his refusal to fill in the blanks on what had happened. He kept holding out on her, but Grandpa wasn't as invested in stonewalling as Dad.

"Keeping the truth from me forever isn't doing me any good. Eventually one of you has to cave, and I know you want to fill me in. It's been ten years, Grandpa. Don't I deserve closure?"

"That's why I brought this, but you beat me to the punch." He slid a blue file folder across the table to her. "It won't give you everything, but I believe you being back here will bring some things up. I wasn't here that night. Just you, Lizzie, and your mother, and you're the only one who can tell what really happened."

"She was here the whole time but..." Emilie looked away from her grandfather, unwilling to think about her sister.

"But she's in Cedar Terrace and won't tell us either." He sighed. "But your father isn't here, and I'm done capitulating."

Emilie raised an eyebrow. "Capitulating?"

"An argument between your father and I." Ephraim dismissed her question with a wave of his hand.

"If you say so."

"If this house gets to you—" Grandpa continued undeterred.

"I told you I'm fine."

"I know you are. But if it does, just get out for a bit. You haven't been back in a long time. Take a walk. Call Andromeda."

"Visit Mama." Ephraim's eyes jumped to Emilie's at the words.

"I wrote it down in the folder. So you can find her if you want to," Grandpa said carefully.

Emilie nodded but stayed quiet. The thought of visiting Mama's gravestone hurt, but it was overdue.

"Thank you, but that's..." She bit her lip and then met his eyes. "I want to see Liz."

Grandpa's breath stuttered, but he nodded anyway. "You're sure? I can call and make sure you're on the list."

Emilie tipped her head back, and a stressed breath escaped in a long hiss. She looked down, examining her nails, trying to ignore the staccato beat of her heart. "Yeah it's—" She pressed her lips together in a firm line. "I can't come back here and not go see her. She's... She'd be so upset if she found out." She nodded to herself. "This is just...a lot."

"Well, I'm right across town. Call me if you need me."

"I will."

He let her comment stand even though they both knew she was lying.

4

DANI

Dani tugged her jacket closed against the cool morning breeze and kept an eye out for the farmhouse where the veilblade was rumored to hide. Breakfast should have been her first stop after weeks on the road, but she opted for a quick hike through the woods near her motel. It spit her out on the street where the Black house stood and gave her time to take a proper peek at it. She needed to get a better scope of the town as well. Rolling in at three a.m. after driving for ten hours hadn't done her perception any favors.

With sentinels, talented, and hunter history, she wanted eyes on the place in daylight. Good thing too, because it was almost falling in on itself. Set back from the street behind a wooden fence weathered by time, the house had seen better days. A two-story farmhouse with a wraparound porch, she saw how it might have been beautiful once. Now, with broken windows and paint-stripped boards, it looked like trouble.

Dani wandered up to the fence, eyes soaking in every detail. When she got inside tonight, she'd need as much help as she could get. She wrapped her hands on the ragged wood, and a splinter stabbed into her hand.

With nobody else on the street, she wasn't too worried about bleeding. If one wanted to use someone's blood against them it had to be fresh, and she doubted she'd bled enough to be worth it. That's why she'd aimed for this time of day. No passersby to ask awkward questions or catch her while she scoped out the house. Good thing too, because she needed to work a little mojo of her own.

Talented had an internal reservoir of power they called on, while casters used contracts or totems that gave them abilities past the norm. For hunters, the process worked a bit different. You used charms, components, things you drew magic off of. Dani had it all in spades—her own protective collection. She reached a hand under her collar and pulled out the effigy of an eye, a slider where the eyelid rested. Holding it, she pinned her eyes on the house and slid the lid to an open position.

The farmhouse lit up like a rave as it glowed. Runes webbed over the entire house, shining in a rainbow of colors. She gritted her teeth and tried to pick them all apart, but it was impossible. So many she didn't recognize. The shapes and symbols were far enough away from one another that if she played her cards right she'd be able to sneak past. It'd mean making a salve to hide her from the magic protecting the place, but it was doable. Dani slid the eye charm shut again and tucked it back out of sight. She blinked a few times to clear her vision and get her bearings.

Joe had sent her up here with nothing more than a few rumors in her pocket. There had been no guarantee Dani would find anything. The amount of magic laid over the house convinced her there was at least something inside. The question was whether it was the veil-blade or not.

Her stomach growled, reminding her she needed to eat breakfast. If there was a decent joint, it'd give her the chance to get a snapshot of the people in town, help her figure out who had placed the runes and spellwork. It was too much for just one person, even a skilled talented, to have done it all on their own. She'd bet at least two of them, maybe more.

She set a brisk pace, heading for the center of Dawson. Down the street and across another, and things no longer resembled the shell of a town she'd driven into last night. She passed a few shopfronts just opening business for the day, before finding a diner on the corner.

Inside, she snagged a booth without having to wait and put in her order. When the coffee showed up on the table, she took a sip and peered around. It bustled with the mid-morning crowd. Mornings weren't her jam most of the time—unless you counted breakfast, which was the tastiest meal of the day. It looked like someone had plucked it right up and out from 1950s Americana, complete with a chrome bar and neon lights.

Life on the road meant convenience was king. It'd been fast food and instant whatever for too many weeks again. Graham would've smacked her upside the head. Her metabolism had always been out of control, and her body had a habit of eating itself when she didn't feed it enough.

Which was the perfect excuse for the almost obscene amount of breakfast she'd arrayed on the table in front of her. French toast, eggs, bacon, a blueberry muffin sliced in half and grilled, sausage, and hash browns. It was more than she needed, but she was hungry, and it'd take time to go through what Joe gave her on the veilblade, along with getting a read on the town.

With a booth to herself, it was easy to scope out everything going on inside. One could never tell with small towns. She still wasn't over that hamlet in Connecticut crawling with revenants.

The diner brimmed with people, but the conversation was a hushed burble: a few trees down at the south of town, stats about the high school football team, news from the family who didn't live there anymore. Nothing out of the ordinary...except for the table two spots over.

Three men bent together, their voices low. Dani picked up a few words, something about a coincidence and a return. Combine that with the way their eyes had followed her when she took her seat, and it made the hair at the back of her neck bristle.

She'd watched them until her breakfast showed up. There were players in every place she took a job. If they mattered, they'd come to her. Not like she was here on a slash-and-dash call, anyway. Now was the time to dig into the details. Her top priority was finding the veilblade.

"New in town?" Dani's eyes flicked up at the voice of the dark-skinned man from the table, leaning back over his chair and looking at her with a smile.

He had warm brown eyes, short locss that fell at the perfect angle, and cheekbones sharp enough to slice. Dressed in a pressed blue collared shirt, with a navy vest over it, and sleeves folded up to his elbows, he cut a dashing figure. Something about him screamed he was *other*. This was not a hundred percent USDA human. Maybe fae, something with juice, that was for sure.

"Rolled in last night. Or this morning. Guess it depends on how you look at it," Dani answered with a grin. She leaned back and popped a piece of muffin into her mouth with a twitch of an eyebrow. Looked like she'd found one player in town already. Usually took longer, but she wasn't complaining.

"That'd explain it. I'm Mercurious Mews, but please, call me Merc."

Dani let the smirk linger on her lips, but felt a charm at her clavicle warming against her skin. The charms were all spelled, each one serving a specific purpose, and there were more than a dozen strung on the necklaces she wore. This one warned her he was trying to work some kind of mojo on her, but he was not talented and not a caster. That left one option: *sentinel.*

"Dani." She took his outstretched hand and shook it with a sharp smile. "Doubt I'll be in town long though."

"Shame. I think you'd fit right in." He leaned back with casual elegance.

"Heh." She choked out a light laugh. Small towns were where she worked, not where she wanted to settle down. Her idea of home didn't involve getting lost in the mountains.

"You don't agree?" His lips quirked up into a half smirk.

"A bit too slow for my speed," she hedged.

"Is it?" Merc cocked his head. "I wouldn't judge so fast if I were you."

"Is that so?" Dani leaned back against her booth, poking at her breakfast.

"I think you might know that though, eh?" He flashed an impish smile at her. "If you have questions, come find me. My bookshop is right around the corner." He gestured with his thumb before winking. "Stay safe, Dani."

Dani watched as he strolled out of the diner. The pulsing warmth of the charm faded away as he exited. No two ways about it, that was the most charming sentinel she'd ever met. Most of them were stuffier. *Am I getting in over my head?* A protector sniffing her out before she'd even gotten her bearings did not bode well.

This complicated things, and Dani hated complicated. Her only lead on the veilblade was the hunter's farmhouse, but it was thin. She wasn't used to sentinels being so friendly, but he might have more concrete answers for her.

Dani left money on the table and headed toward the bookstore. Dawson was quaint, with mom and pop shops littered along the street and pedestrians going about their day. Except that's all there were. Even the rust belt had a decrepit old McDonald's, or hell, a Walmart with shuttered doors. Small business might be the backbone of America, but this was just weird.

Her arrival last night had been eerie too. Dawson looked half abandoned and worse for wear, but on this main stretch it reminded her of nothing so much as Mayberry. It sent warning bells ringing in her mind. Something about this town was off. Everyone seemed to be watching, waiting for her to make a move. She turned the corner at the end of the block and found Merc's bookstore with a tall narrow doorway and a broad plate-glass window.

Inside it was brighter than she'd imagined. Half of the shop was contemporary titles, but the aroma of ink and old pages permeated the room. Small protections hidden from easy view crowded the moldings: discrete runes that blended into a windowsill, a witchball hanging behind a plant above the window, little touches that folks who weren't in the know would completely overlook.

"Well, that didn't take long," Merc said, strolling out from a door at the back of the bookstore.

"I've got an itinerary to keep to." She sauntered through the aisle with one hand dancing along the titles.

Time to see whether Merc was worth his salt. Sentinel or not, he'd have his own strengths, and she needed to suss them out before she went any further. No point in crossing him if she didn't have to.

"Not here on the pleasure tour, eh?" He blinked, slow and lazy.

"Not so much. Bit of a work-a-holic. It's a personal failing."

"Mmmhmm."

The charm at her clavicle warmed back up again. No way to tell if it was because he was working mojo or whether it reacted to proximity. It was a new addition to her collection.

"I'm a big fan of obscure texts. You wouldn't happen to have a catalog handy?" She let the words drop and watched Merc's face to see which of them would break first.

He looked at her; she looked at him, and then he grinned and shook his head. "I'll admit you're good." He rolled his eyes. "Talent recognizes talent." He turned and beckoned her to follow with a fluid wave of one hand.

She scowled and waited for a beat before following. The back door led into a narrow corridor with several doors off of it. He walked through the first doorway on the right, and Dani entered a dragon's trove of treasure.

Relics rested in globes, grimoires and histories on pedestals. Objects lay protected behind spelled glass. Magic pulsed so strong, even Dani could feel it. The air practically hummed. Wards etched along the walls and moldings kept the energy from leaking out and alerting the rest of the world to its presence.

Tall shelves filled with books and arcane trinkets pressed against the walls. A large wooden table dominated the back third of the room, with more books shelved behind it. Several smaller shelves created aisles in the front. There was more magic, more knowledge locked in this single area than she'd ever seen. Graham would have drooled. It even piqued Dani's fancy, much as she tried to keep a straight face.

"Oh. That's—oh my."

"It does tend to impress. I have a sense for these things."

"Do you?" Dani feigned ignorance. Better to let him out himself rather than giving up any intel she didn't have to. She needed allies, but not at the expense of her own secrets.

"We don't get many unexpected visitors." He strolled past and down aisles of heirlooms and contraptions.

"I never would have guessed."

"It's by design." He shot an inscrutable look over one shoulder.

"So the crummy digs at the edge of town and my GPS being convinced this place wasn't here were on purpose."

"More or less. Dawson's a special kind of place. Surprised that you're here honestly." He turned at a table and frowned at her. She watched the gears in his mind move, trying to work something out.

"No formal creds to help me along the way. The depth of what I don't know..." Dani shrugged and ducked her head, playing bashful.

Merc might be a sentinel, but he was a man first, and if experience had taught her anything, it was that men loved explaining things to women. It was an easy game to play. He watched her act but didn't move. A small furrow appeared between his eyes.

"You're serious."

Dani let his words hang in the air and felt the weight of his gaze on her. He was waiting for her to fess up, probing her for the untruth. Except that there wasn't one.

To fool the supernatural, you had to do it correctly. Blend the lie and the truth together so neat you couldn't pick apart where one stopped and the next began. There was plenty she didn't know and more about Dawson in particular. She leaned on that sliver of ignorance.

"Right. So you're self-taught then." He enunciated each word. Dani could taste the shape of the words in the air, unfamiliar and sharp on his tongue. She'd struck a nerve all right.

"More or less. I had a partner. He got out of the life." Granted, he'd died and not retired, but lies of omission didn't count.

"Mmmhmm. That would explain a few things." He huffed out a breath and plucked a book off the shelf behind him. "You don't even know." He licked one finger and thumbed through without looking down at the pages. "Where you are?" He smirked, pleased with himself. "What you are?"

Dani's lip curled up in a snarl, and she took a step back from the table. She didn't play the threatening games that sentinels, talented, and casters all played with each other. The urge to pull her piece made her palm itch, but once one pulled a weapon, they had to use it.

If she could avoid killing a damned sentinel that was always the right call. When one killed a protector, things got hairy. She already had Spectre on her ass, she didn't need trouble. Not that the sentiment ever stopped trouble from finding her. She gritted her teeth and breathed out through her nose.

"You know, threats? Not your best call." The words sounded calm, but she was poised to strike out if she needed to. It was what she did best.

"Threats? That wasn't a threat." Merc went quiet. A stillness stole over his frame and made every instinct inside her scream to life. The charms warned her of magic—and not small-time shit either. His eyes slipped shut, and his body went still as stone. When they reopened, they didn't look right, no longer human. Instead, twin flames of grey-brown power burned from inside of him. "Now this could be a threat." He shrugged. "If you weren't one of us, anyway."

He chuckled, and the flames disappeared. His power slipped back to that internal well, a chalice made of flesh to hold power beyond measure. "But I needed to get you to stop playing dumb." He rolled his eyes and then flipped the book so it was facing Dani. She looked at it like it might try to bite her.

"Something happened. Maybe recently..." He shot her a curious glance. "Maybe not so recently. Something strange. Beyond normal. Something supernatural."

"I'm listening." She took a hesitant step closer, still strung too tight.

"There are the things you know, the things you thought you knew, and the truth." He gestured to the book and took a seat. She grabbed a chair and dropped into it, body tilted away from him and the table, close enough that she still had a shot on him, far enough away she was out of arm's reach. Not that it mattered with magic.

"There is the shadow and the veil. Those who know and those who don't. Talent, tragedy, legacy..." He smiled gently. "I'm guessing tragedy if you're self-taught."

"Tragedy." Dani agreed in a hoarse voice. "I'm skilled at what I do."

"You're a hunter."

"I am...adept at killing the monsters that snack on people." She smiled, a vicious, bloodthirsty smile. She might have been a bystander once, but grudges made her angry, and instead of getting dead, she'd gotten even. With all but Spectre, at least. But she was of a mind to remedy that.

Merc's eyes narrowed. "You call tragedy, but it doesn't quite fit does it? A hand-me-down suit. Too long in the leg I think. But I can't take it from you. You play the game well."

"It's kinda my job."

"Well. When it rains it pours. I assume you came to suss me out? Or was there more?"

"I'm in town for a job."

Merc frowned and sat back with a look of consternation on his face. "You're here for a job?"

"Mm. Rumor is you've got a shiny weapon hiding somewhere in this town. My guess is it's at the old hunter farmhouse."

Merc's eyes flicked to the door behind Dani, his mouth pressed into a hard, white line. "The Black house."

Her leg twitched at the same time, but she kept a straight face. "From what I hear, when they bailed they left some things behind."

"It wasn't a planned departure, if that's what you're getting at."

"You aren't denying the veilblade is in town, I see."

"Dawson hides all sorts of peculiarities."

"Don't go getting cagey on me now, slugger." Dani tapped one finger against the table between them.

"I can't answer your question. The house might have what you're looking for. Might not. I don't track that sort of thing. Not as if anyone can check anyway."

"What do you mean?"

"Wards protect the Black house. Nobody can get in, so it's possible there's a veilblade hidden in there somewhere. I wouldn't bet on it, but it's a waste of your time." He leaned back on his chair until it balanced on two legs and plucked another tome off the shelf. "Here, this should explain more. Consider it a gift of sorts." He cocked his head and grimaced. "Sadly, I need to cut our chat short. I'll see you out."

He ushered her out of the room, through the front of the shop, and out onto the street before closing and locking the door behind her. *Could this town get any weirder?* Dani shook her head and took a better look at the book in her hands. Apparently, she'd be doing a hefty bit of research after all.

5

EMILIE

Emilie always imagined Dawson frozen in time, a place where things never changed, and the ones that did were small, incremental, and easy to miss. It was a town where people left doors unlocked and children walked to school without hovering parents worrying if they would make it. Once she moved, she'd been afraid to come back and find that the rose-colored memories were all a lie.

Along the main thoroughfare, the new shopfronts stuck out, a marker that this was not the same town it had been when she'd been a kid. Certain as time marched on for her, it marched on for Dawson.

Not everything had shifted, though. The diner still stood stalwart and unchanged, and at the end of the block was the Java Bean—slinging coffee and indie music for twenty years now. Emilie got a double-shot vanilla latte and took one of the patio tables, letting the drink warm her up on the chilly October morning.

She had made it through her first evening home without waking up in a cold sweat. She'd tossed and turned half the night, dreams of whispered voices putting her on edge, but it wasn't terrible, so far as disturbed sleep went. It was better than the screamers. This had been almost pleasant in comparison.

Looking down the picturesque street, she couldn't help but remember the last time she had been in town was Mama's funeral. A hazy, indistinct memory of black-clad figures and a casket tugged at her. She had never returned to visit the gravestone, something she planned on rectifying today. She needed time first to gather herself before reopening any old wounds.

"Emilie Lockgrove?"

A familiar voice jolted her out of her thoughts, and she looked up to see who had recognized her. "Huh?"

"Ho-ly shit. You came back!"

"Andry?" Emilie jumped up for a hug, half shocked.

Andromeda Mews was tall, Black, and beautiful. She wore her hair shaved down to the skin on one side, the rest in long locss adorned with clips and charms. She had a sharp, angular face with light-brown eyes that Emilie remembered. But there were new piercings since the last time they'd seen each other. It had been ten years, plenty of aborted trips, missed phone calls, and regrets. And in a single moment all that vanished. Andry shot her a wicked smile and joined Emilie.

"Never thought I'd see you back here."

"Make that two of us." Emilie looked away for a second. "But it's time. I mean, I should have come home a long time ago. It's been a decade, and it was just a house and a fire." She shook her head and spoke too fast, hands fluttering against the table as she tried to convince herself.

"If you say so," Andry said with a pointed look.

"I…" Emilie took a sip of her coffee, frustrated.

"Spit it out. If you can't tell me, then who can you? Hmm?" She waggled her eyebrows and smiled.

Emilie held out for a second before a burble of laughter erupted up and out of her. "Fiiiine. I came to check on Grandpa. But also just… I can't let the fire rule my life forever. If coming back here is what I have to do, then I'll cope." She shrugged.

Andry narrowed her eyes but didn't reply for a long moment. "Is everything fine though?"

Emilie looked away as she searched for the right words. "He mentioned something about doctor visits, but he won't tell me anything. I think he's sick, but he worries, and Dad is...well...you know."

"Yeah, he hasn't changed much." Andry wrinkled her nose and shook her head.

"What about you? Didn't end up...going somewhere else?" Emilie frowned, grasping for a memory that was fuzzy and out of focus.

"Nah. Couldn't get out." She tapped at the table between them. "It's not all bad though. Merc and I bought up a building, opened our own shops after all."

"Really? That's amazing! You always wanted your own place. Just enough space to keep Merc from driving you insane, right?"

"You have no idea. Having a twin brother is not always what it's made out to be. You should stop in later. I'm right across the street." Andry smiled and gestured with a thumb over one shoulder. "So what about you? What *has* Emilie Lockgrove been getting up to for the last few years?"

"Nothing as fantastic as you." Emilie looked away and took a sip of her latte. She didn't want to talk about late rent or the car she fought to keep on the road. "I had a cottage down by Annapolis, spent a lot of time in coffee shops, worked a series of ultimately terrible jobs while I got a mostly useless degree. " She splayed her hands on the table to hide the tremor in them.

"Mmm." Andry gave her a discerning look but let the lie hang in the air. "So how long are you back in town for?"

"Not sure. Why?"

"I mean, we have years' worth of catching up, obviously." She grinned. "I need to know how much time I have."

"Well, I have to check that Grandpa is taking care of himself, and the lease on my cottage was up. So I'm here at least until I find a new place to live." *One I can afford and not get kicked out of.*

"Inter-esting." An alarm on Andry's phone went off, and she swore under her breath. "My delivery truck just arrived. I gotta go unload the crates at the shop." Her eyes flitted across the street to a window filled with an explosion of plants. "But I'm gonna finish this latte while we talk before I head back."

"I can agree to a plan like that."

"So Annapolis? What happened to leaving Maryland behind, seeing the whole world instead of this little slice?"

"Turns out moving states is pricier than I thought."

She'd spent years refusing money from her father. Disappearing from Dawson meant freedom from Dad and his guilt, from Lizzie and her instability. She'd never gotten far, but a few hours away was better than not at all.

"Mm." Andry took a sip of her drink and looked over her shoulder as someone rapped on the door of her shop. "Shit. Business calls! Come see me later, yeah? I'm not kidding about needing to catch up." She winked and hurried over to her shopfront.

"I'll...do that." Emilie sighed and tipped her head back in frustration.

The apothecary stood on a corner lot, glass windows alive with green plants in a dozen varieties. She found it strange that Andry was still kicking around town. She'd wanted out of Dawson as much as Emilie had. The two of them had spent hours making plans of the places they'd go, the things they would do. All of that disappeared after the fire, when Emilie ran away without ever looking back at the people she'd abandoned.

You're being ridiculous, Emilie, she chided herself and got to her feet, tossed her trash, and headed toward the cemetery where Mama waited. The thought of a granite stone sent a bolt of ice through her heart. But she couldn't avoid it anymore; she wouldn't. After all these years, if anyone deserved a visit, it was Mama. Mama, who she hadn't been able to protect. She'd been avoiding it for years, but she'd always known that eventually she'd give in. How could she not?

Dawson's graveyard was old, filled with crypts and mausoleums toward the back half of the lot where the church stood before it burned down in the '70s. It didn't take long to find the place where her family's remains rested: a tall mausoleum with white and black bricks. Mama though, she was in the ground. Emilie counted off one relative after another as she walked along, aunts, uncles, a grandmother who'd passed years before Emilie was born. And then there was Mama's stone.

"Catherine Lockgrove. Devoted wife and mother. May the river take you to rest on misty shores of silence." Her breath stuttered out in a harsh exhale.

The words weren't enough, none of this was. It had never been enough because Mama had died, and then Emilie's own brain had stolen away so many of her memories. All she had was this slab of rock with a name and dates inscribed, and no peace to be found from any of it. She wanted to leave the haunting of her unremembered past behind her where it damn well belonged as she tried to build a life.

One finger danced over the words chiseled into the marker, black stone with white script. Dad had paid out for it and it showed.

"I'm sorry." She laughed bitterly and looked up at the sky. "Look at me talking to a rock. But fuck it. Closure." She shook her head and gazed back down at the gravestone. It was ridiculous, but she also felt like she was about to rip her heart out of her chest. "I know I took forever to come visit you, and I never should have let it go on this long." Around her the trees rustled. Leaves swirled in a small maelstrom taken by the wind in a single gust.

"I couldn't face coming back at first. Not—not when I woke up. And then it was just easier, you being here, for me to stay away." She huffed out a breath and knelt down. "I'm sorry I wasn't there to protect you, Mama, and I'm sorry it took me so long to come see you. I love you. Wish you were still here, with me." She blinked against tears trying to escape her eyes and pulled a silver token out of one pocket and put it on the base of the gravestone. "I'll try to come again before I leave. Promise." She nodded and pressed her forehead against the stone as tears tracked over cheeks.

After a few long minutes, she wiped her face and sat onto her heels. The torrent of emotion left her hollow, made it easier to focus, and she traced a hand over the gravestone again. Somehow, leaving was harder than getting here. Emilie tucked a pale strand of hair behind one ear and stood up. Her heart wasn't lighter. The reminder that Mama died because she was late arriving home weighed her down. There were reasons this wound refused to heal no matter how she tried to clean it out.

When she looked to the left where the brutal stone structure of the mausoleum sat on a small hill, there was a woman standing at the doorway. Emilie frowned and heaved herself back to her feet, brushing the dirt and leaves off her knees. The figure, with her long waves of dark hair, was familiar. She waved at Emilie before turning and walking out of sight and into the building.

Around her the air turned cold, the blustery weather only getting worse. The wind cut, even through the bomber jacket she'd thrown on before leaving the house. Instinct said this was a bad idea—turn back because you do not follow the freaky silhouette of a woman you may or may not know into a damned tomb. That was fodder for horror movies.

"And we, Emilie Lockgrove, are not monster-movie bait. We survive, which means avoiding the weird shit while facing the truck-load of personal trauma that has accumulated over ten years."

Still, she broke away from the path and headed up to the mausoleum. The door was unlocked, but the padlock wasn't broken. So that was a good sign. It was the Lockgrove Family crypt, capital L, capital F. Since Dad seemed to be out of town, it was her problem. It didn't make this a better idea, but the wind was picking up, and if animals got in and nested in there, Emilie would never hear the end of it.

Ten years since she left home and closer to twenty since she'd been inside this place, Emilie had forgotten how bizarre it was. She pulled out her phone for a bit of light before trotting down the short staircase into the room proper. A pair of couches faced each other against different walls. There were small lamps and tables, as though you might entertain here. Past that was the crypt where the interred remains of her relatives rested.

Past the crypts and columbaria niches for remains, the back wall was a massive mosaic. She'd never quite understood what it was, but Grandpa had told her it was a spark. Blue and gold panes arranged like something bursting to life. It filled the whole back wall, making it clear there were no other exists. One way in, one way out.

Nobody else was down here in this silent place, just Emilie, and the longer she stood still the more her skin crawled. Cobwebs were heavy in the corners, and if anyone had been down here in the last six months she'd eat her (nonexistent) hat. But she had seen someone. If her mind wanted to play tricks on her at home, that was one thing. Full blown visual hallucinations while she was out and about were not part of the deal.

They needed to not be happening because that meant new symptoms. And new symptoms led to being wrangled back inpatient again, more therapy, more meds that didn't work. She'd returned home to confront her trauma and put it behind her, not open the box for fresh monsters her brain had concocted to start crawling out.

"Hello?" Her voice echoed as though the room was much larger than it was. "Look, I saw you come down here."

Emilie hesitated. The back half of the mausoleum wasn't lit up, and it looked like bulbs had burned out. If somebody wanted to, they could hide in one of those dark corners. No way could she leave this place wide open. She needed to lock the door behind her. Which meant she had to check and make sure nobody was hiding there.

Even as she walked across the room, her brain screamed at her. This was not a good idea. This was what crazy people did, like when she saw obituaries for someone who got killed and their bodies weren't found for weeks and weeks. If some crazed junkie was in here, then she was probably the least equipped person on the planet to handle it. Letting the crypt sit unlocked wasn't an option though, and if there was somebody down here, she couldn't in good conscience lock them in.

"Not looking to call the cops or anything, but you can't be down here. I mean, how did you even get the door open?" Emilie kept talking, trying to keep her nerve.

But there was nothing, no sound of the wind from outside, not that insistent buzzing, not claws on cement or another person's breath to stir the air. It was quiet as a grave. Emilie passed the halfway mark, and her heart jumped into her throat. She got a few steps closer to the back, and a light stuttered to life above her. A handsbreadth away from the wall and the incontrovertible truth hit her in the face. Nobody else was here.

Fear of a different kind washed over her. She might be cracking up worse than she'd thought. Just to her left were names chiseled into the rock of their crypts, small areas for gifts and mementos. "Marie Deveraux..." Emilie read the words, trying to steady herself. The wind screamed at the door atop the stairs. It slammed shut and all the lights guttered out, her phone dying along with them.

"Shit." Emilie grasped at the nameplates in the sudden perfect blackness. There was no up or down or left or right, just the black. Her hands on the wall helped balance her, and she focused on the sensation of recessed letters pounded in stone.

"Time to wake up," a woman's voice spoke into Emilie's ear, accented in French.

Emilie turned on her heel and threw out her arms to find nothing. That was it, she was getting out of here. She tried to find her way toward the front of the mausoleum. Instead, her fingers pressed against the cool glass of the mosaic, and she screamed as something shocked through her. The lights flickered on, and she sprinted to the door. After a desperate moment where she thought her heart might literally pound out of her chest, one foot kicked the bottom of the stairs. She stumbled more than ran up them, practically on all fours, then fumbled for another horrible moment.

Her hands slapped against the handle, stuck in what felt like a horrible slow-motion nightmare as she let herself out of the crypt. When she slammed it closed behind her and threw the lock, she sighed a breath of relief. The autumn day was still and cool around her. Not so much as a leaf fluttered. Where had the wind gone?

Emilie set a brisk pace back home. She wanted to be behind thick walls that, if not comforting, were at least familiar. Familiar and not out in public where people could see her have a meltdown. A nice cup of tea, maybe some movies on her tablet, and she'd get to bed early tonight, not think about any of this.

With her head down and moving as fast as her legs would carry her, she never even saw the dark-haired woman in the leather jacket. They collided just outside of Andry's apothecary. Emilie went down like a sack of bricks, limbs splayed every which way, but at least the woman didn't follow her to the ground. And she kept her purchases from being destroyed. As if this day hadn't already been rough enough, now this.

"I'm so sorry," Emilie babbled as she scrambled to her knees. "I wasn't watching where I was going, and I ran right into you, and—" She stopped babbling as she looked up at a gorgeous dark-haired woman with golden-brown eyes that danced in the afternoon sunlight.

"Hey, hey, hey. I'm fine. You took a serious spill though. Want some help up?" On top of being gorgeous, she had a nice alto voice to go with it, smoky like good whiskey.

"Uh, yeah." Emilie took the proffered hand and got to her feet. As she did, a flash of something crashed through her mind. The Black farmhouse strobing in a bright, harsh light, blood-coated walls, and a shadow made flesh. She gasped and let go of the woman's hand. "Thanks for your help. And sorry. Again. I didn't mean to crash into you. Have a good one, okay?" Her voice teetered on the edge of something, and Emilie knew she needed to get home soon, or she'd be paying for it.

She found she had to look up into the tall, athletic woman's eyes a bit. Though her gaze was intense and probing, it held nothing predatory or cruel. In fact, it was nice in a way, really nice.

"I'm Dani. Look, are you sure you're all right?"

"I'm having a day, but I'll be fine." She grimaced and shook her head, trying to find a shred of composure. "Emilie. Emilie Lockgrove. Listen, this is just...not the time. Sorry. Again."

She had pushed herself too far and felt stretched thin. But Dani's hand had been warm, callused fingertips pressed against Emilie's palm, and she was gorgeous in the way only punk rock girls with their leather and studs could be. If not for the graveyard and mausoleum, she might have stayed, seen if she could buy the other woman a coffee, find out who she was and what a woman who looked like that was doing in a town like this.

Instead, she felt like a piece of rope unraveling strand by strand. Emilie didn't know what would happen when the last string broke and fell to nothing.

Rather than pretending she was okay, she took off for home, confused and mortified. What in the hell had that been? Crazy flashes meant more hallucinations. She should call Grandpa, tell him what was going on. He'd always been on her side and not anyone else's. But she didn't want to unload this on him.

Mama had seen things, and heard them. It would have been hard to miss when Emilie was younger. One couldn't mention Catherine Lockgrove in town without rumors of mediums and ghosts and other nonsense.

Terror struck her down the middle at the thought that she might start to hear voices that didn't exist, carry on as if she was barely in the real world, like Mama. To the Lockgrove family, Mama had been unwell. Depending on the month, she was either a talented psychic or a person lost in delusions, but to society at large she'd been Catherine Deveraux, a medium capable of speaking to the dead.

Emilie didn't know what she wanted, but it wasn't that. Before the thought could spiral further out of control, the shadow of Lockgrove house fell over her. She let herself in and then collapsed back against the door.

There was only so much she could take. As if her life hadn't been a mess before she got here. After Grandpa's last heart attack she was almost positive he wasn't telling her the whole truth, Dad was still distant on his best days, and she had no idea how she would afford a new place on her shoestring budget. She didn't need more things going wrong.

By the time dusk fell outside, Emilie managed to convince herself that she'd just gotten spooked at the cemetery. She had been emotional, and at Mama's grave, and sometimes a person's eyes played tricks on them. That was her story, and she would stick with it for as long as possible because anything else was lunacy.

After dinner she flipped through the albums Grandpa had dropped off, photos of her parents, of seances her mother had held when she was younger, of the whole family together. Emilie slammed the album shut and put it on the table. She couldn't deal with this, not tonight. After this afternoon had left her nerves still buzzing, she didn't need any extra stress. The same infernal noise in her ears again.

From the main hallway a door banged shut, and Emilie frowned. She'd checked the doors and windows to make sure nothing was unlocked. When she headed toward the sound, she saw a dark-haired feminine figure walk into Mama's greenroom, the door swinging shut behind her.

Emilie wobbled in place. She'd locked the house when she arrived home. Nobody was in the house. That woman looked familiar.

Anxiety thrumming through her like a live wire, Emilie opened the door and gasped. The room shimmered, a mirage in the desert. Lit by sunlight, plants in red and green and blue were in full bloom around her. A slim dark-haired woman stood humming to herself, faced away from her.

"Mama?"

"I'm sorry sweetling, but no." She smiled and turned to look at Emilie. "I'm your Grandmama Marie." She paused and narrowed her eyes. "You and I, we need to have a bit of a chat."

Emilie's jaw dropped. "Oh wow. I am...hallucinating." Seeing visions of someone in the distance or talking to yourself was one thing, but this was next level.

"You're not hallucinating." Marie shot her a deadpan look.

"Says my hallucination." Emilie returned the look in kind as she took a hesitant step into the room.

"I'm sorry it has to be this way," Marie said with a shake of her head. "I'd hoped we'd have more time, but that isn't the case."

"What do you mean?"

"There is to know...and not to know." Marie's voice grew in power, and it vibrated around Emilie, roaring through her bones. "You can never unknow. But knowledge can be hidden away. Bound." Emilie clamped her hands over her ears, but the words thundered through her. "To bind is to hide when you cannot fight. To free the bound is to loose the hound so it may rend flesh."

Fear and panic clawed at Emilie's throat, forcing her to hyperventilate. There was no way any of this could be real, and yet she didn't know how it couldn't be. She scrabbled out of the room and kicked the door shut. Marie's voice followed her.

"Turn the key and let the door open. What was bound be freed, the forgotten remembered. Time to mend the rift, Emilie. The bladesinger will require your aid at the Black house."

Emilie scrambled backwards across the floor until she hit a wall, chest heaving. *It's happened. I've finally snapped.* But there had to be a way to check, to prove that this wasn't just her mind playing tricks. Maybe Mama hadn't been as crazy as Dad had always insisted. That was preferable to the alternative, that she was crazy. Behind her, the front door threw itself open, and her eyes popped wide. She turned to see the cool night as it beckoned her. She stumbled to her feet and out the door.

She had two choices: believe she had gone insane or that something else was going on. It wasn't like it'd be out-of-place in this town, anyway. There were more ghost stories than people in Dawson, but listening to a scary story at a sleepover and believing you were seeing ghosts and visions, that was a whole different level.

Dad and Grandpa had told her Mama was sick, crazy for talking to things that weren't there. But there had been moments, things she couldn't have known, that the spirits had told her. Emilie believed Grandpa, but if Grandmama Marie wasn't a hallucination, didn't that make it possible that they'd lied to her, that Mama had been less sick and more gifted somehow? Nothing made sense, and Emilie's head was reeling. There was the shape of something elusive just beyond her grasp, another memory she didn't have access to.

And there were still three images seared onto her brain from when that woman—Dani—had helped her up to her feet. The Black house, lit up like it hadn't been since she was a little girl, blood on the walls, and a shadow that reminded her of the night of the fire for some reason.

If she was crazy, then she'd drive over there and nothing would happen. It'd just be what it had always been: a farmhouse that had been beautiful, and loved, and now sat empty, desolate, like it had for as long as Emilie remembered.

And if the impossible was true? That Dad lied to her about Mama, and that there was something more going on? If that was real, then the house would be alive and her visions were real. Emilie closed her eyes and exhaled, letting the wind rush over her while she tried to figure out what to do.

She'd stopped trusting herself, her instincts, a long time ago. It had been up to Dad and Grandpa to rebuild her life, to steer her through the troubled period of the trauma. If she wanted to face her past, it meant believing in herself for the first time in years.

So she got in the car and headed to the other side of town.

6

DANI

Dani ran her thumb along the razor edge of her favorite knife as she scanned the tools she'd arrayed for tonight's job: knives and her handgun waiting in sheaths and holsters, and a full set of lockpicks in case she needed them. Without backup, she would be relying on only herself. In the strictest sense, that was frowned upon. Hunting was a dangerous gig. Working solo was a great way to wind up as a spirit when you died slow and alone. Good thing Dani had a talent for surviving. It let her walk away with scratches and bruises while she left behind the bodies of too many people she loved. Better she stick to herself now, not drag anyone down with her.

She rubbed a hand over her mouth and peeked out the window one last time. The sun reached out with fingers of red and orange as it disappeared over the horizon. The cool wind from this afternoon had kicked back up. Lucky her, too, since it meant nobody would look twice at her black sweater, cap, and pants. Dani had dressed for the job, but if the weather wanted to help her out, she wouldn't argue. Anonymity was the goal. She double-checked her bag, made sure she'd snagged a flashlight, and headed out as the sun settled down beyond the horizon.

An unfamiliar truck out front of an abandoned house was going to bring up questions if the job went bad, so she'd opted to go the long way. It was all of a ten-minute hike, and she could cover it in half that time at a sprint if it came down to it.

This town put her teeth on edge, friendly sentinels, a farmhouse locked down better than anything she'd ever run across, and the Lockgrove family in tow too. The youngest one, Emilie, had barreled right into her earlier. Poor girl had had been flustered by something. Dani didn't know what, and the zap of power when she helped her out was unexpected. Made sense, but she wasn't well known like her father or her gramps. Names like that weren't common, though, not the way Black was.

The thought brought her back to reality. She needed to concentrate on the house, not every weird thing in this forgotten little hamlet of a town. The place would be locked down, and it was warded tight enough even a sentinel didn't want to touch it. That on its own was worrisome. The job wasn't out of her league, but it was disconcerting.

The path through the trees spit her out behind the Black house. In the dark, with the wind howling against her ears, it looked even less hospitable than it had in the daylight. The moon reflected off broken windows, and she could make out missing shingles on the roof without turning on her flashlight.

She ambled closer and watched as wards gleamed into light against the house. Each stacked on top of the next, the symbols made of circles and hard lines that contained powerful magic. An arcane alphabet, an entire language spoken only by talented and casters. Graham's salve let her see them as they writhed and crawled along every available surface of the house. There were more than she could hope to identify. Only some of them mattered to hunters, and Dani focused on those.

Stay away. Do not cross. You are not welcome here. Invade this boundary and perish. Some of them would only invoke an idle distaste, but there were always one or two wards that she couldn't translate, and they were the most dangerous. She'd seen wards burn people to ash when they weren't protected. The salve would protect her from the wards, but not what they were hiding from the world.

This was a truly stupid idea, but it didn't matter anymore. She needed the veilblade from where it was hidden inside. A few wards—capable of blowing her limb from limb if she screwed up—wouldn't stop her. From everything she'd found, the Black house had sat empty now for over a decade. One of the oldest surviving homes on this side of town, nobody wanted to see it torn down. Didn't mean they'd been trying to keep it up, either, with no owner anywhere in sight.

The place was coming apart at the seams. A wraparound porch sagged, boards cracked from the strain, and only two windows had survived the test of time. More were broken, jagged teeth shining against the darkness. The yard was unkempt, grown wild from years without being tended. No fence stood to block off passersby, only wards to keep trespassers away. It seemed like it worked though.

Dani kept her pace slow and steady as she closed the distance to the back door. Something about the house was familiar, déjà vu striking her hard. She shook it off, telling herself one haunted house looked a lot like the next, even if this one shared her last name.

The back porch sagged under ruined bones of patio furniture left to rot. Glass sparkled along the ground, scattered into long overgrown garden plots. Shame. Someone loved this place once. There was a small statue of a woman with a curved sword adorned with wards for health, prosperity, and security that had cracked into pieces. It all resonated with her charms. Magic poured into the land and the house alike. *What exactly happened here?* Wards blackened and cracked like this didn't happen because of time or neglect. Their destruction had been deliberate.

The stairs creaked under her weight but didn't break. Small favors. She couldn't ask for much more, especially in a house held together by nothing but rot and tragedy. There was only a simple lock on the door, easy to pick, which meant she didn't need to worry about slicing herself open breaking a window. She'd done that once and almost bled out on the way to the damn hospital. It had been a rookie mistake and not one she could afford when working by herself.

The door was wooden, half sunken into the frame, but the upper third was glass and let her see into the dark house. When she opened it, small wards in silver and gold whorls flared and then faded out of sight again. It'd be better if she knew what they were for, or what might happen when she crossed them, but there was no turning back now.

One step into the house and the spark of freshly awoken magic crackled along her skin, tasting her, testing to see if she'd flee. Maybe a ward to warn off intruders? Anticipation rose in her belly, a flame of want that tore through her and made her palm itch for the heft of a blade. The charms that detected magic warmed her skin, keeping her grounded.

The predator place in her head didn't need weapons. She was the weapon. The knives and guns she carried were just modifiers. Her eyes danced along the floors and walls, matching it to the floor plans she'd found. She knew where there had been bedrooms and bath-rooms. But houses were so much more than that, more than wood and bricks. Emotion and experience sank into the bones of a struc-ture and changed it on a fundamental level.

Dani stepped into the house, and the back door clicked shut behind her. The air was heavy, thicker than it should have been. Outside, the wind screamed and the telltale patter of rain started against the windows. It was background noise against a room as hushed as a tomb, as though it had lain untouched since its last owners fled from the town.

Her breathing sounded too loud in the quiet. Nothing moved, and wards shimmered at the edges of her vision, etched into the doors, walls, even the baseboards. The taste of magic was heavy in the air too, ash and blood thick enough she could taste copper in the air.

In the kitchen, a hand-written recipe still sat out on a counter, pinned under a dusty glass mixing bowl. Bowls and plates still crouched in the cabinets. Half-packed boxes and stacks of books had been pulled off the shelves. *Were they surprised when the end came?*

Hunting was a bloody job, and plenty of folks died ugly. Some of them did in their own homes. Dani moved quick and quiet, going from room to room. If she had a weapon capable of dispatching real monsters, ones more than flesh and blood, where would she hide it?

Not in plain sight. No, that wouldn't make any sense. Appearances mattered. You'd want a special spot to drop it. Every hunter worth their salt had something. A closet, a hidden room, a trap door that led to a cache, a place to hide your secrets.

She turned a corner and stopped dead in her tracks. A pile of half packed boxes sat next to a door. Above them the wall had been gouged with a trio of ragged claw marks. It didn't explain why the Blacks had been packing, but if something had attacked them, the quick exit made sense. Further down the hall a chunk of plaster was missing, letting her see the remains of a bathroom. Splintered shards of bannister were scattered along the floor next to the stairs.

This was the place where everything in this house changed, where it had gone from a home to a tomb. She crouched next to the stairs, looking at the floorboards. Deep gouges marred them, and old traces of blood tracked up the stairs. Maybe a safe room up on the second floor?

A charm heated against her skin, and Dani's eyes trailed up the stairs. She wasn't alone.

"Knock, knock. Anybody home?" She set one foot on the first stair, and the house came alive around her.

The walls trembled, floors swelling underfoot like the ocean in a storm. A roar vibrated the air above her, and lights flickered wildly even though they didn't have power anymore. Doors slammed open and shut, and she took a quick two-step back toward the wall. With the way the floors were bucking, she'd end up with a broken leg instead of making it up the stairs. She slipped her blessed iron knife out of its sheath with ease and curled her fist around the handle, steadying herself.

Whatever was waiting in this house, she'd just woken it up.

7

EMILIE

Rain pounded against the pavement and Emilie's car in a torrent that turned visibility into almost nothing. In between the swish and flick of her windshield wipers, the clouds were a dark, roiling mass in the sky above her. She skidded around turns and whipped across town, accelerating as something under her skin screamed to go faster.

The Black farmhouse appeared to the left, and she swerved to the curb and threw her car into park. Rain splattered down in a quick staccato rhythm making it impossible to see much of anything. A sharp pain at the back of her neck pulled her toward the house, something pawing at her from under her sternum. She stepped out of the car, eyes pinned on her destination as her feet slapped onto solid ground.

A massive peal of thunder shook around her, and lightning struck somewhere close by, throwing everything into sharp relief. The sky above lit up, and she saw the house silhouetted for a fraction of a second. Signs and sigils glowed and writhed along the planks like something out of a movie. She blinked, and the farmhouse shifted. The place didn't look the way it had a second ago; it looked wrong.

The Black house had been a wraith in the neighborhood, slowing falling into itself year after year. Now the windows were mouths filled with tiny rows of needled teeth saturated in blood.

What. The hell.

Emilie shook her head, trying to hold on to her composure and failing miserably. The home was hungry, a truth that resonated down to the marrow of her bones. Scarlet lights flashed from inside. She whimpered.

Rain soaked her down to the bone.

"I'm hallucinating. I'm standing outside in the middle of a thunderstorm, hallucinating about a haunted house."

Emilie fought to control her breathing as she took another step, and then that same feeling tugging her forward. She hurtled down the path as thunder shook the ground.

The storm had reduced the old wooden fence to kindling, tossed halfway across the yard. She tripped, almost falling, and felt phantom hands pull her upright and then linger, tugging at her clothes and hair, urging her forward. Every logical bone left in her body screamed at her not to give in. She'd seen enough movies to know those who ran into haunted houses died terribly. But something deep inside wouldn't let her stop.

She stumbled up the stairs and fell against the doorframe, legs giving out. Her vision exploded as more of the strange markings winked into light, scarlet letters in a language she couldn't read. The door popped open, and she fell inside. She hadn't been expecting it and stumbled for a few steps before crashing down and skidding to a stop against a wall.

Rainwater puddled around her on the floor. Her head throbbed from the second serious dive she'd taken in eight hours. It took a few moments for her eyes to adjust, and when they did, her throat worked convulsively. Dark smears of blood marred the walls, gleaming somehow in the darkness.

She let out a shuddering breath and tried to get ahold of herself. This had to be an illusion, nobody had been here in years, not since

Grandpa closed the place up. She almost had a memory of it, but couldn't quite grasp it.

She reached toward the wall, hand quivering above withered wallpaper. Instead of the gore it looked like, the paper was dry and fell to the ground when she brushed it. The blood wasn't real. Static swelled around her, overwhelming her senses. She squeezed her eyes shut, muscles clenched tight as a vise as she concentrated. Voices broke through the noise, distant and distorted like a bad radio signal.

A man's voice called out, too distant to hear, and then was gone. The static cut off abruptly, and she popped open one eye in a wince, expecting the noise to return. Instead, the woman she'd crashed into this afternoon was staring at her and brandishing a knife.

"Hey, hey, hey!" Emilie threw up her hands to show she didn't have a weapon. "No stabbing. I'm just…this thing happened, and now I'm here. I know I ran into you earlier, but it'd be super cool if you didn't stab me." She scooted backwards again until she managed to get her feet back under her and stood up.

"Right. Because shit wasn't already off the rails." Dani tipped her head back with a sigh and slipped the knife into a sheath on her hip.

"Look, I know this looks crazy. I mean, who just shows up in the middle of the ni—" From upstairs something took a heavy step. It echoed across the floorboard as dust and detritus cascaded from the ceiling. Emilie stopped mid-sentence, eyes drawn up to the second floor. Even over the rain, she could hear someone muttering, the voice distinctly male.

"Crazy does not begin to cover it." Dani grabbed at Emilie's arm.

"Okay. I mean I know what this looks like—"

"You look out of your league, and I don't have time for a bystander tonight." Dani shot Emilie a disgruntled glare.

"I'm not a—a—"

"Bystander?" Dani raised an eyebrow.

Emilie sputtered and let herself be dragged forward a few steps toward the door. "I can't really explain how or why, but we need to be —not here."

"That's my line."

"What?" Emilie frowned and shook her head in confusion.

"Nothing." Dani scowled. "I appreciate the gesture, but I'm not here for my health, and you are in my way."

"What are you talking about?"

Dani narrowed her eyes. "You're Emilie Lockgrove, right?"

"Yeah? What about it?" She shrugged out of the other woman's grip and took a step back.

"Of the *talented* Lockgrove?" Dani made a swishy motion with her fingers, and something familiar reached out from the memories she didn't have access to.

We are a family of many talents my darling. Yours haven't all woken up, I don't think. Dad's voice drifted through her mind, and Emilie blanched. When had he said that to her? And why?

"When you say talented..."

"Magic. Monsters. Shadows and demons and witches and wards," Dani deadpanned. "You must know. No way were you raised by Ephraim freaking Lockgrove and his son without getting some kind of mojo to hold on to." Dani shook her head, and irritation flared in her eyes. She took Emilie's arm again then frog-marched her toward the front door. "Look. No offense, but I'm not playing babysitter tonight, Lockgrove or not. You gotta beat feet."

"Beat fee— No. Something is going on here."

"Yeah. I'm at work, and you're in my way. It's cool. I have a solution: you leave, and I do my job." The woman smiled, feral and full of teeth, and heat rushed through Emilie, desire strong enough that she couldn't stop the flush from breaking across her cheeks. Dani was tall and lean and *so* Emilie's type it was impossible to ignore. The temptation to fan herself was overwhelming.

Emilie shook her arm free for the second time and planted her feet, not wanting to look Dani in the eyes and be swayed by the magnetic force she was putting out. If she didn't want to go, then the other woman probably couldn't make her if she went all dead weight on her. Emilie's solid frame versus Dani's lithe body gave her the advantage in that aspect.

From upstairs, something heavy moved and distracted her. Dani used the opening to manhandle her with a painful pressure point on the back of her arm, moving her closer to the front door. But when Dani grabbed it, the knob wouldn't turn. She shook it with all her strength, and it didn't move an inch, which was weird, considering it had been hanging on its hinges. Now it might as well have been sealed shut. Something deep inside Emilie knew with a horrible certainty that this house was haunted.

The ponderous movement continued above them as floorboards creaked out in the hallway.

"The hell?" The noise distracted Dani from her efforts to extricate Emilie from the house.

Emilie kept looking up toward the second floor. There was something up there. It felt...monstrous. Crazy as that sounded, even in her head, she had no other words for it. Emotions roiled from it, and somehow she could feel them, taste them in the air. "Do you hear that?"

Dani looked over and met Emilie's eyes before tracking the slow movement up on the second floor. "Oh."

"Oh? What is oh?" Emilie stepped back away from the stairwell and deeper into the house. "This place has been abandoned since, since..."

"Since the Black family took off into the night as if fleeing something monstrous?" Dani inquired with a curious lilt to her voice.

"Something like that. It happened when I was a kid. But that's not the point!"

Emilie backed away as Dani pursued her, step for step. Heat sparked between them with each movement. Ghosts and magic and monsters weren't real. If they were, Grandpa would have told her. Wouldn't he? Emilie's back hit the wall, and she swallowed a squeak. Dani was nearly pressed against her, somehow far more intimidating than her frame should have been able to manage. She felt the line of Dani's body and had to resist the urge to take a better look. One arm braced against the wall above her head, toned biceps bulging. Emilie would have been lying to herself if she pretended she wasn't ridiculously into her, even if this was the middle of what was turning into the strangest night she'd had in years.

"What is the point then?" Dani asked.

"Someone—or something—told me to come here." Emilie raised a finger trying to make her point.

"Who?"

"That's not important, is it?" Emilie asked, eyes too wide as she tried to evade the question. Somehow, "My dead several times great-grandmother told me to," didn't quite have the right ring to it. That and it seemed like a sure-fire way to make the only person she had been into in a long time run fast and far.

"Then what is?"

"See, that's where things get complicated." She chuckled lightly and smiled awkwardly at Dani. She was completely off her game because the other woman was a stone-cold fox, but what she should have been paying attention to were the noises from upstairs—not the words coming out of her mouth.

"Oh yes, because they're so simple right now." Dani stared at Emilie for a long moment. Was that appraisal in her eyes, attraction?

"Is sarcasm really the best option for us?"

"Us? There is no us. There is me, here to get something done, and there is you who busted in on me." Dani enunciated with a flourish of the blade in her hand.

"When I ran into you earlier, well, I mean, when you helped me up—"

"On the street."

"Yeah. I saw something."

Dani cocked her head and watched Emilie closer. "You wanna elaborate on that?"

"There was you, and a thing made of smoke, and one of those glyphs—"

"Wards." Dani corrected her in a soft voice that brooked no disagreement.

"Yeah, one in red. Dark, dark, red."

"Blood wards." Dani swore under her breath and took a step back. "And you have no clue what's going on?"

"Not really, no. Do I look like I'm in the loop?"

"Blood wards mean we are both in deep shit."

Dread rolled over Emilie in a slow, inexorable wave as the landing at the top of the stairs creaked ominously.

"There's...something in this house. I can hear it, up there." Her gaze flicked up toward the ceiling again, afraid of what she might see.

"So I noticed," Dani muttered and then frowned. "Back toward the kitchen." She gestured, and Emilie took the lead farther into the heart of the house.

The buzz from earlier returned. It skittered like electricity off her skin and burrowed down to the bone until it vibrated in her teeth. Instead of trying to ignore it this time, she leaned into the sensation. A pair of voices argued back and forth, an old man, infuriated and screaming, and a desperate younger man. But only one of them wanted her attention. The younger voice called her name over and over.

The signal cleared up, but the buzzing along her skin was still there. The world swayed around her, ground rushing at her face. Dani grabbed her by the waist but couldn't stop the momentum as Emilie fell and took her down to the ground in a rough tangle of limbs.

"You have to open the basement door, Emilie. Only you. Blood calls to blood."

The words rang clarion inside her head, as though someone were speaking right next to her. She gasped, a sweet, cool inhale to lungs that hadn't been doing their job.

"Oh no you don't. I need you to not pass out because I do not have time to haul you outside tonight." Dani's voice was furious next to her.

Emilie extricated herself from the other woman's warm, enticing limbs, and coughed, getting her feet back underneath her. "I'm fine. Or I'll be fine."

"If I'm stuck with you, that means you follow my lead, and I have to find—"

"In the basement." Emilie took a step forward and a phantom hand guided her to where she needed to go. "We need to get to the basement." She looked back over her shoulder to see Dani watching her carefully.

"There wasn't a basement on the blueprints for this place."

"I think I know where it is."

"Have you ever been here before?"

"No. I have a feeling, or something."

"Or something?" Dani repeated.

"Yeah, I hear... I think those blood wards things are on the basement door. Blood calls to blood." She frowned. She didn't know how to explain the knowledge that those particular wards belonged to her Grandpa, and that they weren't a danger to her.

"I'm not saying you're wrong, but that is one hell of a gamble."

She didn't argue or call her crazy. "How so?" Emilie asked, toeing her way down the hallway, letting instincts she'd ignored for a decade bloom back into life.

"Blood wards are nasty, or they can be. If you aren't the right bloodline, they can kill you."

"Oh that's...oh." Either she was playing along for some reason, or she believed her. That either meant magic was real, or Dani was crazy too. Emilie shook her head and stopped. To her left there was a cabinet that didn't sit flush with the wall. "I thought the entrance would be here." She frowned, confused as she stared at it.

"Not surprising." Dani pushed past and pried at the one edge until it popped up and away from the plaster. Behind it was an ornate door with wards written large all over it. They moved and writhed against each another. Magic, they were real, honest honest-to-goodness magic.

"Jeeesus." Dani whistled low. "Would you look at those." She shook her head and took a step back, giving Emilie a look that said "do what you will."

"You see them too?" Emilie whispered, afraid of the answer either way.

"Of course."

One hand tapped at her thigh too fast. A sneaky voice said this was a delusion, her mind coming up with lies to deal with a truth too difficult to understand.

Her fingers trembled as she reached forward. Dani's hesitancy was catching, and it would be just Emilie's luck to find out about magic only to die the same day. She breathed out in a slow, steady stream, sensed someone invisible standing with her. She grasped the knob. Crimson wards glowed against the wood and then melted away.

"Here goes nothing." She pulled the door open to a narrow stairway, and when nothing happened, she took a step forward.

Dani followed her, lighting their way with a flashlight. The door fell shut behind them. All around, tiny lights flared to life, wards visible next to balls of light in palest blue and white that lit the landing.

Emilie looked back and noticed it had three sets of locks. She locked them all, just in case and just in time. As she threw the last lock, a force slammed into the door, rattling it in its frame. Emilie stumbled back with a yelp.

"Looks like the only way through is down." Dani nodded her head as though this was normal for her. She started down the steps and Emilie rushed to follow.

Even with the terror and confusion, she found herself watching the sway of Dani's hips, or maybe it was in part *because* of the terror and confusion. She wanted to smack herself. What kind of person was she to be checking out this woman at a time like this? The kind with a pulse? The distraction helped calm her. She sighed at herself, but followed after a moment. Behind her the locks continued to rattle as something threw itself against the door, making her jump and pick up her pace.

At the bottom of the stairs lay a large oval landing. In front of them stood a pair of black double doors.

"Is it locked?"

"Hmm? No, I don't think so." Dani frowned.

"There aren't any wards on these." Emilie got to the landing and approached the doors. Hesitantly, she reached out and pressed a palm against the dark wood.

When she didn't fall down dead at the motion, Dani tried the other door. It swung open without a sound. Emilie watched as Dani stepped through, and tried not to think about how big of a mistake it might be as she followed her.

8

DANI

Dani stepped through the doorway and stopped short with Emilie on her heels. The basement was cool without being musty. Weapon racks lined one wall, brimming with blades and guns. When she fantasized about putting down roots and building an arsenal, this was what it looked like. She threw a glance back at the door and noticed a trio of iron bars mounted next to it. Considering the pounding from the main floor, she took the time to push the bars down. *No point in a security system if you didn't use it.*

If this family had something to hide, she figured it'd be down here. Unlike the rest of the house, someone had ransacked this room. Files were thrown across a scarred wooden table, and bullet casings were scattered on the floor by a weapons locker. It was no easy call where she'd find a mystical monster-killing knife.

Emilie passed her, wide eyed. Dani wanted to keep her eyes on this girl. She was willing to believe Emilie didn't know what was going on for now, but it didn't make a lick of sense, not with the magical pedigree that followed her last name around. At least she was cute. She appeared as defenseless as a fawn, but was undeniably cute.

Things would be easier if Dani was alone, but it would have taken her hours to find her way down here. They must have left it off the blueprints on purpose. The blood wards would have come later when they were sealing the house up.

Dani bit the inside of her cheek and tried not to consider this might be another dead end. The spirit upstairs was concerning, if it was a spirit, but not a total surprise all considered. She had an iron blade if it got confrontational, but she didn't have her whole kit to cleanse anyone tonight. She waited with bated breath, but the noise upstairs paused. It might still be trouble, but they weren't on the run for the moment.

She walked over to the table, curious to see if there was anything useful in the files. Moving as quickly as she could, she rifled through the handwritten pages. Between the slanted script and the mess someone had left them in, it was incomprehensible.

Emilie's presence threw her off her game too. She narrowed her eyes and watched as the woman wandered aimlessly through the basement, jumping at every noise. She was shorter than Dani, curvy, with wisps of white-blonde hair that framed her face and captivating pale blue eyes. She'd caught the flash of red on her cheeks earlier, and she respected the way she'd held her ground upstairs. The problem was that the hunter knew how to sniff out trouble, and that's exactly what she was looking at.

Damned if she isn't my kind of trouble though.

Dani wished she'd been able to kick her out of the house and send her back home, but with Spectre on her tail, she was out of time. She needed to stay professional, and she hated professional. It was so damned boring compared to the alternative. Being a hunter meant enjoying herself while murdering monsters. Anything else was a waste.

"Why are you here?"

Emilie whipped around at Dani's question. Her eyes flicked back and forth. Dani scowled, there was something off about this girl.

"I didn't have much choice in the matter," Emilie hedged.

"Darlin', I hunt monsters, for a living. Try me."

Emilie's eyes widened, making Dani think she didn't know about monsters. Great, that was just great.

"I don't actually know what's going on here." Her gaze slipped away from Dani.

"So you make a habit of just showing up at abandoned houses in the middle of the night and knowing where hidden rooms are?" Dani scoffed. "Well bless your heart."

"It's been. A weird. Day."

"I'm gonna need more than that." Dani smirked with a turn of her head and wondered if it was just anger she saw cascading through those pale blue eyes. Emilie had some fire for sure.

"Okay. Fine." Emilie bit out the words. "My life is in pieces, my grandpa might be dying, I got locked in my family's crypt in super creepy circumstances, and I'm seeing things. And if that wasn't enough? My several times great-grandmother appeared and told me to come here. Except she has been dead since before I was born. Why don't you tell me how that makes any sense?" Emilie flailed her arms around and shook her head.

Dani let a cold, flat mask slip over her features. This would be easier if Emilie was playing her, but her gut twisted, warning her that she'd missed something. The blade, Emilie, the Black family...it all fit together somehow, but she didn't have the whole picture.

"I mean, you're a Lockgrove right? Magic and talents? They're your family's bread and butter. If you missed it you gotta be about as dense as it comes because..." She trailed off.

"My memory is what you'd call a problem. I don't remember a lot from...before ten years ago."

"Why does that matter?"

Emilie shot her a dirty look, and Dani managed not to roll her eyes, barely. The wheels in her head turned. She had two basic options: trust Emilie, or tie her up in a corner until she found the veilblade.

"It matters because I don't know what's real! Oh, your mama was crazy, Emile! Except maybe she wasn't!" The last part turned into a shout. Emilie closed her eyes, face relaxing as she seemed to compose herself—a touch—before she went on. "And oh, it was the fire that caused the memory loss, but I'm remembering things that don't match!" Emilie paced back and forth, intermittently yelling and throwing her arms in the air as she did. "And there's this weird static, and I can hear voices inside of it. Voices!" She turned and stared at Dani, and one of her eyes twitched. "And it was crazy, so I came here. To prove to myself I wasn't crazy. And I'm not because the house was lit up and there is blood on the walls and someone keeps whispering to me and this can't be real!" The last bit turned into another shout, almost a scream really. She collapsed into a chair at the table and thunked her head against the wood.

Dani watched her, trying to gauge her response. She was still tempted to tie up the woman and get back to work, except that Emilie's description fit a talent sparking up—even if it was late as hell. Most of the time talents showed up during the end of puberty at the latest. No way was Emilie younger than twenty-four or twenty-five. One of Dani's hands played with the hilt of the consecrated iron blade strapped to her hip.

She was locked in a basement with a talented who didn't know what she was, and something nasty waited for them both upstairs. This night just kept getting better and better. But Dawson wasn't any weirder than her usual gigs. She believed Emilie, and if it could help Dani get closer to that weapon, it'd be worth the risk.

She'd heard of unskilled psychics hearing "static" when they tried to reach beyond the veil, but a true medium? They were a different case altogether. There weren't many running around anymore, not since Spectre murdered the last of the Deveraux a generation back.

"Okay, here's the thing. In general, I try to be nice." Dani shrugged. "Sometimes. But we don't have that kind of time tonight. Ghosts and monsters are real. Witches: real. Things that eat people and don't leave so much as bones behind: real."

Emilie shifted uneasily, and something crossed behind her eyes, a shadow, a gleam of understanding maybe. That or she was checking Dani out on the down-low. Wouldn't be the first time with a bystander, wouldn't be the last. People tended to find the whole hunter thing attractive. Something about it felt different, though, more genuine and deeper. The possibility sent an unexpected thrill through her.

"I got a lead on this house about a weapon I need, but I think there is something more going on here because two plus two isn't adding up to four."

"What do you mean, something more?"

"You've got some talents hidden under the skin there." She pushed a finger against one of Emilie's arms. Her soft skin shot another thrill through Dani.

The woman blushed and tilted her head a bit to hide it behind her hair. Damn, she was too cute for Dani's own good. "Talents?" she asked in a voice that was a bit breathy.

"Ma-gic, talent. That static, it isn't static." Dani cocked her head. "You're probably hearing dead people. From the—" She gestured about them. "—beyond or whatever. From the other side of the veil."

"I mean...wouldn't I have known? Wouldn't this have come up before?" Emilie shook her head and gesticulated wildly.

"You should have." Dani gave her a long look, trying to measure the internal strength of this woman she'd only just met. "Unless something blocked them out."

"What does that mean?"

"Sometimes a talent gets fried when you push too far. Not my department, to be honest. Doesn't explain why your family sent you here, but it is what it is."

Emilie chuckled, a dark raw sound. "There's this...one voice here. That's how I found the basement. He led me here."

"He?"

"I don't have a name, just a voice. A phantom hand pushed me in the right direction."

"Okay. Okay, okay." Dani paced back and forth, scanning the room. "I don't know what's up with tonight, but if you help me, maybe I can help you. I'm here for a weapon, a specific knife."

"A weapon." Emilie's voice sounded distant. "You need the veilblade."

"How...?"

"Voices. In my head." She blinked slowly.

Dani scowled. "They tell you where to find it?"

"Down here somewhere?" She followed the question with another frown and a shake of her head. "The signal isn't strong enough. It was...but it's gone fuzzy."

Dani left Emilie at the table and took a more thorough look at the room she'd barred them inside of. Only one way in and one way out from the looks of it, with shelves and cabinets set against two walls and another taken up by weapon storage. Some shelves were filled with herbs and various odds and ends, but not what she was looking for. Around her, the air grew thicker, heavier.

"Do you feel that?" She pulled at her collar, neck slick with sweat, and looked at where Emilie sat. Emilie's head cocked, one hand held up to her ear like she was trying to listen to something. She winced as if whatever she heard wasn't good. "Did you hear me?" Dani pressed.

"What?" Emilie blinked and sat up, meeting Dani's eyes. "Sorry, I thought the static had come back, but it hasn't. It's crackling like..."

"Fire." Dani finished Emilie's sentence for her and grabbed her by the arm, pulling her out of the chair.

The air in front of the door shimmered, and a slim crack in the world appeared. Tiny grey wisps of smoke drifted out from it. Her heart hammered in her chest. She'd seen this before, and it could only mean one thing. The fracture turned red, and the smell of brimstone and old death crept into the room around them.

"Did you miss me, Dani?" A cultured baritone voice wafted through the rift, and her blood ran cold.

No. Graham's dead body flashed before her eyes. No way had he tracked her down. Dani had been careful, so damned cautious. She'd used wards and charms and every ointment and oil she'd ever discovered. Tiny plumes of flame sipped at the air, lapping from the rift as something dark and viscous dripped onto the ground. It didn't matter how he found her, only that he had. There wasn't much time. That rift would open wide soon enough, and either Spectre, or one of his wraiths, would slink through. She needed that blade *right now*.

"So quiet," his voice drifted through the rift. He chuckled and goosebumps ran up her arms. She ushered Emilie behind her and pressed the two of them back until they hit the wall. If he'd come here for Dani, there was no reason for him to notice she wasn't alone. Not unless he came through himself.

"No witty banter this time? I'm hurt." He tsked, and she looked over her shoulder and put a finger up to her lips. "Or do you just miss your friend?" He cackled, and she winced as though someone had raked nails down a chalkboard. Nobody talked about her Graham like that, nobody.

"Go to hell."

"There we go." His delight was unnerving as all hell.

Dani couldn't wait to gut him and watch the light in his eyes die out once and for all. Part of her wanted to reach through the rift and yank him out. Another part was terrified of what he might do to Emilie and her if he made it through.

"That's the little hunter that could."

Dani rolled her eyes. "So clever. However do you stay so sharp?"

"I thought it might be you. Only a matter of time until somebody triggered this wee trap of mine."

"What's that supposed to mean?" She ambled away from Emilie, keeping an eye on the rift and the blackness pouring out from it.

She gestured at Emilie to check the cabinets over by the arsenal. The others hadn't yielded any results, and she didn't have any spare weapons to hand off when things got bloody. Spectre's wraiths—his personal nightmare creations powered by magic and created from darkness—were his front line of defense.

"Did you make a new friend, Dani?" He tsked. "That was a bad choice. You remember how the last one died, now don't you?" Emilie's movement must have caught his attention.

Emilie stared back at her, terror written all over her face. Dani didn't know what to do. She wasn't used to dealing with this degree of messed up by herself, and she wasn't prepped to handle a wraith, not the kind Spectre could throw out. The rift stood between them and the door, growing wider by the moment, and something was moving on the other side.

9

EMILIE

Emilie watched in horror as the tear continued to grow larger. She opened her mouth to speak and then clamped it shut again. Her hands trembled, her calves wobbled, and voices in her head echoed and ricocheted without rhyme or reason. Viscous, dark fluid dripped onto the floor, and something else was coming. The rift was wide enough that she could almost see a shadow made of undulating coils waiting for the opportunity to slip through.

Another moment passed, and wet tendrils of a greasy looking substance and smoke slithered into the world followed by loops of glistening serpentine scales. Dani had turned from an agitated young woman into a weapon made of flesh, a grey-silver knife in her hand. Something in Emilie knew it wouldn't be enough, not against that oily mess.

Worse, the voice Dani bantered back and forth with as they edged through the room was familiar. *Where do I recognize him from?* The memory stayed locked behind the door in her mind, but something about it struck a chord she couldn't argue with. It belonged to someone important. Important how, she wasn't sure, but she had a feeling it wasn't good.

The world around her slowed as she backed into a cabinet next to the weapons arsenal. She watched the snake-thing ease its way into the basement inch by inch.

She needed to remember who the voice belonged to. It was from before the fire and Mama screaming. She'd stuffed it down into a box never to be opened. Never, ever, ever. Except it was here, the voice that haunted her nightmares as Mama died over and over again, a voice from her dreams and her childhood, and one she didn't bloody well remember.

Her breath came too fast, becoming panting gasps she couldn't control. If she kept going, she'd hyperventilate and pass out, and then they'd both be screwed. As though things were going according to plan. The joke was on the universe, she'd never had a plan, just cause and effect, one action tumbling into the next until she arrived here.

The sound of cold laughter ripped open old wounds, made the past come spilling out into the now as though a door in her head was opened. Trauma and pain and tragedy washed over her in a wave. The pressure around her shifted, and her ears popped. One moment there was the low buzz of static, and the next it disappeared.

"Emilie. Emilie, you have to get the blade. It's hidden in the rear of the cabinet. But you need to give it to Dani, and you need to do it now! Damnit! CAN YOU HEAR ME!?"

She jumped, and the world crashed back to life.

She saw Dani as she bantered, getting closer to the snake thing, attracting its attention away from Emilie. The wheels had come off the wagon, and nothing sat right anymore, but someone was next to her. Ben. Benjamin Black. The name floated into her head as though she'd known it all along. Maybe she had. It became easy to feel his presence as he hovered over her.

His words broke through, and she scrambled into motion. When she turned on her heel, a floor to ceiling cabinet she hadn't noticed before glowed. Chiseled wards gleamed against dark wood, but she ignored them and grabbed the doors. The wards flared a bright red at her touch; more blood wards. After a moment of tingling beneath her skin, the doors gave into her frantic tugging, as if they recognized her. Inside the cabinet were rows of boxes. Without touching them she knew none of them were what she needed.

"Calm now. Easy does it. All the way in the back there's a secret compartment. You'll feel it." The hairs on her arm rose as Ben guided her hand to the switch surrounded by more blood wards.

This time when his presence faded away, the heat of the room rose and swallowed her. Emilie moved boxes out of the way until she fumbled at the mechanism, gratified at the small pop when it caught.

A muttered curse made her look back. The snake creature had dislodged itself from the rift, oiling looking coils undulating across the floor toward Dani. The thing was unclean on a fundamental level. Something out of a nightmare, its sinuous length led to a warped head with too many teeth. More of the slick substance coated every inch of the creature's body, pooling on the ground and spreading across the floor.

Dani moved almost too fast to follow. The blade in her hand was a silver blur, slashing back and forth. Each shot hit its mark, carving thin wounds against the bulk of the beast. Instead of blood, all it did was leave weak pale lines. Her weapon was clearly not strong enough to get the job done.

Emilie shook her head and dove into the cabinet, frantic hands grasping at the edge of the hidden compartment. A single item wrapped in dark cloth rested inside, and she grabbed it and scrambled backwards. The silky material dropped to the side, revealing a long, pale-handled blade. Calling it a knife or a dagger would have been wrong, inadequate. The blade was a gleaming promise of lethal force.

She turned back to get her bearings. She kept to the wall, skirting the large dark puddle on the floor and coming into sight of the snake-thing for the first time. Pale grey eyes met her own, and that damnable voice thundered around her.

"Well, well, well. What do we have here?" Emilie noticed the smile, the absolute joy in his tone, and it nailed her to the spot.

The door in her mind hiding everything she'd survived creaked further open. She knew him, and however she did, it tied into that night, the evening of the fire, when her life burned to ash.

"I've been looking for you. I didn't expect this, though. Tell me, sweetling, do you remember me yet?" Emilie was so struck by the voice, trying to place it, desperate to remember, that she almost didn't notice the snake-thing. Its dark coils undulated, preparing to spring.

"Looking for...me?" She whispered the words under her breath, each exhalation a knife under her ribs as panic reared up inside of her.

"Oh yes, dear one. You slipped right through my fingers, but you'll recall me soon enough."

The snake hissed, and it broke through the fog in Emilie's mind. She yelled Dani's name and chucked the blade, cloth and all, as hard as she could. The snake's tail slammed into her ribs, and her body cracked into a wall, knocking the wind from her. Her vision went spotty and dark around the edges. The world turned to a stop-motion picture as she tried to remember how to breathe.

Dani missed the veilblade, and it clattered to the floor as the snake reared above her. Emilie fought to sit back up, and her head lolled on her shoulders. From inside the rift came an inhuman scream.

The door in her mind opened wider, and she tried not to whimper. The tear lit up at its edges, air catching on fire where there wasn't any fuel. He was coming, the man who spoke through the snake-thing. After ten years, he was coming for her. She just didn't remember who he was or why he had been looking for her. But she knew one thing, she was terrified as all hell.

10

EMILIE

ani's outstretched fingers missed the shroud Emilie chucked at her, and it skidded across the floor, out of reach by mere inches. Silky cloth slipped away and revealed a gleaming silver blade, the veilblade. Power was sunk into the essence of the weapon, and even Dani felt it ripple through the air.

She had no time to think about why someone had wrapped it up tight. Spectre screamed from behind the rift as the snake-wraith slammed Emilie into the wall. She wasn't sure why he couldn't make it through on his own. She only cared that he couldn't. But that could change at any moment. Dani seized the opportunity and surged toward the veilblade. He recognized the little medium, and it distracted him. It wouldn't last. He'd chased her for months now. This was his big chance to get her, and no doubt two for one sounded like a better deal to him, but if he thought she'd make it easy, he had another thing coming. Anger swelled inside of her, her constant companion. Spectre didn't get to win, not if she had anything to say about it.

She skidded to stop, swiping the blade off the floor in a fluid motion. As she pulled it from its sheath, it came alive and glowed like a captive sun. Tendrils of magic lapped up her arm, tasting her skin and deciding if she was worthy. The light disappeared, and magic pulsed deep within. The snake hissed behind her, and Dani pivoted, dropping into a crouch.

A blanket of calm settled over her. With a proper weapon, it was time for the slice of the blade, the scream of a body pushed to the brink, time for the bloody place inside her head, a temple to hunting. Her right hand gripped the veilblade tight and let it hang low against her thigh. Muscles trembled, anticipation churning through her.

In front of her, the wraith rose on thick, inky coils. A hood flashed out around razor-sharp teeth, patterns in gold and scarlet breaking up the blackness of its flesh. She recognized those markings. She'd seen them last in Alabama. It hissed again, ichor dripping from its mouth, and she snarled back. A strand of magic still connected it to Spectre on the other side. Separating them was her one shot.

It snapped at her, and Dani danced backwards, drawing it away from the tear. She needed to stretch its resources as far as the dimensions of the room allowed. The wraith coiled and then sprang at her. Small sidesteps gave her better range as she eluded a flurry of strikes.

The snake slid past, and she swiped out with the blade, hitting nothing but air. She was close, but not enough to take a chunk out of its hide. She darted forward, leaped over a thick strand of oily flesh, and turned on her heel at the last moment. The veilblade slashed out, a bright-white blur in the yellow light. This time she hit her mark. The snake screamed as she effortlessly sliced through ebony scales.

A spray of blood splattered against the floor. The wound knit itself in moments. She slid under another coil and avoided the too-close snap of jaws next to her head. She hammered the blade into flesh above her and ripped a long lateral line along its belly. It screamed again. Spectre echoed the noise, frustration and spite seasoning his voice.

The snake recoiled, twisting and turning to hide the wounded sections from the kiss of her knife. Beyond it, the rift shimmered, smaller than it had been. It took juice to open that tear and to keep his pet alive. Even the bogeyman didn't have an unlimited well of power to tap. He was burning through his reserves to take her out from a distance.

Emilie groaned, and Dani let out a small relieved breath that the impact hadn't killed her. Plenty of hunters went down from less. One wrong hit, and it was all over, no matter who you were.

A wet splat from the rift refocused her on the task at hand as another dark loop of smoke-flesh dropped to the floor. Spectre was trying to feed it more mass. It pulled itself taut, stretching away from her and the breach. Her vision narrowed to a pinprick. She had a perfect shot.

Dani exploded into motion. The knife in her hand ceased to be a weapon. It became an extension of herself. When she hit the connection between beast and master, the impact jarred her whole arm. She grunted and freed the blade with a tug that sent a spray of blood into the air. This time, no fast-action healing jumped to work. The snake screamed and writhed, coiling to strike at her. Dani kept hacking, once, twice, and on the third blow the link was severed. The monster melted as it lunged for her, nothing but fetid breath hitting her. The rift sizzled and disappeared.

She took a few steps away from the puddle of black liquid left behind and then dropped to her knees. She still clutched the veil-blade in one hand. She looked at it in disbelief, not a speck of blood or gore touched it. The rest of her wasn't so lucky.

Her pants and jacket were covered in maroon stains—nothing new there—and dark ichor from the ooze caked the soles of her boots. Dani made her way over to the other woman, moving slower than she had been a minute ago.

Emilie slouched against the wall, watching with a shell-shocked expression on her face. She was too pale, eyes like dark wounds, but then Dani was never cheerful after getting thrown into a wall either.

"Can I say..." Emilie shook her head. "This was not the plan when I showed up tonight."

"You had a plan?"

"No. But that's...beside the point."

"You doin' okay down there, killer?" Dani gave her a half smile and raised an eyebrow. Emilie might not be a heavy hitter, but after tonight, it was clear by a long shot she wasn't a bystander.

"There's only one of you, and the world isn't a stop-motion picture anymore, so I think I'm good. I hurt but not 'oh god it's broken and I'm dying hurt.'"

"You know the difference?"

"Yes." Emilie's voice was flat. Dani knew a shut-down when she heard it. She would let her keep her secrets.

"I couldn't have done this without you."

"Thank Ben."

"Ben?"

"Yeah. He used to live here. Thank him. I never would have found the compartment otherwise." Her eyes shifted.

"There's something else." Dani waited a beat. "I mean, other than the massive snake monster I just murdered the shit out of."

"That...voice, the one beyond the—" She gestured to the other side of the room where the rift had been. "—rip or whatever. I recognized it."

"Yeah?" Dani turned and fetched the cloth the veilblade had been wrapped in.

"Yeah..." Emilie trailed off.

Dani decided not to pry. Staying in this town wasn't mandatory; she had what she'd come for. It'd be easy to disappear before dawn. Except that Spectre recognized Emilie. Even if she didn't remember him, there was something there. She had her weapon, but it felt as though she'd trudged into a trap. If the Lockgrove family had tussled with the bogeyman, then maybe they'd wanna pitch in and help her take him out. She avoided talented, but if they shared a grudge, she could make an exception.

Upstairs, another series of heavy thumps rocked the door that led down to the basement. Dani ignored the noise and tucked the veilblade into the inner pocket of her jacket. No point in advertising what she'd found down here. She helped Emilie to her feet.

"You expecting company?"

"Not so much." Emilie's eyes were pinned to the ceiling.

"Well, fuck. I don't think there's another way out."

The door upstairs slammed open and Dani flinched. Nothing easy to deal with would have blown it away like that. She touched the hilt of the veilblade but waited to draw it. A pair of feet pounded down the stairs, and Dani slid in front of Emilie. Anything that came for them would have to get through her first.

The bars that sealed the doorway fell away, and the double doors swung open, revealing Mercurious, the sentinel bookstore owner. Not quite what she'd expected. His face was wild, and a pale blue shirt wrinkled around the collar hugged his chest.

"What are you two doing down here?" he snapped and looked at the remaining residue on the floor. "Oh, that's not good."

"I handled it," Dani said and shot Emilie a look over her shoulder.

"Uh huh." Merc said.

"I did ask about the house."

Merc shot her a dirty look and then glanced at Emilie, who still looked woozy. "Is she okay?"

"Took a nasty hit when things went sideways."

"You wanna elaborate?"

"Not really. Kinda tired after dispatching the wraith." She shrugged.

"How did you even get in here? There were four layers of glamours and wards."

"I'm a professional." Dani didn't want to admit that she thought something fishy was going on too. There were too many coincidences about this house. "And Emilie's a Lockgrove. She waved off the blood wards." She smiled viciously.

"That's not— Wait, Emilie broke them?"

"Yes. I did." Emilie bit out the words.

"Emilie—"

"Did you know?"

"Phillip's going to kill me for this." Merc tipped his head to the ceiling and let out a long-suffering sigh. "By the time I found out something was up, you were gone. You want to blame somebody? Talk to your father."

"Yeah, well, he isn't here right now is he?"

"No, but your grandfather is on the other side of town. And Ephraim hates keeping secrets from you."

"Great, you two know each other." Dani shook her head. "Small town and all, I guess. Well that saves time. Not to be the bearer of bad news or anything, but we have a bigger problem,"

"Oh?" Mercurious turned back to Dani, eyes narrowing.

"Did you know what was down here?"

"You mean Spectre's snake?" he asked, voice level.

"Yeah, I—"

"Spectre." Emilie whispered the name. "I recognized his voice but I don't..."

"Nobody was supposed to get in," Merc explained, eyes jumping between them. "Ephraim locked this place down. My pops helped too. It was basically Ben's final wish. I'm surprised you two are alive." He rubbed a hand along his jaw.

"Well, we are," Dani said, intent on getting all three of them out of there. "Look, we're outta here. You're late to the party."

She took Emilie by the elbow. Merc ducked under her other arm and helped support her as they made their way up the stairs. The storm had passed, and Emilie shook as tears tracked down her face. Dani walked her down to the street and paused. Better to cut and run, it would be a kindness, but she couldn't make herself do it. Emilie needed someone, and right now that was her.

"Did you drive here?"

Emilie blinked slowly, and her pale eyes settled on Dani. "Uh, yeah. From my house." She gestured. "Across town."

"I don't think you should drive right now." Understatement of the century.

"I...yeah...you're...it's..." Fresh tears welled in Emilie's eyes, pulling at Dani's heartstrings in all the right ways. "They hid it away. They took my magic and bound it and told me I was crazy," she said, words tumbling out of her mouth in a grief-stricken deluge. Dani recognized the sentiment.

"Do you want me to drive you home?" Dani asked, voice soft. Kinder than usual.

"What time is it?" Emilie looked up at the sky, the moon still obscured by the clouds as they scudded past.

"It's gotta be at least two." Dani cocked her head. "Maybe closer to three. Why don't you let me drive you back to my motel room? You can crash for a few hours and then go home once your head clears. Someone should keep an eye on you in case you have a concussion."

Emilie nodded and handed over a pair of keys she had clipped to her belt. "I mean, you don't have to."

Dani steered her into the car. She walked around to the other side and looked over the top of the car, back at the house. When she rolled up, it had been a carcass. What sat there now looked normal, if outdated. She bit her lip and then looked into the car with a frown.

"Wait here for just a sec, okay?"

With a thrust of her head and a harsh look, she told Merc to take a walk with her. They stopped on the sidewalk. "What the hell was that, Merc?"

His jaw tightened, and his eyes darkened. "That was what Spectre left behind the night he attacked the Blacks. A calling card of his."

"I asked you about this place, and you shut me down. What part of keeping the balance means leaving me in the dark when I come right out and ask?"

"It was a miscalculation, not an attack. I didn't know how bad it actually was in there. It was closed up by my parents and Ephraim Lockgrove. It was inherited in this condition."

"Fine, but don't think I'm done with you." She looked back to the car to make sure Emilie hadn't wandered off. "I'm taking Emilie back to my motel room tonight. Poor thing's been through the wringer."

"I'm not sure that's the best idea."

"Yeah, well I'm not sure I give a damn what you think right now." Dani scoffed. "She just walked into a clusterfuck, and the only reason she ain't dead in that basement is because I happened to already be around. I don't know what kind of cut-rate operation y'all are running

around here, but I'd lock it down before somebody winds up dead."
She shook her head and returned to the car.

It only took a few minutes to get over to the motel. Dani concentrated on remembering the turns from earlier in the day, while Emilie sat still as a statue. Shock had that effect. She'd give her a few hours to deal, but then Dani wanted answers. Later, Merc needed to answer a few pointed questions as well.

She pulled into the motel and helped Emilie to her room. She watched as the medium lay down on the far bed. In a few short minutes, her breathing evened out, and she fell asleep. Dani took a seat at the kitchenette, poured herself a glass of whiskey, and tried to relax.

She pulled the veilblade out from her jacket and laid it out on the table next to the book Merc had given her. Now that Emilie was asleep, Dani needed to think. That had been a house of hunters who'd run from Spectre years and years ago. She had a sinking suspicion it was the same year the paramedics found her wandering, lost and bloody, too young to say much, and no parents or guardians nearby.

Next to her on the floor, a beat-up canvas backpack slouched against her chair. Graham's pack. Inside was the file folder with everything they'd ever hunted down about her family. She'd been discovered just a few miles outside of Dawson. It wasn't too bold of a jump to think she might have been a Black. Was that what Merc had meant when he asked if she knew who she was?

And then there was Emilie. Dani didn't do shit like this, didn't bring people home and let them crash out of the kindness of her heart. There was no reason the pale-haired woman ought to have brought anything to the surface, and yet here they were. In sleep, her lovely face had smoothed out, and Dani realized how tightly she held herself while awake. At least for now the woman could relax, get some rest, especially with her chalk wards protecting the room. This woman stirred her in a way she was afraid to admit, even to herself.

She sipped the whiskey, feeling like she'd ended up with more questions and problems than before.

11

EMILIE

Sleep only helped so much. Emilie had dreamt of deep shadows and cold laughter and a door that creaked open slowly. Disturbed sleep wasn't anything new, but she'd always thought the nightmares were figments of her imagination.

Dad and Grandpa told her she'd forgotten because of the fire—a trauma that had irreparably changed her. They'd lied.

Now she remembered: Mama teaching her how to tune the radio in her mind that let her speak to the dead; Dad showing her how to read wards, helping her trace them on window panes as they recharged spells to protect their home from danger; Dad binding her, tucking her power into a box and hiding away the key.

The fire delineated her perception, before and after. Everything had changed; it couldn't ever be the same. She gauged every experience against that pain, convinced herself that since she'd survived that, nothing the world threw at her would keep her down. Now in the wake of some of her memories returning, the fragile foundation of her life began to crumble, a sandcastle drowned by the tide.

Dad had told her Mama was crazy, that the sickness ran in her family, but he'd known the truth. And Grandpa, for all his help, had backed Dad up. They'd hidden her magic, bound the things that made her different, and let her consider herself broken, flawed.

No wonder Dad pushed so hard to keep her out of Dawson. If she hadn't come back, she might never have found out what they'd done.

They'd hospitalized her, medicated her. But worst of all, Emilie didn't understand why. What had she done that Dad felt the need to lock her whole world away, amputate her abilities, and leave her a stranger in her own life? What could be so terrible that they meted out this judgement?

A rock settled in her chest as she tried to find some rhyme or reason. The strange static that had followed her since she got home changed. The signal seemed to be coming from far away, not the way Ben sounded last night. It was all snippets of conversation that lacked any context.

Dad was still MIA, off on one of his mysterious trips. She needed to talk to Grandpa. Her stomach churned and roiled. He was supposed to be the one she trusted. The idea that she'd been wrong for a decade while he perpetrated this fraud, it would have been ludicrous a few hours ago. Now, there was no way to tell. Not without facing him.

Dani lay crashed out in the other bed. It was rude to leave, but Emilie needed answers now. She looked over at the other woman. All those sharp edges from the fight were smoothed by sleep, dark hair mussed around her. Her wild beauty made Emilie's breath catch in her throat. Dani hadn't had to help her after what had happened, but she had. She was the only reason Emilie had gotten out of that house alive, but before she could ask her why, she needed to confront her grandfather. Hesitation gripped her, but Emilie let herself out the door into a grey overcast day that fit her mood.

Grandpa lived a short drive away in a rancher that backed up to the tree line. He bought it when Dad got married, said the house was too big for just him. Growing up, his place became a home away from home. She tried to hold on to the thought as anger froze her heart, encasing it in icy shards that pushed her onwards. He'd lied to her, and she wanted answers. She needed to know the why, as though it could calm the anger that suffused her.

She parked the car and let out a long breath. When she got to the front door, it was unlocked. Not surprising. The man took being an early bird to a whole new level. If she crossed the threshold, there'd be no turning back. It meant accusing Grandpa of withholding the truth from her even while he had answered her late night calls and helped her when she came up short on rent and been there for her every time she'd called.

She clenched her teeth and walked through the doorway. Why would Grandpa do anything to make her life more difficult after Mama's death, even while he constantly tried to lure her home to Dawson again? She didn't deserve this. Not now and not when she had been seventeen.

She passed through the living room to the back porch, where he liked to watch the sun rise over the trees in the morning. The door sat open, two coffee mugs sitting on the table between the chairs. Emilie stopped short on trembling legs. Inside her chest, her heart broke into tiny pieces.

"I've been expecting you. I caught it as soon as those wards faded away from the Black house." His voice didn't tremble, but it was quieter than she was used to.

She slipped out the door and into the empty chair, grabbing a blanket from the back and pulling it around her shoulders like a shield. Instead of answering, she picked up the coffee cup and let the heat warm up her hands. She wanted all the help she could get for what was next.

"I'm glad you came," Grandpa said, his gaze pinned on the horizon. Emilie turned so she could watch him as he spoke.

They had the same eyes, blue-grey storm clouds. Mama called them ghost eyes. Anger and sorrow warred inside of her chest, hollowing her out.

"When Spectre attacked the Black family, we thought it was a one-off, thought we could just board up the house and keep anyone from triggering the spells in the basement." He shook his head.

"That was years before Spectre came for Catherine. We thought we could protect her." Grief colored his voice, peppered every syllable in pain.

"That's not why I'm here." Her voice trembled, and she hated it. She wanted to hear what he was saying but not as much as she wanted answers.

"Patience my girl. It all fits together. Spectre and Dawson, Black, Lockgrove, Deveraux."

"D-deveraux?"

"Mmm. Your mother's maiden name. I suppose the binding stole that from you too."

"Why then? Why do this? And then lie... For years you and Dad both lied. And I don't—I don't understand why."

"That isn't an easy question to answer." Emilie tried to interrupt, but he held up a hand quiet her. "I'll explain what I can, but I don't have the whole picture. I doubt anyone but your father does. He's been hunting the Valkyrie, looking for a way to fix his mistakes"

"What do you mean?"

"I couldn't stop your father from casting the binding." A harsh laugh ground out of him. "Phillip cast it while I was gone, and by the time I saw what he'd done, it was too late. He shook his head, lip half curled into a snarl. "The spell had already taken hold."

"Why?"

"What do you remember about the night of the fire?" He turned and watched her, eyes troubled.

"Someone screaming, and smoke so thick it looked like ink, and a...shadow that was a man, but not. It's scrambled."

"And the name Deveraux?"

"It's familiar...but I'm not positive?"

"They were your mama's kin. An old talented family." His gaze drifted back to her. "Capable of magic. Mediums and psychics who could reach past the veil. A most powerful gift...until something killed them. One by one."

"That's why Mama never talked about her family."

"Yes. Catherine was one of the last. Not quite a full blown

medium, but adept at speaking to the dead. Until the curse found her, same as every other Deveraux for over a hundred years."

Emilie tried to swallow, but her throat was dry. Her hands shook, and she clasped them together. "When you say medium—"

"You remember the séances your mother would hold? When she'd speak to those who had gone on?"

Emilie licked her lips, let her gaze drift to the tops of the trees, and tried to clear her frazzled mind, if only for a moment. "And I got what? What Mama had?"

"You, my dear, received the brunt of the Deveraux talent. Stronger than anyone who lived in my lifetime at least." He shook his head. "The things you heard, the people you saw. Gifted beyond measure, my dearest." He winked. "Have been since the day you stood up and claimed the world as your own. And that made life uniquely dangerous for you."

"Dangerous how?"

"For over a century, the Deveraux mediums were killed. The community said it was a curse, but the longer it endured..." Grandpa lowered his head and stared down at his open palms.

"So I was in danger because of the curse? I don't...understand. How did Mama...do what she did then?"

"When your parents got married, Phillip knew that Catherine was a Deveraux, but she'd learned to shield her abilities, hide what she was. The bloodline had been weakening for generations—"

"They went underground?"

"Yes. The family bound themselves, hid, and joined those without even a spark of magic. It didn't protect them in the long run, but they tried. And your mother became more adept at it than most."

"But?" Emilie heard the way he held back, saw the tension in his shoulders.

"Phillip and I, we thought it was an actual spell. Something attached to the bloodline, a preternatural pox upon them, but the curse wasn't a casting—it was a man. Now he calls himself Spectre, but that wasn't always his name."

Small birds sang in the distance, the morning crisp and cool around them. She didn't want nice weather. She wanted a storm to equal the one that billowed in her chest. "I heard him," she rasped. "Last night in that basement. That's when I remembered for real, that and when Merc broke in to 'save' us," she said, making quotation marks with her hands. "Why do I remember his voice?"

Grandpa's face soured. "Because he was there the night of the fire." He tipped his head back to the sky. "And before that too, I think. After Phillip realized, he wasn't well, Emilie. It terrified him. Because if Spectre had found Catherine when her gifts were so mild, there was no doubt it would only be a matter of time until he came for you too."

"I don't remember any of that."

"It'll come back now that the binding is breaking down. When your father cast, he didn't understand what he was doing. Not entirely." Storm clouds broke out across his face, his lip curling in anger. "It locked your talents away, but it also shut all of your memories of magic away with it." He shook his head and took a sip of his coffee.

Emilie followed suit, trying to understand what her grandfather was telling her. She was still angry. It thrummed along her nerves and straightened her spine, making it hard to stay calm. The more Grandpa talked, the angrier she got, though not at him.

"Why didn't you tell me? I mean okay, Dad casting this sounds plausible enough after last night. Spectre hunting down mediums and killing Mama I even get somehow. But why let me believe she was crazy? That I was? What did I ever do to deserve something like that?"

"The binding that your father cast, it wasn't a small thing." He gritted his teeth. "Breaking that kind of magic might have damaged you and broken your mind, forced you to remember before you were ready." He shook his head and turned back to the horizon. "That, I couldn't do."

Emilie swallowed, and tears began to sting at her eyes. "All those years. All of those therapists and medications and nightmares…" Emilie peered down to find tears dripping down her face and onto her knuckles.

"I did what I could, what your father refused to. I tried to get you back here where your mind would do the work. Every time you triggered a memory, the binding failed a little more."

"Why bind it? Why keep me so far away? None of it makes sense and it just—it isn't fair!"

"You've heard the phrase ignorance is bliss, but knowledge is power, yes?" Grandpa sighed and his eyes went distant. "In your case it became a shield. *Armor.* Spectre hunted the Deveraux by seeking out their abilities somehow, like a supernatural bloodhound. The binding kept your talents locked up and your memories with them. If you didn't remember them, you couldn't use them, and without those, he couldn't find you. It was the worst solution, but it kept you with us."

"Alive and trapped like a bird in a cage."

"But alive."

"And what about when the binding broke?"

"They aren't permanent solutions. It was only a matter of time." He licked at his lips again. "Your father swore he had a plan, a weapon that even Spectre couldn't hold up to, but he wouldn't tell me anymore than that. You can see how well that all worked out."

Emilie cursed under her breath and took a sip of her coffee, lukewarm now but still better than nothing. All of this was too much, too fast, and none of it meshed with the world she'd lived in for the last decade. She wanted Dad here, wanted to look him in the eye and make him answer for making her life a living hell. She wanted to demand to know what his damn plan had been. But as usual, he was nowhere to be found.

"Where is he? I thought he'd be here this time of year. He might not have wanted me home, but he isn't... I mean, he's not avoiding me...is he?"

"I doubt it." Grandpa composed himself and shot her a dark look. "Your father isn't the type."

"That's not an answer!" Emilie threw off the blanket and paced across the porch. "Where is he?"

"I don't know." Grandpa pursed his lips and met her eyes. "He told me he had a lead but he didn't want to jinx it. And then he disappeared, as he's wont to do. I haven't been able to track him down since," he bit out.

"What am I supposed to do here? I was home because everything else is terrible. I didn't have a choice and now...all of this? Dad? Missing. Mama? Murdered. The binding...I mean. How do I...?"

A hysterical cackle burbled out of her. She felt vindicated and hollowed out all at the same time. Nothing was right or real or made any sense.

"I wish I knew."

"No. That doesn't get to be your answer. Not this time, not for this. You knew it was dangerous, and you let this happen. I was a kid, not even eighteen yet, and you left me with Dad, even knowing what he's like. You've always known." She glared at him, hoping her eyes spoke the volumes there weren't words for.

"I can't fix this. But I think you met the person who can."

Emilie squinted, not sure at first who he meant. "You mean Dani?"

"Yes."

"She only came here for the veilblade, and she got that. I don't get the feeling she wants to stick around."

He nodded. "She came for a weapon, but ask what that weapon is for."

"You think she's hunting Spectre?" Emilie turned wide eyes to her grandpa.

"I do, and if she is who I think she is, the hunter will have a horse in this race too."

"That's cryptic, and I'm really over cryptic." She sighed and pinned her grandpa with an exasperated look. "Why would she even help?"

"It is what hunters do, but offering a bounty is never a bad look either. She's got a weapon capable of killing Spectre and his wraiths, and a grudge. If he's coming for you, why not stack the deck in your favor?"

"What makes her so capable?"

"The veilblade." Grandpa rubbed at his forehead. "They're not run-of-the-mill weapons. I haven't seen one in a very long time."

"You still aren't telling me everything!" Emilie shook her head.

"I'm old and full of secrets." He sipped at his cup of coffee. "And dropping too much on you at once would be cruel. However, I'm not going anywhere."

"You aren't lying?" She narrowed her eyes.

"Only by omission."

The words made her want to throw something at him. Had he been anyone else in the world, she might have. "I suppose I ought to go talk to Dani then."

Grandpa nodded. "I think you should. Maybe the two of you can manage what no one else could."

12

DANI

Dani heard gravel kick across the parking lot as someone parked out front. A quick peek through the curtains showed Emilie's pale head climbing out of her car. She hadn't been sure that the little talented would come back after leaving earlier this morning. The other woman had proved herself as an asset instead of an obstacle last night. Unexpected, but not unwelcome.

She opened the door before Emilie could knock and lounged against the frame with a cocky smile. "Wasn't sure I'd be seeing you again. No note. I was heartbroken," she teased.

Emilie smiled, wan and worn thin, but still far too hot for Dani's own good. Poor girl had been through the wringer. The last thing she needed at the moment was Dani checking her out.

"I needed to speak to my grandpa, work some things out." She licked lips and then offered coffee in to-go containers. "But I brought back caffeine, which should count for something?"

"C'mon in, killer." Dani winked and waved her back into the room.

Emilie left one cup on the kitchenette and sat down with the other. She played with the lid before taking a long drink. Dani watched her, taken by the way her entire body relaxed at the first sip, eyes slipping shut as she sighed.

"So how'd the talk with your gramps go?" Dani snagged her drink and sipped at it while watching the other woman.

"It was something. A lot, I mean."

"And yet, you're back here and not at home."

"Yeah well. Last night, what happened…" Emilie's gaze bounced back and forth. "It broke some things open."

"You don't say." Dani raised an eyebrow.

"That voice, on the other side of…that tear. I recognized it."

"You're not alone there." She bit at her lip, curious about how a woman who seemed ignorant of the depth of her innate talents would know the likes of Spectre.

"The veilblade—that's why you came to town, right?" Emilie looked up, a bright glint in her captivating eyes.

"Mmm."

"See my grandpa thinks you're hunting Spectre, and that's why you needed it. And if that's the case, then I need your help."

"Help how?" Dani asked coolly, sipping her coffee.

"I need you to make sure he doesn't kill me."

"Why does he want you dead? How does he even know you?" Even more questions crowded her mind: How had Emilie found the veilblade? How had she found the basement when she was running blind?

"My mama's side of the family are—were—mediums. Deveraux." She shook her head and looked at the ceiling. "Spectre has been hunting us for a long time, and after he—after Mama died—my dad did a binding on me. To hide me from him."

"Hol-y shit." Dani raked a hand through her hair. "Well that'd explain…a lot, actually."

"Once it unravels all the way, he'll find me, and nobody in my family seems to survive that. My grandpa said you might be willing to help."

Working for free was rarely a good gig. Plenty of bad barreling at you with no payoff? Not Dani's modus operandi when she had a choice. However, Spectre was already her target. If he was looking for Emilie, and not her, maybe there was a shot. Worst came to worst, the medium could be bait. She hated herself for the thought the moment it emerged, but she couldn't deny it might work.

"Say I wanted to help." She took another sip of coffee. "I wouldn't be the first person to try and put that bastard down. Never seems to take."

"The veilblade. It's different somehow. And my dad has spent a decade trying to kill him, so I might be able to find out more."

Dani leaned back in her chair, weighed the pros and the cons.

Emilie leaned forward, the cup gripped tight in her hands. "My family has money. They're willing to pay a bounty. If you want the job." Her voice rode the edge of desperation.

"What? To be your bodyguard?" Dani drawled, eyes on the medium, gauging each reaction.

"I don't care about me." Emilie winced. "I mean—don't get me wrong. It's not like I have a death wish, the opposite really, but if I have a target on my back, no way do I make it out alive. Maybe... maybe with your help, and the veilblade, I have a chance."

"So a job with a bounty."

"Yeah. You can even come and stay at my house." Her eyes roamed the water-stained walls. "It's safer. Covered in wards and protections."

"Sounds like better digs than this place for sure."

"The minute the binding snaps, Spectre will find me. He's got a... read on the Deveraux bloodline somehow. You can't protect me if you aren't there. And it'll ensure that when he comes, you can do your thing."

"Do you understand just how nasty he is? Look, I'm down to crash at your pad, take the job, make sure the bogeyman stops moving and breathing. But this isn't something small. This is..." Dani trailed off, shaking her head.

Memories of Alabama streamed through her mind, the scream of metal as it rent, Graham's gurgle as his breath died away, flames and burning rubber as she ran, desperate to escape with her life. She took another sip from her coffee to try and camouflage her shaking hands.

"It shouldn't be small." Emilie's mouth turned to a hard white line, eyes gone paler than before. "He killed my mama. He's the reason Dad stole my life. I can't let him win."

"Okay then." Dani nodded. That, she could get behind. "I need to pack up all my gear and check out. Just text me the address and I'll meet you back at your place?"

"Sure. Dawson's small, it's easy to find."

A little thrill went through Dani at the idea of staying at Emilie's place. But this wasn't a hookup or one night stand. She would have to keep her wits about her. If she didn't, one, or both of them, might not survive.

DANI PARKED her truck across the street from Merc's shop and eyed the avenue. Yesterday, she'd opted for low profile, but by now every player in town would realize something was up. A person didn't break down glamours and wards like the ones they'd busted through last night without people noticing. She needed more answers, and at least some of them would be in the back room of that bookstore.

The air outside was sharp, but her leather jacket blunted its edge. She'd tucked the veilblade into an inside pocket. Dani traced it's outline through the fabric, taking comfort from its presence.

When she ducked into the bookstore, there was no sign of Merc. She took a few careful steps inside and looked around. It didn't seem right to have the front door unlocked, nobody manning the shop— small town or not.

The door that led back to the hallway and backroom sat slightly ajar, and through it she heard the murmur of two voices. She crept closer, keeping her footfalls light as she listened. Either they weren't concerned about being overheard, or this shop had great acoustics, because it was easy to eavesdrop, despite their hushed voices.

"You noticed it last night?" said a woman's voice.

"Of course I did. I found Emilie and that hunter, Dani." Merc's voice was lower but easier to hear.

"Dani...you don't think...?"

"That she's a Black? Little Daniella come back home after twenty years?" Merc clucked. "It's possible. I wouldn't have expected it, but when I got there the wraith was gone."

An electric shock radiated down Dani's arm. She'd told very few people her full name. Only Joe and Graham knew it, and here it was being bandied about like it was nothing. The idea that this was the place she'd come from, that the Black house last night had been her home once, was almost too much to digest.

"What do you mean gone?" the woman's voice snapped,

"The rift wasn't there anymore, only residue. Both of them looked as though they'd been through hell."

"How did they pull that off? Pops never had the juice to touch that thing. It nearly killed Ephraim when he found it! It's why they locked the house down the way they did."

"Ephraim's said for years that the Black mantle waited down there. That's why Spectre left behind his little friend," Merc murmured.

"And what? You think a hunter managed to find it? Seriously?"

"She wasn't alone. Emilie was with her."

Dani had known that Merc was holding something back, but it was another thing to wander into a conversation about her. Her upper lip curled into a snarl, but she stayed quiet and continued eavesdropping.

"Phillip bound her talents," he continued.

"Oh, don't be like that, Merc. Ephraim has been swearing for a decade that if he could just get her back here, it'd wither on the damn vine."

"So Emilie helped her uncover the hidden blade? Nobody could find it, you know, back in the day."

"She's a new element, back in town for the first time since the fire. You remember how strong she was, and that was before any of us had come fully into our strengths."

"It'd mean she reached past the binding to talk to someone, and that means one of the Blacks, somebody who lived there." Her voice was sharp and desperate.

"It was Ben, if anyone."

There was a heavy pause. "If Dani is Daniella, there's nothing Ben wouldn't do to help her. That blade? It's hers by birthright and bloodline."

"Rude."

"Okay fine, I'm sure she's a stellar hunter too, but you know how those prick mages cast the spell on hunters at the Watchtower."

Someone snorted. "In any case, this is dangerous, brother."

"The town hasn't been active in years. Not like this. Not since Catherine—"

"All the birds are coming home to roost. It was only a matter of time. We always knew that." The woman's voice was insistent but gentle as she pushed.

"They better hope they can figure it out before he gets here, or this won't end well."

Another long pause stretched out. "When does it ever?"

The conversation lulled, and Dani hustled carefully to the front door. She wasn't about to clue Merc into the fact that she'd heard that little exchange, especially considering she was a major point of inter-est. *Daniella Black*. Her name echoed through her mind, pounded along next to her pulse. Was he right? Had she been walking through her childhood home?

Her palm itched, missing the heft of a weapon. Through her pocket, the veilblade warmed up, and she caressed its shape, taking comfort from it. She didn't have all the details she needed to work in this town, and it was getting old. She shut the door. Louder this time.

"Just a sec!"

Yesterday, Merc had been dressed immaculately. Today he was still in a pressed shirt, vest, and slacks, but the clothing was rumpled.

It was clear he'd had a tie and then abandoned it. He looked around wildly, but settled when he saw her at the doorway. *Who was he expecting? And why is he pleased that it's me?*

"Dani, back so soon?" He leaned against the doorframe with a smile.

If Emilie hadn't charmed her so thoroughly, she would have thought he was cute. He certainly thought he was.

"Well, you ran off on me last time. Bad manners, don't cha know?"

"I did give you a present."

"Never been a big book gal, but it does have a certain heft to it." Dani wandered toward the back, fingers playing over the spines of shelved books.

"Something tells me this has more to do with last night though. Hmm?"

"Oh, I have questions, loads of questions." Dani stopped and pinned him with a dark look.

"Not so strange in a town like Dawson, but I may have answers to at least some of what you are asking. To the back room?"

"After you," Dani agreed and followed him back.

They assumed the same positions, Merc flanked by bookshelves behind the table, and her standing out in the open. She knew he was a sentinel and could lash out if he wanted, but the bulk between them helped to settle her nerves.

"So where do you want to begin?" he asked.

"Well. Let's start here." She pulled out the cloth-covered blade and laid it down between them. With a few swift movements, she unwrapped it.

Merc gaped at it and then up at her. "You're just carrying a veil-blade around like it's nothing?"

"Finders keepers." Dani shrugged enigmatically. Better to get more information from him before she went spilling her guts.

"It's been a very long time since this has been out in the open air. May I?"

"By all means." She gestured and Merc reached out to touch the blade.

A small electric shock jumped between the veilblade and his extended fingers. He froze. Merc's eyes slipped shut, and the air got thick and heavy. He was working something, all right. The moment passed, and he pulled away from the weapon.

"So it accepted you then." He nodded. "Yeah, I guess there is a lot to talk about. Where to begin? What do you know about veilblades?"

"Not sure what you mean." Dani frowned. "They're nastier than a normal blade. Even consecration doesn't hold a candle to it."

"Well, that's a start. They were the first and most brilliant weapons, built to strike back against the darkness, forged on mountain anvils. Relics, imbued with magic to fight the things that pass through the veil."

Dani whistled low. Joe hadn't mentioned any of that.

"These are artifacts from the days when the Watchtower still stood guard. There weren't many, and only a handful survived."

"Why?"

"Over the years, disaster and corruption have claimed more than their fair share. Spellwork binds the blade to a bloodline. These weapons are passed from one generation to the next." He narrowed his eyes. "You used it last night?"

"Yeah. Was sort of in the thick of it." She shook her head and shrugged.

He nodded. "For you to handle it, you'd have to be a Black. Do you understand what I'm saying?" His voice was soft, sympathetic. Dani hated it, the saccharine quality trying to make up for what she'd never had.

"That I rolled into town looking for a weapon and found a long-lost family. That's ridiculous," she scoffed.

He exhaled in a slow stream and met her eyes. "The thing is, that blade? It was one of two that I knew the whereabouts of. Valkyrie has the other. The only way you could have used it is if you were Ben's daughter."

"My father," she breathed. Dani's world slid sideways. Part of her stayed focused, asking the questions she needed answers for, but she'd mostly tuned out.

"Yes." He shook his head. "You saw what happened when I tried to touch it?"

"The shocks? Yeah. Why…?"

"The magic in a veilblade chooses its master. It allows a hunter to claim the mantle of bladesinger. Ben didn't have the stomach for it, so his father never gave him the opportunity."

"The hell is that supposed to mean?" she growled, protective of a man she couldn't even remember.

"Hunters who take on the mantle…" Merc frowned and tipped his head back, looking for the right words. "It isn't an easy path, and those who begin down it unprepared for what it entails don't survive long." He raised an eyebrow. "Your mother was one of the best hunters Dawson had ever seen, but your father didn't have the taste for it. The families that have veilblades, they go back to the first fights against darkness. The blades choose who wields them." He smiled. "Bladesingers are vicious fighters."

"I've heard the term before, but I thought it was just…rumor."

He raised an eyebrow. "You hunt monsters, live on the edges of the world, fight things nobody believes are real. And when you find a weapon capable of handling the worst, you think the name is a bit much?"

"I mean, when you put it like that," she grumbled.

"Okay," Merc said. "Riddle me this. You've been hunting for a long time now. Have you ever gotten injured? Broken bones? Brain injuries?" He watched her, waiting for an answer.

"No. Luck and skill." She grinned, but a frenetic energy buzzed at the edge of her vision.

"That's what they all say. Bladesingers, even before their blade finds them, they're more. Not talented, or sentinel, but *more*, faster, stronger, more capable of taking it on the chin."

Dani took a step away from the table and paced. It wasn't like what he was saying was completely out of the park. She'd heard rumors before about hunters who were more like legends. One only needed to hang out in a hub for so long before somebody got drunk and pulled out stories of Valkyrie.

"Why me?"

Merc paused, clearly weighing his words before he spoke. "Because you're the last Black. If not you, then the blade would have found another line. They always do. But so many of the weapons have been lost, to fire and flood, murder and mayhem, to betrayal and deeds best not spoken of. Each one is imbued with its own magic, changing and becoming almost symbiotic with the bladesinger who wields it. They are a fiercely guarded treasure, one that hunters have protected alongside their other secrets." He shook his head. "Sometimes things go wrong."

Dani swallowed and tried to think. She'd searched for her family for years, ran into one dead end right after the next. To find them now? When they were gone and it left her with nothing to hold on to? It tore the old wound open.

Hunting had been the one thing in the world she'd understood down to the marrow of her bones. She loved the hunt, the rush of adrenaline, the killing blow, and she was good at it. She thought she'd chosen it, a way to declare herself as her own person. The idea she had been following in unseen footsteps was eerie, as though she'd never had a choice but to become a hunter.

"Is that why Spectre came for them?" She ran a hand through her long hair. "My parents, I mean. The house, it was a wreck. Like they'd been packing, but the gouges in the walls...and Emilie said she saw old blood."

"My pops thought so. He was the sentinel here before my sister and I were initiated. He and Ephraim found the wreckage a few days after, and Spectre's gift in the basement. But no sign of your parents or you."

"Why us?" Dani jumped to her feet, pacing back and forth.

"Most veilblades are gone." Merc frowned sympathetically. "By striking at the Blacks, Spectre was destroying the last well-known hunter bloodline to have possession of one."

"Was it me? Did he—I mean..."

"You're asking if he was coming for you? No, you were too young to be anywhere near his radar. Your mother, Valerie, was a pistol.

She'd crossed him, and between that and being a bladesinger through her own right..." He trailed off and frowned.

"And me coming back now?"

"Coincidence."

"I don't really believe in those. There's something more going on in this town."

"That's almost always true here in Dawson. Most of the population knows of the darkness in the world, the things that hide in shadows. Dawson acts as an enclave in that way. Just one of the many reasons we discourage tourists."

"Can the veilblade kill Spectre?"

"I don't know. Truly." Merc gave her a long look. "But if Emilie's bindings are unraveling, it's only a matter of time until he appears."

"Why? Why here? Why does he want the Deverauxs dead?"

"All questions I don't have the answers to." He rubbed at the back of his neck. "I wish that I did. Phillip Lockgrove might, but he's not in town."

"Yeah and isn't that convenient," Dani muttered to herself. "Do you have details on anything about Spectre and the Deverauxs?"

"Not enough. It comes from something that happened before any of us were born. I wish I could help you more."

"Are you sure?"

"Yes, sadly. Distrust me all you like." When she shot him a look at the comment, he raised an eyebrow. "I saw your face when you realized I was a sentinel. Most hunters dislike my kind, but keeping the peace in Dawson is my priority."

"And if blood runs in the street when Spectre comes for Emilie?"

"It wouldn't be the first time." He paused and met her eyes. "But I doubt you'll find my sister and I are as neutral as our cohorts would prefer."

"Good to know." Dani nodded and folded the cloth back around the veilblade before tucking it back into her jacket. "Thanks for your help."

"Mm. I'll be here if you need me again."

She left Merc behind and headed back out to her truck. It was too bright out after the dim lighting in the back room, but she forced her squinted eyes to take in the quiet streets of town. It appeared sleepy, quaint even, but now she knew it concealed much more than it revealed. What was worse, she'd just walked out of the one place she thought she might find answers with nothing but more questions.

13

EMILIE

Emilie's gaze slid along the polished wooden floors and familiar furniture in the living room. Grandpa would have let her crash with him if she'd wanted to. He'd made up a room for her when she was nine and updated it every few years so she always had a place to run to if things got hard, but running away was no longer an option. Hiding at his house would only delay the inevitable.

She wandered room to room, seeing if any of them triggered memories. Only two places had set her off since coming back to this house: upstairs in the workshop, and down here in the green room. The two rooms where she'd been closest to Mama were also where her talents broke past the binding.

"She's been trying to reach you for so long, it was just easier in those rooms," a woman said. Though the voice was behind her, her gut told her nobody else would be able to hear her. She jumped, spinning on her heels.

The woman she'd seen in the greenroom last night stood there. In the dark, she'd seemed mysterious, but now with rays of light hitting her, the resemblance was easy to notice. She shared Mama's coloring, tanned skin and chestnut hair, but the shape of her face, her nose, those were just like Emilie's.

"Who...?"

"I'm Marie Deveraux." She watched Emilie and waited.

"Grandmama Marie. Was that you at..."

"The crypt? Yes. I didn't mean to frighten you, but we weren't sure how fast the binding would unravel. Whether you'd hear or see first." Marie cocked her head as she watched her.

Emilie kept her eyes on Marie. "Why trap me then?"

"To force the issue." Marie's face was a cold, assured mask. "No time to play nice, not if the monster found your father already. It isn't fair to you, but life rarely is. We thought you might prefer being alive to being comfortable." Her mouth turned into a frown, as though the words were distasteful.

"And last night?"

"A necessary catalyst. Daniella would have discovered the basement with or without your help, but the Lockgrove blood wards probably would have killed her. And she never would have located the veilblade in time. We need all the pieces in play to do this." Marie's eyes slid away as she wandered around Emilie.

"Daniella...?"

"Dani. The hunter." Marie pinned her with a wry look. "Her full name is Daniella. Black. And she is necessary."

"To do what?"

"Oh my dear, I thought that was obvious. We will kill Spectre once and for all. But to do that, we need everyone."

"What are you even talking about? Okay, okay. I know Spectre killed Mama, that he wants my head on a pike, but what I don't understand is why. Why us, why this, why any of what is going on here?"

"That is a long story and not one I can tell you yet."

"Seriously? I swear you and Grandpa are both terrible! I'm stuck in the middle with no details, and nobody alive or dead wants to admit it's my life on the line!" Emilie slapped her thigh, and the sound reverberated through the room around them.

"Still miles to go before you sleep, and the more you learn the faster the binding unravels. Once it's gone, well and gone, Spectre will come for you. And if you and Daniella are not ready?" Marie shook her head and naked fear showed in her eyes. "He'll kill her in front of you, and he will hurt you in ways you can't understand right now. If you and Daniella do not end him, I don't think anyone ever will." Her voice was sharp as a knife inside Emilie's head, and it cut down and into her like a brand.

"So it comes down to us?" Emilie made a helpless sound. "That's not right. That's not fair. We didn't— I didn't ask for any of this!"

"None of us did. That I can promise. None of the Deveraux talented burned out of their homes and killed by Spectre deserved what happened to them, but it happened anyway. The world is not fair, and you know that already."

Emilie made a small noise and buried her head in her hands. Two days ago, her biggest problem was coming back to this house, facing Mama's death, the fire, and all of her lost memories. This was so much bigger than she'd ever feared. She wanted to run away, run until nothing but a distant memory haunted her.

It was never that easy. Even when she'd run from the fire, the past came back for her. Finding out what that freedom cost? It wasn't worth the price she'd paid. The ignorance hadn't been worth it. Every moment she spent in Dawson drove that further home. She'd thought nothing remained behind but memories and pain, but hiding from Spectre cost her so much more than that, and she wasn't sure how to process all of this and move forward. Lying down to die certainly wasn't an option. If it was, she'd have left this world a long, long time ago. No. The only real option was to keep limping forward. Marie didn't want to tell her, dead or not, but Dad had been researching for years to find how all of this started, figure out how to end it.

The world might knock her down, again, and again, and again. It had cursed her, bound her talents, killed her mother, and stolen her memories, but only Emilie got to decide if she stayed down.

Dani would be here soon, and if nothing else, she'd need a place where she could stow her gear and crash later tonight. That was doable. She compartmentalized the rest and focused on getting a room set up for Dani.

When she sat back up, Marie was gone and the house was quiet around her. Emilie was glad too. Grandmama or not, Marie was working an angle. She trooped up to the second floor. Once upon a time, Mama kept plenty of beds open for anyone who might need them. The house had buzzed with people.

Whether Dad redecorated after the fire was the real question. If worst came to worst, she'd take the master and put Dani in her room, but that seemed kind of creepy. Not what she wanted to do if there was any choice in the matter. When Emilie got up to the second floor and opened the door to the larger of the guest rooms, draped furniture greeted her. It was dustier than it had any right to be, but it would work.

Emilie took the time to make up the room for Dani. She had a feeling it was unnecessary, that Dani would sleep on the couch if there weren't any other options, but it was something to do, something productive. She needed that today, needed something solid to plant her feet on. So the sheets got tossed into the hallway, furniture wiped down with disinfecting wipes she found under the sink, and with fresh bedding, it looked like an actual room. If there had been flowers in the house, she would have tossed a few into a vase and dropped them on the windowsill, but it'd do. Either way, it was miles better than the roach motel on the edge of town.

A knock at the front door drew Emilie up and out of the cleaning frenzy she'd gotten stuck in. Mama would have been proud. She took the stairs two at a time and opened the door to find Dani standing with a few bags slung over her shoulder.

Dani looked like a still from a movie, afternoon sun silhouetted behind her and a cocky grin lighting up her face. Her dark hair curled wildly at her shoulders, and her eyes caught the light, turning more gold than brown. Emilie smiled dumbly for a second before getting ahold of herself and waving her inside, trying not to look smitten as she did so. "Get checked out okay?"

"Yeah, you do it enough and it's an art form of getting out of dodge with no problems." Dani flashed an easy grin and then took in the place with wide eyes. "Quite the digs you got here. Gotta say, when you said your house, I was not expecting…this."

"Yeah. My family is a little ostentatious sometimes." Emilie closed the door and leaned back against it.

"Sometimes?" Dani asked with a sly smile that made Emilie's heart beat faster.

"Okay, most of the time. Grandpa isn't as bad as Dad though. Maybe it skips a generation." She smiled. Cleaning out that room might have done her more good than she wagered on. "I made up a bedroom for you upstairs, figured we'd just order Chinese or something for dinner."

"Sounds good to me. Lead the way." Dani gestured.

"The house is gigantic, but most of the rooms don't get used anymore," she explained, leading Dani up to the second floor. "When my mom was still alive, it was a different story, but Dad's more of an obsessive recluse than an entertainer." She opened the door to the bedroom and let Dani pass her into the room.

"This is…" Dani's voice trailed off, and she dropped her bags onto the bed with a heavy thump.

"A guest room. Meant for guests." Emilie tried not to fidget where she stood. "No big deal."

Dani turned and gave her a long, searching look. "I guess I'm just not used to decent digs, that's all. Living on the road gets rough, but it is what it is."

"Well, I'm glad you're here with me." Emilie shrugged. "This house is too big for just one person."

"Your dad's been here alone for years though, right?"

"Only technically. He's always traveling for work, or he said it was work, anyway. Might have been more than that. I don't know."

"Hmm. Lockgrove Antiquities, right?"

"Yeah. The auction house has all sorts of things." Emilie shrugged. "I was supposed to apprentice with Dad but it didn't work out." She said it flippantly, but it hurt even more now with what she'd learned. Before the fire, the plan had been for her to take charge of the auction house, learn the trade from Dad and then take over in a few years—the same way Grandpa had taught him before handing over the reins. The family business was just another casualty of the fire.

"Anyway, why don't you get settled in, then I'll show you the rest of the place." She bit at the nail of her thumb, watching Dani with a brief smile. Either she was brilliant for inviting this woman into her house or completely mad. She couldn't quite decide which.

"I'm good for the mo'." Dani huffed a laugh, raising an eyebrow as she leaned back on the bed. Her head lolled as she looked out the window for a moment before meeting Emilie's eyes again. "Used to living out of my truck half the time, so this is...different. Good different, but still different." One hand clutched at the coverlet on the bed, and Emilie had to try not to whimper out loud. Dani was intoxicating. Just standing here felt a little bit like being drunk, but not incapacitated. There was a wildness that drew her in, something she could never capture but only appreciate from a distance.

"So, tour!" Emilie shook her head, hoping that Dani couldn't see the flush creeping up her neck. She led Dani back out into the hall and pointed out rooms on the floor. "The front bedroom was Mama's workshop once upon a time, guest room, guest room, guest room, my room, bathroom, your room, master. Stairs go up to the third floor."

"What's up there?"

"Mama used it as a séance space, but I haven't been up there since I got home." Emilie shrugged and headed up the stairs. They were creakier than the main stairs and narrower too. These hadn't gotten a facelift like the parts of the house built for public consumption. It looked more or less like how she remembered it. Tall cabinets sat against two of the walls, filled with components, candles, and other bits and pieces. A small table sat with a charcoal runner draped over it. Glossy wooden floors shone beneath tall windows that let in the late afternoon light. In the corner, a ladder led up to the roof, the tallest point of the house, where Emilie spent hours pretending to be anywhere but here.

She frowned, standing up here, a headache starting somewhere behind her eyes and reverberating through her skull. Memories crowded at the forefront of her head, blurring her vision for a moment, and she wavered in place. Dani reached out and grabbed her lightly, the contact sending a spark through her.

"I'm good." Emilie licked her lips and shook her head. "Memories are pesky." She nodded, swallowing a sigh when Dani moved past her into the room. "Only Mama, Dad, and Grandpa spent much time on the third floor."

It was a sacred space built for more complicated spellwork, for ritual work. The kind a person didn't want two young talented to intrude on by accident.

Funny to think back on that now, so many years later. She'd lost so much, but that was one of the few memories the binding allowed her to keep: standing on top of the world, watching the sunset and wishing to be someone else. It hadn't worked out the way she'd thought back then though. Things rarely did, even if one didn't have their life stuffed into a box to protect them.

Magic filled this room from top to bottom, and it resonated with Emilie. It distracted her enough that she walked halfway across the floor before she noticed the circle. It was ten feet in circumference and burned down into the wood of the floor so deep that grooves marred the floorboards. Emilie stopped short. She knew without being told that this was where Dad had worked the binding. It had left behind evidence of spellwork so strong that it had torn into his ritual space.

"So this is—" She swallowed against a lump in her throat and turned back to Dani, putting her back to that circle and everything it represented. "—a ritual space. A place for big magic." She rocked on her heels and looked back at the hunter.

Dani was watching her with a narrowed gaze, and there was a fierce intelligence lurking in her golden-brown eyes. "Just being here brings all that rushing to the surface?" Her head tilted to one side, sizing her up.

"Not all of it, but some of it. Last night? When Spectre started talking, it was like a door in my head cracking open. I think it started to snap the binding, give me back bits and pieces."

"Isn't that kind of convenient?"

"For who? Certainly not for me." Emilie squared her shoulders. "I'm just taking this as it comes. I can't tell you much more than that." She shook her head and ushered Dani back down the stairs and onto the main floor. "Down here is the complicated part. The floor plan is wacky, but you've got the kitchen, green room, living room, dining room, study, library, and sickroom. We have a basement too, but it's just filled with boxes."

"Damn girl." Dani shook her head. "This place is a damned palace." Dani whistled long and low. "You said your pops protected it?"

Emilie frowned, a memory popping up of Dad pointing out the ways the house kept them safe, a place to hole up against the things that waited out in the night. "As protected as it gets. Wards, glyphs, salt poured into the foundation and the fence on the property line." She rubbed at one temple, suddenly wishing she had some aspirin. She was glad for the clarity her returning memories were delivering, but that didn't mean they were easy to process when they dropped on her like this.

"Least that's something I don't have to do for once." Dani relaxed a little bit as she kept looking around.

"Huh?"

"My car has wards, but every room needs prepped. Chalk works most of the time, but I took a while to figure that out."

"Yeah, this place was passed down through the family. A place of safety. A man's home is his castle or something." Emilie shrugged and looked down before turning her gaze back to Dani, watching from under her lashes.

"Definitely takes the edge off of things." Dani's lips turned into a devilish smirk. "So does this burb have any decent delivery options?" She sauntered past Emilie, meeting her eyes as she swished toward the kitchen.

Was she flirting? She'd never been much of a flirt, and it had been a long time since she'd managed to catch anyone's attention. Dani was just relaxed and being friendly. That had to be it, because anything else was kind of ludicrous. Someone who looked like that definitely didn't hit on someone like her. "So, Chinese for dinner?" She moved past Dani to pull out a menu from a drawer next to the sink.

Emilie unfolded it and leaned over the counter, circling the items she had in mind. She could feel Dani's eyes on her. Was her gaze always that *intense*, or was this a fever dream?

"Agreed." Dani's arm reached across the counter to point to the food she wanted to order. "Here."

Her finger tapped on the paper, tracing a line across. It was stupid, such a small little gesture, but when Emilie looked up, Dani was watching intently, lips curved into a smirk. For the second time, she caught the other woman gauging her, but this time it stirred something inside her chest other than anxiety, liquid heat.

"I'm gonna go catch a shower while you order, if that's cool?" Dani quirked an eyebrow as if daring her to think of what she'd be doing in there.

"Yeah. I'll um... I'll let you know when food gets here." Her voice was squeaky at first before evening out.

As she watched Dani turn the corner into the living room, her heart thundered up and into her throat. Being around the other woman felt a little bit like going insane as she tried to break down every tiny movement or snatch of eye contact.

Dani wasn't doing any of this because she had to. There was a freedom in her choices, something Emilie envied and was drawn to in equal measure. Maybe she'd have been able to write it off if not for last night, but after being rescued from a literal monster, there was no denying it. She was smitten, and only time would tell if it would end in disaster.

14

EMILIE

Emilie... I'm waiting for you.

Emilie startled awake, unsure if she'd fallen all the way asleep to begin with. Falling asleep fast was not a skill she'd ever learned. She sat up in bed, tried to get her bearings.

She was back at home, in the Lockgrove family home. Thin shafts of moonlight broke through the window, leaving tiny rectangles of light that slanted toward the door. Wind knocked against the glass, rattling the shutters outside.

The room didn't look right though. It was too hazy. A thin sheen lay over the walls and the floor. She blinked and saw phantoms of flame that walked up the walls. Around her, voices spoke, one on top of the other in quiet, indistinct tones. They were louder than she remembered hearing before. The mumble sounded all around her. She wondered if maybe it was a dream.

Come on now, sleepyhead. Surely you remember me of all of them? a male voice spoke, clarion against the murmur of other voices. It curled around her, familiar and foreign in equal measure.

She swung her feet to the floor and flinched. The wood wasn't cool to the touch. It was warm, alive, as though the house was a living, breathing creature and she existed deep in its belly. She brushed the thought away and tried to get a hold of herself, ignoring the intrusive thoughts. None of this made any sense, but magic operated differently than logic, she was figuring out. Or would that be remembering?

She looked back toward her bed and about jumped out of her skin. Or would have, except that her damn body was still lying on the bed, chest rising and falling as she breathed. She felt an iron band close around her chest as panic throttled her. Was she dead? No. No, her body breathing proved that much. Somehow, she'd slipped her skin.

Don't panic. Remember. This isn't new. You've done this before.

The voice calmed her, kicked her brain into high gear. *Astral projection.* It made sense, and it might explain what was going on. It came back to her in a rush, another piece unlocking. Astral projection was when a talented projected their psyche past the physical into the in-between. the edge of the veil. It was a tricky maneuver, one that required time. Training. Not something that happened by accident. To pass beyond the veil, even just a step or two, was dangerous, the most dangerous thing a medium could do. That was why even those who had the ability didn't do it often. It was far too easy for something that lived in the cold dark to find a person and take a bite. She heard old lessons from Mama and Dad, echoing in her ears, warning her against it, but it seemed so long ago and far away.

From upstairs, something pulled at her, a curious magnetism that drew her out of her room and into the hallway. The voices of the dead quieted as she wandered away from her body. The house looked like itself, and not, all at the same time. It felt like walking an old trail in a new season.

Wisps and memories of people flitted past her. Ephemeral shadows lost in time, they looped through actions again and again, forever. If she paid attention to one, they came into focus, but it was like watching a movie, unable to interact. From downstairs, the haunting melody of a badly tuned piano and a woman sobbing drifted up. But that wasn't her priority.

For once, it was curiosity that drove her forward, kept her moving through the hall past Dani's quiet snores and over to the small staircase. Glyphs and wards etched into the walls flared and faded with the pulse of the house. They served as comforting reminders that she was safe here, in her body or not.

Downstairs, there was a sharp thud, and the sobbing cut off. In its absence, she heard Grandmama Marie call out to her, but it was impossible to decipher from halfway up to the third floor. Strange. She knew she ought to listen to what the ghost had to say, but the pull continued to paw at her from under the door at the top of the stairs, where a faint glow emanated.

It's not important. It can wait. You trust me, don't you?

He was right, whoever he was. She'd see what Grandmama wanted after she found out what was upstairs. A slam from downstairs rattled the walls, but she continued up the stairs. Emilie heard Dani slip out of her room and down the stairs, as easy to ignore as the voices were.

She didn't open the door so much as pass through it like she was a ghost herself. Inside, it blazed like high noon. Wards layered three thick in thin, precise script shimmered on every surface from floor to ceiling. A rainbow of colors danced from inside the cabinets, and the shade of a little girl playing with a doll murmured from the far corner. In the middle of the room, a circle burned into the floor lit up a rusty orange-red that flared like fire.

The circle called her to her, weak compared to the magnetism that had drawn her out of her room. She took a hesitant step forward, wondering what might happen if she crossed the threshold of magic.

Would it snap the binding? Break her into pieces and put her back together again, this time with the memories that eluded her? Humpty Dumpty in the flesh.

I was wondering when you might fiinally come home. An elegant, dark haired man appeared from behind one of the cabinets. Tall and handsome, he had dark curls of hair against pale skin and bright blue eyes that burned like gemstones. This was the man that kept speaking to her. Dressed in an antiquated suit, it was clear he was long dead. Not that it mattered.

Somewhere deep inside her, a sharp pain bloomed, and she remembered: Henry. His name was Henry, and he'd been her first friend from beyond the grave. Memories assaulted her: them talking together, his playful demeanor, the way he'd always been there when she needed him, even if he didn't have a pulse anymore.

"I remember you."

Well, I'd certainly hope so. It'd be terribly rude to forget me, even after staying away for so long. His voice was an elegant purr, and he gestured with each word, another language, spoken with his hands instead of his voice.

"I had my reasons."

Mmm. So I gathered. Do you remember, then? He moved closer and looked down at her. *I'd think so, seeing you not quite in your body and all. But then, one never can be sure.*

"Some things." Her eyes drifted from him back to the circle. "Not everything."

You know, you could. He moved closer, placing light hands on her shoulders. It was cold, not like the way his voice rubbed along her all soft and elegant. This was sharper. She ought to pay attention. And yet, his whisper urged her to step forward.

Take the step, break the binding. Cross the circle and return to me. Return to him. Her eyes drifted along the floor again. She understood now what it was as it called to her. Magic reaching out to magic. Grandpa warned her it was dangerous. Grandmama Marie had said it was the last thing keeping Spectre from finding her.

But that voice…it was so familiar, a memory she couldn't quite grasp. Something was wrong here. She stopped and Henry's hands dug into her shoulders.

You don't want to? I thought you wanted to know, wanted more than anything to remember?

"Not like this." She shook her head and dug in her heels.

From the second floor someone called her name, but it wasn't important, not when she was up here. Looking at the magic that kept her caged, she tried desperately to remember what she had forgotten.

Wasn't it her choice? Didn't she get to decide what happened? How it happened?

I've been looking for you for so long... His voice was a caress that dripped down her spine, and Emilie moved forward a few inches, toes almost touching the border of the circle. Someone walked the edges of the room, sticking to the shadows. *I thought you'd forgotten me, forgotten all of our time together.*

The shadows were too thick, and the way he spoke, the accent at the edge of his words, Emilie recognized it. She'd heard it, recently. She racked her brain, fighting the urge to take that last step, break past the barrier and unleash all of those lost memories like a torrent in her mind.

Let Spectre find her.

Emilie's eyes went wide, and some of the haze that had drifted over her faded away. His voice—Henry sounded like Spectre. The hands at her shoulders evaporated, and Henry disappeared. But something, someone, still lurked in the darkness. While she remained in her body, the binding kept her safe from Spectre, but the veil was a dangerous place for an untrained medium.

The pull remained, asking her to bend forward just a little, take such a tiny step it wouldn't even be noticeable. And then she'd be free from this cage made of magic and amnesia. Wasn't the truth worth the price? Who was to say that Spectre would find her? Didn't she deserve the truth?

Such a little thing, to cross the boundary. All she'd have to do is reach out. Just pass her fingers through that curtain of magic and find the truth they'd locked away from her. Emilie raised a hand and watched it tremble in front of her eyes as that seductive thought whispered to her.

Something moved in her periphery, followed by a hiss of frustration. Someone pounded up the stairs and then she was being yanked backwards by the shoulders. She felt herself falling out of the door, back down the stairs, through the halls, into her bedroom, past Dani who was shaking her.

Emilie's eyes popped open as she crashed into her body. She

sucked in a wild gasp. Dani jumped back from her, eyes wide. She felt the ache from how tightly Dani had been holding her as she had shaken her.

"You need to wake up. Something happened."

"What?" Emilie blinked, trying to get her bearings. Whether it was the astral projection or something else, being thrown back into her body jarred her.

"Something happened, downstairs. I think you need to come and see." She took another step back toward the door.

Emilie swung her legs over the side of the bed and then stopped in her tracks. All she'd worn to bed was a threadbare T-shirt that clung to her ample curves, a cartoon raccoon on the front. She snatched at her robe and tried to shrug it on before Dani could see her.

"What time is it?"

"I heard something from downstairs. It woke me up."

"Probably the storm door. It never latched right."

"Yeah. I don't think it's ever gonna latch right again."

"What is that supposed to mean?"

"Oh, it's shredded," Dani said matter-of-factly.

Emilie's mouth popped open, and she shut it, flabbergasted. The storm door to the kitchen from the backyard was a massive, solid steel slab Dad had installed to protect the house from flooding during bad storms. They rated it for hurricane-force winds. Nothing should have been able to tear that thing apart.

"Yeah, see, that's the face I made."

"You are not exactly engendering me with confidence here."

She stopped at the doorway and turned around with a devilish smirk. "I don't know what that word means, but you should probably come down and see. It's not good. Also, the raccoon is cute." Dani winked and left Emilie standing there, a red flush creeping up her neck like ivy.

15

DANI

Neon lights on the oven read 5:47, and outside the sky was gray as night faded towards the weak promise of dawn. They'd cleaned up after dinner and wiped down the counters. Everything still sat where they'd left it...except the back door was cracked open just enough for the early morning air to make the room cooler than usual.

Dani let Emilie pass her to open the kitchen door the rest of the way. Where earlier a solid storm door stood, now only wreckage remained. Only the top third still hung onto the hinges. Torn and mangled chunks lay strewn across the backyard.

The damage had been bad enough when she'd seen it from inside. Emilie froze, eyes pinned on the door and what lay beyond it, horror writ large in every tense muscle. Dani knew she was trying to take in the wreckage, her brain train to put things back where they belonged. Where they'd never fit back together properly again.

Another layer of security had been torn away from her. Dani felt for her, she did, but this was not the time for kid gloves. Not Emilie's fault, Dani knew, but it was clearer than ever that they were on the clock and running behind. Emilie turned back to look at Dani, face drawn, questions swimming in her pale blue eyes. Dani's chest ached as she remembered the unique pain that came when the illusion of safety was shattered. It was necessary, but seeing the desolation in her eyes didn't make that easier to bear.

"I don't know what did it," Dani's voice echoed in the cavernous kitchen, "but the real show is outside."

Emilie turned back to the door and ducked under the remains. Dani followed, not touching the mangled door either. The backyard was half wild, covered in leaves and ending with a fence at the tree line.

Fog hung low over the grass, thick and ominous. Chunks of twisted gray metal had torn into the grass and gouged wide furrows into the ground. Shrubs lay torn up along the fence line and scattered about the yard. Dani wasn't sure how she'd slept through this kind of destruction. Standing out here with the cool air hitting her skin, her instincts screamed danger.

A charm burned at her clavicle, and she pulled it away from her skin before it singed her—it wouldn't have been the first time. Dani stuck close to the back door, glad for the wards along the perimeter of the house. They were probably the only reason they hadn't had an unexpected visitor *inside* as they slept. Still, it was better that Emilie saw, that she understood they were not in the free and clear even if the house had protections in place.

"This is..." Emilie looked from the twisted metal up to the windows on the third floor. "We should get back into the house."

"Agreed." Dani waited for Emilie to pass her and then walked back into the house and locked the door. Couldn't hurt.

"Coffee, coffee, coffee," Emilie murmured under her breath. She bustled around the kitchen and had a pot brewing within a few short minutes.

"You really didn't hear anything?" Dani raised an eyebrow.

Emilie's eyes shifted to her uneasily. "I heard things, but...uh, I wasn't...I mean..."

"Spit it out already."

"I think Spectre called me up out of my body and tried to get me to break the binding that way?" Emilie grimaced as she poured two cups of coffee.

Dani snagged hers off the table and took a careful sip. "I'm gonna need you to explain that one."

Her brow furrowed in concentration as if she struggled to free the information from behind a wall. Eventually, the look smoothed away and she spoke. "So, some mediums can spirit-walk, astral project, whatever you wanna call it."

"Yeah, I've seen it done. Takes time and space and inner peace or some shit."

"Usually I'd agree with you." Emilie twitched and coffee sloshed onto her hand. She didn't seem to notice. "Except that I fell asleep in my body and then woke up outside of it. So, you know." She laughed nervously and took a seat at the kitchen table.

"That's a thing?"

"Apparently." Emilie shook her head rapidly and picked at the hem of her shirt. "I've never done anything like it. I'm not sure how to explain it but..."

"But what?"

"I saw an old spirit. Something was off about him, but in the shadows..." Emilie frowned. "I recognized another voice with his. I'd swear...I'd swear I heard Spectre upstairs. But it was like he couldn't... see me. Somehow."

Dani stared at her. *This was bad. In a 'the monster knows where we're sleeping' sort of way.* Her understanding of bindings was limited, but she'd gathered enough about the way Spectre hunted. He followed the talent, and if Emilie couldn't access hers, then she stayed hidden, but it looked like they couldn't even depend on that as she started remembering and her talent broke through.

"Are you fucking with me?"

"No." Emilie shook her head, pale hair arcing out around her face.

Dani paced back and forth across the length of the kitchen. "Spectre drew you out of your body, and you think it's what? Super cool?" She shot Emilie a dirty look.

"No, of course not. It isn't." Emilie tipped her head back and let out a strangled yell. "What I'm saying is that I think he's....moving through the veil somehow. The spirit I saw, Henry, I remember him. But it was like...he wasn't himself somehow."

"Uh, huh." Sarcasm was her natural defense. A huge part of her felt bad for using it against Emilie when she was clearly struggling, but right now she needed anything she could get, anything that would drive out the sound of Graham's gurgling breaths.

Emilie frowned and took another long sip of coffee. "There's a reason nobody has killed him."

"Hasn't been for lack of trying."

"Yeah, but he's got a reason for what he's doing. What if that's connected to the reason nobody can kill him?"

"That's a pretty big fucking jump." Dani scoffed and took a sip of her coffee to distract herself.

"Yeah, but what if I'm right?"

Dani stared at Emilie and tried not to be cruel. It wasn't that what she was saying was out of the question. Getting one's hopes up or pinning the plan on a jump like that was dangerous, though. If they overlooked details, somebody could end up dead. She winced at the thought, Graham's face flashing through her mind before she pushed it to the side.

In the few moments she'd been distracted, Emilie had drifted off into her own little world. She turned and cocked her head. The air grew thick, heavy with the smell of ozone and sandalwood. Emilie's head dropped below her shoulders, and she took a deep, shuddering breath. When she sat back up, the ozone smell faded, but the air was still thick. Dani curled her lip, aggravated that she'd let herself come down unarmed and under-prepared. Several of her charms heated in unison, warming her skin through her shirt. Emilie's eyes popped open, and Dani's lip quivered.

Not Emilie's eyes, dark honey brown, whiskey-gold eyes. Graham's eyes looked at her out of the wrong face. A strangled whimper fought its way past her lips.

"Miss me, troublemaker?" His voice came from Emilie's lips. It was strange and wrong, but she'd thought she would never hear that voice again. Memories rolled over her, all the barbs from Alabama fresh again in her mind. But this time those eyes weren't glassy and lifeless, they were just in the wrong head.

"Hey now. No cryin' on the job, remember? Rules are rules, and I don't have long."

Dani sat down hard. "I remember," she answered with a weak laugh.

"You have to tell Emilie the truth about why you came to town. And about Alabama."

"No."

"There isn't time. He's coming for you, same as her. Two prizes for the price of one, and she's on the right track. The answer is in what happened and who was there. So play nice, huh? For me?" Graham winked, and then Dani watched as he faded out and away from her.

Emilie gasped, hands scrabbling against the table for purchase. She sat there for a long moment and then looked at Dani again, pale eyed once more. Her chest heaved, trying to get air, trying to get a grasp on herself.

Dani sat stock-still, every muscle rigid. Graham was dead and gone, nothing but charred bones and ashes, not even enough to bury. She knew, she'd circled back to check after. Most people didn't get the opportunity to speak to the people they lost after they crossed over. Mediums, real ones, weren't a common talent. It wasn't enough either. A glimpse of Graham, and then he was gone again. It felt like having her insides scooped out.

She waited for the question she knew was coming. When Emilie asked, and Dani knew she would, she didn't know what to say. What could she say? She'd worked side by side with Graham for years. He'd been the person who knew her best, better even than Joe. Losing him had been like losing a limb. Graham taught her how to survive this life, how to make her own sanctified shells, patched up her wounds, and joked with her, been her best friend and her favorite person. What could she say to any of that? There was no explaining it.

"Who..." Emilie's voice stuttered.

"Graham," Dani said, licking her lips to banish the hoarse tone from her voice. "His name was Graham." She frowned and looked at her knuckles on the table. "He was my partner, my best friend."

She didn't want to say more, didn't want to open that can of worms. Maybe he'd have been more if things had been different, but they weren't. She'd buried all this for a reason, please and thank you. She'd sworn to herself not to open it until the job was done and Spectre was dead.

"And now he's dead."

"And now he's dead," Dani agreed and drained the dregs of her coffee. She waited a beat, Graham's voice ringing in her ears. "We ran together, hunted together. And then Alabama happened."

"Alabama?"

"Yeah. Couple of months back, we worked a job. Graham did the background, I did the deed, but it wasn't what we thought it was. It was Spectre." She rubbed at her face with both hands, unsure of where to even begin. She dropped them away and looked back at the other woman.

"We need help." Emilie's eyes were too bright in her face. "I think we need to call my grandpa.

"Why?"

"Because that, whatever that was, it's never happened before." Emilie's jaw went tight.

"I've heard of it before." Dani leaned back in her chair. "Ain't common. But some mediums can channel the dead." Her lips twisted.

"Yeah, well I heard what he said. About Spectre and about me. So maybe Grandpa can help. It's better than nothing. And neither of us know what did that to the back door." Emilie's gaze shifted to the locked kitchen door. Through the window panes the remains of the storm door were easy to see.

"You trust him?"

Emilie bit her lip. "Yeah. He tried, in his own way. He tried." She got up and took the empty cups to the sink and turned on the faucet.

"Is he gonna give up the details we need?"

"I think he can point us in the right direction. He said Dad had been trying to figure everything out, but I haven't had time to check his office or the library." Emilie finished washing out the cups and put them on the rack to dry.

"Besides. I want breakfast."

THEY'D WAITED for the sun to finish coming up before heading into Dawson to meet Ephraim at the diner. The sun in the sky meant better visibility on anything sneaking up on them. Whatever comfort Dani had wrangled before bed disappeared by the time they took the back corner booth at the diner.

The worst of the early morning rush had ducked out by then, leaving just a few tables filled with people who spoke in hushed voices and didn't look up. They hadn't even paid attention when the trio took their seats and ordered breakfast. Dani liked it better this way. Anonymity would keep them alive if they played their cards right. Emilie and Ephraim chatted about this and that until the food came, and then he pinned Emilie with his pale blue eyes.

"You said you needed help."

"Last night was weird." Emilie picked at her food.

"Weird how?"

"Well, somebody snatched Emilie up out of her body, and the kitchen storm door is in pieces," Dani said with a sharp smile.

"What? The binding?"

"Is still here. Kind of," Emilie said, pushing food around her plate.

"Anything else?" Ephraim sighed and ran a hand along the length of the Formica table. His eyes bounced between them as he worked something out.

"So, are we just not gonna talk about Spectre?" Dani broke in. She rapped her knuckles on the table. "He's been after me for months, and he knows who killed his little pet in that room."

Ephraim met her eyes, and she glared right back. They needed to come to an understanding. She wasn't his granddaughter and wasn't impressed by a talented, even one with a reputation like his. And as much as she liked Emilie, they didn't have time to be gentle about this.

"You've been his quarry all these months." Ephraim frowned.

"Since last year in Alabama."

"When he lit back up again," Ephraim agreed. "He'd been off grid for a few years. That's the first time anyone caught wind of him since he tussled with Valkyrie." His eyes flickered past Dani when he said it. "Nobody figured out why he popped up. Nothing but ruins left behind him."

"Don't I know it," Dani muttered and bit into a chunk of bacon with zeal.

"I'll tell you what I can, but I need something first."

Dani swore and tipped her head against the vinyl headrest of the bench. She saw what he wanted from the glint in his eye, information for information, and he wanted what everyone had since Alabama, details about what had happened, how things had gone so wrong that two veteran hunters got hosed.

"You want to know what happened." She dropped her head back down. Dani needed to look him in the eye and do this. "I don't like going around sharing my wounded soul."

"I wouldn't ask if it didn't matter."

"You think he has a network?"

"He has more than just him, has to after all these years. I've studied this monster for a long time, and I've had the misfortune before of underestimating his abilities and reach."

Dani sighed, wishing she'd just left this town, and Emilie—hot though she was—to their own devices. Fine. If they wanted the story, she'd tell them all of it, every terrible moment that she'd survived and how she hit the ground running after. She'd had a lot of bad days, but that one? It took the cake.

"We holed up in this little town in Alabama. Cypress Springs, or some shit like that. Mining town once, but when the jobs left, the town died. Graham got a call from a contact nearby, got all fired up over it. He found us the job, and I went along with it because that's how things worked..."

16

DANI

CYPRESS SPRINGS, ALABAMA,
THIRTEEN MONTHS AGO

The truck bed gleamed, charms and knives lined up within it and catching the sunlight. It refracted up onto Graham's face, bouncing off the lenses of his wire-framed glasses and illuminating his golden-brown eyes behind them.

"It's a lesser wraith. One that slipped its leash along the way somewhere." He shrugged his broad shoulders and glanced at her before looking away.

"Isn't that kind of above our paygrade?"

He stretched his tall frame up to its full height. "Not always. Not this time anyway."

"If you say so. I follow your lead." She grinned and tossed a small blade into the air, catching it in a spin.

Dark locks of hair bounced around his bronze skin and trailed down his back as he shook his head. A sharp smile curved his lips. "Only when you feel like it."

"Whatever. So what are we looking at, oh wise one?" Dani mocked with a raised eyebrow.

Graham sighed dramatically but closed the spell book he'd had open in his lap and put it to the side. "Few buildings have burned up, nothing inhabited, but moving closer. A few casualties, but not many, mostly vagrants."

"So nobody gives a damn." Dani rolled her eyes and spat at the ground.

"Better than double-digit bodies."

"Yeah, but not by much." Dani's smile evaporated, and she looked along the lonely stretch of road next to their truck. She hated showing up once the body count started. It felt more like being a gravedigger than a hunter sometimes.

"With a wraith, even a lesser, we're lucky."

"How'd you ID it already? We haven't even rolled into town yet."

"I got a call. And I've seen these sorts before." His eyes slid away from hers, and Dani's lips pressed together in a tight line.

She wanted to grill him for more info on how he'd identified it, or why he seemed so gung ho when they'd been four states away when the call came in. But it'd do nothing but make him clam up. Dani just needed to remember for the next time he got drunk. Graham was always chatty with a few drinks in him. Otherwise, she'd never have gotten anything about his past out of him—years hunting together or not.

"Don't make that face. I know what I'm doing." He shook his head but wouldn't meet her eyes.

"I know, I know. How dangerous are we talking here?"

"Nasty. But so long as we're prepared, it'll be fine. Not so potent once they're out of range of their masters." He reached for another book and cracked it open, eyes scanning the page, looking for something.

"And this one slipped its leash?" She pushed, hoping for details.

"Or whoever created it let it run loose. Either way." He snapped the book shut and looked over at her.

"And you're sure it's operating solo?" She pressed him, searching his face for any sign of subterfuge.

"Yeah."

"Because if it isn't—"

"I said it was on its own, didn't I?" Graham snapped and then grimaced.

"Sorry. We stick clear of talented for reasons, right?"

"Like I said, there aren't any in this town."

"Okay." Dani put the knives back in their sheaths one at a time, prepped for the last leg of this trip. "So what's the game plan?"

"We're gonna summon it and then kill it."

"Seriously?" Dani turned and looked at Graham like he'd grown a second head.

"It's the only way. A Greater Circle will make sure it doesn't go anywhere."

"Doesn't that break the cardinal 'don't fuck with talented' rule?" With a grimace, Dani threw her knife into the board propped up against the tire. "They're your rules and we follow them but G—"

"We don't have a choice." His tone didn't brook any argument. "It's old business, and it is what it is. Besides, none of them will waste their time on a wraith they didn't create."

"Is that why we came?" Dani raised an eyebrow and snatched her blade out of the plywood.

"We came because we got a call. And this is our job, remember?"

"Yeah, I remember. I just prefer monsters made of flesh and blood, is all." She frowned and rubbed at her forehead. Later, they'd hash this shit out later.

THE WAREHOUSE GRAHAM had chosen sat out on the outskirts of town. The road that led to it was paved with gravel instead of asphalt, and the truck jumped over every bump and divot. It was an abandoned, grey hulk of a building, jagged holes where windows had once been. It'd been years since it had been abandoned, and it loomed, the ghost of industry past.

Inside, rusty machinery lay strewn about with trash and papers that carpeted the floor. The broken windows let in enough light, but the LED panels in the truck would come in handy after sundown.

Three sets of ladders around the room led up to a catwalk that hugged the walls of the room. From the looks of it, nobody had been here for a long, long time.

"This'll work fine." Graham's voice echoed through the building, distorted as it bounced off the walls around them.

"I'm on LED duty?"

"Yeah, we're gonna need all of them for this place. I gotta get the circle set before dark."

She took the time to set each light so it focused on Graham's circle, illuminating it in sickly, unnatural light. It was better to focus on the equipment than what Graham was about to do. Watching as he bled himself to get the mojo flowing wasn't something she enjoyed. She went outside to collect her thoughts and retreat to the quiet place in her head. It gave her a bit of time to watch the sun sink down against the horizon, painting the world red and orange as it disappeared.

The two of them showed up when there were already bodies on the ground. That came as part of the job. After all, it was hard to tell if something was hunting people without victims. Sometimes, when they were lucky, there was a bounty waiting on the far side. Mostly, it was a lot of get it done and get out of dodge before the locals clued in to what was going on.

Then there were jobs like this, jobs where somebody in the know got a heads-up and reached out. Usually they were small things, a poltergeist here, a revenant there, but wraiths were something else, and how Graham was acting put her on edge. It was like something else was on the line. She heard it in his voice.

Graham handled the magic, and she was the muscle. That meant wraiths landed in her department. They didn't go down easy, and magic rolled off them like water off a duck's back, but blessed or consecrated blades cut right through them. Inside, Graham chanted, guttural syllables floating out the doorway.

She pulled one of her blades from its scabbard and ran her thumb along the curve of its edge. When Graham's voice got louder and the wind picked up, she jumped down to the ground and rolled her shoulders. Time to get to work.

Graham, and the massive circle he'd painted onto the floor, were in the middle of the space. Shadows clung at the corners of the room, but Dani already knew what hid there. That was the point of preparing early. His voice dropped low when she walked into the building, air thick as he summoned the wraith into his circle. All she had to do now was wait. Still, it was weird that Graham wanted to get this done so quick. She was used to a week just to case a joint. He always said the devil was in the details. *So why does he seem rushed?*

There would be time enough for details, and getting the truth of why Graham had been so dead set on taking this job, when Alabama was in the taillights. Graham finished the incantation, and the glyphs traced around the edge of the circle glowed in sequence for a moment before the circle snapped to life.

Thick, dark smoke billowed up from the floor and poured into the circle. It obscured whatever was hiding. The smell of burnt flesh and death filled the room. Inside the boundary, something more substantial than vapor moved. When it ran into the glyphs at the edge, a bright cross hatch of gold appeared, trapping it. Graham backed away and took the shotgun she'd loaded for him. Dani grinned, all teeth, and pulled a knife from her thigh sheath. Its heft was familiar in her hand, worn leather gone soft from use.

She stalked around the edge, careful not to cross the border. Not yet, not until she saw the wraith inside. Wraiths weren't always bright, but like any predator, they tracked movement. It moved again, and she saw its form silhouetted against the smoke. It's shape was vaguely humanoid, with two arms and two legs, but with thick growths along the shoulders and head.

"H-hello!? Is anyone out there? I need help!" A man's panicked voice cried out from inside the circle, breaking into coughing and hacking.

It sounded warped, not quite right, but if she'd been walking past, she'd have rushed in to help. That was the point. She dropped into a fighting stance but didn't move closer. She whistled, a low sound that faded almost as soon as she made it.

The figure moved at her too fast. In the blink of an eye, it changed from being a vague outline to a screaming monster. It hit the edge of the circle and slammed into the magic netting that held it.

Grey pockmarked skin stretched too tight against its sharp bones, a bad attempt at something almost human. As it shrieked and clawed, bright orange cross-hatched burns seared into its face. The screams were the wrong pitch, the squeal of a wounded animal. Nothing sentient. Nothing capable of reason.

Dani burst forward into the circle and slashed it across the torso. She juked to the left and flipped the blade in her hand, jamming it up and into the monster's chest cavity. It threw itself back from her with the knife still lodged in its hulking mass. Wild screams echoed around them as it tore at its own flesh.

Dani took a quick step away from the wraith, retreating outside the circle. She didn't want to get caught as it flailed. The wraith backpedaled, legs moving too fast and catapulting it into the other side of the circle. The binding flared again, and the smell of cooking meat broke through the thick air.

She'd thought the gut shot was a killing blow, but the way it was thrashing made her second-guess herself. The other consecrated blade appeared in her hand, and she crouched to go back in for round two when Graham grabbed her by the shoulder. He yanked her back, his eyes wide.

"Something's wrong. We've got to—" Graham's frantic voice cut off as the wraith screamed a death cry.

The circle glowed white hot, meticulous lines and glyphs melting together before it shattered, mesh falling to the floor and burning its way into the foundation. Small gouts of flame climbed out of the meshwork and caught on the floor. The fire acted like a living, breathing thing that crawled along the ceilings and the walls and consumed everything in its path. Smoke choked her, acrid and thick. But Graham had one hand wrapped around her wrist in a vise-tight grip, grounding her, pulling her behind him.

Fire filled the warehouse in seconds. It moved faster than should have been possible as it ran up pillars and jumped with abandon from the floor, to the railing, and to the ceiling. Thunderclaps shook the air around her. Dani realized after a moment it was laughter, booming, malicious peals of laughter that made dread curl up in her belly, hot and fetid.

Graham continued yelling and pulling at her arm, but she couldn't hear what he was saying as the flames roared around them.

Finally his voice broke through the noise. "We've gotta go, Dani! It was a trap! HE'S COMING!"

"Who is coming!?" Dani tried to catch her breath, and a coughing fit wracked her lungs. She pulled her shirt up, covering her nose, and ducked low, moving as fast as possible.

"The wraith wasn't leashed, he marked it. Someone marked the damn thing, and Spectre is coming."

Panic bleated in her ears. Warped perception made everything louder, bigger. The twenty feet from the circle to the door felt like miles. Hot embers burned away strands of hair, and the smoke made every breath hurt. Heavy coughs wracked her frame. They needed to get out, but smoke obscured everything as Graham dragged her toward what she hoped was the door.

The smoke cleared enough for her to see the double doors, and she moved up next to Graham. He reached to open them, and a roar shook the building. The ground bucked underfoot, flames leaped for the ceiling, and the catwalk above the doors sheared away from the wall in a scream of metal. She grabbed the back of Graham's collar with her free hand and yanked him backwards. They both tumbled to the ground. In front of them a heap of rusted metal blocked their exit.

Above them in a corner, the walls cracked and smoke escaped in a steady stream. Dani stood back up, wild eyed, and a moment later Graham appeared out of the smoke and grabbed her by the elbow. She could see the hatch work inside the circle of magic still glowing and fueling more flames.

"The other door!"

Another coughing fit made her double over, and she had to hold her shirt over her face again. Her heart pounded in her ears. She became convinced this was the end. Graham ducked down and ran. Dani followed suit, close on his heels as beams crashed down around them and decrepit machinery turned red from the heat. They dodged the worst of it and gave the circle a wide berth.

Another molten chunk of catwalk came screaming down to the ground and took out one wall. A bestial snarl followed it, sending a cold chill down Dani's back. Fortunately, she and Graham had been working together a long time, and they moved together by instinct.

Back to back, they surveyed the room. She palmed another blade from one of her sheaths and took it in hand, glad that Graham had the shotgun.

Her eyes danced back and forth until she spotted the smoke billow out of the way of a large shape. It looked like something between a wolf and a big cat. Dani spotted two more as they moved, silent and careful. They were hunting, and she was the prey. Graham moved forward so slowly, it was barely noticeable. Dani stayed with him, keeping their backs pressed in a firm line.

The monsters slipped out of the flames, shadows made real. They were black as pitch, with glowing jewels for eyes and markings in gold along their backs. She tapped Graham's thigh twice and then rolled toward the closest beast. It swiped at her with a massive paw. She dodged and slashed out with her blade. The blessed iron passed right through the shadow, no sizzle, no scream, no distortion. She might as well have waved her arm at it.

The beast skidded to a halt and turned its head to stare her down. The shotgun fired off to her left, and another beast snarled from her blind spot. Graham hip checked her, and she tumbled away from the fray.

Dani skidded across the floor, crashing through a cloud of smoke that parted like a gray curtain around her. The shadows didn't chase her, and Graham's scream told her why. She scrabbled for purchase and surged back to her feet. The door was right behind her, close enough she could have turned and run through it. But that was not an option, not without Graham. Malicious laughter echoed around her, bouncing off every surface. It chased her as she swung her arms through the air, trying to clear away the smoke.

From somewhere ahead there came a cold, cultured man's voice. "Gra-ham. How nice to see you again. It's been *so* long."

Graham snarled as giant chunks of ceiling rained down, clearing the smoke. For a moment, she saw him collapsed on the ground. She had to get closer. She had to help him, *save him*. Another cough choked her, and she gasped, desperate for air. Time was almost up.

A pillar to her right crashed to the floor and took out a massive section of the wall. Smoke and flame whooshed toward the fresh air. It cleared things out enough she could see everything in front of her but blocked her from getting closer.

Graham was a tumble of limbs on the floor, and his eyes burned a dark gold. His stomach was a mess of gore, and blood shone wet on the ground beneath him. The shadows had torn him to pieces.

Horror, followed on its heels by shock, tripped through her body. Tendrils of bloody magic gleamed, slick and wet, out of the puddle below Graham. In ten years, Dani had only seen this once: sanguimancy. The ability to use one's own blood as a weapon. Unfortunately, the more a person used it, the faster they died.

She watched as the tendrils helped him to his feet. A tall figure emerged from the flames behind him. He was taller than Graham by a head, and slim, with a hood that didn't quite obscure his face. He had a bone structure and a way of holding himself that said he had been handsome once. Not anymore. His skin was too pale and peeled away from the muscle and bone in thick patches in contrast to long curls of dark hair. Worst of all were his eyes, a perfect black, cold and cruel.

Graham gave him a bloody, ferocious smile. His eyes glowed even brighter, two pieces of burning topaz imbued with magic. He met Dani's gaze and nodded before jerking his chin at the door behind her, using shorthand to say what he wouldn't with words.

Run. But she couldn't move. Dani couldn't make herself take the opening he'd provided her. Instead, she took a step toward him.

Burning lumber and debris blocked her from going any closer. She searched frantically for a way around.

The figure glided to Graham and lifted him without any effort at all. Her partner let out a strangled cry of fury, and dozens of spears made of blood slammed from him into the hooded man. He staggered but didn't let go.

Instead, gouts of flame erupted from him, boiling away Graham's dark skin. He screamed, a strangled, bloody sound. Dani fell to the ground and scrambled backwards on all fours, limbs propelling her as fast as she could go. She was still watching when Graham stopped screaming and his eyes went dark, when the figure snapped his neck and dropped him like he was a bag of trash. Graham's blank eyes stared at her across the floor of the warehouse through the flames and drifting cinders.

She slammed back against the door. Scrambling up, she turned and pushed the door open. Smoke billowed out into the cool air, and she collapsed onto the gravel, gulping in fresh air and trying not to puke. The truck was still a good fifty feet away, and if she wanted to get to it she needed to run, now. Right fucking now. But she couldn't make her legs work because all she could see were Graham's dead eyes.

The figure screamed, and Dani snarled in response. She managed to get her legs back up under her. Graham deserved better than this. She couldn't kill the bastard right now. Her fingers grasped her throwing knife, pulling it from a hidden sheath. It was stupid. A little consecrated blade wasn't going to do what Graham's magic hadn't, but she didn't care. She had to try to hurt the bastard. Her heart screamed at her for vengeance. With deadly aim, she let the knife fly.

She was running before she heard the wet thunk of metal meeting flesh. His scream ended in a hiss. "Dani. I'll find you. Just like I found Graham. You can't run forever!" He laughed behind her as she kicked gravel under her feet.

The air burned like needles in her throat, and she couldn't hear anything over her sobs. Tears dripped down her face, obscuring her vision, but she got into the truck and tore ass out of there. She drove north out of town, away from Alabama. She had no idea where she was going or whether he was following her. She didn't know anything except that Graham was dead and she'd just seen the face of evil, and she had to run. Run, and run, and run, and hope that she was faster.

WHEN DANI LOOKED BACK UP at Ephraim, her nerves felt raw and her throat was thick. But she wouldn't cry over Graham again, not here with people who'd never known him, who she barely knew. That didn't make telling her story any less painful. "So there you have it, what happened in Alabama, straight from the source." The words sounded bitter, and she didn't care. He had forced it out of her. She didn't have to be nice about it.

"Thank you. Truly." Ephraim sighed. "Graham was a talented young man. I'm sorry that Spectre got the drop on him like that. It shouldn't have happened that way."

"You knew him?" Dani shook her head, confusion making her head fuzzy on top of the grief.

"I know a great many people, as you might expect. But there's only been one sanguimancer born in the last seventy years. I helped to train him." His eyes skittered to the side. "And then I helped him to disappear from the talented community."

"Is that why he started hunting? He wouldn't..." Dani clenched her jaw, trying to find the right words.

"It was. The magical version of witness protection, in a manner of speaking." Ephraim sighed and shook his head slightly. "I am sorry for making you relive that, but I needed to know what drew him back out."

"Can you help us?"

"Not as much you'd hope, but I'm not your only resource in this town. I know where Phillip has hidden the research that you need, and I know of two sentinels willing to aid you as best they can."

"Well. That's a start."

17

EMILIE

They'd left Grandpa behind in the diner, and Emilie was only slightly less frustrated than she'd been this morning. She had hoped talking to him would give them what they needed to deal with Spectre. She could sense the danger crawling closer. With every moment, the binding frayed a little more and the talents inside her bloomed, reaching for the light denied them for so many years. The morning hadn't been a total loss; he'd told them where Dad hid his notes. If he was half as meticulous in this as he was at the auction house, she'd bet there'd be plenty to parse through.

Dani stopped her slow amble and turned back to Emilie with a stoic mask on her face. "You think the sentinels will help?"

Emilie shook herself, breaking the torpor and the memory loose. "Merc and Andry? Yeah. They don't *exactly* follow the rules most sentinels stick to. Their family has been here as long as mine. They can help us figure out why he's hunting us, so we can turn the tables."

"How do you know that?" Dani tipped her head and narrowed her eyes but waited for Emilie to catch up before she started walking again.

"The rules thing? It's a point of contention with the family. The rumor was always that they had fae blood that gave them an out, but I don't know if it's true or not." Emilie scratched at the back of her neck. Reclaiming these memories was uncomfortable when some things came easily and others were still shrouded.

"Okay then." Dani nodded.

The hunter's face was drawn, and she gritted her teeth, unhappy with this turn of events. Emilie probably would have felt the same if they swapped places. Being asked to dredge up the worst night of your life, relive it for the details hiding in the scrollwork at the edges wasn't fair. None of this was fair, but it was their lot, and Emilie had long ago learned how to deal when nothing worked how it should.

"They might have details about Spectre that Dad missed." Emilie rolled her shoulders, acutely aware that the street had emptied around them. It gave her an eerie feeling, as though the town were holding its breath and waiting for something to happen.

"Oh?"

"Their gran, she was the town historian for a long, long time."

"And we're nosy," Andry announced from behind Emilie. "We like to know all the things." The trees that separated the sidewalk from the street rustled in response to her announcement, boughs reaching toward her gently.

"Find all the secrets Dawson tries to hide from us," Merc added. "Handy trait in this line of business." He cocked his head, and small fissures in the sidewalk at his feet sealed themselves back up until they looked brand new again.

She whipped around at the sound and clutched at her chest while Dani nearly snarled. The twins had snuck up behind her. It stirred up a memory that made it almost feel like old times. Those two could sneak up on a ghost without getting caught. They stood shoulder to shoulder with easy smiles. They looked like two sides of the same coin.

"Good to see some things never change," Emilie answered and shook her head.

"With Gran retired in Georgia, somebody had to take over." Andry shrugged and twisted her lips into a wry smile.

"It is sort of our job to keep an eye on things in Dawson," Merc added with a pointed look.

"And you waited until now because...?" Emilie asked, irritation coloring her voice.

Andry's smile turned into a smirk. "Because they bound you up like a trussed deer—"

"And Phillip told me you might die if we tried to break it early." Merc cut his sister off.

Andry frowned and elbowed Merc as she moved past him. "We didn't want to stay quiet—"

"It's more complic—"

"I *said*, we didn't want to stay quiet," Andry hissed at her brother with a sharp glare. She sighed and turned back to Emilie. "We're here to help now. Besides, Phillip's stash of research? It's extensive. You're gonna need help." She waggled her eyebrows suggestively, and the tree branches rustled again in agreement.

Emilie bit her lip, trying to make the right call. Her knee-jerk reaction was anger, pure and white-hot if they'd been in on this too. But she pushed it aside. This was Andry and Merc. They never would have gone along with it to appease her father. It almost made up for the lies and the distance, almost.

"And why should we trust you?" Dani asked from behind Emilie, voice cold as ice. "Last I checked, your boy there didn't have the deets to help us out."

Andry's smile vanished, and she turned to Merc with a bewildered expression. "She came by the shop?"

"After our talk."

"Uh huh." Andry closed her eyes and shook her head. "Merc likes to play by the rules, and the rules say we shouldn't influence the outcome of events."

"Andromeda..."

"No." Andry's eyes flashed as she turned to her brother. "Not this time. Not with *him*." She took a deep breath and turned to Emilie and Dani. "I don't follow those rules."

"Andr—"

"I said no! They owe me. If the council gets a hair up their ass, they can come see Dawson for themselves instead of hiding three thousand miles away." She reached up to the nearby tree, caressing a new leaf as it unfurled and reached for her.

Merc opened his mouth like he wanted to say something more, but seemed to think better of it and shut it again. He slouched and gestured for his sister to lead the way.

"See. I knew you'd see it my way." She smiled and looked at Emilie. "Ephraim tell you where Phillip's hiding his research?" She started to walk but then waited for Emilie to follow.

"More or less." She hurried to catch up, heading for the parking lot around the corner.

"Good." Andry nodded and shot her an approving look over one shoulder.

"Don't you two have like...shops to run?" Dani raised an eyebrow.

"We closed for the day," Merc said, gesturing as he pointedly looked up and down the deserted street. "You might have noticed. Nobody wants to come out today."

"Must be something in the air," Dani muttered and turned the corner toward her truck.

Emilie followed her, intent on getting back to the house and getting behind the wards. If whatever had torn up the storm door rolled through town, there wasn't anything to hide them, only the stringy remains of the binding working as a curse and a boon at the same time.

It was another block down to where they'd parked, and they still didn't pass any other pedestrians. Emilie couldn't remember the last time things had been this empty, and it only ratcheted her anxiety up another notch. When they got to the truck, she turned to the twins and licked her lips nervously.

"There's something else. Other than Dad's research, I mean." Emilie shifted her eyes to Merc. "Last night something shredded the storm door."

"The storm door?" Merc frowned and took a step closer. "But only the door."

"It didn't break through the wards," Dani added. "If that's what you were asking." She placed a gentle hand on Emilie's shoulder, and it sent shocks through her, but she stayed still and watched for Merc's reaction. If she didn't move, maybe Dani would leave her hand there. Emilie could feel the calluses on her palm through her T-shirt. The contact was small and perfectly innocent, but it was like electricity sparking across her skin. How long had it been since someone had touched her like this and made her heart skip a beat? She didn't remember.

Merc shifted uneasily. She had never been as close to him as she was to Andry, so there was no way to pinpoint what was on his mind, but Emilie could tell it wasn't good.

"Not quite what I was asking, but it answers the question well enough." Merc put his hands in his pockets and rocked back on his heels, face smoothed into a neutral mask. "I suppose our help is more necessary than I wagered."

"Told you so," Andry shot back at her brother. She rolled her eyes and turned back to Emilie. "Your family never does anything the easy way. Why would they start now, right?" She smiled. "Why don't we head back to the house so Merc can see the door before we get to work?"

THE YARD LOOKED SO MUCH WORSE than it had this morning. Without fog to obscure the damage, it was impossible to ignore the torn shreds of metal driven into the earth at strange angles. Emilie watched as Dani lingered next to the kitchen door, sitting on the stairs. Andry wandered toward the tree line and tutted under her breath. Merc made a beeline for the largest chunk of metal in the yard.

She joined Dani, avoiding the grimy residue of violence that surrounded the shreds of the door. It didn't feel safe back here, not anymore, as though this intrusion had stripped any remaining security. Something invaded that sanctity, and it made her skin crawl, made her feel small and afraid. Standing next to Dani, whether it was rational or not, helped. It took the edge off the wrongness of the yard, gave her the tiniest spark of normalcy, of safety.

Merc crouched down and reached a few fingers toward the wreckage. He didn't touch it though. *Curious. Maybe he felt the residue that clung to it as well.*

"This happened last night?" He turned toward them, one of his thick locss dropping along the side of his face.

"Somewhere between last night and very early this morning," Dani answered, taking a step closer to Emilie, eyes still pinned on Merc. "Something loud woke me up. When I came down, this is what I found." Her mouth thinned into a white line, and she crossed her arms over her chest. "Except when I came down, part of the yard was on fire. Or had been. Hard to tell."

"And then Emilie woke up?"

"I got her up too."

"You know she's always slept like the dead," Andry added over one shoulder, still standing at the far reaches of the backyard.

"Had to shake her awake," Dani said with a small smile as she caught Emilie's eye.

For just a moment it was like they were having a normal conversation, catching each other's eyes from across a crowded room. But it was gone in a flash, replaced by this nightmare Emilie couldn't seem to escape.

"But neither of you heard anything from outside?"

"A door slammed, but that's what woke me up." Dani shrugged. "Why does it matter? Something obviously happened."

"That door never latched right," Andry said. "Never wanted to stay shut. It always used to bang during storms. Probably why Emilie didn't wake up. She's used to it—was used to it."

"It matters because there is magic all over this yard, and I'm trying to figure out if someone cast a dampener over the house before they showed up," Merc said, brushing a few specks of dirt from his trousers as he stood.

"That's not small potatoes," Dani said.

"Exactly." Merc gestured back to the house. "There's nothing else out here for us at the moment. We might as well head back inside."

"Yes, because your opinion is the only one that matters." Andry rolled her eyes and stalked past her brother as he gaped at her.

"I'm a fan of inside," Emilie said, taking a half step backwards toward the remaining door.

"I agree, unless you have something to add, Andry?"

"Whatever tore that door off the hinges bolted in a hurry." She clucked her tongue. "Tore through half the grove trying to get out of here. Lucky Ephraim warded this place so tight after the renovations."

"So what? You were just being quarrelsome about going back in?"

"Don't forget they need both our help, hmm?" She gave him a pointed look before walking back through the kitchen door into the house.

"So yes, you were being quarrelsome." Merc sighed as Emilie locked the backdoor behind them all.

"It's easier for you."

"Oh, is that so?"

"Stone. Doesn't. Scream." Andromeda narrowed her eyes and pointed at her brother fiercely. "It's different with stone and metal. They'll talk to you, but they aren't alive." Her upper lip curled. "But that's not how it works for the green things and they are— screaming."

"You're a hortimancer?" Dani asked, interjecting herself between the twins.

Some tension drained out of Andry's face as she calmed back down. "I...technically—"

"Sentinels don't use the same terminology," Merc offered.

"But sort of. They would have called me a green witch two hundred years ago. Plants like me. The green things talk to me, but it goes both ways. I can hear them when nobody else can and..." Andromeda gestured toward the trees in the backyard, "it's always worse with trees. They're old and settled, time for them is slow and steady. This is a massacre, and they're wounded. It's not easy." She rubbed at her shoulder and then met Emilie's eyes. "Gimme a few minutes? Merc's got details for you anyway, I think." She raised an eyebrow and wandered out of the kitchen.

"Do ya, Merc?" Dani turned on her heel to face him.

Emilie watched it all with a bemused look on her face. It was nice to have someone on her side again, and the thought sent heat rising through her chest. She knew it was unadvisable to get attached to Dani, but her heart didn't seem to care much.

"In a manner of speaking. It was a wraith that ripped its way through the door. I got the story out of those twisted curls of steel in the grass." He deadpanned. "And because I've seen this kind of thing before."

Emilie flinched. She couldn't help herself. The comment hit like a punch to the gut. It may have been Spectre. She tried to play off the reaction, hoping nobody had been paying too much attention. She ducked her head and then started for the coffee maker. Sure, three pots in and it was barely one in the afternoon wasn't exactly 'healthy' per se, but things were going haywire and she needed the distraction.

The longer they stood here and just chatted, the closer Spectre got. After what happened in the attic before she'd woken up, his voice still echoed through her ears. Worse, that echo didn't do what it should have. It didn't frighten her. That voice was a caress, an old friend long forgotten. Disconcerting didn't even begin to cover it. When she returned with the coffee pot, she took the opportunity to touch Dani's arm, lifting the pot with a questioning look.

Shooting her a smile that warmed her to her core, Dani nodded. Emilie left her hand on the woman's arm a bit longer than was necessary. The warmth of Dani's skin and the strong cords of muscle beneath comforted Emilie in a way nothing else seemed to be able to do.

"So I didn't imagine the way the yard felt, right?" Dani asked as she rubbed one palm against her jeans. "I didn't even get close to touching anything."

"Residue from the magic," Merc answered. "All power has a taste.

For wraiths created from forbidden power and necromantic energy, it feels like this. There are dark paths that a talented can walk."

"Places we don't go," Andry's voice added quietly from the doorway as she reappeared.

"Places nobody in their right mind goes."

"For good reason." The twins finished each other's sentences, one person speaking with two voices. Emilie shivered as power echoed through their voices and curled along her spine.

"That's not the most helpful thing you've said today," Dani said, aggravation rising above the sarcasm thick in her tone. "So somebody was throwing serious magic at the house, cool. But that's not the priority here because we know who would have been doing it." She threw up her hands and paced back and forth across the linoleum tiles. "Spectre has been out for my blood for fuckin' months. He knows Emilie is back in town, just can't get his mitts on her yet."

"It's all connected," Merc murmured.

"Connected how? See, this is what I mean. This cloak and dagger sentinel bullshit!"

"It's about history," Andromeda interrupted. "Spectre wasn't always Spectre. He got his start right here in the little town of Dawson. It should be in Phillip's notes."

"Grandpa said it was in the back office," Emilie said with a frown. "But I don't know what that means."

"You've never seen it?" Andry's jaw dropped, and then she clamped it shut again. "Right. Decade. Of course you haven't. Man, you are gonna flip."

"You have?" Emilie looked over the coffee maker as it gurgled and raised an eyebrow.

"Yeah. I was helping your dad put two and two together to get the whole story. Or as much of it as we could anyhow." Andromeda ushered everyone out of the kitchen and toward the study.

It was the one room in the house Emilie hadn't been compelled to rummage through since returning home. Dad's study was his quiet place in the house when Mama had been entertaining, not a place for little girls—not even quiet ones that wanted to curl up and read a book where nobody was likely to find them.

Andromeda threw open the door without any compunction and marched across the room to where a bookshelf was built into the wall. Emilie followed hesitantly, Merc and Dani not far behind. She gasped as wards flared brightly in the room.

It was a rainbow of shimmering colors built into everything, at least as many as the attic had, and packed so tight they were almost on top of one another; protection from fire, far-seeing, death, madness, casters, and plenty more she didn't recognize. Each one was clear and bright, and it took a long minute for her to catch her breath.

"You okay, killer?" Dani put her hands on Emilie's shoulders and peered around to get a look at her face.

The touch grounded her, helped her think. "Yeah it's just—bright." Emilie squeezed her eyes shut and shook her head. When she reopened them the wards were still easy to pick out, but they no longer burned like small stars in her vision.

"It's a lot, I know." Andry turned and looked at Emilie, concerned, before her eyes flicked to her brother.

"Yeah, we need to get to work." He pressed his lips together in a firm line.

Emilie turned to Mercurious. "Wanna explain?"

"The more you use your abilities, the looser the binding gets, the stronger they are..."

"Which means one step closer to Spectre finding me," Emilie responded with a sigh.

Merc nodded, face grim. Andry distracted her from asking him anything else with a muffled squeak. The bookshelf she'd been fiddling with popped open and revealed a doorway into a room. Emilie gaped as she walked over cautiously, drinking in the sight. A doorway wreathed in scarlet wards prefaced a long, narrow room crammed with research. Books, leather-bound folios, and loose papers were filed away on three long shelves. A small desk held a stack of black notebooks, each one labeled with a date range on the spine. She recognized her father's cramped handwriting, one note-book on top of the next.

"Does everyone in this town have a back room full of goodies?" Dani called from behind her. "I mean, damn people."

"Most of them. Places like Dawson attract people that have secrets," Merc answered.

Emilie looked back over her shoulder to see Andry watching her with kind eyes. "How do I know what's important?" she asked, voice bordering on hopeless.

"Grab the notebooks. Nobody else can go in unless we wanna get zapped."

"Blood wards?"

"And then some. Grab the notebooks. We ought to get started."

Emilie snatched the notebooks off the table and handed most of them off to Andry. If she'd had the time, she would have spent days in here going through everything. There was more here than research about Spectre alone, and her curiosity begged her to dig deeper. Her father had locked it away for a reason, but there was no time to ponder why, or what it might contain. This was the magical equiva-lent of a safe, and she wanted to believe that the information hidden away was here for the right reasons.

Bless Dad and his obsession. It might save her life, even if her fury at the binding hadn't faded in the least. He might have been a para-noid, angry man, but he wasn't stupid. From behind her she heard Andry and Merc talking. Dani caught her gaze, and they shared a long, meaningful look, one that fortified her.

Time to get to work.

18

DANI

Dani groaned and leaned back from the long dining table to scrub at her face. They'd been at this for hours. Phillip's journals had cross-referenced books from his private study and the main library. Then came charts and lists that made her eyesight blur the longer she stared at them. Fighting and killing she excelled at. Research, not so much.

"Anybody else feel like their eyes might melt right out of their faces?" Her voice bordered on desperate, but right now she didn't care.

She needed to get up and move around, do more than just jot down notes and hope they found the link when Phillip hadn't been able to pull it off in a damned decade. Hope wouldn't solve their problems. When Spectre showed up, Dani would survive. That was kinda her gig—being the last woman standing. Even when she didn't want to be. What she needed to do was figure out how to keep everyone else alive.

"A break for food wouldn't be the worst thing ever," Andromeda admitted with a sigh. "We need more time."

"Even if we had all the time in the world, we still might not put things together one hundred percent." Merc shook his head. "Too much time gone by, too many people dead."

"Okay, then," Emilie said, standing up. "That's how we put it together. I can...talk to the ones who aren't here anymore. I mean, in theory."

"That's not a good idea." Merc stood up on the other side of the table, eyes wide. "You push those boundaries and whatever's left—"

"Might snap. I'm very aware!" Emilie barked and moved away from the table, leaving all of her careful notes behind. "You think I forgot? It's the only thing I can think about since I got back here." She let out a harsh bark of laughter. "My head is the one on the chopping block, and it's my memories and abilities that got locked away." She stamped out of the room, hair flying around her face.

Dani raised an eyebrow and leaned back in her chair. "Was that the plan or...?" She gestured after Emilie. The instinct to go after her nearly had Dani standing up. But the hunter in her needed answers, and the hunter won out.

"Not helping." He glared at her, while Andromeda trailed Emilie up the stairs.

A flash of jealousy tried to rear its ugly head in Dani, but she stamped it down, hard. Now was not the time.

"You've known the girl for years, right? You didn't see this coming?"

"Emilie attached herself to my sister's hip, not mine." He rolled his eyes. "Notice I'm not the one running after her to talk her down."

"Is she wrong, though?" Dani gestured at the table between them. "I mean, we've got ten years' worth of research and digging, and we're still lost." She shook her head.

"Are you and Emilie both out of your damn minds?" Merc gave her a wild-eyed look like she'd just proposed eating bugs. "Every time she stretches the talent inside her, a little more of the binding gets eaten away."

"No shit, Sherlock. Sitting still and twiddling her thumbs isn't doing her any good either." She rubbed at her temples.

"She's alive, isn't she?"

"Surviving and living? Not the same thing. We can't stop her, and it might come down to her talents. There has to be a reason he's so gung ho on having her, right?"

"There are several." He waited a beat before continuing. "Spectre is a creature of history. I might not know where he came from, but I know he's crossed the Lockgrove and the Deveraux lines. He holds a grudge."

"He's like the carnival pony, everybody is taking a ride." Dani pinned her gaze on the ceiling and sighed.

"I know Emilie can't control what or who reaches out to her. But she doesn't need to accelerate the process." He frowned. "You of all people should understand that."

"And why is that?" Dani said in a too-quiet voice.

A tic in Merc's jaw popped, and he took a long breath. "Because I know about Alabama."

"How?" she asked in a soft murmur. It was a word sharpened to a vicious, killing edge. Heat pooled in her belly. There were only so many ways somebody could have put together what happened in that warehouse. Sentinels might have access to more information than a hunter, but they didn't know everything.

"Does the how really matter?" He cocked his head, one of his locs falling over his eyes. It was almost cute. It also kind of made her want to punch him in the face.

"It matters." She ground her teeth together, heard the click in her jaw from the pressure.

"A few sentinels put two and two together when they investigated it." He leaned against the doorway, arms crossed defensively.

"Why would sentinels care? It wasn't in anybody's territory."

"Because a necromancer killed a sanguimancer. You can't have thought it would go without being investigated." Merc tilted his head and watched her.

"You mean Graham." Dani made a noise low in her throat. Her chest burned, and she grasped for a weapon she didn't have, fingers clenched so tight her nails bit into her palm. "He had a name." She pushed herself to her feet, unable to continue sitting still.

"I do." Merc blinked.

"And what? They didn't know I was there? Or did they just not care?" She paced back and forth, shaking her head.

"I doubt anyone knew who you were, or that you were even alive." He shrugged his shoulders in an elegant gesture.

"So they didn't care." Dani paused and turned back to him, jaw so tight it ached.

"Graham hadn't made contact with anyone in the talented community for a long time, and he'd been an associate of some very nasty people once." Merc paused and raised an eyebrow. "I know you don't want to hear this, but you weren't crucial to what they were investigating."

"Why am I not surprised?" She snarled and slammed her hands down. "Sentinels never want to get their hands dirty. Hunters are first on the scene, and then we die, and we're not *crucial to your investigation*." She snarled and tipped her head back. This day wouldn't stop tearing open this old wound, and she was over it.

"Our job is keeping some kind of balance between the world you and I live in, and the one most bystanders do," Merc said carefully, stepping out from the doorway. "I'm not sure what you want me to say here."

"Right. Keeping the balance, or whatever the hell that means. As though living people aren't dying while you play at neutrality." She punctuated her words by jabbing at him with her index finger.

"It is what it is," Merc agreed curtly.

"Why are you so spooked about Spectre coming back to town then? Not like you're a target."

"Because," Andromeda announced from the doorway, "every time that son of a bitch comes to town, people die."

"What do you mean?"

"Spectre has been a plague on this town for two hundred years, since he was born."

"And you're just now sharing with the class?" Dani snarled.

"Merc will fill you in. I'm taking Emilie upstairs. Her dead family is talking to her again." Andry winced and disappeared again.

"The hell is up with you people and holding out? I mean, seriously." One of Dani's eyes twitched. "What part of working together do you not grasp?" She let herself sink back into a chair, eyes pinned on Merc.

"There. Are. Rules." Merc slapped a hand down onto the table. "Sentinels aren't like talented or hunters. We don't have a choice. There is no running away. No matter how bad some of us may want to." He made a disgusted noise.

Her head went quiet, red breaking across her vision for just a moment. A blade flashed in her hand, and she felt her face slip into an icy mask. "Rules don't matter." She slammed her blade into the table between them. "Not all of us had the *option* of staying neutral when a monster is on the loose."

"To you. Because you're a hunter. There are consequences for *our* actions." His eyes flashed as he ignored her comment about neutrality. "But that's beside the point. Even we don't have the full story about Spectre. We know how he was born, but we don't know why he won't bloody well die." He looked away.

"Fine." Dani bit the word out and snatched her blade out of the table. "So tell me all about his tragic backstory." Dani leaned back in her chair and inspected the blade for damage before sheathing it again. The table was still covered in all the books that intersected with Phillip's research.

"Several families founded Dawson. Lockgrove, Black, Hawthorne, Deveraux, they were all here." Merc pointed at old photos.

Dani whistled. "Those are some..."

"Powerful families?" Merc nodded. "Yeah. There were others, but they didn't survive, or stay." He cleared his throat but kept going. "Vincent Hawthorne wanted to marry Amelia Deveraux."

"She wasn't interested?" Dani peered down at a photo of Amelia. With her pale hair, she had the same coloring as Emilie. The resemblance bordered on eerie.

"Not so much, no. He didn't take the rejection well, and something happened. A fire started, and it almost ate the town alive." Merc paged through several books until he found the obituary records with dozens of names listed.

"And?"

"When the dust cleared, dozens of people were dead, and it had leveled half of Dawson. The Hawthorne home burned to the ground. Amelia and Marie Devereaux were missing, along with Peter Black and a half dozen others." Dani pulled one of the books closer and looked through the names.

"And this Vincent guy?"

"Everyone says Vincent died in the fire. In a manner of speaking, that's true. The Hawthorne family died in the blaze. The man who emerged from the flames was more than half mad and obsessed with finding Amelia." Merc backed away from the table with a sigh.

"You're saying, what? That Vincent Hawthorne is Spectre?" Dani frowned. No way was it this easy. Then again, this town was in the middle of nowhere, and if not for a very specific rumor, she'd never have found it.

"Yes. You know about the dark paths a talented can walk?"

"Kind of hard to miss. I kill them when they do." She met Merc's eyes, challenged him to ask.

"Spectre *ran* down them. Unsurprising with his talents for fire and death." Merc shook his head and looked down. "He broke every taboo for power, seeking to beat death."

"Still."

"I told you I knew where he was born, but that's where everything gets murky."

"Murky how?" Dani leaned back on her chair, balancing it on two legs.

"Everyone assumed that Amelia, Vincent, and Peter were among the dead, but there weren't any bodies. A few months later Peter Black shows back up and tells everyone he was escorting Amelia to her new life with family further south. A way to get her away without anyone following them." Merc started to rifle through the books and old photos again, searching for something.

"Guessing things didn't shake down that way." Dani leaned forward, biting at her lip.

"A few years later, Marie Deveraux shows up with Amelia's body. They only discussed what happened behind closed doors, but it had to do with Spectre. A few more years down the road, the Deveraux mediums started to die." He pulled out photos of Amelia's funeral and the original Deveraux mausoleum.

"Wait did...did Spectre kill her? Amelia I mean." Dani frowned, the gears in her head trying to put the puzzle together.

"Marie said no." Merc's face darkened, and he went quiet for a long minute. "He tried, but she escaped and died after. Said she'd rather be dead then belong to him, but..."

"But what?"

"Marie crossed the veil. Emilie used to talk about her when we were younger. A few other Deveraux have been seen after crossing, but there is no Amelia. Nobody knows what happened to her spirit."

"You said Spectre has talents in fire and necromancy right? Why didn't he just raise Amelia?"

"Her body was in no condition to hold a soul, and the ability to channel one is...beyond rare. Amelia had the gift, but I don't know of a living medium who can do it now, much less back then." Merc shook his head.

Dani jumped up and paced in slow, measured footsteps across the dining room. Sitting still was driving her insane. Information overload fried her brain, and they still weren't any closer to figuring out Spectre's deal. Knowing where he'd gotten his evil little start was helpful background and all, but it didn't give them a weakness to exploit and take him down with once and for all.

The reason the bastard was such a bogeyman was because he wouldn't stay dead. Every hunter worth their salt had heard stories. Joe watched him get plugged with sanctified rounds. Another left him crippled in a burning building. But he always came back.

Fires, possessive douchebags, and monsters that wouldn't stay dead. This, right here, was why she had spent most of her time hunting monsters and not talented. This time it was different, though. Dani had always been a sucker for a pretty face and a sob story, and the Lockgrove medium had both in spades. But it was more than that. Lying to the world was a shade easier than lying to herself. Graham deserved more than what he'd gotten. From the world, from her. She had to kill Spectre, for both of them.

"Fine. How does it fit together, then? This town, the Deveraux curse, Spectre? Lockgrove, Deveraux, Black, and Hawthorne? Don't it seem a little too neat and clean to you?"

"I don't know." He held up a hand. "I know that's not what you want me to say. It's not what I want to say, but it is the truth. It's all connected. There are threads, but I don't have the whole picture any more than you do."

"Nobody does." Dani's lip curled into a snarl. "Nobody alive has the answers we need." She met Merc's eyes.

"Don't you dare say it again. Keeping her away from him is more important."

"Is it though?" Dani asked. "Is that supposed to protect her? You? The balance? I mean, you can hack a wraith to pieces with a consecrated blade, but it takes forever. The veilblade goes through like they're made of butter."

"I don't like where your head is going."

"I'm just fulfilling my duties as a bladesinger. Didn't you say this was my calling?" She scoffed.

"Dani..."

"We need details, and the dead seem to be the only people who have 'em. Nothing in the world is meant to be undying. If Emilie needs to talk to the whole fucking cemetery to find out how Spectre gets put six feet under and stays there, then I'll dig up the bodies to do it."

"She does that and the binding might sn—"

"He's coming for her. One way or another." She shifted her weight, tried for tact. "I saw him in Alabama and he was not...looking fresh."

"You saw him?" Merc leaned forward eagerly.

Dani met his eyes, loath to reveal anything about that night if she didn't need to. To hell with it. She'd already opened the wound once today. Might as well go for broke while she was at it. "Yeah. He's kind of decaying."

"Well, maybe everything wasn't as ineffectual as we thought." Merc's voice was a murmur, but Dani caught what he was saying.

She watched him, felt her lip curl and twitch as his eyes flickered back and forth, working out a puzzle she didn't have access to. She didn't think he'd even realized that he had spoken out loud. The door slammed out front, and Dani jumped to her feet. She reached for a knife, but stopped herself when she heard a familiar voice.

"Is my granddaughter hiding somewhere around here?" Ephraim's voice echoed as he wandered into the kitchen, looking frazzled.

"She passed out." Andromeda appeared behind Ephraim and gave Dani a nod over the old man's shoulder. "A lot to process."

"It was only a matter of time. Thank Phillip for that." His lip curled, disgust written all over his face.

"Did you find something after breakfast?" Dani asked, hoping to find out why he was here so they could get back on track.

"In a manner of speaking."

"Spit it out then. We're kinda busy here."

"I was due at the Terrace." His eyes shifted over to Merc.

"The hell does that mean?"

"There's a...chance that someone else has details Emilie doesn't."

"And?"

Ephraim's jaw tightened. "Emilie hasn't seen her sister Elizabeth since before leaving town."

"Why not?"

Ephraim sighed again and shared a look with Andromeda. A question lingered in the air between them. Emilie hadn't mentioned a sister. Nobody had. These people were driving her up the damn wall. This was why she preferred working with hunters, if she worked with anyone at all. More and more, she only trusted herself. Graham had known about Dawson and the Blacks. Everyone in this town was swimming in secrets they didn't want to share. Shining a light on people's dark little secrets wasn't anything new. Part and parcel of being a hunter.

"Sharing secret looks isn't going to help things any."

"It's complicated," Ephraim hedged.

"You keep saying that as though it's some kind of explanation, but it isn't. I don't care about this town, or your family secrets, or why the hell you keep looking at each other, but I know for a fact there is shit you aren't telling me. And at this point? I'm over it." Dani folded her arms and glared at the three of them.

"Emilie is younger than Elizabeth. Just a year and change, not enough for them to be separate from each other's lives, but those two girls were as different as they come. Emilie was quiet and loved her books, and Elizabeth…" He swallowed hard and a look of pain passed over his face. "You couldn't keep her in the house or out of trouble." He trailed off again, and Dani tried not to roll her eyes. "Elizabeth was here that night, she usually avoided Catherine's séances. I don't know why that night was different. She refused to tell me, and I don't know whether she ever told Phillip, but I know she never saw Emilie again after the fire."

"Why?"

"Because Elizabeth didn't walk away." Ephraim's shoulders slumped.

"She took the brunt of it." Andromeda took a step forward and put a hand on Ephraim's shoulder. "That's what I always thought, anyway. Liz, she was a force of nature, but you didn't mess with her little sister. After the fire, Emilie woke up, but they put Liz in a medically induced coma for a while. And when she woke up…she wasn't all herself anymore."

"He took a bite out of her." Ephraim's voice brimmed with rage again. "Spectre took a bite out of my granddaughter, and she never recovered. Not entirely."

"Where is she?" Dani asked, voice gentler than it had been a few minutes ago.

"Cedar Terrace." Ephraim clenched a fist against one thigh. "It's a private hospital with facilities for talented who've been…wounded."

"What do you mean?"

"He means that they built Cedar Terrace to house psych patients who also happen to be talented. They diagnosed Liz with schizophrenia when she was fifteen, three years before the fire." Andromeda shook her head. "After that night, she was never the same."

"We tried to bring her home." Ephraim's voice was so quiet. "Emilie had left town already, thanks to Phillip's handiwork. But it didn't pan out."

"Didn't pan out?"

"She attacked Phillip, told him she needed to see Emilie, had to tell her what the shadow man had done, that Emilie didn't remember she was in danger." Ephraim tipped his head back, anguish rolling off him in thick waves.

"So you locked her up and threw away the key? Not real big on dealing with problems in this family, huh?"

"We didn't have a choice," he answered in a dull voice. "Elizabeth's last outburst sent Phillip to the hospital, and then they admitted her to Cedar Terrace. We'd hoped it would be a short stay. It wasn't her first time."

"But that wasn't the case this go-round?"

"No, it wasn't. She wasn't—isn't—stable enough to come home. It's...safer. For her and for us this way." He kept shaking his head, words becoming shorter and further apart.

"So why bring her up? Elizabeth, I mean."

"She's been adamant for years that the only person she wanted to see or speak to was Emilie, insisted that there was something she had to tell her about that night. Neither I, nor Phillip, nor anyone else has ever got her to open up about it."

"Isn't that asking a lot from Emilie, though? I mean..." Dani cocked her head and looked at Ephraim.

"It's important," Emilie's voice sounded from the doorway behind Andromeda. "Lizzie said she didn't want to tell me unless I asked. But that I had to come see her to ask. She wouldn't tell me in her letters."

"Letters?" Dani frowned. "People still do that?"

"They weren't ever regular." Emilie crossed into the room and took a seat at the table, picking at the old wood. "But it was how we kept in touch. Liz didn't like the phone, since there wasn't much privacy. She never talked about the fire until her last letter. She told me that if I wanted answers, I had to come see her in person. I had to ask."

"Is that why you came back?" Dani asked, moving closer.

"Partially, I guess." Emilie scratched at her face. "I just thought she was being dramatic—mad that I never came to see her."

"But now?"

"Now I think she knows something." Emilie looked up to Dani, fear naked in her eyes. "And I'm afraid of what it is."

She reached a hand down, gripping the little medium's shoulder. "You don't have to do this alone. I've got your back, killer." She smiled and knew she was damning herself as she did. Somehow, Emilie had crept past all of her careful defenses, started to become more than a job.

She wanted to protect her, and if this last year had taught her anything, it was to trust her instinct.

19

EMILIE

Eyes pinned out the window, Emilie watched as the trees and asphalt blended into a green and black blur. The rumble of the engine and Dani's quiet grumbles as she drove helped to keep her frayed nerves from spiraling into panic. It'd been easy to avoid visiting Liz, even when she knew it wasn't the right thing to do. Seeing her would have meant braving Cedar Terrace again, something she'd sworn she'd never do. Now, on the way to the hospital, nausea roiled heavy and acidic in her stomach.

It seemed like all the women in her family had spent time at Cedar Terrace at one point or another. Liz had spent more than her fair share, in and out for treatment from the day they'd diagnosed her. But Mama had too. And after the binding? When she woke up with so many of her memories gone, Emilie spent the better part of two months there. Of course, at the time she hadn't known it was a place for talented. It wasn't fair to judge the entire place on that history, but she couldn't ignore it either.

Questions, and questions, and questions. She needed the answers that Liz had, but not like this, not the pain, not the resurfacing memories, not the certainty that somehow her sister's fate was her fault. One way or another, the truth would come out. Better to face it head on instead of hiding from it this time around.

The sight of Cedar Terrace made fear curl in her chest and calcify as they drove toward the gate. It was a brute of a building, dark brick with rolling lawns, too many trees, and an imposing iron fence boasting spiked ridges. The complex was comprised of three rings— secure facilities to house talented in need of help.

The sight stole her breath and made her lungs ache, but when Dani reached out and took her hand, some of that eased. Although she knew better, she fought the fear that this would be the time she'd enter the gates and they'd keep her there. Just like Lizzie. According to Merc, the whole hospital complex operated under a serious dampening field. One way to control a talented who had lost their mind was to remove access to their talents. It was a different binding, but no better than the one her father had wrapped her up in.

They crossed through the gate and drove up the sloping drive. A heavy cloak of nothingness draped over Emilie's shoulders, weighing her down as it muffled her senses. They passed clusters of group homes and halfway houses as they climbed the hill. Soon they drove beyond the threshold of a second gate, this one a less aesthetic grey concrete.

They followed the signs for the long-term facility and took a left off the main road to where a small visitor parking lot sat. The second ring had moderate security and housed long-term residents. At the top of the hill stood an old prison complex, now serving the most dangerous patients. Emilie's eyes strayed up the hill and lingered on the barbed wire that topped ten-foot-tall chain-link fences.

Emilie sat exposed, nerves stripped raw and bloody. Being back brought back memories she wished had stayed gone: Mama scream-ing, strapped down; Lizzie, silent and still. And her own stints here hadn't been a grand time either. All of it washed together.

"You holdin' it together over there?" Dani asked softly.

"I—yeah. It's just...a lot."

"Yeah. Nobody told me this place was a fortress."

"Not all of it is." She pointed uphill with her chin. "Up there used to be a prison once."

"Gonna be okay?" She reached out again, one finger running across Emilie's knuckle in a whisper of flesh.

"I have to be." Emilie rubbed at her forehead. "I'd hoped I'd never have to come back here again, though."

"You've been more than once?"

"Yeah. Mama, Liz, and me...we all had to visit for different things, different times." Something in her jaw jumped, and she clenched it tighter, trying to will herself to have a spine of steel, even though she felt like jelly.

"Rough." Dani turned to look at her. "Sure you wanna do this?"

"No." Emilie shook her head and then turned to face Dani head on. "Spectre's already come at me once while I was asleep. We got lucky last night, but it isn't gonna last. It's gotta be today, while we still have time."

"Glad to hear you say it." Dani bared her teeth, and it fell somewhere between a smile and a show of aggression. "But this place is fuckin' off-putting." She rubbed a hand up and down her arm.

"It's the dampening field."

"Yeah, that's what the wonder twins called it."

Emilie laughed in a sharp bark, a surprise even to her. But the moniker fit too well for it not to be funny. "Okay, now that's funny." She settled down and shook her head. "Thank you. I know you don't owe me anything but—"

"Don't mention it. Everybody needs someone on their side." Dani winked and then opened up her door and hopped out of the truck.

Emilie followed her and looked up at the building. Of all the places in the world she wanted to be, this was at the bottom of that list. But she owed it to Liz to come see her and finally find out what she needed to say. Back at home she had a sheaf of letters from Liz, handwritten. She'd asked her to come home. She'd begged for a visit without telling her why. Looking up at the building, the weight of all of it crashed down on her.

Row after row of windows glinted like dark eyes against the red brick and white columns, a beast waiting to gobble up the unsuspecting. Places like this had history, and it wasn't all good. Not everyone who checked in checked back out, and the graveyard out back punctuated that particular point.

Walking up to the glass doors, Dani was a comforting presence at her side. The twins staunchly refused to visit. The dampening field here was too difficult to deal with, they had claimed. Emilie couldn't blame them. The more vibrant the ability, the harder it clamped down they said, and it was clamping down mighty hard on her. She'd never noticed it before. Now the silence deafened her.

It only took a moment to check in at the front desk. Grandpa must have called ahead because nobody blinked at her or Dani. That man planned for every contingency. It was probably why he was still alive.

The secretary gave them directions to her sister's room, but after one wrong turn Emilie got mixed up and got them lost. Long empty hallways seemed to lead nowhere, and staircases appeared and disappeared without rhyme or reason. On every floor, melancholy voices drifted and echoed past them. It made Emilie's skin crawl. She'd been a voice once, disembodied, lost, trapped.

"Do you have any clue where we are?" Dani asked, boots clicking out a steady rhythm against old tiled floors.

"We're over by the east wing, I think?" She scratched at the back of her head and looked for some kind of sign that might help to point them in the right direction. "This place was never easy to navigate, and I think they've updated since the last time I was here." She shook her head. "Not helpful. I know."

They rounded a corner and finally found a directory encased in Plexiglass and mounted to the wall next to another staircase. It might as well have been written in ancient Greek.

"I think we wanna go this way." Dani squinted at the map and then looked down a long hallway, trying to find their route.

"You might be right." Emilie looked between the map and down the hallway. "We're on the right floor, aren't we?"

"Looks like. See, we followed this hallway from the main stair..." One finger traced across the map, charting out their course. "And we're here at this small one. Just gotta go over two wards, and we should dead-end there." Dani tapped one finger against her temple, flashing Emilie a grin. "I've got it covered. HHS puts out the worst maps on the planet. You can read those, you can read anything."

"HHS?" Emilie looked over, confusion written on her face.

"Department of Health and Human Services." Dani shrugged. "Foster system meant I spent plenty of time in spots with maps just as bad."

They continued down the hallway, Dani a half step in front. Dread slowed Emilie's footsteps and bone-deep anxiety flowed through her. Her internal radio was silent, the dial spinning back and forth, looking for a signal blocked by the dampening field. It didn't strip away her abilities or erase them, just wrapped her in enough insulation that there was no way to access them. More than that, she couldn't shake the peculiar feeling of being watched, even though she couldn't see anyone else in the hallway with them. If there was a spirit here, the blinders kept her from seeing them. It wouldn't surprise her though. A place like this had to have restless dead.

Dani paused in front of her and turned. Somehow, the hunter was becoming someone that Emilie trusted. She was sharp and hard in a way that Emilie had never pulled off. But she also got her in a way that nobody else did, not even the people that she desperately wished understood her. On impulse, she closed the distance between them and took Dani's hand. A brief spark jumped between them, and Emilie felt it strike down to her core. Dani didn't pull away, instead smirked with a tug of her lips and tightened her grip around Emilie's hand. Maybe the hunter wanted somebody to reach out as much as Emilie needed to do it. Dani started down the hallway again, tugging her along in her wake.

Heat suffused her. She didn't know what it was, but something about Dani put her at ease, even here. It was easier to let Dani lead them so she didn't have to pay attention to their surroundings. A turn here, a turn there, all while she kept her eyes on the ground and concentrated on putting one foot in front of the other. Liz had been there the night Spectre came and everything went wrong. She'd forgotten, or almost forgotten.

She never asked why her sister went from being independent to being a full-time resident of Cedar Terrace. Her stomach curdled, acid reaching for her throat. She'd never even tried to find a time to visit. Had something in the binding caused that, or was it all on her? If her father had worked something that made her not want to come see her own sister, she'd never forgive him.

Dani stopped short, and Emilie followed suit, looking up and around them. They'd come to a pair of double doors with a nurses' station set off to one side. Emilie's breath hitched in her chest as a fine tremble worked its way down one arm. One wrong move and she'd snap and fall to pieces. No way did she want to walk through those doors and ask what had really happened the night Mama died. But she didn't have a choice. The past would come back for her. Closing her eyes would only ensure she didn't see the shape of it until it was too late. She had to face her sister, face her past, and face herself. The realization didn't make it easier to bear.

"You ready, killer?" Dani squeezed her hand and met her eyes.

Warmth spread from Dani's palm into hers, giving her strength. "No. I don't really have a choice, though. Not really." She scuffed one shoe against the tired gray linoleum. "What if it's a mistake? Or she won't tell me? Or…"

"No way to tell. But this place don't help. The dampener or whatever. Your gramps wouldn't have sent us out here if there wasn't a reason, right?"

"Right. Right. There's just this terrible feeling sunk into my bones."

"Hey now. I'm right here, and I don't go out in public unarmed." She waggled her eyebrows and closed the distance between them. The heat that had started in Emilie's palm spread throughout her body. If they weren't in the middle of a magical institution…

"Seriously?" Emilie's eyes went wide. "We are at a psych facility." She threw a look back over her shoulder as though an orderly were watching them, looking for a reason to drop them into a room of their own, one without a doorknob on the inside.

"Not my first rodeo. Trust me, okay?" She placed her hands on Emilie's shoulders, riveting her to the spot. "I've got your back, even if the orderlies get handsy." She winked. "Let's do this thing, and then we'll be back behind wards before it gets dark, yeah?"

"Yeah." Emilie sighed.

She concentrated on Dani's hands on her shoulders, the way she smelled, how she held herself. Being strong didn't come easy to Emilie. It was easier to run and hide from the problem. But in this moment she had a chance to do it differently, to follow Dani's lead and see where it took her.

Dani must have seen something in her eyes because she took a step back. She was still close, but not holding her in place. It was time to stand up on her own two feet and face her sister. So Emilie stepped forward, hit the buzzer, and waited for a long minute before the door creaked open.

A receptionist instructed them to take a seat in the visitors' area. It was a small room with a water cooler and a half dozen chairs. It could have been any waiting room in any doctor's office.

"So this whole ass hospital is for talented?" Dani dropped into a chair across from Emilie and lounged in it.

"Kind of. Talented, sentinels, some casters and hunters too." She fidgeted, unable to get comfortable, still convinced they'd try to hospitalize her as well.

"Really?"

"It's private, so you have to know somebody, but yeah. It was part of the Dawson outreach. Trying to make a place where people like us didn't have to hide what we were all the time." She attempted a weak smile. "The results haven't always been fantastic." Most it came back to her in broken memories, the rest Andry had filled her in on.

"Interesting." Dani tsked and dropped her head back against a wall.

"I guess? Wait. Are you just...trying to distract me?"

"Maybe. I admit nothing. Besides, getting the deets on this place is way better than sitting here twiddling my thumbs while you drive yourself insane." She blinked, face far too placid.

Guilt wormed into Emilie's chest, hot and heavy. If she'd listened to Grandpa, she'd have come home years ago. Instead, she had pushed this aside until it all came swarming at her at once. Maybe it would have been different. Maybe she would have had time to slowly piece this together instead of being surrounded and outnumbered by the things she needed to know but didn't. She should have known better. Instead, she'd hidden in Crownsville and pretended things weren't tacitly terrible and always falling apart around her no matter how hard she tried to rebuild them time and time and time again.

"Emilie Lockgrove?"

"Yeah, that's me." Emilie rose, and they followed the fresh-faced nurse out of the waiting room.

Across the hall was another room, built for visits like this. Emilie paused at the door, giving Dani a long look. The hunter didn't smile, but Emilie saw the confidence and support in her eyes, which was better. At a slight nod from Dani, who leaned against the door in a non-verbal signal that she would be right there, Emilie walked in alone. The room boasted warm walls with photos, a scatter of tables and comfortable chairs, with a small bookcase that dominated one corner—every item exuded warmth. It was as generic as any psych unit she could imagine, even if this one was classier than most. She'd had her fair share of visits behind locked doors in the years since the fire to know quality when she saw it.

Liz sat across the room in an overstuffed armchair pressed against the far wall. If it had been possible for Emilie's heart to turn to stone and shatter against the floor, it would have. The years had been kinder to her than to Liz. Her sister, who had always been tall and lean and sharp, looked like a ghost of the girl she remembered. Now Liz was a dark reflection of Emilie, haunted by the night they'd both survived. She was too thin, cheeks sunken, collar bone and cheekbones pressed against parchment-thin skin. Her long dark hair was pulled back in a lank braid that draped over the arm of the chair and framed dark, luminous eyes. Thick burn scars circled either wrist, crawled up her arms, and ran along the column of her neck.

"Emi." Liz's voice was hoarse, but she sounded so happy.

Emilie edged closer. She heard the nurse exit behind her and close the door. She looked over her shoulder and saw Dani lurking outside, watching through the window, close enough to get to her, but far enough away to give her some privacy with her sister. She appreciated the gesture and looked back to Liz.

"Liz...hey." She smiled and felt tears in her eyes.

"Took you...long enough." Her words were slow but steady.

"I've always been hardheaded."

"Isn't that the truth?" Liz smiled and occupied her hands with the bulk of a yarn blanket in her lap. "Do you remember what Dad did yet?" She pinned sharp eyes on Emilie.

"The binding?" She shook her head. "Yeah, I remember, kind of."

"Wondered how long it'd take. Do you remember the shadow man yet?"

Emilie frowned at the way Liz's voice changed, how her eyes became hooded, dissecting her the way a hawk looked at a baby bunny it was considering eating. "The shadow man?" Emilie asked and pulled at the neck of her shirt.

"You know who I'm talking about." Lizzie's voice was low and dark,

Emilie felt something stir in the shadows behind her. It had to be her nerves. "Do you mean...do you mean Spectre?" Her voice was a hushed whisper, words unwillingly torn from her throat.

"Mmm. He never forgot you." Liz turned like she'd heard something from outside, but nothing moved, not even a breeze to stir the leaves on the trees. "But you don't remember that night. That's why you're here."

"I'm here because I wanted to see you, needed to."

"Because of that night." Liz's voice shifted again, a singsong tone that made the hair at the back of Emilie's neck stand straight up.

"The binding shut it away."

"Not surprised. It was a special night, Emi, remember? Mama was gonna let you help during the séance, and I was home again. Daddy wasn't there because Grampa needed help at the condo…"

"It's like watercolors." Emilie scooted closer to Liz and ignored the feeling that something was wrong. She needed answers. "I can see the shape, but not the detail. I get frames here or there, like a slide from a movie, but no context. I don't know how to put it together."

"You were never any good at puzzles."

"Could be worse."

"True." Liz's eyes slid away, lighting on the far corner where thick shadows had pooled just out of the afternoon light. "You're running out of time, aren't you?" She turned back to Emilie. "Is that why you came? Not because you wanted to?"

"No." Emilie leaned in further, trying to find the words. "I mean, also yes. But it's just happening this way. I always wanted to come visit but…"

"It meant coming home. Daddy probably wove something extra into the binding to help keep you away. I told him it was a bad idea because the monster would still find you, but he didn't want to listen."

"He never wants to listen."

"You have to listen. Don't look at the shadows, just listen." She clenched the blanket so tight that her knuckles turned white. "The shadow man knew about you before that night. Mama didn't know who he was, and neither did you because he gave a different name. He was fond of you, the shadow man. But only because you have her coloring. He wants to keep you *for her*." Terror suffused her words, and Emilie inched closer, unsure of what to do, what to say.

Liz's gaze bounced around the room. She refused to look in a single place for more than a second or two. The whites of her eyes showed, swallowing her dark brown irises. Emilie saw the echo of the sister she'd known, but that Elizabeth was gone. The fire broke them both in different ways, but Liz had taken it harder. And she hadn't been stable to begin with.

"Was the shadow man Spectre?"

"One face, lots of names. Took him time to find the ones he liked.

But he always had time." She paused and looked at Emilie dead in the eyes. "When you rip off the Band-Aid, he'll be there. He bit me because he couldn't reach you. Remember? But he has a poison bite, and I never grew back the parts that burned away."

"What are you saying?"

"He let me stay as a warning to Daddy. Could have gobbled me up, but he didn't. He needed us, and Daddy hurt him so bad that night. So he wanted to hurt him back. Tricksy, tricksy monster." Horror flooded Emilie, fresh and numbing as ice on her soul. Liz sighed and closed her eyes for a moment.

Emilie closed the last bit of distance between the two of them, coming so close they were nearly touching. Out of the corner of her eye, shadows crawled along the floor. Liz surged forward and took Emilie's hands in her own, too warm, like she'd been struck with fever. Her eyes popped back open so wide that her pupil took up almost her whole eye. A tiny bloom of flame appeared in her eyes, and Liz started to scream. In an instant, she ceased to be human and billowed into a plume of flame made of flesh and death. Lizzie's hands were still wrapped around Emilie, and she couldn't free herself as her sister screamed and writhed. A man started to laugh, his voice bouncing off the walls around them.

20

DANI

Dani leaned against the doorframe and took another peek through the window. Emilie was still talking to her sister. Whatever she had to say must have been worth the wait. Standing out here, she felt like an interloper. Dani barely knew the girl, and here she was, hanging out and watching her emotional reunion with her sister. On the outside, looking in. Nothing she wasn't used to.

The weight of the veilblade in her pocket brought her comfort from the heebie-jeebies this whole joint gave her, yet another reason she was glad to be a hunter and not talented. Being locked up in a place specifically built to smother your magic seemed like a special hell.

She took another look down the hall and then peeked over one shoulder back into the room again. Emilie and Elizabeth sat in a pool of light with shadows everywhere else around them. Dani stopped as her mind tried to process it and failed miserably.

"Fuck!" She groped for the handle, but threw the door open a half second too late.

Everything froze in front of her for a long moment, details seared onto her retina. Shadows crawled along the walls, pooled in corners, and twined around Elizabeth, giving Emilie a wide berth. Those shadows fled from the onslaught of flames as Elizabeth turned from a woman to a creature of fire and death.

Dani jolted forward and grabbed Emilie around the middle, dragging her back and away from her sister. She slapped at tiny flames burning on Emilie's clothing as they fled the room. Emilie screamed her sister's name over and over again. Adrenaline gave Dani a stupid amount of strength, allowing her to practically fireman carry Emilie out. She stopped fighting, her screams reducing to whimpering, which was somehow worse. Hearing her pain caused Dani pain, but she shoved it down. She didn't have time for it now if she was going to save Emilie's life.

Out in the hallway, an alarm screamed violently. A red light strobed, and everything erupted into chaos. Someone ran past. From behind them, flames crawled out of the room and danced along the ceiling. In mere moments the flames had become an inferno that engulfed everything in the room. A man screamed in the distance, and Dani heard laughter. That capricious chuckle made her growl and bare her teeth. She'd recognize Spectre's cruelty anywhere.

She tugged hard on Emilie's arm. "Come on, we've gotta go. Now!" she commanded. The harshness broke through Emilie's shock enough to propel her into motion. Dani could feel bad about it later. Right now she was happy it got her moving.

This wasn't possible, not here. There wasn't supposed to be any magic. That was the whole damn point of the dampening field, of why they kept so many people here. She swallowed convulsively but continued running, one fact glaringly obvious. It had been a trap. And if she hadn't been there, it would have worked. It would have worked, and Emilie would have died.

They burst past the receptionist's desk and out into the main hallway. People ran back and forth, and more sirens screamed, echoing against one another. Spectre's fires moved fast, and Dani wasn't taking any chances. They kept moving.

"The whole damn place is going up! Get everyone out! No way to tell what wards will hold!" yelled a man carrying an extinguisher as he ran past.

The panic that had been hiding under her sternum burst into action. "Time to go! Come on, Emilie! Time to fucking GO!" She took off as fast as her legs would carry her, still holding onto Emilie's hand like a lifeline.

Emilie stumbled through the first few steps before she caught her balance and almost kept pace. Almost. Dani chanced a look back and saw the dazed look in Emilie's eyes. She looked more like an animal fleeing the fire than a person. Smoke began to curl around their feet, and Dani kept propelling them forward. If they stopped moving, they were dead. The map from earlier was pinned on the inside of Dani's eyeballs, and she used it to guide them past the staircases that wouldn't get them all the way out of the building.

The smoke curling around them grew thicker and rose higher, drying out her throat and burning her eyes. Screams ricocheted through hallways that now resembled a horror movie more than of a hospital. Dani dug her heels in as a chunk of ceiling rained down, cutting off the route she'd been taking. Whirlwinds of dust and detritus made the air too thick to breathe as fire turned it to liquid heat.

They were almost out of options. It was either backtrack toward the fire, or head up the staircase they'd just passed. Dani chose up and hoped she was quick enough that they could outrun the flames.

Up a floor, the air was clearer, but it wouldn't be for long. Flames licked under closed doors, smoke crawling along the floor. Dani coughed again and pulled her shirt up over her mouth and nose. They took the corridor at a sprint and turned a blind corner to a hallway hazy with smoke. Flames curled, indistinct inside clouds of dark smoke, while the strobe of the alarm lights confused things further. Everything looked alien in the grey haze.

Dani squinted at the dim green glow of an EXIT sign at the stairwell. It gleamed like a beacon, and she took off again, Emilie half running, half being dragged along for the ride. The metallic taste of panic flooded Dani's mouth as another wall collapsed behind them.

She could not afford to panic until they were outside of this hellish maze. If she panicked, they died. And they would not die; she wouldn't let them.

They hit the doors to the steps with a thump that reverberated. A moment later they spilled down into the stairwell. The air here was clear, clear enough at least, and Dani took the stairs two at a time. Smoke followed from behind, filling their footsteps as though it chased them personally.

Adrenaline burned away the fear, and clean air let her think. Dani was built for life or death scenarios. This she understood more than old grudges, or family drama, or any of the other shit Dawson seemed to have in spades. Terror bayed at her from a distance, but for now, in this moment, she held it at a distance They thundered down the staircase, past walls saturated with fire, and into even more smoke.

She could barely breathe, couldn't see, and heard nothing but the crackle of flames eating everything they touched. Dani did the only thing she could. She held onto Emilie's hand as though they were the last people left in the world as flames licked at her skin and singed loose hairs from her face.

To the left, a hallway led further into the bowels of the hospital where fire roared along every surface, bodies left on the floor where some kind of machinery had blown up. To the right lay the doors to freedom and life. Dani crashed into the doors and they stumbled out into the fresh air, holding onto one another like lifelines.

The fresh air stabbed needles into her throat with each breath. Dani let Emilie tug her over onto the grass where other survivors were watching the horror show. Sirens from firetrucks blared as they barreled up the long drive toward the catastrophe. Dani coughed and fell to the ground, trying to catch her breath as she turned. Flames jumped out of half the windows of the hospital. In some places, the bricks had turned red from the heat. Around them, patients and staff alike watched in hushed horror.

It had all happened too fast, just like Alabama. The way the fire moved, even if she hadn't heard him laughing over the chaos in the first few moments, she would have known. His fingers were all over this cataclysm. Heavy coughs wracked her, and she doubled over, choking as she hacked up black slime. Looking over at Emilie, she realized it wasn't *just* like Alabama. This time she hadn't failed so cataclysmically in saving someone she cared about. Emilie was hacking up a lung, no longer holding on to Dani for dear life, but still close.

Paramedics followed on the heels of fire trucks as they started the arduous task of treating everyone. There were too many people, and Dani didn't know any of them. The bone deep certainty that this had been a trap, one built specifically to snag Emilie, tugged at her again, and Dani struggled to her feet.

They needed to go before something else happened. If she was wrong, then they'd check in at a hospital somewhere. But if she wasn't? There was no way to keep Emilie safe out here. They were sitting ducks.

"Slow and steady. Don't make any waves, but we need to get out of here."

She shouldered Emilie and got them to her truck. It lay far enough back in the lot they avoided the emergency crews as they followed a long arterial service road. It ran parallel to the main road, and they weren't alone. Vehicles queued in front of them as the hospital evacuated. Dani kept her eye on the rearview mirror, convinced there was more to this.

They passed the gate and Emilie collapsed, a massive sigh whooshing out of her. One hand clutched the side of her head, and she whimpered again, a small, pitiable sound. Dani didn't pay any mind. She couldn't. Nothing else mattered until that place was no longer in the rearview mirror.

21

EMILIE

Emilie counted in her head, each number slow and steady. *One.* They were in the truck. Dani was driving. *Two.* Her stomach roiled and turned with every bump in the road as they raced away from Cedar Terrace. *Three.* Lizzie was dead, and it was all her fault, and she'd never be able to fix this. *Not now, not ever.*

She tucked her head between her legs and dry heaved, desperate to get ahold of herself. The truck swerved to the side of the road, and gravel kicked up under the carriage as Dani stomped the breaks. Emilie had the door open before they'd come to a full stop. She jumped up and ran for the bushes.

She only made it to the back tire as her stomach emptied itself. Bile roiled in her, and acid splashed the back of her throat. The air tasted too sweet after the fire, and she couldn't catch her breath. She could still smell charred flesh like a barbecue. Except the meat had been her sister.

Emilie whimpered and pounded her thigh. She needed to pull herself together. She couldn't snap now. Lizzie wouldn't want that. She spat on the ground and breathed out slowly through her nose.

Sirens wailed in the distance, headed toward the hospital, as she caught her breath. The fire left her skin flushed, too sensitive where it had singed away her hair. Trees blocked the truck from seeing the hospital complex, but the sky glowed red as a black cloud reached for the horizon.

Emilie ran a hand through her hair and breathed out as she stared at it. It was only a matter of time before everyone in the area heard about the fire. Nobody around here could ever keep their mouths shut, and they'd be able to see that haze in the sky for miles.

Everything in her head was scrambled. One moment she couldn't breathe, remembering the look in Liz's eyes as she went up in flames, and the next she was staring at the horizon, wondering how far the haze could be seen from. She'd heard someone. As Liz screamed and Dani dragged her backwards out into the hallway, she'd heard someone laughing, as though this were funny.

Like it was a game.

It was a spell that had done it. It had to be. But she didn't know how that could happen at Cedar Terrace. Lizzie was screaming inside her head, forever screaming. It didn't make sense. Emilie was always going to come and see her sister. Kill Liz to hurt Emilie and what, why? If Dani hadn't been there, there was no way she would have made it out alive. The binding might have still been intact, but she'd have still been dead.

How long would it take him to figure out that the fire hadn't worked, that they'd escaped? It wasn't as though he could find her. Not yet anyhow. But he could see the fire, and he'd know she had been there. Could he use the catastrophe he'd caused like a radar to track her?

The realization hit her that while he couldn't find her, the same might not be true for Dani. Emilie scrambled back into the truck. They needed to get back behind the wards to regroup.

"We need to get back to the house. We need to get back now."

She strapped in as Dani took off back toward the house. It felt like something watched them from the woods, tracking them. The veil radio was quieter than it had been when she crossed the boundary of the dampening field, no voices, no static. That could mean she was being paranoid, and that nothing was actually following them, but the what-ifs coiled around her, a python squeezing its prey.

Emilie trusted Dani not to slam them into a tree, so she kept her eyes out the back window. A few times she saw bushes move, but they were driving quickly enough that it was impossible to make anything out before they were out of sight.

"Did you see something?" Dani asked, noticing her jumpiness.

"No, but I swear there's something out there." Emilie blinked against exhaustion, adrenaline bitter in her mouth as she held onto the seats.

"Wouldn't surprise me." Dani white-knuckled the steering wheel. "That was a trap."

"I noticed." Emilie shot Dani a quick look.

"And you think he might try to gank you while you're out in the open?" Dani shook her head and frowned.

"He knew I was at that hospital, so if he can get to me before I'm back behind wards..."

"Then it wouldn't matter that he can't track you by magic. Let's get you home." Dani gunned the engine and took a turn, tires screeching. For a moment, something thick and made of shadows that defied physics appeared along the tree line, but then it vanished, and Emilie couldn't be positive she'd seen anything at all.

Dawson had safeguards and protections that would make it more difficult for wraiths to follow them. They were close to the town limits. All they needed to do was get back inside the house. The home had become a cage, but it was a safe cage.

Nothing about any of this was okay, and the closer she got to safety, the more jumbled up it got. Mama was screaming and Liz was screaming and everything was fire, and she couldn't get that chuckle from Spectre out of her head. It'd been haunting her nightmares for years. One life-altering fire blurred into the next, culminating in the death of someone else she'd loved. Worse, he'd been doing this for decades, for centuries even. He stole away the women in her family, burning them alive while he laughed. The terror thrumming through her bones was the same terror her family had lived with for generations, trauma passed unerringly from mother to daughter.

You remind him of what it was to be human. To love someone more than yourself, Grandma Marie's husky, accented voice murmured into Emilie's ear. *You remind him of what he used to be.*

Emilie blinked, confused. *You and Amelia Deveraux share more than just talents; you have her coloring too. It's part of why he's wanted you differently than the others.*

The words made horror ring clarion inside of Emilie's head. Dad's research said he burned the Deveraux women because they would reveal his secrets, but it was more than that. Something teased just out of her reach, and her mind wasn't putting the pieces together, even though they were all right there. This kind of hatred, there was more than fear behind it. It was as if Spectre had never loved or cared for anything other than himself to begin with. To fan the flames of hatred and cunning like that? It needed fuel, something to keep him going through all the years that passed them by.

"With me, sugar?"

"What?" Emilie blinked and started. "Yeah, I guess I drifted off. Or something."

"Okay." Dani gave her a concerned look but didn't push the issue.

They'd pulled into the driveway at the house. With wards around them, something inside of her relaxed. They weren't safe in the strictest sense of the word, but at least they weren't exposed anymore. That was worth something at least.

"I keep seeing Liz's eyes." *And hearing her voice as she screamed and burned.*

Hysteria closed in around her, everything becoming too bright, too harsh. Liz's death fell around her, a weighted shroud that she would never be able to shrug off. Without adrenaline to fuel her, she felt lighter, empty and hollowed out. All that remained was the wisp of a girl who was far too easy to burn away until nothing was left, nothing at all. Her hands flailed at the door and got it open, but her body didn't want to work right. The world was fuzzy around the edges, and it took Emilie a long moment to realize she'd started to cry. Exhaustion reared up and captured her, but she needed to get into the house. She needed to call Grandpa.

"Hey, hey, hey, I got you. I got you," Dani said. Warm hands helped her out of the truck and made sure she kept her feet under her as she stumbled into the house.

Emilie held onto her like a lifeline, the only thing in her world that made sense right now. Even if that didn't make sense either. How was Dani keeping it together? Spectre'd killed Graham. She'd seen this before. Emilie barely noticed when Dani got her on the couch. She said something, but Emilie couldn't make it out. She was just so tired, so she stopped fighting it and sleep claimed her in moments.

22

DANI

Whiskey mellowed Dani out, smoothed her rough edges, made the flames of the fire less distinct. Emilie was still out on the couch, but she'd stopped whimpering and crying in her sleep. Lucky. For her it'd been weeks of waking up screaming to nightmares of fire after Graham's murder. Two fingers of bourbon let her focus, so the adrenaline tapered away instead of making her feel like she might explode into a million pieces. It wasn't enough to get a buzz, but enough to take the edge off. She also needed something to calm her nerves after looking at the news. Volunteer firefighters had hosed down the hospital and saved the complex, but people still died, and that was on her. It was Dani's responsibility to protect people from Spectre, and she'd screwed the pooch again.

The alcohol blunted the sting, blurred the edges and kept the weight from turning her into Atlas carrying the world. It hadn't always been difficult like this. Nostalgia begged her to leave this job, Spectre, and Emilie behind. He had turned Elizabeth into a trap made of flesh and bone, and she didn't want any part of that madness. But she wasn't sure she had a choice in the matter.

Graham would have said this was the job. It didn't matter what it turned into; you worked the job until it was finished, protected the bystander. If she bailed, Emilie was as good as dead. Dani's eyes settled over the woman on the couch. Liquid heat pooled through her limbs as she watched her sleep. Emilie was smart, but that'd only take her so far. She'd always be a medium, always be talented. With Spectre on her tail, even Ephraim and the sentinels couldn't guarantee her survival.

It didn't help matters that nobody was answering their damn phones. She hadn't been able to get anyone on the line since putting Emilie down. It didn't sit right, but no way were they in on what had happened this afternoon. Spectre was playing a giant game of chess with them, and nobody had noticed until tonight. Elizabeth lived in that hospital for almost a decade. That was a long time for a spell to wait for the right trigger. He was prepared, and he had a plan, and Dani didn't know what cards he held.

They'd been playing defense. That forced them to react to the moves Spectre made, and it left them at a serious disadvantage. They needed to strike back and stop letting him call the shots.

Emilie wasn't lying to her, she was certain of that. But Dani's trust didn't extend to the sentinels or Ephraim. They had their own cards to play. Ephraim wanted to play "kind old coot," but a person didn't get to his age without a few skeletons in the closet. Andromeda and Merc were playing it close to the chest too.

She wanted Spectre dead, maybe more than anyone else. If there was a weapon that could get the job done, she was holding it. But if she was wrong? Dani didn't want to gamble with Emilie's life.

There was no way of knowing what exactly would happen if Emilie stripped away the binding. It was risky, and Dani's head wasn't on the chopping block. Whether she broke the binding or it frayed away all traumatic-like, Spectre was coming for her. This was their chance to be smart instead of running headlong into danger, again.

Pity. Dani preferred the running.

Minutes ticked by, and the creeping suspicion that something more was going on crept up her spine. No word came from anyone else. Whatever had been following them from the hospital had peeled off once they'd crossed the town limits. It made her wonder if it had veered off to deal with someone else.

From the other room, a flat tone sounded from the TV, followed by a newscaster's voice. "We interrupt this broadcast to report live from the Dawson town limits, where a gas main has ruptured."

Dani skidded into the other room to see the TV portraying fire shooting along the road they'd crossed not even two hours ago. "This comes just hours after the Cedar Terrace hospital complex caught fire. Bill, is there any indication whether the two might be related?"

"We've got no indications right now, but we will be updating over the course of the night, Karen. Local authorities are asking residents to shelter in place and stay off the streets if possible while they try to contain the fire."

Dani swore and bit at her thumbnail. This was not good, not good at all. Shelter-in-place orders meant that even if Spectre did try to come for them, there wasn't anywhere to go. There were only two routes out of Dawson, and she'd bet dollars to donuts something had happened to the other exit too. Trapped in Dawson with no good way out of town wasn't what she wanted to hear. Dani didn't like being in rooms without two exits. It made it too easy to get cornered.

She exhaled slowly, blowing air out of her nose, and muted the TV. They had switched over to other local news, nothing that she needed to concern herself with, not while there were more pressing things to deal with.

Frustrated, she pulled her phone out and called Mercurious for the third time in the last hour. It rang three times and then went to voicemail. So either he was ignoring her or he couldn't answer. Not good in either case. She couldn't leave Emilie here alone, and if she'd read things right, going outside could well be a death sentence.

Something moved in the living room, and she darted in, hair flying around her face. She wasn't taking any more chances. She should have known better. She knew what a slimy piece of work Spectre was. That kind of trick was right up his alley, the bastard.

When she turned into the living room, a breath she hadn't realized she was holding whooshed out of her. No calamity awaited, just

Emilie sitting up on the couch, blinking, owl eyed with a blanket wrapped around her shoulders.

"Welcome back, killer." Her voice was a bit kinder than usual, but she figured trauma warranted kid gloves, or at least not sandpaper ones.

"Thanks." Emilie coughed.

"Water?"

"Yeah."

Dani headed to the kitchen, Emilie's padded footfalls following behind. The house breathed around them, but it was still too quiet. None of this made any fucking sense, and her instincts were screaming at her. Wards or not, protected house or not, they were sitting ducks. Dani didn't play bait. Not now and not ever.

Thoughts crowded her mind as she got Emilie a tall glass of water and handed it over. Maybe booby traps could help. She could put a few of them down at the doors and windows to make sure nothing shady happened while they slept. That might work, or it might blow up one of the others when they finally crawled back into contact. If they showed up at all.

"Where are the others?" Emilie asked.

"I don't know. I can't get in touch." Dani ran a hand through her hair.

Emilie's eyes twitched and she turned her head, putting her glass onto the counter. "That's not right."

"Agreed, but I can't get ahold of anybody."

"So you just sat around—"

"I wasn't leaving you alone." Dani flicked her eyes over to the muted television. "And then a gas main blew up at the town limits."

Emilie staggered but caught herself on a chair at the kitchen table. Her eyes bored into Dani's, asking the question that she didn't have the answer to. *Was it Spectre? Probably.* Her mind spiraled into terrible possibilities again, and Dani tried to ignore it as best she could.

"The way we came in." Emilie turned her head to the side, like she was listening to someone, and then nodded. "We have to find them."

"Find who? I really hope you're not asking me to leave the protected house to go looking for people who aren't answering their phones."

"I don't think they did it on purpose." A worried mask fit over Emilie's features. Dani swore. She'd always been a sucker for a pretty girl asking for help.

"There are shelter-in-place orders." Dani couldn't believe she was trying to convince her to listen to the authorities.

"Fire and police are local to the town, and they're not gonna stop me." Emilie sighed, stood up, and started wandering through the house looking for something.

Dani marveled at the fierce look on her sweet face. "Seriously?"

"Small town, old families. We have our perks." Emilie's voice was light but strained. "Have you seen my shoes?"

"Why? Why go after them right now?" Dani shook her head and followed the crazy blonde woman back into the living room.

"Because I can't break the binding by myself. Grandpa might have gone dark if he got a lead on Dad...but not Andry. I need you to trust me on this one." She shook her head, and errant strands of pale hair fell over her face.

Dani bit her lip and met her eyes. It would be so easy to reach out right now, cup her face, and kiss her until she forgot she wanted to leave the house. Her hand twitched, and Emilie raised an eyebrow. Daring her to try and stop her from what she needed to do. It was hot, and aggravating, and she couldn't remember the last time someone had been able to do this to her.

Emilie's fierce gaze pinned her to the spot. She went on. "We're out of time, and I can feel it even if I can't explain it. Andry is our best bet to help me break the binding without losing my mind in the process."

Dani sighed again and wondered how she got herself into these situations on such a regular basis. "If it was Spectre, it's not gonna be a cakewalk out there." No way did she want to go out there unless it was to run far and fast from this town, this job. But something inside screamed it could be their chance to get Spectre.

If they were playing a massive game of chess, Emilie was the queen. They were low on reserves, and they needed every piece on the board just to survive. He'd expect them to hole up in this house, protected by wards. Out there, they were vulnerable, but it was more open, giving them room to maneuver if it came down to it.

"I know." Emilie's hands twisted at the blanket she'd carried into the kitchen with her. "But they wouldn't ignore our calls with everything going on, not on purpose. Something is wrong." She grimaced. "I can feel it."

"Fine." Dani scowled but resigned herself to what came next. "Do you know how to use a gun?"

23

DANI

The night took on a thick, dense quality that Dani could have done without. Spectre liked his wraiths black as pitch, which made them easy to hide out along the edges of buildings or crouched in shrubs. They crossed down through Emilie's neighborhood without running into anyone or anything.

She knew it wouldn't last.

With the veilblade strapped to her thigh and a shotgun in her hands, she wasn't taking any chances. Emilie had a pistol for the same reason. Every little bit counted, and this way she was armed in case they got separated. She'd expected to find movement, but so far they'd seen nothing. No people or animals moved along the street. Instead of putting her at ease, it made the hairs at the back of her neck stand up straight.

After traveling street after empty street, they finally pressed against a brick building around the corner from Andromeda's shop. Dani stole a look over at Emilie. Her pale hair glinted from the streetlights, the Beretta almost invisible in her hands. The girl might not have looked like much of a threat, but she was taking everything in stride, and that made her hot as hell to Dani.

A few blocks away from the apothecary and the main drag of

town, every instinct in her began to scream. Her charms burned as they warned of danger, a lot of damn danger.

The breeze barely stirred the leaves on the trees, but it was like a fog of violence lingered on every street. The entire world held its breath for what came next.

Dani put a finger to her lips, took a deep breath, and then peered around the corner. Street lights threw shallow pools of light that refracted off glass storefronts and illuminated writhing shadows. The quaint small town she'd visited in daylight had been swallowed by an inky darkness.

The spell-shadows crawled along every surface as they oozed into the world and away from the light. As far as she knew, there wasn't really a name for the little bastards. She called them pets. They worked off a hive mind and reported back to Spectre. They were how he had been tracking her all this time, a lesson she'd learned the hard way. Between Dani and the apothecary, the world crawled with them. It would be impossible to go in without being detected.

Dani ducked back around and gestured for Emilie to move to the far side of the building. Her instincts had been right, but even armed up like they were, there was no way she and Emilie could get there going through the front door. Even then, there was no way to tell if Andromeda or Mercurious were even there.

This had been a bad idea from the onset, and she knew it. But she'd also seen the look in Emilie's eyes. If she'd balked, Emilie would have come out here by herself. She probably would have gotten swarmed by the pets too. Little bastards would have eaten her alive.

"What did you see?" Emilie peered past Dani's shoulder toward the street.

"Nothing good." Dani put a hand on the other woman's arm, keeping her away from the street. "Spectre's pets are crawling all over the damned street. Is there another way to the shop?"

"Not really?" Emilie frowned, mouth in a tight white line. "We can cut through the alley, but it's not direct."

"But it'd get us closer, right?" No way were they gonna be able to get all the way to the shop without running into trouble. But the more they could avoid, the better.

"By a block or so."

"I'll take it. Where do we go?"

Emilie hunched over and traced out a tiny grid of main street in the dirt at their feet. The alleyway in front would lead them along the back of the block where the shadow minions were crawling, provided they weren't lurking back there too. It seemed like they were more of a deterrent to anybody stupid enough to be out on the streets tonight. It was working.

Dani stepped past Emilie and peeked around the corner along their new route. Without the street lamps, it was hard to tell what was waiting for them.

"Is it clear?" Emilie put one hand on Dani's shoulder and tried to peek over to see.

"Maybe," Dani hedged and ducked back around the building again. "Okay, here's the deal. I'm gonna take lead. You stick to my heels. And if I shoot..." She met Emilie's eyes, trying to get her to understand how serious this was. "...then you shoot."

Emilie went pale, but nodded. The hand not on her gun quivered, and Dani ignored it. The woman would either shoot when the time came, or she wouldn't. She'd seen hunters who'd trained for years freeze up when shit hit the fan. And she'd watched a fourteen year old jump on the back of a vampire and nearly wrench its fucking head off. There was no way to tell until push came to shove.

"You're positive you want to do this?"

"I don't want to, but it's necessary." The quiver in her hands stopped, voice a hard line. *Well, that settles that then, doesn't it?*

One step around the corner, and then another, and another. With every impact of her boots on the pavement, Dani expected an attack, shadows that swarmed with pale eyes and too many limbs. Another step and she expected wraiths made of shadows and death. Another step and she waited for the scream of a beast that did not exist anywhere but inside the mind of a depraved lunatic. But nothing happened. Ten feet, twenty, fifty, and they'd made it from one end of the alley to the next, quiet as ghosts. They were playing cat and mouse, and somehow they'd gotten this far undetected.

There was a strategy here that she wasn't seeing. If things were this empty, this easy, it meant one of two things. Either Spectre's attention was elsewhere, which was probably a bad sign. Or they were playing right into his hands, which was worse.

They had one more block to cover, and this time no alley to dart across and hide themselves in. Dani peeked around the corner to check, and again there were perfectly measured street lights that dotted either side of the road. No shadows clung anywhere they didn't belong, but a thick pool of darkness swept from a building a half block to the left.

She turned and met Emilie's eyes, reached out with one hand. "When I go, you go. Don't look back. Don't think. Fuck, if you can avoid it, don't goddamn breathe. You hear me?"

"I hear you."

Dani started them out at an easy trot as they took the corner, gunning for the shop a block down. They passed the pool, and whatever lingered inside it stirred with a steady hiss. She started to run, her boots pounding the pavement as they tried to outrun whatever had been keeping watch. The thing screamed behind them, and Dani's lip curled.

She slowed by a half step and let Emilie pass her, the shadow closer than was strictly safe. Dani pivoted on one heel, braced her stance, and fired the shotgun into center mass.

Normal slugs probably wouldn't have done much, but she'd loaded up her special shells. Salt, rosemary, lead, silver, and another dozen herbs all ground into ammunition meant to stop monsters in their tracks. From ten feet away, there wasn't time for the shell to expand. It hit the quivering mass of darkness and exploded out the other side.

Emilie flinched. Dani felt her lips pull up into that dark, blood-thirsty grin Graham had always told her she possessed. She let out a whoop as the shadow turned to smoke and melted away to nothing. She turned back and pumped the shotgun. She had no clue what they'd be running into when they turned the corner, but they were in the shit now and she was going to be prepared.

Another corner and they were back to Main Street. To the right, pets still swarmed every open surface. To the left, there was nothing but the shop waiting for them. Dani grabbed Emilie's open hand and kept them moving. Her lungs burned, and blood rushed to the surface of her thighs as she pressed on. She pulled Emilie along with her, unwilling to leave her behind by even a step.

She stumbled to a stop a few feet in front of the apothecary, nearly falling to her knees. The glass windows had cracked, black ooze hanging wet and glistening on them. The scent of copper filled the air. The door to the shop was torn to shreds. Droplets of shadow clung stubbornly to shards of wood. Dani knew what it looked like when a pack of pets got their teeth into something. It was what they'd find inside that she wasn't sure about.

She pulled up her gun as she searched for movement. Emilie growled low in her throat. It was good to see she was made of stronger stuff than Dani had wagered. Behind them, shadows still swarmed but refused to come closer. A sudden explosion of sound came from inside the shop. A woman snarled, followed by the croaking howl of a wraith, and Dani snapped back into action. Emilie had a half step on her, but Dani passed her once they got into the shattered interior of the shop.

Dirt, the remains of plants, and glass covered the floor. It crunched underfoot with each step. The shotgun was comfortable in her hands, braced against her shoulder. Three steps in, something howled from the back of the shop, a raspy sound that filled the room and made the floorboards shudder. Something cracked, and a woman screamed in anger.

Without a moment to think, Dani vaulted over a ruined door and found more of the ooze in the hallway. Her boots slipped in the ichor, just as a wraith made of grey smoke and flame slammed a door open and crashed into the wall with a snarl. Bright artificial light flooded around it from the doorway, macabre ooze now easy to see.

Dani took quick aim and fired her gun.

The wraith screamed and tried to scramble away, away from the light and Dani's gun. Except there was nowhere to go. She strode forward, pumping the shotgun to load up another shell. One shell in the chamber, six left. She snarled. This was what she trained for. Another step forward and the shadow scrabbled against the floor, massive claws gouging the wood. Another shot and it screamed and flailed onto its back. This is what she lived for, this moment when the monster became the hunted. Dani racked another round into the chamber when Andromeda appeared out of the doorway.

Her dark skin glowed, a green aura that rose off her, long locs arcing around her head in a halo. Her eyes burned bright, and the hairs on Dani's arms stood on end as she watched, one arm flung out to keep Emilie behind her.

Andromeda didn't even spare them a glance. Around her, a carpet of living things grew, crawling out of the room. Thick vines wrapped around her limbs, while flowers as big as a clenched fist bloomed in bright, vivid colors, a greenhouse come to life around her. She moved forward, and a carpet of moss spread with each step, eating the black ooze. Andromeda spoke a forgotten language, syllables guttural and harsh as she spat them out, and thrust a hand forward.

Light exploded out from her palm. A phantom wind chased it and pinned the shadow up against the door at the end of the hall. The edges of the wraith melted away as it snarled, howling at the power annihilating it. Dani stepped up to Andromeda's side, feeling the soft crush of plant life under her boots. Another shell into center mass from point-blank, and the shadow dissolved.

Nothing remained but the ichor that had given it form. The wind died along with the green light that had veiled Andromeda. The sentinel gasped, a violent shudder vibrating her bones. The air lost its weight as the sentinel dropped to one knee, Emilie surging forward to catch her.

Dani helped Emilie drag Andromeda into the back room. Green coated the walls. Vines and exotic plants twined around bookshelves and bloomed out of every crevice. Emilie got Andromeda sat down in a corner, and the two of them spoke in hushed whispers back and forth.

Near the back of the room, a small pool of dark ichor remained. Unnatural flowers bloomed in black and purple above it, stalks soaking up the poison as they grew. If they grew? Dani wasn't really sure how it all worked.

They weren't safe here, might not be safe anywhere in Dawson, but Dani needed to move them. Spectre's creations were getting stronger, and she didn't want to see what he'd come up with next. Even if she had the veilblade.

No way was she letting Emilie push them across town. Andromeda didn't look great, and if Spectre could drain a sentinel without even being here himself? That was a bad, bad sign. It was time to fall back. The rest of her kit was back at the house. She was good. Hell, she was one of the best working the East Coast from the way Joe talked. But even she wasn't good enough to handle a group of these suckers alone. It was time to go.

"Okay. I'm good, I'm good." Andromeda shook her head and stood up with barely a wobble in her footsteps. "What are you two doing here, though? You're supposed to be up at the house—"

"What are *we* doing here?" Dani's eyes flashed, and she took an angry step forward, one finger pointed at Andromeda.

"We're here…" Emilie shot her a warning glance and continued in a calmer tone. "Because Spectre used my sister to try to kill me." Her voice wavered, eyes fever bright in a too-pale face. "And it's time to find out why."

"You want to break the binding? Tonight? Are you crazy?"

From outside somewhere, a wraith howled again, a long sound that made ice climb up her spine. Dani shuddered and snapped back to the problem at hand. "We don't have time. We have to get back to the house. Now."

"There are—"

"The attack demolished your wards. Pets got to the ones outside. That's how you had company. Now we have to go." She shook her head, rose, and hucked it back out to the front of the shop, Emilie and

Andromeda following at her heels. She led them into a night that had somehow gotten darker in their absence.

Even the slight breeze died off, flames at the horizon no longer burning orange. A blanket of darkness lay over the street. Dani didn't want to go out there. Out there was something that wanted to take a bite out of her. And without even the light of the moon to help guide their way? It was not a chance she was excited to take.

Emilie and Andromeda flanked her a moment later, hesitancy rolling off them in waves. The three women stood there as though waiting for the darkness to pass. But Dani knew it wouldn't. It would grow thicker and darker until Spectre's shadows began to bleed into existence. Desperate times called for desperate measures.

Dani reached back into her knapsack and pulled out her flares. They'd be a beacon for anything on the street, but it was a necessary evil to see their surroundings. If they got lucky, the flare would burn bright enough that nothing would want to get close. If not, she'd send the girls running and stay back to deal. It wouldn't be the first time.

She dragged one of the flares along the jagged remains of the doorframe and then chucked it onto the street in front of the shop. She needed to know what was hiding in the darkness. A dull red glow threw out a fifteen foot arc of light, and from the edges, dozens of eyes blinked back at them. Pale eyes and grey teeth shone bright against the darkness.

Nothing moved in. Those horrible, slitted eyes glowing with a hungry menace just watched and waited. Dani ushered Andromeda and Emilie back the way they'd come, along the side of the building, snapping another flare to life.

Twice they tried to take a turn, and twice they ran into walls of wraiths. They needed to escape downtown, get back up and into Emilie's neighborhood where there was some cover. Spectre wouldn't have blacked out all of Dawson. He was trying to funnel them into a trap, and Dani wasn't about to make it easy.

"Run," she snarled and tossed a flare into the wall of wraiths. They screamed in a single high-pitched whine that bled together and nailed her in place for a long second. She cringed under the sound of it until the fire swept across them and gave her an opening to take off running. The smell and flames worked as a deterrent to keep the pets from giving chase, but she knew it wouldn't last long or do much damage. Emilie and Andromeda sprinted ahead of her in the darkness, knowing each twist and turn to take to get them closer to safety. Glass crashed to the ground behind them, and Dani spared a glance backwards. A wraith that looked like something between a wolf and a panther took chase. The shotgun firm in her hands, Dani pivoted and took a knee.

Three bounds of massive paws hit the ground. Dani waited until fetid breath that made her gag wafted across her face, then pulled the trigger. The wraith screamed low and long, turning to dark smoke as it died. She pumped the shotgun and took off running again.

They'd come back up to the neighborhood a different way than on the way down. From here she saw Lockgrove house as it loomed against a sliver of moon. They were only a few hundred feet away if they cut across the backyard. All the three of them needed to do was get back behind the wards where they could wait out Spectre until daylight.

"Tricksy girls." From behind Dani in the darkness, a voice slithered over her skin. Her blood went cold. She turned, slowly, to see Spectre emerge from the darkness flanked by a pair of wraiths.

He looked better than in Alabama, tall and broad-shouldered with wavy dark hair that sat against his collar. Dani saw why he'd have been a catch back in the day, with a straight nose and pale skin. It was his eyes that ruined the illusion, cold black eyes with no flicker of humanity in them. His wraiths were just as bad. Furred lupine spines thickened into massive forepaws with wicked claws. Vicious heads somewhere between a hippo and an alligator with small yellow eyes and too many teeth perched atop muscled shoulders. Pale markings in runes striped their skin in white and grey.

"Emilie, run." Dani's eyes went wide, and she snarled as she dug her feet into the loose dirt, the shotgun steady in her hands as she watched him.

A violent smile slashed his face open, and the monster that called himself Spectre spoke up. "Are you sure you want to, Emilie? Didn't you miss me?"

Andromeda cried out, and Dani heard the thwack of a body hitting the ground. When she took a glance over her shoulder, Emilie was in an unconscious heap, Andromeda hauling her into a fireman's carry. Their eyes met and they understood each other perfectly. Dani would stand rear guard. She could trust Andromeda to get Emilie back to the house, behind the wards where she could be protected.

She turned back, ready to spray Spectre in the face, even if it only annoyed him. But he'd disappeared, only the monsters he'd brought along remained. Dani growled and fired the shotgun. At this range, it didn't do the devastating damage she'd hoped for, but the beasts focused on her. *Good.* Focusing on her meant Emilie was safe. *Safer.*

Falling back in a situation like this was critical, let her partner cover her and then cover them, back and forth, like a dance. Keep firing to make sure the wraiths didn't close distance and get a nasty swipe on her. Without backup it was doable. It just wasn't easy.

One step forward and she racked another shell into the chamber and fired, again and again. Each step was another shot as she ran through her ammunition. In the time it took to close the distance to the first wraith, the sanctified shells had torn it to pieces. It smoked out as she dropped the shotgun. In the sheath on her thigh, the veil-blade burned like a brand, begged her to unsheathe it, let it do what they had forged it for.

Another one was close, and she took off running toward the wraith, letting her momentum pull her into a long slide as the monster swiped at where she'd been a moment ago. Her toes dug into the ground as she pulled the veilblade from its sheath. It was a living star in her hand, made of fire and death, pure in the way only a fatal blow could be.

Behind the wraith, the lights at the Lockgrove house flickered on, one after another. Andromeda had done it.

The nightmare wraith turned to face her, massive head snapping back and forth as it scented the air. It seemed to be trying to work out which way she'd move next. She tucked the blade along her forearm, obscuring it from the wraith. Small eyes might mean it didn't see the way she expected. Her chest heaved, breath coming harder with each exhalation.

Body folded into a forward roll, she slashed out with her blade as it launched itself at her. Ragged claws tore into her shoulder and sent her careening to the ground. Unforgiving gravel ground into her cheek, knocked the wind out of her, and made it hard to pull in another breath. Agony speared her but there was no time to think.

She rolled to the side and got her feet under her, and flipped the veilblade in her hand, letting it rest at her side. Her left arm hung wrong, dislocated and throbbing.

The wraith favored one side where she'd scored a long lateral wound that tore it open. She'd done damage, but not enough. It snarled, and she took a careful step back, and then another. The frightened part of her screamed that she should turn and run, that little piece of the girl she had been once. But the hunter in her smothered it with a decade of experience on the job. If she turned her back to it, then it'd take off after her. Best case, it'd be fifty feet before claws raked her from shoulder to hip. It would expect her to run, a monster like this *wanted* her to run.

Dani wasn't about to do anything it would like. Her right hand tightened around the blade, hoping she'd done enough damage to it that it wouldn't be able to move as fast as it had moments ago. It was her one shining hope right now. She surged forward, opening up her left side as she did so. The wraith took the bait, and at the last second she juked to the right, veilblade crashing into his belly. It slipped in easily enough, and skin charred as it cut through the bulk of the beast.

The wraith screamed, jumping backwards and pulling her along. It threw her off balance as the blade tore free, a wet explosion of blood and viscera splattering onto her and the pavement alike. It lunged forward and she stabbed in, hand nearly sinking into the flesh before she danced backwards again.

Fast, but not fast enough. Wicked teeth sank into her side, excruciating pain burning through her as she stabbed it again, and again, and again. She slashed at its throat and stumbled backwards, grey streamers flying at the periphery of her vision. It fell to the ground with a gurgle and faded to nothing. Pain flashed through her, cold and sharp. That was a bad sign, a very bad sign. She turned, one arm still hanging limp, the other wrapped around the veilblade, dripping with dark blood. Agony echoed through her bones with every step.

In front of her loomed the Lockgrove house. She had to protect Emilie. Spectre had seen her. He'd be coming for her.

The house gleamed, a bright beacon on top of the hill, but it looked wavy in her vision. Smoke, maybe? Her legs felt like lead, and she barely made it off of the asphalt and onto the grass. It was slippery, dew from the day coating it, and she stumbled, losing her footing. Dani landed in a heap on the ground and couldn't get her feet back under her again. Fifty feet lay between her and the door. There was a med kit in her pack, if she could get back to the house. Her legs fought gravity, fought the pain that consumed her with every beat of her heart. Her useless arm pressed against the wound, wet hot blood flooding from her as it stained the grass.

If she wanted to survive, she needed to put pressure on the wound. But nobody was coming to help her, and no way in hell was she dropping the veilblade. So instead, she half pushed, half army crawled. Every breath was excruciating, and when her vision went blurry, Dani realized she'd started to cry. She couldn't die, not yet. She had to help Emilie, had to avenge Graham.

Somehow, she made it up to the back door, but the knob was out of her reach. She panted and pressed her back against the door. From somewhere along the tree line, an aborted yelp sounded, and she could hear panicked voices from out front, more trouble coming. She needed to warn Andromeda and Emilie, but it all just seemed so far away.

Dani glanced down at herself and tried to swallow the whimper. Her side was a wreck of ruined flesh, dark blood coating the ground under her. Even if she got to the med kit, there was no fixing that. Numbly, she realized that she was dying. Her vision narrowed as light flared along the tree line, more grey swallowing everything moment by moment.

Her eyes were so heavy. All she wanted to do was close them for a moment. If she could rest for just a few minutes, she'd have the strength to get back up, at least get the door open and warn them, tell them something was coming. She fought the urge to close them but her head thudded dully against the door. The pain leveled out, as though it had become part of her, no longer something to worry about.

Hunters didn't sleep on the job, but they died on it.

She'd die here, in this little two-horse town with no one who cared about her in a hundred-mile radius, without ever avenging Graham, nothing more than another tally on Spectre's unending list of victims. Had she been cocky? To think she, of all people, could take down the bogeyman?

A harsh laugh bubbled out of her, and she choked on it, blood in her mouth. When she spat, it fell into the puddle of blood that had grown around her. Dimly, she heard someone call out, but she couldn't answer. It was too late. She'd made all the wrong choices. She gripped the veilblade tighter, and it pulsed warmly in her hand as her eyes slipped shut and darkness swallowed her.

24

EMILIE

It was his eyes that did it, black as pitch and cold as midnight on the shortest day of the year. They dragged her in, mesmerized her and froze her to the spot. His gaze left her a quivering rabbit, trapped by the hypnotizing snake as it pondered what to do with her.

Emilie saw Spectre. And Spectre saw her. And then everything was grey. She felt herself fall, and snap, and shatter. A thousand Emilies all at once, bound and unbound. A girl trapped by her past, a girl who feared the future, a girl who had never known the reach of the talents which lurked deep inside of her. Magic that yearned for the sweet absolution of night and darkness, the veil of stars hung low over a purple sky.

Their eyes met, and the stars aligned, and Emilie crashed herself against the rocks of a binding already worn thin by time, circumstance, and ability. It felt like a bomb going off in her chest, the pain a bright, violent flower that bloomed inside of her and burned away everything. She forgot and remembered a hundred times in the space of her body falling to the ground. But what was a body for a medium? Nothing more than a sheath to the spirit, and her mind fled down, and down, and into itself until she forgot where she was and who she was, and everything that had happened. It all fell away until she was nothing, and there was nothing, except the pieces of a woman scattered on the floor.

When the woman realized that she was a person, she sat surrounded by nothing but thick grey smoke. *No.* Not smoke. Fog, thick enough that she could make patterns by swinging her arms through the air. Dense whorls of silver and grey obscured everything and left vague outlines of shapes in the distance. She felt the curve of her body, but it carried no weight, as though she were as insubstantial as smoke.

In the distance, she heard voices and she knew them somehow. But there was no familiarity, no spark that told her who they were or who she was, nothing but a girl. The remains of something that had been whole once, now nothing more than a reflection shattered into a million pieces.

Are we more than the sum of our parts? Or just pieces of a puzzle, never finished, always evolving into something more. Something different.

The fog cleared enough that she could see a woman facing away from her. She was tall and curvy, with waves of dark hair that cascaded down her back. She didn't turn as she spoke, but her voice carried. Every word made the fog clear a bit more. It didn't reveal anything, she could see farther, a perfect white expanse that reached on forever.

The clarity gave her something though, almost a memory. There had been something worth doing, an important task, one that mattered. But concentrating didn't do her any good. Only a blank slate lay where once the rest of her had been. She was missing pieces, but that knowledge didn't help her. It didn't do anything but make her realize that she wasn't herself, whoever that might be.

"Oh darling, you fought so well. But some fights are not meant to be won or lost. The price we pay for knowledge is high. For you, I think, it will be higher than most."

The woman's voice was kind, soft, with a lilting French accent that colored every word. So familiar. This voice had been with her since the early days, when she had been small and quiet, when she was little more than large eyes that watched, and open ears that heard what nobody else did. Not even Mama could see Marie.

"So you do remember me. Then perhaps it isn't all lost. Not yet."

The woman turned with a small smile, but it looked sad on her face. She had tanned skin and warm eyes, and the woman knew her. *Grandmama.* She was the first voice, the voice that had spoken to her since before there was memory. She'd shown her the secret rooms of the house, steered her away from the voice of the dark man. Grandmama stepped closer, and she stood up, unfurling herself in a body that wasn't real.

"It's time to remember, sweetling. Time to pick up the pieces of yourself. Just remember. Remember…"

Her voice faded along with her body, scattered like drops of water falling during a thunderstorm, and everything changed. The perfect void of white grew darker. Fog turned to smoke that burned her eyes and choked her breath. Cinders rained down around her, smearing along her skin and piling on the ground. Drifts of things burned away long ago by fire and flame, and death and destruction surrounded her.

FIRE. Memories pushed at her, the seductive voice of a man made of shadow, the scream of fire that ate at Mama's bones. A single orange aura bloomed in Lizzie's eyes. It burned its way through her mind, roaring as it consumed everything she had been or would be. But even fire requires fuel.

She remembered a thousand moments, eyes slipping shut as ash danced around her. The flames danced and writhed in memory and mind. But they did not kiss her skin or melt her bones. Inside her chest, the perfect cold of glacial ice came alive, sheathed her in armor that glistened and did not melt in the fury. Heat threw itself at her, along with a man's voice that cursed and cried and battered against that armor. But her glacial armor did not crack or crumble under the pressure.

The cold kiss of death and what lay beyond the veil encapsulated her body and mind. It protected what she had always been, what she had to be by virtue of what lay inside her. She was a nesting doll made of flesh to hide the talents that had grown in a garden bereft of light.

The fire died, and the woman felt her finger twitch. When she reopened her eyes, the flames disappeared. The perfect white was gone too, black scorch marks everywhere, except for the two feet around her. Instead, there was a puddle of water around her, cold and calming, protecting her.

Voices rang out, clamorous and chaotic, voices she knew. There were also voices she didn't know, the cries of those trapped beyond the veil, wrapped up in their pain, their pasts, and the things left undone.

"Bindings are not to be used lightly. There are consequences..."

"Hide, Emilie. Hide or run. If you don't run, you'll die. I can't lose all of you. I won't, do you hear me?"

"You have to hide from him. Hide from the shadow man..."

"He said he loved me...said he needed me..."

Emilie. Her name was Emilie. It fit, the perfect pair of jeans worn to the shape of her body. The name fluttered inside of her, and she knew it as her own. The woman remembered. Her name on Mama's lips and Dad's, and on *his.* Emilie Lockgrove. She was the last surviving Deveraux, imbued with the gifts that came easily to the women in her family.

But her legacy didn't belong to Mama and Grandmama alone, and she knew that now. Her early gifts had been so strong that nobody ever looked further, a child who heard the voices of the dead, who could slip her skin like a snake, a child capable of channeling those long gone. All gifts given to her by the blood of a medium.

But Emilie's gifts went further. A strand of Dad's line, locked in her DNA: ice. The cold that protected her core kept the binding from stripping away everything she'd been. She could feel the space where the ice had frozen that piece of her solid, the chill of the grave deep in her core.

Ice and death. Those were her gifts. A woman who could hear those gone and dead for decades. A woman who could share her body with the departed, straddling the two worlds, bringing them together like no one else could, like no medium born in the last century was capable of. She was a voice for the voiceless. And now, she could hear all the voices blocked by the binding.

Dad thought it would protect her, keep her safe from Spectre and his curse, keep her from dying in flame and ruin like Mama and her mother before her, and hers before her. Back and back and back to the beginning. He thought that, if he had the time, he could unravel it all. It was nothing more than a tangled skein of yarn that required time and diligence. But he'd had it all wrong. They all had.

To know how it ends, she had to know how it started. In the space between two breaths, a man became a monster, incapable of death. Emilie wasn't a weapon. She was a conduit. The understanding pulsed inside her, knowledge that to find herself, all the pieces scattered to the wind, she had to return to the beginning.

Once upon a time, there was a town where talented did not have to hide. They named it Dawson, and as it grew, people heard its call and came from far and wide. And amongst those who came was a dark man with eyes like pitch and a woman who stood on either side of the veil, pale haired and pale eyed.

And the man coveted the woman as though she were a jewel, clutched in greedy hands and hidden from the light. She didn't want him though, and tried to hide from the man. So he took her, not knowing that she had allies. Allies with sharp blades and iron hearts.

The man hid the woman, bound her with rope and magic to hide her from her friends, but he could not hide forever and they found him. He fought them, and lit the world on fire. And in the cinders, they found the woman and released her, and she ran. But once again, the man found her, and this time no blades got her in time.

And in her dying words, she breathed to life a curse that would follow the man who had become a monster. A geas born from blood and pain, to follow him for all of his years. Never would he see her again. Never would he cross the veil and find peace. Never, never, never. The man, in his rage, became the flame and the shadow, intent to destroy her bloodline, an attempt to free himself and claim her as he'd always wanted.

Emilie knew about the ways the truth could be twisted and

warped over the years. A dying woman could beg for freedom from the man who had hunted her, and in her pain and her power, bring to life a curse on a man who became a monster. Had she known what she was doing? Amelia Deveraux, when she spat those words out at him, did she know what she wrought?

"And never the twain shall meet." Marie's kind voice echoed around her, out loud instead of in her head. Maybe it was this place that allowed her to do it, this strange in between. Her story still ricocheted across Emilie's mind like a bullet. "He'd hunted her for so long, and blood magic—death magic is powerful. Mediums stand with one foot in either world, both sides of the veil at their fingertips. She used that power to ensure that he could never follow her, but there are consequences for big magic."

A scream rent the air, the voice of a woman driven beyond madness, fear, or hate. It was raw and broken and lonely, words lost in the cacophony. It cut off as quickly as it had appeared and left Emilie wondering who it belonged to.

"Amelia," Marie explained. "My sister. The one he wanted but could not have. Her magic keeps her tethered, forcing her to watch what Spectre does to her daughters. So long as Spectre lives, she remains trapped in between. And no matter how many times he is killed by mortal hands, he cannot die, thanks to her curse."

"What?" Emilie felt her bottom lip tremble. "What are you saying?"

"Spectre doesn't want to kill you. Not in the way you think. Remember. Remember all of it. Not her past. Yours."

Marie's voice faded, and Emilie knew she was alone again, alone in a vast expanse that was her mind, where there was nothing but time, time to find all the pieces she had lost. Memories circled and closed in, coming home to roost as they settled back into place.

She hid alone in the back corner of the library while Mama held séances up on the third floor. The house was noisy with spirits that only she could hear, so loud that Grandmama got drowned out. It was the first time that Henry came to see her.

She could never quite see him, but she could hear him, and he was real enough that if she'd wanted, he could have slipped into her skin. But that was dangerous, and Mama got sad when she did it, so Emilie kept the walls in her head built up high. Those walls protected her from what hid in the veil is what Mama said, but it seemed a little wacky to Emilie, who could hear so much more than Mama.

He found her hidden in the deepest corner, cloaked by thick velvet curtains, with her hands clamped over her ears, trying to drown out the people in the veil who heard Mama's call. He was kind and curious, and able to teach her how to quiet them down. His name was Henry, but some people called him Shadow. So he became the Shadow Man, her best friend. And if he was a spirit, then who needed to know, really? He only came around when she was alone, anyhow, never showing up when Grandmama, or Dad, or Lizzie were around. He was her special friend, and that was all that mattered.

Watching her childhood play out across the cinema of her mind left Emilie nauseated. She watched Spectre find her when she was still so young and so naïve. He taught her and groomed her through the eyes of a lonely child who wanted a friend more than anything else in the world.

It wasn't until Andromeda and Mercurious became a part of her life that he faded away. And even then, she could now see where he had watched, seething, as they had stolen her away from him. Day by day, month by month, year by year.

Fifteen and sobbing her eyes out. Michael Jones had broken her heart, asked Mary Kline to the dance, even though they'd been dating. She had thought he'd been special, someone she could give herself to. But he'd betrayed her, and the twins were across the country for vacation. She had no one to talk to, no one who could understand.

And then Henry was there. Before she even realized it, her tears slowed and then stopped when she spotted him in the corner. "Why didn't he love me?"

"Because people are monsters. But I would never hurt you."

"I know. But you're a spirit. You aren't a person."

"Am I now?"

Those words echoed back through her head. Am I now? Am I

now? *Am I now?* Three little words that she hadn't even noticed. She'd been in the throes of her first heartbreak. Looking back, it was impossible to miss. More conversations like this one filtered through her, drips and dribbles of things that struck horror into her. He'd once promised to take her away, and in her own way, she'd loved him.

She loved him in the way only someone young and blind could. He'd been so careful, taken his time and groomed her. He made her care about him in a way that turned her stomach. That she had forgotten this horrified her. It had been too much to remember after the fire. Who would want to remember something like this?

She'd wanted to leave this town behind, to run away to where nobody knew her and she could start all over. She wanted away from talents and spirits and a family history that haunted her every step in Dawson. She wanted life on her own terms, without all the conditions that this town brought with it. The distance would let her outrun the talents inside of her. And he'd led her down that path, encouraging it every step of the way. Why not? The further from Grandmama and Dad and Grandpa she was, the easier she'd be to snare in his trap.

And the more she remembered, the closer she got to that night, the one she couldn't remember and yet had haunted her for ten years. The night Mama died.

THE COLD SNAP made it feel like autumn had finally shown up. Sharp air almost tasted like snow, almost. She was running late getting home after getting a flat tire back in town. She had to leave the dang 4x4 where it was with a jack holding it in place until morning. Rules were rules.

And in the Lockgrove house, séance decompression was mandatory. Mama'd held one of the bigger gatherings in the last few years, and she'd need help to get back to herself. Emilie shook her head and tucked her chin to her chest, moving a little quicker. Liz had said she was staying in, so at the very least someone was there. Mama wasn't alone in the house with all the spirits. She couldn't hear or speak to most of them, anyway. Most were too old for anyone but Emilie to hear their whispers along the carpets and walls. They were little more than echoes.

When she got up to the house, it was still dark, not entirely strange considering Mama preferred candlelight for her ceremonies. But no extra cars meant everyone had bailed already. Liz should have turned everything back on by now.

The house was too quiet inside, muffled artificial silence, like someone was trying to cast a spell for quiet but doing so clumsily. Through the floor, she could hear a pair of people talking in Mama's study. That must be where Liz had her cornered.

She dropped her hat and jacket next to the door and realized that there was a flicker of light dancing along the stairwell. With one hand, she flicked the light switch at the base, but nothing happened. Kind of creepy, but it was still quiet. The power must be out again. Not unheard of in a house this old. Dad kept insisting he'd upgrade the wiring, get the whole place redone. It never happened, but he kept talking about it.

Emilie sighed and started up the stairs, stopping halfway. She could distinctly recognize both of the voices speaking now, but it wasn't Mama and Liz. Liz crouched at the top of the stairs, peering around the bannister.

Mama was talking to Shadow Man, to Henry. She froze, unsure of what to do or say. She'd assumed he was an old spirit and that was why he'd never shown up when Mama was around. But there was a hard edge to his words she'd never heard before when the two of them were speaking. It frightened her. She had the sudden feeling he'd been a forbidden secret and she'd been ferreted out.

"Something's wrong." Liz glanced over her shoulder and met Emilie's eyes. "She stopped the séance early, kicked everybody out, and now she's in her study talking to somebody. But Emilie, something is wrong. I can feel it."

"What do you mean wrong?"

"Mama's not coming back right..." Liz's voice trailed off as the door to Mama's study opened a few inches wider.

Mama and Shadow were still talking in hushed voices, but the quicksilver back and forth of conversation was easier to pick apart now. Emilie passed her sister on the stairs and headed for the door. If it was Shadow Man, she'd explain to Mama. Emilie knew him, and if he was as old as she'd thought, maybe that was what had tripped Mama up. She'd overextended before, talking to spirits past her range.

Liz followed a half-step behind, hesitant but unwilling to let Emilie go by herself. It was unnecessary this time, but she appreciated it all the same. When they got close to the door, the voices stopped, Mama cutting off mid-sentence. Emilie could almost feel the weight of their gaze through the wood of the door. It unnerved her, but she wasn't going to back down. If Mama was off, they needed to deal with it before it got any worse. Otherwise, she'd have to visit Cedar Terrace again, and nobody wanted that, least of all Mama.

Gentle fingers pushed open the door. Whatever she had been expecting to see, it was not this. Dozens and dozens of candles in jars and on candelabras blazed like a starry night in the room. Shadows jumped along the walls and ceiling, and they made the hair on the back of Emilie's neck stand on end.

An orange halo silhouetted Mama, but she was standing wrong. It took a long moment for Emilie's eyes to adjust, and it wasn't until Liz dug her hand into Emilie's arm, squeezing it too tight, that she realized they weren't playing a trick on her.

Her mother's limbs sat at odd angles. Tendons stood out in tight relief on her neck, her eyes were too wide in a pale face, bare pinpricks of color in a sea of white. Her mouth was pulled into the tight rictus of a smile that was more sinister than sweet.

Not Mama, her talents whispered to her, the spirits in the house finally speaking up.

Liz slid past Emilie and put one foot in front of her sister, a small gesture, but unmistakable.

"Emilie...darling." Mama's head cocked to one side, arms dancing at her sides, a morbid facsimile of a ventriloquist dummy. Thin loops of shadow writhed around her, articulating her limbs. Behind her, a tall form wreathed in shadows watched. "There's someone here for you." Her voice was off-key and saccharine sweet. And it was wrong. Wrong, wrong, wrong.

Liz stopped pretending and slid in front of Emilie. A ball of something sizzled in one palm. "You let go of our mama."

Emilie gasped, the realization that Liz could see him shocking through her.

"Out of the way, girl," Henry spoke through Mama, his voice laid over her. "Emilie. Emilie sweetheart, it's time to go. You want to come with me, don't you? Don't you?"

The part of her that had told Henry about her desire to run away and disappear recoiled, horror roiling through her. It had been a dream, one she'd shared with her friend. He was just a spirit stuck to this house like so many others. But it was becoming clear that he wasn't a spirit like others. If he was a spirit at all.

She shook her head, tears spilling over her cheeks. Mama's eyes bulged, and she couldn't seem to breathe properly, a thin drip of blood slid from one nostril. Henry snarled and several things happened all at once.

Mama dropped like a puppet with its strings cut. She hit the floor in a heap and then began to scream in a long unending wail. Emilie tried to run toward her mother, but Liz threw out her left arm and clotheslined her. The shadow swiped at the place her head had been only a moment ago, and Liz shoved the sizzling ball of energy into its mass. It split in two, and Emilie watched as one shadow threw her sister against one wall and the other wrapped around her mother's neck.

"Nononononononono," Emilie muttered to herself, eyes too wild because this was mad. It was insane. This was not happening. She had to get to Liz, and they had to get Mama because Henry had gone mad.

Mama's voice cut off with a loud crack as Emilie got her hands around Liz's middle. Fire crawled before them, consuming everything it touched and making the room burn brighter. Mama stared with dead eyes, and Emilie swallowed a scream, pulling frantically at her sister.

In her panic, the walls Mama had taught her to keep up at all times fell. Her shields lay useless. Suddenly, Henry wasn't himself. He grew tall and broad, with pale skin and a sharp nose. He was handsome, and she recognized him, not as Henry the Shadow Man, but Vincent Hawthorne. She swallowed a whimper and tried harder to pull Liz back and out into the hallway.

Her Henry was the monster who killed Amelia and burned half of Dawson to the ground once upon a time. Flames bit at her clothes, and she slapped at them. Once they were over the threshold, she got her arms under Liz's shoulders and scrambled backwards as hard and as fast as she could. They had to get away from him, and they had to get out of the house, and Mama was dead, and Dad wasn't here. Her mind scrambled in a loop before she tripped over the carpet, running and falling backwards with Liz's weight on top of her.

Fire erupted from Mama's study, eating the house alive. They were trapped in a nightmare, and Emilie had to get them out. It took another long minute to fight out from under Liz's weight. From the stairs, she heard Dad cry out, and then he was racing past as if they weren't there on the ground.

Smoke and tears made it hard to see, but she kept her arms around her sister, trying to get them to the stairs. Dad was casting at the top of his lungs, incantations flying, but it was too late. She turned the corner at the bannister. Something surged at her out of the smoke, and Emilie lost her balance. She fell backwards down the stairs, and everything became pain and fire until it went black.

THE MEMORY of that night settled down into her bones, and Emilie felt the weight of it clamp down around her shoulders. Such a heavy memory, no wonder she hadn't wanted to remember.

A wild laugh tried to force its way past her lips. She was afraid that if she started to laugh, she'd never stop. She'd be left here in this void, filled with the memories that the binding had locked away. If she had known what was waiting, hidden deep inside her own mind, would she have still come home? Did she want to know what came after?

The understanding settled around her until she reclaimed all of it. She was trapped here in her own mind, and there was one more memory she was missing. One big one. One that wasn't going to be any easier to stomach than seeing Mama die. She didn't want to remember anything more. Maybe it would be better to stay here, hide inside herself until the body withered and faded away, and she became a spirit to float along.

Except she already knew that hiding wasn't an option, not really. It would only mean that she was easier to find. There was no binding hiding her from Spectre now. He'd come for her. That he'd waited as long as he had already was surprising enough. Although it made sense if he'd been working his wiles for as long as he had. She had to face that last memory. Blinking against tears, she waited while it returned.

Her skin felt stretched too tight, and she was freezing. So incredibly cold, even though a chill had never once in her life bothered her before this. The nurses kept telling her it was because the fire had burned her badly enough that it exposed the nerves under her skin. All Emilie knew was that it was excruciating. It seemed like it was the only thing that punched through the pain of losing Mama and Liz getting shipped up to the ICU.

Emilie was alone here. Her own private room was slowly turning into a personal hell as the night of the fire played over and over in her head, a loop that always ended the same way. Mama's scream cut off, the fireball trying to engulf her, and choking smoke before it went black.

It had been her fault. Dad wouldn't say it, but it was and she knew it. She'd welcomed Henry, told him everything for years, and years, and years. Compared to Liz, she'd gotten off easy. There were some burns on her shoulders and back, but nothing like her sister. Not like Mama either. Dad and Grandpa had been swapping visiting her and Liz, and every time Dad came in it felt like her throat would seal itself shut. She didn't know how to tell him it was all her fault. She didn't know if she could.

What a coward. She never told Mama about Shadow, and at the moment that her shields went down, she'd seen him. She'd seen the face he'd spent so much effort hiding. No wonder. Grandmama had told her all about Vincent Hawthorne and what he'd done, that he'd turned into a monster that hunted their family. She'd been a fool not to know Shadow for who he was, as Spectre.

The door swung open, and Dad entered, dark hair in absolute disarray. His eyes were too wild, and he hadn't shaved in days. Her mind chanted at her again. "Your fault. Your fault. Your fault..."

"Emi, sweetheart, you're awake. I'm glad." He looked back over one shoulder as though he wasn't supposed to be here. She couldn't remember if that was true. Grandpa had been spending more time with her, but the pain meds they'd put her on made time pass in strange ways.

"We have to talk while there's still time." He paced back and forth before pulling a chair up to her bedside.

"Grandpa's supposed to be by, I thought." Emilie struggled to sit up, head too foggy by half. Why was he talking about this now? Why not wait for Grandpa to come by?

"Later, later." He shook his head, eyes wild. "I know what happened. I know he came for the two of you. But it's okay."

"Dad, I—"

"No, you have to listen. He will come for you. He can't get you here. Wards stop that, but you aren't safe. But I have a plan. I can hide you from him. I promise."

"Dad, what are you talking about?"

"Hide. Hide or run. Those are the only choices, and I won't lose all three of you, do you hear me? I won't! The binding will work. It has to work."

"Grandpa said magic like that has consequences..." Emilie frowned, trying to remember why Grandpa had been so upset last time she'd seen him.

"It doesn't matter. Consequences don't matter if you're dead, do you hear me?" He stood up so fast that the chair went skittering across the floor. "Let me do this."

"Daddy I—"

"I would never do anything that let you get hurt if I could help it. Do you trust me?"

"Of course I do. I—"

"Then I will fix this." He nodded and started speaking more to himself than anything. *"I can fix this."*

Emilie stood there as the pieces of herself shifted back into place. She had thought getting the truth would give her peace, solace, allow her to see what had happened and how to move on. But it was the opposite. Her heart felt like it had turned to granite inside her chest.

Dad had come to her while she was drugged up and convinced her the binding was the only way. With the memory now in her possession, she was angrier than she'd been before at his distance. This was so much worse and in every possible way. He'd already known what he wanted to do, and he'd strong-armed her into it when she was weak and vulnerable and tearing herself to pieces.

He'd said he could fix this. Maybe he'd even believed it, but his actions had stolen away her life. As many terrible memories as had beamed themselves back to where she could access them, there were sweeter ones too, of Mama and Grandmama, Grandpa and Liz, memories of him too, before the fire. But the sepia tone of those long ago moments were wiped out by what he'd done.

25

DANI

Everything hurt. The dry ache of the desert burned at the back of her throat, raw and patchy. Her bones creaked, rising through desiccated flesh as it vibrated along her. Head filled with cotton, skin stretched too tight, absolutely everything hurt.

Dani cracked open her eyes with a Herculean effort. Too weak to even sit all the way up, she found herself in an unfamiliar room. A worn blue quilt covered her. Narrow walls and a popcorn ceiling greeted her as she looked around. She tried to get her bearings, but her vision blurred around the edges as though she'd been asleep for too long. She didn't see any clues about where she was.

Dani closed her eyes and then heaved out a shaking breath before she shimmied herself up to a sitting position. It didn't help much, and it hurt like a bitch. Every inch of her body throbbed with pain, screaming at her to close her eyes and never open them again.

Good thing she'd never been one to listen to directions, even when her body was the one doing the talking. Every breath was sharp, needles stabbing through her lungs and out her back. The quilt laid over her fell down around her hips, and she could see the darkness of her own flesh under the sheath of a white sheet.

None of this tracked. She'd been as good as dead out back. That kind of wound... Even if it had happened in the middle of a damned ER, there was no coming back from that kind of damage. So how was she sitting here, healed up? Her eyes scanned the room again and found a few things.

The veilblade sat on a small wooden table to her left, within reach, and wards danced along the moldings up next to the ceiling. There was no way to tell what they did from this distance, but that meant it was a talented house, or it had been once.

This was all bad. Her heart beat a staccato rhythm in her chest. She didn't know where she was or who's mercy she might be at. But she had the veilblade, and she was wearing her own clothes. Didn't fix the problem, but it helped.

It took a long minute to catch her breath and even longer to get her feet on the floor as she sat up. Exhaustion bleated in her ears like she'd been running for miles. With the veilblade in her hands, some of her tension bled away.

When she stood up, her whole body swayed, threatening to throw her back in bed. She had to hold herself steady by leaning against the bed. She'd taken two shuffling steps and nearly fell when Andromeda stepped through the narrow door at the front of the room.

"Oh, thank God you're awake." Dark smudges bruised under her eyes, and she looked wan, worn out. "We weren't sure if you'd pull through there for a while."

"You're the reason I'm still breathing?" Dani let herself fall to a seat on the bed and hoped the sentinel couldn't see the way she fought for every breath.

"Yeah. And it wasn't easy." Andromeda leaned against the door-jamb. "You barely had a pulse when they found you." Her eyes slipped past the open door out the hallway. There was something she wasn't saying.

"How..." Dani shook her head and pinned Andry with a concerned look. "I saw those wounds. No way did I come back from that. No way." Fear sat heavy at the back of her throat, choking Dani as she tried to ask the question. *Was I dead? Did I die?*

"A few more minutes and you'd have been past even my skills." Andromeda smirked and raised an eyebrow. "I am a woman of many gifts." She nodded to the veilblade with her chin. "Magic in that blade wasn't about to let go either."

"You're saying what? The veilblade kept me kicking?"

"Yes." Andromeda nodded her head. "There are reasons bladesingers are so tough."

Dani frowned, mouth pressed in a hard line as uneasiness coursed through her. The sentinel was being cagey about what had happened after she'd gone down. No way was it that simple, and she needed details. Knowledge was how she stayed kicking. "How long was I out? Is Emilie okay? Spectre was..." Dani grit her teeth. "What. Did. I. Miss?"

"All hell is breaking loose. You've been down for a few days. Emilie's here. There's a lot to catch up on." A flurry of emotions crossed Andromeda's face.

Hearing Emilie was here sent a wave of relief through her. She hid it, not wanting to show her cards until she knew the situation. "Like how I'm alive?"

"Like how you're alive," Andromeda echoed.

She waved Andromeda out of the room. "Let's get on with this. I need to see Emilie."

With a nod, Andromeda left the room. "Yes, but first we need to chat. I'll let you get dressed, unless you want help?"

The sharp look Dani gave her had her backing out of the room and closing the door behind her. Dani was stubborn enough that getting changed wasn't a team sport. It probably should have been if the ache in her arms from pulling on jeans and a fresh shirt were any indication. Motivation to see Emilie gave her strength. She tucked her charms under her shirt, but that was as far as her energy took her. She was still wobbly on her feet, but every step got easier. Still, when she opened the door and Andromeda waited on the other side, relief flooded her. "You keep looking at me like I'm some kind of science experiment."

"It happens."

"It happens?" Dani snuck a look down the hall to make sure they were still alone. "This—" She gestured to her side. "—this does not just happen. Not without some serious mojo. Serious, serious mojo."

Andromeda clucked her tongue. "I told you, woman of many gifts. The blade kept you alive, and I made an executive decision to put you back together again."

Dani chewed her lip, watching the sentinel, waiting for the other shoe to drop. She'd always figured herself as a decent judge of character—necessary when half of the job was reading people—but the sentinel standing in front of her didn't make any of her internal bells and whistles go off. She wanted to trust the woman. Hell, she owed Andromeda her life. But there was something she was holding onto, and Dani figured it had to be a bombshell of epic magnitude. "Fine. I asked inside, but exactly how long was I out?"

"Better part of a week. Tonight would have made it five days."

"Five DAYS?" Dani braced herself against the wall. "How is that even possible?"

"Magic." Andromeda smiled beatifically. "Besides, after we got you stabilized you were the easy one."

"The easy one?" Dani felt her stomach clench, and she blanched.

"I told you. All hell is breaking loose out there." Andromeda tipped her head.

"And now it's time to chat about it." Dani grit her teeth, held tight to her composure.

"Look, this isn't the way I'd have done it, but we are outta options. Phillip, Ephraim, Merc and..." Andry clenched her teeth but continued in a harsh whisper. "...and we need to catch you up."

Her stomach dropped at Emilie's exclusion from that group. "And what? A cute little chat is how we do it? Drop the cloak and dagger bullshit, why don't you? You said Emilie is here, but is she all right?"

"She's sleeping. A lot has happened." Andromeda's nose flared as she glared at Dani. "We're still in the Lockgrove house because it's the safest place in town. You have your weapons and your own clothes. But half measures won't cut it, and we need to get you up to speed."

The woman in her wanted to demand to see Emilie first, but the hunter in her knew they had to debrief. "Fine." Dani waved her arm, gesturing for Andromeda to lead the way. The sentinel waited for a long beat, scoffed, and walked down the hallway. Dani followed, keeping close to the wall in case her legs tried to give out on her.

Andromeda turned into the dining room, and Dani took an extra moment to compose herself. The burble of low conversation died off as she entered. Merc, Andromeda, and Ephraim all had seats at the long wood table. In the doorway to the kitchen was a tall, slim man with dark eyes and white-blonde hair. Looking at him, she knew this had to be Phillip Lockgrove, and she locked eyes with him, glaring balefully. If things had been different, she'd have read him the riot act, but she wanted to get this over with so she could make sure Emilie was okay with her own two eyes. Phillip sneered at her like she was a bug to be squashed, and Dani wished she'd brought the veil-blade out with her.

"Welcome back." Ephraim's thin lips quirked into a small smile that accentuated the wrinkles around his eyes, and he gestured to an empty chair. For a second, she just stood there, tempted to keep standing out of sheer spite.

"I hear everyone wants to have a little chat." She pulled out a chair and dropped into it with a scowl. Her side pulled at her, sharp pain that stole her breath, not that she was about to share that information.

"A lot has happened."

"Stop saying that! I get it!" Her free hand beat a staccato rhythm on the wooden table. She wanted to get up, pace, anything to keep from sitting still, but for once, she listened to the throb of her body as it attempted to knit itself back together. "I want to know what happened, all of it."

The room went silent, quiet enough that Dani could pick out the breathing of the others. And then it exploded as everyone started talking at once.

"We got stuck dealing with—"

"I saw the fire from the road but—"

"By then everything was going up—"

"...time I got there—"

"One at a time! C'mon guys! I know this isn't your first rodeo," Dani snapped.

Ephraim held up a hand, and everyone else in the room went quiet and let him take the lead. "After you and Emilie left for the hospital, I received a call from a contact with Phillip's whereabouts." His lips thinned as he glanced at his son. "When I found him, we hightailed it back to town, but I saw the fire from the road, rerouted to the hospital, but by the time I got there the blaze was out and you two were gone." He nodded to Merc.

"We got stuck dealing with an incident on the far side of town. A rock slide, not enough to cause much damage..."

"But enough to block the road from being used." Andry's eyes flashed. "There's barely any signal over that way." She met Dani's eyes.

An explanation for their lack of communication, which, okay, was fair. But it didn't make Dani any fonder of her.

"By the time we got back to town, everything was going up in flames. Andry and I split up. I went to get Ephraim and Phillip across town," Merc said and nodded to his sister.

"And I went back to make sure our building didn't go up, where you found me."

"So it was what? A perfect frickin' storm to keep everyone distracted while he cornered Emilie?" She slapped the table with a snarl. "I was with her when Spectre killed Elizabeth, or did you just forget about your other granddaughter? I got her back here, and we couldn't get in touch with any of you. Do you have any idea what that was like?"

"I can't imagine what that was like for you, but please, don't think my grace under pressure has anything at all to do with the lives of my granddaughters. Vincent has been playing this game for a very long time with the lives of people I love, and he caught us." Ephraim's voice was even, but fire blazed in his eyes.

Dani sat back in her chair and looked Ephraim dead in the eye. Stuck in this room filled with perfectly good explanations, they were still skirting around who wasn't in the room. "If you care so much, then where is Emilie? Did she even make it back to the house, or are you lying to me about that?" Dani looked around, gesturing.

"I'm not going to put up with this nonsense," Phillip announced from his perch.

"Nonsense? I ask if your daughter is alive, and it's nonsense?" She whipped to look at Phillip again and really wished he'd give her an excuse to punch him.

"She'd have been fine if she just stayed at home." His voice was prim, and he stared down his nose at her, nostrils flaring as if he smelled something foul.

"What happened to Emilie is *on you*." Ephraim's kind demeanor had vanished. His voice whipped through the room as ice coated the chair and the table in front of him. "*You* tricked her into the binding and hid *everything* from her! Be glad you are my son because anyone else would pay for a transgression of such depth." Ephraim stood with a loud clatter as a chair fell over.

Dani sucked in a breath and scooted back from the table, wide eyed. Phillip cowered to the edge of the room, and Andromeda scooted closer to her brother. Ephraim continued to glare at his son while he grabbed his chair and sat back down. The ice was melting or evaporating against the table as though it had never been there to begin with. She knew he was a powerhouse talented, but seeing it in person punctuated the point.

"Where is Emilie?" Dani's voice sounded quiet after the pissing match between the Lockgrove men, but it carried. She didn't give a rat's ass about their squabble. She wanted to make sure her little medium was okay.

Ephraim collapsed with a sigh, and Phillip wilted even further. Merc's eyes slotted to his sister, and her eyes went to the ceiling.

"Emilie is upstairs. She didn't wake back up."

"What exactly do you mean?"

"She means that when Spectre saw Emilie, and Emilie saw Spectre, the binding snapped, snapped the exact way I was trying to avoid." Ephraim shook his head.

"She's in a kind of...magical coma," Andry explained gently. "We can't wake her up. The only person who can do that is Emilie, but..."

"But? What the hell is 'but'?"

Merc reached across the table and grabbed his sister's hand before looking at Dani. "But the longer she's under, the less likely she wakes up. Same as any coma."

"I see."

Dani clenched her fists against the leg of her jeans, trying to control herself and gauge the responses of everyone around her. None of this was okay. There was no way of even knowing if Spectre could be properly killed, but she bet if she cut him into pieces and put every piece in a lead and silver-lined box, it would take him decades to put himself back together.

If Emilie didn't wake up from this, or if she woke up wrong, it would be the least of what she would do to him. And when she finished with him, her piece-of-work father could answer for his sins. That woman had never screwed over anybody, not truly. She didn't deserve a lifetime trapped inside her own mind like a prison.

"Oh, I wouldn't go underestimating my Emilie," Ephraim said, not unkindly. "Girl has a stubborn streak a mile wide and three deep. She needs time to put herself back together, same as you did. Her wounds are simply harder to see."

"This is a thing? I mean, don't get me wrong, but none of this seems okay. How is she even alive right now?" Dani looked from one person to the next.

"This happens," Merc said in a kind voice. "Bindings are not small things." He shot Phillip a nasty look. "And Emilie's was a complicated affair. When it snapped, it broke her mind, and unless she can put it back together, she won't wake up. She's alive because Andromeda is very skilled at what she does." The compassion in his voice bled through.

She shook her head and jumped to her feet, pacing back and forth. Her side throbbed, sharp and vicious, and this time she couldn't help the wince that broke her face in half. A slow, painful moment made her sit back down, and a readjustment eased the pain, but there was no forgetting about it, no way to hide it from the room. Andromeda scowled and raised an eyebrow.

"I need to take a look at your side." She stood up and crossed the room until she was leaning against the table looking down at Dani.

The hunter knew that look, intimately. Every hunter who had gotten laid up and needed help to get back on their feet knew it. It didn't matter whether it was a doctor, nurse, whatever. Every person with a knack for putting people back together got that gleam in their eye when a charge was acting up before they were back on their feet. "Yeaaah, I figured that was only a matter of time."

"Hey now. I was nice. I let you get all caught up first. C'mon, lemme take a look while this lot make a late breakfast, hmm?" Andromeda motioned for Dani to head back to her sick room.

She rose and left the table, but not because she planned on going back to her sick room. "Let me see Emilie, then I'll rest."

The walk up to the second floor seemed to take forever. Emilie was too small and pale in the big bed. Dani stood in the doorway, watching her for a few minutes, trying to settle her nerves. She wanted to sit down on the bed, talk to Emilie, beg her to wake up.

Instead, she stepped inside and took a seat next to the bed. The little medium looked so small, so frail, and Dani hated it. Emilie was stubborn, not some waif to waste away outside of her body. She swiped at her face with one hand and leaned forward on her knees.

"Hey, killer." Her voice cracked a little, and she cleared her throat. "Sorry it's been a few days. I went down hard, but I'm back now. So, if you're still in there, we need you back too. I told you I'd protect you from Spectre, so you need to let me keep that promise." She nodded more to herself than anyone else.

One hand reached across the bed, ghosting over Emilie's knuckles in a facsimile of an embrace. "We're not gonna let him get away with this, okay? So come back when you can. We'll be here. *I'll be here.*" She exhaled long and slow.

Andromeda was waiting out in the hallway, and no doubt she'd heard all of this, but right now, Dani didn't care. Seeing Emilie laid out like this was shifting her priorities, but one thing stayed the same.

Spectre had to die. She wouldn't let him be the reason she'd lost two people.

Her examination didn't take long, but one look beneath the bandages made it all real somehow. The ragged wound that had tried to kill her looked like something healed years ago. White scar tissue in a knot at the side of her abdomen, small spiderweb cracks of white and pale pink stretching across the taut brown flesh of her stomach.

"I get magic and bladesingers, or whatever. But seriously, how the fuck am I alive?" Dani didn't mince words between the two of them the way she would have out in the dining room.

"You're not gonna like the answer."

"Why is that?"

"Because I don't have a clear one." Andromeda's lips twisted as she poked and prodded at tender flesh. "Bladesingers heal faster than mundanes. It's like a...weird line of magic, but it's nothing you can control the way a talented does."

"Well, I don't like that at all."

"I told you." Andromeda clucked her tongue with a dark look. "You're mostly healed up. Compared to when you went down...well, you're in good shape. A few more hours, maybe another day or so, and you should be back to new. But you need to take it easy until then."

"So the pain is what? Gonna disappear if I take a nap?"

"Basically." Andromeda shrugged. "You're healing as soon as you take a hit. Sleeping just makes it easier for your body, since it doesn't have as much to deal with. You also need to eat. Fuel and all that. I'd bring you a plate, but I have a feeling that getting you to lie back down is gonna be like pulling teeth, so you can come grab something from the kitchen if you want." She walked to the door in a fluid motion. "There's more to delve into, anyway."

With a pointed look, Andromeda departed. More to take in, as though Emilie being in a magic-ass coma wasn't enough. She pulled up her tank again and looked at the scar on her stomach. That should have been the product of months' worth of healing. She'd watched hunters bleed out and die in minutes from a hit like that. How had her guts even stayed in her damn body? Not to mention the infection she should have picked up from dragging herself across the damn ground?

Dani snorted and let her shirt drop back down. They'd walked right into his trap. He'd known Emilie would spiral after the hospital, and he chased them back to town. Spectre had known she wouldn't be able to get in touch with anyone, thanks to the gas main and the rock slide, and timed everything so that Emilie would insist on finding help to break the binding.

So that he could break it for her. But why? None of it tracked. He wanted Emilie, but she'd been right there. He could have killed all three of them if he'd wanted. Not without a fight, sure, but his wraiths had been nasty enough. So why just break the binding? What was she missing? She could feel Spectre breathing down her neck, waiting for the final pieces to fall into place.

26

DANI

Dani walked out front, hoping fresh air would clear her head. No such luck. It'd turned dark as the middle of the night, even though it was still a few hours until dusk. The wind carried the smell of death and fire, ashes in a silver-grey cyclone that danced across the yard. Standing there, the weight of this job bore down on her.

Upstairs, Emilie still slept. If she could call a coma sleeping. Being outside was better than being in the house, but not by much. Inside, Emilie's people were at each other's throats. Out here the air was charged with something, a storm brewing that didn't have anything to do with weather.

After the conversation this morning, she'd eaten, taken another nap, and woken up to murmured conversations and worried looks. Andromeda and Merc stayed huddled together as they muttered in the green room, while Ephraim and Phillip sat with Emilie as though their presence could will her awake. But she knew better. Even now, Emilie was right where Spectre wanted her. Dani didn't know why, but truthfully, it didn't matter in the long run.

Spectre was a monster, and he wanted Emilie. She might have tried to fight back, but she hadn't been built for fighting. She was made for a life around real people, ones who lifted their faces to the sun, took vacations, and spent days at the beach, those who lived lives that existed beyond the shadows. Dani counted her life in hunts. What could a woman like Emilie know about this kind of life? Worse, there was no way she could possibly want it.

Hunters didn't follow normal rules. They didn't get sunshiny days or vacations on the water. They got an arsenal, nightmares, and the rock-solid understanding that their sacrifice meant people like the ones inside didn't have to get their hands dirty.

That fact should have made her angry, or desperate, or bitter, something. That it didn't was more proof she'd been born, bred, and trained for this life. A life where magic put her back together and she was more alive in the moments bleeding out than she had been in months. The urge to walk back into the house and crack open a cold beer, let the alcohol glaze everything for a few brief minutes, was intense, but that would have to wait until she was out of Dawson and Spectre was another name on her list of dead monsters. It would have to wait until she got retribution for Graham, for the parents she'd never gotten to know, for all of it. He'd killed so many. He'd almost killed her. She wasn't about to let him kill Emilie too.

She'd stand against him to her last breath if that's what it took, same way as her family had before her, the hunters, bladesingers, whatever. They were people willing to pick up a weapon, put themselves wholly in front of the monster, and put it in the damn ground. Like everything else, it would fall to her, alone. As always, she was left standing alone.

"It's not safe out here," Merc said.

"Not safe anywhere." She shot him a quick glance back over one shoulder and then turned her face back to the yard. "But here we are."

"I noticed you didn't spend much time upstairs with Emilie." He crossed the space between them, lounging next to her.

"Not much point. She ain't there right now." Dani turned and caught a better look at Merc.

He was trying to play it casual, but it wasn't working. He never moved much, still as stone. There was something different now though, as though he were waiting for something. She followed his eyes across town where the orange halo of fires still burned. It seemed like every time the fire department got one handled, another appeared. Folks were leaving Dawson fast as their cars could take them. The talented hunkered down, waiting to see where the chips lay when it was all said and done.

"She's still alive, Dani."

"Yeah. Alive and trapped inside her mind. She might wake up in five minutes, she might never wake up. No way to tell, right?" She raised one eyebrow and sent him a cold look.

"You aren't wrong..."

"I'm right. You know it, and I know it. Same as we know that those fires that the firefighters can't put out are Spectre. It's just a matter of time 'til he shows up here looking for his prize." Dani chewed her lip and rocked on her heels.

"So what do you propose we do?" He gestured with a wide arm down at the traffic visible from up here on the hill. "Run like them? Load Emilie into a car and flee?"

"Course not." Dani rolled her eyes. A few roads over, she watched as lights flicked on and then popped back off again. "But sitting and waiting like she's gonna wake up and know what's going on ain't the play either." She rolled her shoulders in vain, an attempt to shift some weight off of them.

"Spectre can't be killed."

"That's what they say." She laughed, a dark broken sound. "Say he's been shot, stabbed, burned, drowned...the works." Dani smiled, a violent gesture. She could see in his eyes, the way he shifted his weight away from her, that her expression unnerved him.

Good. He should be scared, him and anyone else who tries to stop me. "But there's another way, I think. You cut him up into enough pieces, be mighty hard to put himself back together."

"You can't be serious." Merc's eyes went wide at the prospect.

"Can't I?" Dani threw her hands up and pivoted to look Merc in the eye. "I don't know whether it's because you're a sentinel, or it's this damn town, but either way, y'all are willing to what? Hunker down and hope for the best? Wish Emilie back awake again?"

"Sentinels can't interfere." He swore. "You don't get it. Hunters never seem to get it. We're bound to the land we protect and watch over, but our abilities? They cut out if we step out of line."

"Didn't seem to bother Andromeda when she was saving my life."

"Yes, please." He hissed the words between gritted teeth. "Do tell me about how my sister flaunted her abilities."

"So you'd prefer I died?"

"No. That's not—" He pinched the bridge of his nose and sighed. "She'll get away with it, or she'll pay the price. Only time will tell. And she has more leeway anyway, with her talents. But we can't fight back against Spectre unless he attacks one of us direct. We try to and our abilities will fry us."

"You're serious."

"Deadly."

"Well. Explains a little." Dani didn't want to offer him solace, didn't want an olive branch extended. Whatever he might say, sentinels existed for balance. She didn't give a rat's ass about balance. "But sure, whatever. You can't leave and your hands are tied. But theirs?" Her eyes flipped up to the second floor where Ephraim and Phillip sat watch over Emilie's body. "He's gonna come for her. Maybe not today, but soon. And when he does? Somebody has to stop him."

"You think that's you?"

"Do we have another choice? I have the veilblade, and if you and your sister are right, I'm a bladesinger, so I might as well own it."

"The wards will keep her safe."

"Not forever, not from him."

"How do you know?"

"Do you know what hunters call Spectre? They call him the bogeyman. The friggin' bogeyman, Merc. He will burn them out like he's burned out every Deveraux since Amelia escaped his clutches two hundred years ago." Dani shook her head and wrapped one hand around the hilt of the veilblade strapped to her hip. "He doesn't get to win. And he doesn't get her."

"And if you die in the process?"

"Then I die." She spat the words out. "You think I'm afraid of dying? You think this was my first close call? Most hunters don't last ten years if they keep going. I've been hunting the things in the dark for fourteen. It's only a matter of time 'til my number comes up, but if I take him down with me, it's worth it."

The front door creaked as it opened behind them. "I always forget how willing you lot are to sacrifice yourselves," Phillip said as he walked out. "But then it takes what it takes, now doesn't it?" He craned his head and looked down the road. "You won't be alone. I've seen to that much, at least."

"What does that even mean?" Dani looked back over her shoulder, bewildered.

Walking up the hill along the road was a figure silhouetted against the darkness by the shallow pools of light cast by the streetlights. Battle-scarred leathers covered her lean body from neck to ankle, and a long blade rested in its sheath along one leg. Dark hair, cut rakishly short, framed a hard, but beautiful face. Though Dani had never met her before, she knew exactly who she was. Every hunter around knew who she was. Valkyrie was known far and wide. If Spectre was the bogeyman, she was as close as it got to an avenging angel.

"I brought some backup," Phillip said.

"Yeah, I'd say." Dani frowned and turned. "You know Valkyrie?"

Next to her, Merc choked, and an emotion she didn't recognize slid across Phillip's face for an instant before it smoothed back out to that mask. She wanted to ask again but knew it wouldn't do her any good. She thumped Merc on his back until he caught his breath and then pinned Phillip with a deadpan glare until he answered.

"We're acquainted." He smiled faintly, but it looked almost plastered onto his face.

"Maybe there's something decent about you after all." She turned back to the yard, watching Valkyrie's graceful ascent.

27

EMILIE

When she'd woken up last time, free of form or shape or substance, Emilie hadn't known who she was. Or where or what or...any of it. Now she had everything, memories slotting themselves back into place as she rebuilt who she was.

She'd thought that maybe, once she had everything back, she'd wake up, open her eyes in her own body and...what? She didn't know what she expected to happen next. But she wasn't fully in her body anymore. Slowly, breath by breath, she drifted away towards the veil. The veil, the in-between, the river Styx, it had plenty of different names, but they all came down to the same thing. This was the place where a person crossed from life to death. Most people only saw what lingered beyond the veil when they passed over. Even the veil itself was closed off for most people most of the time. Not mediums though. They had one foot in the real world, one beyond in the darkness of death. A living person who straddled the great divide.

That meant she could feel both her connection to the dark maw of death and the strand of vibrance that connected her to the land of the living. Unless she tuned in, it was easy enough to ignore the voices of the spirits lost to the in-between. Usually it stayed quiet here, away from the madness of the real, the hustle of lives being lived every moment.

Something else kept interrupting the calm, shrill screams that broke the silence every few minutes, Amelia's cries, an animal with its leg stuck in a trap. They made everything vibrate when they reverberated through the space before cutting off for a few minutes at a time.

When they came, the screams were deafening, and she had no way to tune them out. It sent everything off-kilter and destroyed the balance until down was up and left was right. Emilie winced as they started again but tracked the noise to its source. It was one thing to know that it was Amelia Deveraux, tormented and trapped, another entirely to hear her scream, a noise more inhuman than anything Emilie had ever heard before. Spirits chose, in the beginning at least, to stay in the veil. For some it was unfinished business or a violent death. For others, it was the need to continue watching over friends and family.

Amelia lacked the luxury of that choice. She'd run from Spectre, tried to escape him, but the blood curse that kept him from dying also kept her from crossing over. Emilie concentrated on the source of the scream and moved toward it. Mist obscured everything around her until it didn't.

Suddenly, a floor of dark glass stretched far ahead. A worn crypt sat in the middle of it, one wall wet with blood. In front of the crypt sat the sunken form of a woman, her skin withered with gaping wounds, her long hair dry as straw.

The screams cut off the moment Emilie's feet touched the floor. Amelia unfurled from her heap on the ground to a standing position and watched Emilie as she approached. Her eyes were hungry predator eyes, but there was still a gleam of something that had been human in them. Healed wounds striped her long skeletal limbs white against the brown, aged skin.

With every step forward, the years peeled off Amelia. The husk of a woman gained muscle and fat, until she looked like she had in life. Emilie's heart stopped in her chest. The resemblance was uncanny. From behind long, white-blonde hair, pale blue eyes watched her with the weight of two centuries. Now she understood why Spectre had let her live so long, why he hadn't lashed out or tried to snare her sooner. He had other plans for her.

Spectre wouldn't give up on *his* medium so easily. So he'd snared Amelia as she died, trapped her here in the veil. Unable to escape him in death, her magic kept him from passing over to follow her. Around one ankle a dark chain of magic held her tight, links driven deep into the glassy ground they stood on. Mediums were rare enough. A medium capable of becoming a conduit? They were once a generation.

"You're Amelia."

"I am? I was. I am." She nodded her head and looked at Emilie like she was a tasty morsel.

"I heard you scream."

"Did you? I think my throat should hurt from screaming so much. But then I'd need a body, and I don't have one. This form is a lie." She gestured to herself. "But he can't reach me here. Fair is fair. I might be trapped, but at least I never have to worry about that." A dark fire lit her eyes. "Not until they try to hurt him, anyway."

"Spectre did this to you? Trapped you in this...place?"

"Spectre?" She cocked her head. "Vincent Hawthorne keeps me here." She spat the words out like poison in her mouth. "He had tricks nobody had seen in decades. But he didn't know what I could do." Amelia paused. "Maybe I didn't know either."

"How did he do it?" Emilie took a few steps closer. "Keep you here?"

"*And never the twain shall meet.*" Amelia looked behind her at her own blood staining the stone of the crypt. She pointed with her chin to a tether around her ankle. "The tether keeps me here. Unable to pass across the river to whatever waits. My curse ensures he can never truly *have* me."

"That's why he can't die." The words slammed into Emilie's chest. Amelia had run from him, but not fast enough, never fast enough. He hadn't been able to catch her, not all the way, just enough to keep using her and keep her trapped.

"He doesn't want to die." Amelia looked around and then continued in a hushed voice. "He wants me to break the curse, but I won't, and the Valkyrie won't. Only a bladesinger can cleave the link, and she won't give him the satisfaction."

"You'd be free." Emilie shook her head. "You'd be able to escape him for good—"

"He could use a medium to call me into their body and lock me there if I pass. I won't do it. I'd rather live out hell in this place." She waved her arms around. "Do you understand? He wants to use you to channel me. Has since the first time he got eyes on you."

"Because I look like you?"

"Amongst other things." Amelia's face shifted, intense eyes too wide in a pale face. "Hiding is the only way."

"No."

"You have to hide."

"No." Emilie stamped her foot and shook her head wildly. "We can kill him, Amelia. For good."

"He'll find me, in the after."

"That's not how it works."

"You don't know."

"I know that no way do you both end up in the same place."

"You need a bladesinger, one who wasn't corrupted like Valkyrie. They're all dead, dead, DEAD! They're dead and passed and I'm trapped here and now, FOREVER!" Amelia's words tripped over each other, coming faster and faster as she started to scream again. A wind cold as the grave swirled in the air around Emilie, arcing her hair into a halo that whipped at her face.

"There is one who can sever the link."

Amelia calmed for a second, if only to argue. "That is no guarantee."

"Daniella Black, daughter of Valerie Black and Ben Black, heir to the first line."

"The Valkyrie's daughter lives." The wind cut out immediately, leaving them once again in an artificial silence, Amelia's voice more hushed than it had been a moment ago. "Fitting then, that she should cleave the bond that holds me here. But Vincent always has a trick up his sleeve. To end him, once and for all, it will take more than a death of the body."

Emilie waited a beat and then answered, heart in her throat. "Tell me."

28

DANI

Downstairs, Dani heard the murmur of voices as Phillip and Valkyrie spoke with the sentinels. She'd come upstairs intending to sit with Emilie for a little while. The room had been occupied, so she'd kept on walking up to the third floor.

It was quieter here than anywhere else in the house, and for the first time in hours she was alone. So much of her life had been spent by herself or with a handful of other people. Being around so many people she didn't know made the hair at the back of her neck stand up.

The tiny fights breaking out between everyone weren't helping either. All of them crashed up against each other as they tried to figure out what came next and whether Emilie was ever going to wake up again. It was only a matter of time until Spectre came for her, and when he did, they didn't really have a plan on what they were going to do.

"I'm not sure where I'm supposed to go next." She spoke out loud to Graham, even though he wasn't there. "I can't wake her up, and I can't hunt him down. I mean, if Valkyrie and her veilblade can't handle him, who am I to think I can?" She rubbed a hand across her jaw, and then touched her veilblade, slung onto her hip.

"What do you think of an old man's opinion then?" Ephraim Lockgrove strolled into the room, looking curious.

"Your reputation does kind of precede you," Dani admitted grudgingly.

Ephraim walked farther into the room, carrying a bottle of whiskey and two tumblers filled with ice.

"Good to know. I'd hate to think I somehow lost my edge." His voice was jovial, but there was something more in his eyes.

Dani almost said no. She wasn't used to dealing with people his age, although the Lockgrove patriarch wasn't anything like any other septuagenarians out there walking the streets. Then again, he'd brought a bottle. How was she supposed to say no?

"Done fighting with Phillip for the moment?" She raised an eyebrow.

"He deserves it." Ephraim shrugged and took a seat on the floor. He poured two fingers of whiskey into each glass and offered her one.

Dani took the glass and sat down across from Ephraim. "So to what do I owe the honor of a one-on-one with Ephraim Lockgrove with..." She paused long enough to savor a sip of her drink "With damn good whiskey?"

He opened his mouth to say something but started coughing. Quickly, he covered his mouth with a handkerchief from his pocket. When he pulled it away, it was speckled scarlet. Dani opened her mouth to ask a question, and Ephraim held up a hand. When he sat back up, his eyes were cloudy with pain.

"As you might be able to tell, I'm not in what anyone would call good health." He smiled, but it was faint and thin.

"Emilie mentioned something about it." Dani narrowed her eyes.

"She doesn't know the extent of it. Neither does Phillip." He took a long sip from his drink.

"And you're telling me? That's messed up." Dani shook her head and took another drink.

"That's neither here nor there. There was always a better-than-average chance that Emilie breaking the binding would start something catastrophic." He smiled and drained his glass, holding it up to the light. "I...wasn't there to protect her after the attack on her mother. I did everything I could, but so long as there was time, I let her stretch it."

"You're out of time."

"I think that's rather evident, yes." He paused and then poured another glass for himself. "I believe that you have an idea for how to protect Emilie from Spectre, how to put him down, and if I can, I'd like to help." He took another sip from the glass.

Dani watched him, barely touching her own glass as he spoke. "How?"

The word reverberated in the space between them. Merc and Andry, and even Valkyrie, had their own motives for the way this would play out. Maybe when she'd started this job, it was to destroy Spectre, but protecting Emilie was at the top of that list too.

"To kill him will mean two fronts," Ephraim explained. "That's why no hunter has ever been able to finish the job. It can't be just his body. Someone will have to force him across the river."

Dani shook her head. "No. I mean that's...that's a death warrant."

"It is." Ephraim laughed and coughed into his handkerchief again. "But I'll be dead in a few months either way."

"This isn't just the kind of thing you spring on someone."

"You know that's what I told my doctor, but here we are." He threw back the rest of his glass and then set it down between them.

"Why me? Of all the people in this house..."

"Because you're a hunter." His eyes skittered away from hers as he said it, but Dani let it go.

"Valkyrie is a hunter."

"Only in the strictest sense. She allowed the magic of the veil-blade and...tragedy, to strip away the human part of herself, the part that made her a hunter and not...what she is."

"I'm not really sure what you mean." Dani finished what was left in her glass and set it on the floor.

"That's a question she'd need to answer." Ephraim frowned and clenched his kerchief in one hand. "You'll make sure that Emilie gets through this. She deserves so much more than the hand that she was dealt."

"I think that's something we can agree on." Dani nodded. "There's something about her." She chuckled again. "Look Ephraim, I can't...I can't promise anything. That's not part of the gig, you know?" She jumped up and paced from one side of the room to the other. "All I can promise is that I'll do my best."

He met her eyes solemnly, and Dani couldn't help but notice how much like Emilie's they looked.

THE DINING ROOM had turned into a war room as they read and reread all the information available, seeking a way to protect Emilie and kill Spectre. Dani didn't think that there was a silver bullet hiding somewhere in old notebooks or historical diaries of talented who had lived and died in fear of the bogeyman. That didn't stop her from trying to figure something out. Phillip had joined her for this session, both of them flipping through page after page of research.

"You aren't going to find the answer to any of your questions in a book," Valkyrie spoke up from the doorway.

Dani pushed back from the table and turned to watch the other woman.

"Spectre worked very hard to try to wipe out any details of who he is behind the mask, how he's alive, why he won't die."

"Tell us something we don't know." Dani shook her head.

"He doesn't want to kill Emilie. He wants to use her, and that makes him far more dangerous."

"Does it?" Phillip asked. "Either way, she's gone."

"The difference is who else leaves this encounter with a pulse. Spectre leaves behind bodies. He always has." Her eyes met Dani's for a moment before turning away.

"We need answers to make a plan." Phillip stood up and leaned back against the table as he tried to get Valkyrie on his side.

"Or we use my plan." Dani's voice was saccharine sweet. "If

Valkyrie and I carve him limb from limb, and cut off every finger on either hand, and remove his tongue...how does he cast?"

A deadly hush fell over the room. Nobody standing here was free of blood on their hands, but what Dani was proposing went the extra mile. In the past, the issue with Spectre was that once someone put him down, he didn't stay there. Her plan would make it impossible for him to put himself back together anytime soon. It was a twisted option, but the best one she'd been able to come up with.

"It's an option," Valkyrie acknowledged. "You'll be more effective than I am, anyway."

Dani cocked her head and made a confused face. "I'm not really sure how that's possible."

"You're an untainted bladesinger. Someone whose mantle is yet untouched by tragedy." Valkyrie's eyes alighted on Dani, and her gaze felt weighty, different somehow. "It gives your power an edge in some ways."

"And yours is corrupted—tainted?" Dani reached to the veilblade at her hip, taking comfort in its presence here.

"For a long time now. I had already taken up the mantle when Spectre killed my family and left me for dead. Had it happened before I took it on, things would have been different." Valkyrie frowned and looked over to Dani before turning on her heel and walking back out of the room again.

Dani jumped to her feet and followed her into the hallway, where she ran into Merc. Valkyrie had disappeared somewhere out of sight. He raised an eyebrow and then drew her back into the greenroom gently.

"Look, there's something here you need to know." He looked down at his hands and then met her eyes again. "Your mother? Valerie Black? She and Valkyrie are the same person—in a manner of speaking, anyway."

Dani's head snapped back out to the hallway. "What am I supposed to do with that?" She wobbled but managed to keep her balance.

Phillip appeared in the doorway to join them, looking kinder than

Dani had seen him up until this point. His eyes alighted on Merc, and then flickered to her, his face caught somewhere between pain and exhaustion.

"Ah. It's time is it?" He nodded. "Valerie Black, when she was still Val, was the kind of hunter they tell stories about. She was born and raised here. My father knew her from the day she was born until the day she disappeared into the night."

"You said when she was still Val." Dani's voice wavered, but it sounded like it was coming from far away. As though she were barely attached to herself in this moment.

Phillip nodded slowly. "I did."

"Could you be more cryptic?" Dani frowned, hand clenched in a fist to ground her here.

"Valerie Black left Dawson the night that Spectre tried to kill her and succeeded in killing your father, Ben." He licked his lips. "She went underground and nobody ever saw her again. But not long after, a bladesinger more vicious than any in over a century showed up."

"Valkyrie." In Norse mythology, the Valkyrie were handmaidens of Odin. They chose the warriors who lived and those who were killed and admitted to Valhalla. Seeing Valkyrie in person, she understood the name.

"Yes." Phillip watched Dani as the earth shifted and crumbled underneath her.

"My mother is dead. Spectre killed her." Dani fought the urge to stamp her foot, unable to wrap her mind around this new truth.

"Valerie is. The woman who was your mother, she died and Valkyrie was born."

"I still don't understand."

"Bladesingers don't die easy. But everything that made Val a person and not a weapon was stripped away from her. She lost her family, thought you'd died, and all she had was her weapon and the drive to kill Spectre."

Dani reached out a hand and grabbed the side of the table. She tried to steady herself as a kaleidoscope of information beat her about the head.

"I know this isn't easy."

"I don't think you have any idea what this feels like."

"Val was one of my friends, one of my best friends. When she died, I spent years trying to hunt her down and got nothing but rumors for my luck."

"She sure as hell showed up when you asked."

"About a month ago, I managed to track her down. We knew it was only a matter of time until the binding on Emilie failed. She was my Hail Mary."

"So you weren't here to help your daughter because you were chasing my mother across the country."

"More or less." He didn't meet Dani's eyes. "I have a file for you, a file and a journal."

"A file."

"Information. Sightings. Everything I managed to dig up after she disappeared. After you both disappeared."

She sighed, and it came out in a shiver, but there wasn't time to focus on her shit right now. Not when Spectre was on the horizon and Emilie was still unconscious. "Thank you...for telling me." Her eyes popped between the two men. "But my family drama can't be a priority right now. We don't have time." Dani swallowed and steeled herself. "I have a plan for how to deal with Spectre, but I need your help."

"I've told you before—"

"Yeah, yeah, yeah, rules blah blah." Dani waved her hand in the air. "Are you allowed to set a trap that would just funnel Spectre and anyone else, ensure there's only one way in, one way out?"

Merc turned his head. "Yeah, I think Andry and I could manage that." He nodded. "What did you have in mind?"

"We only have so many options, and with Emilie still out, those are limited. We can't go chasing him down, and it's only a matter of time until he comes. I just wanna know about and be able to control how he comes in, what he has access to."

The greenroom wasn't in the kind of shape it must have been once, but it still had a large wooden table with a recess filled with dirt. As she talked, Dani sketched out the house and surrounding area in the soil.

There was no choice but to compartmentalize what was going on. She couldn't follow Valkyrie, ask if she was the mother that Dani had dreamed of as a kid. Even though she had a pulse, if she understood Merc right, she'd traded becoming the Valkyrie and the abilities that came with that, for the life she'd had.

Dani couldn't imagine that kind of choice. Her life, her circle, had always been so small. Graham and Joe were family, and she had a few people she could loosely call friends. Losing Graham had unhinged something inside of Dani, left her spinning almost out of control. Coming here had been the one thing to set her straight, between finding the veilblade and running into Emilie.

What would it have taken for her to give up everything that remained and surrender to the hunt? Hadn't she wanted as much in the early days after losing Graham? She couldn't blame her mother, but she couldn't quite understand that kind of motive either.

"It could work, maybe." Merc's voice was rough, resigned to what came next.

Dani fixed them all with a hard, determined look. "I don't think we have any other choices at this point."

29

DANI

After speaking to everyone else in the house, and with dusk fast approaching, Dani was out of options. She'd come upstairs to check on Emilie one last time before everything started. There was no point in dwelling, but if her medium could hear her? It was worth the shot. But now, looking at the woman, it didn't seem right. She was too pale against white sheets, and her chest barely moved as she breathed. Watching her hurt Dani in a way she hadn't expected. This woman had gotten under her armor and touched something inside. How, she had no idea.

Dani pulled a chair close to the bed and tentatively touched the back of Emilie's hand. "I don't know if you can even hear me." She shook her head. "But if you can, then you should know, I think Spectre is coming for you. Maybe we can't kill him, but I have something that looks like a plan if you squint the right way."

She looked down at her hands, trying to find the right words, but they escaped her. This was why she hated sick rooms, always had. Even if this one was a far shot from the antiseptic smell of death that lingered in hospitals no matter how hard you tried to scrub it out.

"He's not gonna get you without a fight. Not while I've still got breath in me." She huffed out a short laugh. "Which I do, thanks to

Andromeda and my apparent healing abilities, the veilblade or what-ever." She tipped her head back. "Not even sure why I'm telling you all of this, to be honest. But we're gonna stop him, and I think we can do it. For real."

She wove her fingers through Emilie's. The pad of her thumb whispered over Emilie's knuckles, and she was struck by how frail the little medium seemed. Dani didn't know how the other woman had wormed her way past her defenses, but she had, and now things were confused. Was she here to protect Emilie, or kill Spectre? Both? Neither?

Outside, something bayed, almost a wolf but warped and distorted in tone. Dani nodded, stood up, and walked to the door. "That's last call, killer. I'll see you on the other side. Or I won't. But I'll do my best to make sure he doesn't get to you. Promise." She opened her mouth only to snap it shut again. There was plenty more to say, but she had a job to do. She leaned over and planted a gentle kiss on Emilie's forehead before walking out of the room.

It lacerated her heart, but the hunter did not look back.

IT WAS one of those perfect autumn nights, dark as dark could be, with clouds to obscure the moon and stars. Sitting on the front stair with a blade in her hand, Dani could feel the moment for what it was: calm before the storm. Usually she didn't notice the moments like this. She had to look back to recognize them.

The air had a sharp edge, wet from the storm moving toward them. It gave everything the tang of ozone, and in the distance over the mountains, lightning cracked across the sky.

In the darkness, it was hard not to twitch at every rustle of green-ery. But Andromeda and Merc had managed one final parting gift before they had to slink back into town where they'd ride out the storm. Sheer cliffs of granite would funnel the wraiths and Spectre up a specific route. Thanks to Andromeda's handy work, trees and bushes intertwined so deeply, not even a jackrabbit with a grudge could break through.

Something snarled from the path, and Dani slotted her eyes toward Phillip where he waited by the side of the house. Valkyrie had her own hiding place, both of them staying quiet until Spectre made his appearance. A moment later, the hum of several generators burst into life, followed by the lights. Bright pools of LED light washed over the yard and lit up every blade of grass.

A trio of wraiths stalked into sight, lupine heads mashed onto lean feline bodies, black as smoke with gold and grey markings seared into their skin. If the things hadn't been so damned terrifying, they might have been beautiful. They were all long sleek lines of muscle and sinew under fur and scales.

Dani let out a long breath. *Finally.* Around the back of the house, the telltale crack and sizzle of flesh meeting magic echoed. Phillip had laid traps all over the damn place, an easy way to make it clear to Spectre that there was only one way into the Lockgrove house now. She unfurled herself from where she'd been sitting on the front stairs, the comfortable weight of the veilblade strapped against her thigh.

She'd armed to the teeth for this fight, the shotgun in her hands and handguns tucked into shoulder holsters. Sweat prickled at the base of her spine. She sauntered into the light and smirked at the beasts where they stood.

"Well, well, well. Are y'all used to showing up uninvited or what?"

One of the beasts crawled forward, belly low as it brushed the grass. Dani stood her ground, watched, waited. Two larger wraiths emerged at her periphery. She imagined steel spikes had been driven through the toes of her boots, keeping her pinned in place.

Show no fear. Give no quarter. Graham's words, Joe's voice echoed through her ears and guided her hands for the showdown of her life.

One of the wraiths snarled low in its throat and raised all the hairs on her arms and the back of her neck. A tiny part of her that was always afraid screamed, begged her to run and flee and never

ever, ever look back again. It always had. And Dani always smothered it.

Fear could be useful, under the right circumstances. It told her when to fight and when to run. But when the chips fell, it couldn't help her, not as fear. She funneled it down and distilled all of that panic and fear into rage. It was a blinding, always burning pit in her stomach, her closest companion.

She heard the sound of heavy paws clawing through thick dirt, something large barreling at her full speed. A wraith the size of a bear roared at her side. Muscles in her thigh twitched, screamed to run, to duck, to move. To do anything! Dani grit her teeth and felt something in her cheek twitch.

The seconds slowed down, and she saw it all happen in slow motion. The wolf snarled, pale teeth in a dark maw, and she met its eyes, yellow and malevolent. Behind them something moved too fast for her to follow, just a blur that gleamed silver, and where it moved, blood gushed in great wild arcs. The smell of fur and sickness was deep in her nose, an overwhelming smell of being gutted that drifted into nothing as Valkyrie sliced it in twain before it smoked out and disappeared.

Two of the wolves dropped in twitching heaps before fading to nothing, and Dani rolled to the ground. A wraith sailed over her head. Before the impact of the ground could reverberate through her bones, she took a shot. Blood and viscera rained down on her, and she rolled to the side, boots digging into the earth as she lunged forward.

Behind her, the monster screamed in agony, but she didn't spare it another look. The weight of another body pressed into her back, and Valkyrie was in the fight.

"You're still up. Good. He'll be here soon." Valkyrie's voice was rough, but Dani heard the violent delight in it. The two of them were cut from the same cloth.

The grass at the edge of the yard bloomed with tiny flames that ran the perimeter. Around them, the prowling wraiths slowed. The air, thick with copper from the blood and bodies, stank. A high whining scream somewhere along the side cut out with another sizzle of magic. Dani took a step forward and away from Valkyrie, eyes tracking back and forth. One wolf dragged itself toward her, and Dani cracked off a shot. Its face disappeared into red mist.

She racked another round into her shotgun and knew it was her last. Valkyrie wandered through the clearing, a long sword flashing through the air as she finished off the wraiths. More howls, more screams, came from the woods and around the side of the house. Magic cracked in response, and she saw bright blooms of color smash against trees and ground alike.

The ground shuddered underfoot, and everything went quiet. Tendrils of shadow crawled their way into the light, long limbs of darkness that reached out and crept closer. Light curled around the edges, unable to penetrate it. Trees rustled and leaves fluttered to the ground even though there was no breeze to cause it.

"Game time," Dani muttered and looked just past the tendrils into the darkness, where a shape waited. "Afraid to come into the light, Spectre?" Her voice had a mocking edge to it.

"Why would the cat fear a mouse?"

"I'm not afraid of you." Lie number one.

"You should be." The hate in his voice slid over her in a hot wave.

He stepped out from the shadows, but they still clung to his broad shoulders, recoiling from the light and hiding in the folds of his clothing. Dani almost didn't recognize him. He had pulled his dark wavy hair back from a face with a strong jaw and straight nose. A tailored black suit with a black overcoat and a high collar completed the look.

He was a far cry from the monster she'd seen in Alabama. He looked less like he'd come for a fight and more like a suitor showing up for a date. Revulsion crawled through Dani's limbs, and she shivered theatrically, mouth pulled into a grimace. His eyes though, those were the same, dark pits of black burning with hatred and mad fire. He looked human. While he played the part well enough on the surface, those eyes gave him away.

"Should I though? I mean, you look like you showed up for a date, man. How fuckin creepy is that?" She shook her head.

He snarled, and the glamour over his features shimmered like a mirage before settling back into place.

"Oh, you can't be serious." She snickered. "Did you put on your finest suit to try to win Emilie over? Cause I kinda think you burned that bridge, and you're not exactly her type." She crinkled her nose. "You should really just go."

"You can't keep her from me."

"I mean, I can try. And the thing is, I'm pretty stubborn. Hell, it's why I'm here tonight, right? I mean, you tried to kill me a few nights ago." She smiled razor sharp. "Seems like it didn't take."

"Emilie will understand. She'll see there isn't any other way, and she'll come to me. And not you, nor anything else can stop me." He smiled, and it made Dani want to vomit.

"I told you, Vincent, my daughter isn't interested." Phillip strolled up from the side of the house, looking like a horror story, his white oxford shirt rolled up to his elbows, blood too bright to miss. It coated his hands and forearms, dripping to the ground. It gave him a savage air that made Dani's comments about going to war in a three-piece suit sting a little bit less.

One of Spectre's hands twitched, the first movement since he'd walked out of the darkness. His face transformed, a mask of rage, and for a second one eye was pure white before the glamour snapped back into place.

"Phillip, I thought I told you last time that if you got in my way, interfered in any way...I'd carve you piece from piece while you screamed the whole way down." He raised an eyebrow. "But I suppose idle threats don't help anyone. Where's Emilie in all of this? I didn't think she'd be too keen on you sacrificing yourself for her." Spectre beamed, and it lit up everything but his eyes. Hands spread wide, he took an easy step forward, and the grass wilted under his feet, sickness bleeding out into the ground.

Under his arms, a pair of wraiths slunk into sight, bellies low to the ground, cats again twining and pressing their dark furred bodies against one another. They formed a shield that would protect him against anything sudden. Dani imagined that in the trees there were dozens of them, all waiting for his signal to reveal themselves.

Spectre's smile turned feral, sharp at the edges as the glamour shuddered again. His eyes flickered past the three of them to the house before settling back onto Dani again. "Or is she still wandering among the shards of herself?" He chuckled. "Bindings can be tricky things now, can't they, Phillip?"

"It doesn't matter, you're not getting into that house," Phillip answered.

"And who will stop me, hmm? A corrupted bladesinger, a hunter, and a second rate talented?" He scoffed.

"Ah, ah, ah." Dani waggled her index finger at him. "No being rude now." She flipped the veilblade in one hand, catching it in a deft motion without tearing her eyes away from him. "After all, we aren't monsters. Well, I mean *we* aren't. You definitely are."

His good cheer vanished at the sight of the knife. It didn't have the searing glow that Valkyrie's curved blade did, but he recognized it. Good. She wanted him off his game. That way, when they started to carve him up, maybe they wouldn't all get immolated at once. It was the little things, really. To her side, Phillip murmured under his breath, and a ball of something formed in one gore-coated palm.

"You shouldn't have that." Spectre kept his eyes on Dani and the veilblade in her hand.

"I disagree." She winked and gestured down the line of her body. "Really just pulls things together outfit wise."

"You aren't going to be so cute when I tear you to pieces."

A wraith leaped toward her in punctuation. Valkyrie took two fluid steps forward and sliced through the thing in midair. Phillip threw a roiling ball of silver energy at Spectre, and it hit with an electric crack. He sneered, and a dark shield snapped into place, but fissures appeared as the shield protected him from the wave of magic that rolled over him.

A fireball exploded as the shield crumbled, flames bursting into life where Spectre had been standing. The light blew away the wraiths, more shadow and magic than flesh. Dani shielded her eyes and listened to him scream. She crouched down, knees bent, toes digging into the dirt. Spectre's scream was a wild sound that humans weren't supposed to make, ragged and shrill.

Around him, small beasts of fire burst into life, wraiths of a different kind altogether. The veilblade pulsed in her hand, and Dani threw herself into motion. Around her, magic crackled as Phillip threw another spell, and in her periphery, she saw the arc of Valkyrie's blade slicing through the fire imps. Dani didn't pay attention to any of that.

Slash, dodge, pivot, a deadly dance that counted time in ragged breaths, pointed out mistakes with death wounds. She'd been training to kill for as long as she could remember. The little fiery imps couldn't touch her.

They burst into smoke as her blade slid through them, a hot knife cutting through butter. An extension of her arm, the perfect weapon sliced through one monster after the next. She counted the breaths between each motion, her body moving on instinct, attuned to the burn as her muscles worked like a well-oiled machine.

She took every opportunity, seized every opening that the little firebugs gave her. The pulse of the blade centered her, made the crackle of burning knuckles and torn jeans inconsequential. It was a target-rich environment, but there were too many of the small devils in between her and Spectre. And he wasn't going to be down for long.

Another spell jumped through the air, and the ground swallowed a dozen of the mutated little monsters. Dani threw her body forward, ignored the burn of flame against exposed skin, and hit Spectre like a sledgehammer. Her shoulder rammed his solar plexus, and she rode him to the ground, veilblade slipping up and under his ribs.

They hit the ground in a tangle. Phillip reached down and grabbed her arm, helping her get away from him. The stab would have killed anyone human, but she watched the flesh knit itself as blood stopped flowing. Spectre started to laugh, blood dribbling out of his mouth.

"I told you. You. Can't. Kill. Me."

Spectre struggled back to his feet. The fight stripped away the glamours and protective spells. He smelled like the grave and looked more like a walking corpse than the handsome mask he'd shown up in.

But he didn't move like a corpse. He was faster than Dani had expected, and he hurled himself at the two of them. She tried to get her feet back under her and failed, legs tapping against the ground with no traction. All she saw was a shadow and a white blur coming at her face before Valkyrie's blade bit through his outstretched arm, severing it from the rest of his body.

He bled fire and shadows, magic connecting the severed limb to the rest of his body with an inky darkness. Against the darkness, Dani spotted a silver tether that hooked around the wrist still attached to his body.

Valkyrie's blade slashed out and ricocheted off the tether, sparks of magic flying, and for a second, Dani swore she heard Ephraim's voice in her ears. *The tether Dani. Break the damn tether!* She scrambled forward on all fours, and in a final desperate swipe, she lashed out. When the blade bit into it, the chill of death crept up her arm, and Spectre screamed, falling backwards. When he hit the ground, he stopped moving. Suddenly Dani could feel the raw ache and burn of the wounds she'd forgotten about in the fray.

The ground underfoot rumbled, and the house behind them groaned from the pressure, a wide fissure cracking up through the foundation. Another loud crack, and Dani watched as the wards that protected the house, and Emilie inside it, faded out.

30

EMILIE

"So that's it then." Emilie looked down at her hands and then back to Amelia. "I thought there was... I mean, I was supposed to be moving on with my life, getting answers, not..."

"This." Amelia nodded. "I know the feeling well."

Emilie blinked and felt the pull of her body from far away. She wondered if she'd ever feel the weight of her skin or the warmth of the sun on her face again. That was looking less and less likely.

Spectre...Vincent...had done so much damage over the years. Starting when he was a boy, he'd hunted Amelia to her death, kept her trapped here in between life and death, going mad because of it. He killed Mama and turned Lizzy into a trap. He killed Graham. So much murder and death and fire and mayhem. All because Amelia hadn't wanted him, because she had tried to escape and live her life. He'd kidnapped her, stalked her, and in the end, even death couldn't free her.

But Emilie could. For a price, she could end it, once and for all. She could assure that Spectre crossed the great divide so even his spirit couldn't break back through. The only question was whether she was willing to pay it. It was so much to ask of one person.

Amelia's voice had shaken when she explained what it would take, what had to be done to handle this. Spectre always had another ace hidden up his sleeve. Killing his body wouldn't get the job done. There was no way to ensure that he crossed the river and didn't lurk in the veil waiting for an opening, a body that he could inhabit until he could worm his way front and center.

No. To ensure that he stayed dead required more. It required a sacrifice, another soul, willing and able to drag him across the border to whatever fate awaited him. That fate didn't matter, not really. Dead was dead. At least once someone passed the veil. Even mediums couldn't reach that far. There was no way to tell what would happen.

"You can't ask me to do this. It's not—it's not fair!" The words exploded out of Emilie.

She wanted to scream. She wanted to run back to her body and keep running for as many years as she could hide from Spectre. It wasn't her time to die, not yet. There was so much she'd wanted to do, and see, and experience, but now it tasted like ashes in her mouth. More than anything, she wanted to explore the possibilities between her and Dani. Something inside that woman drew her like the sun, and she couldn't imagine leaving her. But what kind of life would they have on the run? Dani had been running for so long. It wouldn't be fair to her.

She could either trade her life for Spectre's, or spend a lifetime running from every shadow with every new death weighing down on her conscience. She knew firsthand the devastation he'd wreak trying to hunt her down, but she could be the last one, the last Deveraux medium—the only person who could channel Amelia and let him win his prize.

If she did this, she could rob him of that.

It was the only way. To be sure, she'd have to walk across the Styx and pass through everything the veil offered. It meant cutting her life short and taking him with her along the way. He'd never kill someone else's mother, take their best friend, or leave their sister behind. She could protect them, those nameless, faceless people who he'd kill if she ran, along with the not-so-nameless.

Dani standing in the doorway flashed through her mind, hair wild and eyes gleaming in the late sun. Running wasn't a solution. Hiding wasn't a solution. The only way to keep him from continuing this cycle was to kill him. The thought ran around and around in a circle that Emilie couldn't escape from, and panic consumed her. She didn't want to die. Maybe her life wasn't great, but it was her life.

To give it up for a monster who had done nothing but hurt everyone he'd come into contact with wasn't right, and it wasn't fair, and she didn't want this. But it was her burden to carry. Wasn't that always the way it happened? The air between them shimmered and vibrated and the quiet shattered. Fire roared to life at the edge of the glassy black surface that ringed Amelia's cage, and Emilie flinched.

"If you're right, and she is truly Valkyrie's daughter, then it will be soon. She will break the chain, and when she does, he won't be barred from this place anymore." Amelia gestured to the wall of fire, and Emilie turned to look at it. Through the veil beyond the fire she could see Vincent's face frozen in a rictus of pain, flames consuming his limbs but not killing him, never killing him. "The curse holds him back."

"For now." Ephraim Black appeared next to Emilie with a grave look. "You're alive. Good."

In front of them, Amelia screamed as a laceration in her chest suddenly ripped open. The flames disappeared. Amelia stumbled backwards and fell against the side of the crypt. It was stained in black and maroon, old blood from the wounds Amelia took from the man she'd been unable to escape.

"What's..." Emilie turned to her grandpa.

"The spell, the link. They're attacking Spectre now, and he can't die..."

"... but he can torture Amelia with his wounds." She finished the sentence for him.

"Listen. There's a tether. A link..." She paused for a second, desperate to make the right choice. Run and live, or fight and die. When the chips fell and it all came together, what did she choose? "Dani has to break it. It'll free Amelia, and then I can do what has to be done here. But I need you to tell her because I can't leave until it's done, and it can't be finished until she breaks it." She huffed out a laugh, tears wet in her eyes. "Okay?"

"Emilie…" He searched her eyes, and she saw the moment he came to a conclusion, whatever that might have been.

"Do this for me and I'll explain later." She threw her arms around him, and even without mass, weight, or bodies, felt the warmth she'd always associated with her grandpa. The person she trusted most. "I love you, okay?"

"Okay." He nodded and then he disappeared.

Emilie watched and waited and felt the panic wash away under steady determination. She felt light hands on her shoulder as Grandmama Marie appeared next to her. Her eyes were dark orbs of fire shining in a spectral face, and she looked more like a spirit than she ever had before. Power burned her from the inside out.

"Don't worry, sweetling. You won't be alone when he comes." Her voice echoed, and a swell of cool power swept around them. Different from before but familiar, the Deveraux power multiplied over and over again. One by one, each of the mediums he'd murdered to drive the knife into Amelia appeared around them. They were a circle of Deverauxs that shimmered, some more mist than shape.

Muted sounds of a fight drifted toward them, and Amelia screamed again. More wounds appeared, and one hand dropped away from her body in a gout of blood. The manacle at her ankle glowed bright and then faded away as though it had never been there. Amelia looked up, her wild-eyed gaze flitting all around them before alighting on Emilie.

"Remember. Finish it or we'll meet again." She turned and began running, and with a flash of light, she escaped.

Pale veins of light bled into the floor, the barren darkness being eaten by the veil's power. A wild animal scream cut through everything, and Emilie braced herself for what was coming. Spectre would not pass quietly, and he would follow the line he'd hooked around Amelia to where Emilie waited for him. Without the physical weight of a body, the tells of heart rate or breathing, nothing but emotion filled her, anger, white hot and icy cold until it flowed over.

Spectre wisped into sight. He lacked the wounds he'd carried in life, looking more like his younger self. A dark miasma of oily shadow still clung to him, coiled around his limbs like a serpentine familiar. Part of her wanted to run screaming, but she remembered Amelia's pleas, Marie's hands on her shoulders.

"Emilie. I should have known I'd find you here." His nostrils flared, but he kept a pleasant facade on his face. "Where's Amelia?" He raised an eyebrow and looked backwards over his shoulder, where the bloodstained crypt still stood.

"She's free now."

"What have you done?" His eyes lit with cold fire.

"Nothing. But an uncorrupted veilblade is a beautiful thing."

"Dani," he gritted the words out. "Then this will be easy."

"No. You're not safe from the veil any longer, Vincent. The next time you die, you won't ever wake back up again."

Behind him, the forms of the Deverauxs and other talented winked into sight. Tall women and short women, fat and thin, pale and dark haired, all holding hands, all pinning their eyes on Vincent. Emilie needed to keep his focus on her until they arrived, all of them. The shadows crawled over his torso, reminding her that in the in-between or not, he still wore enchantments to protect himself.

"Why, Emilie? I loved you. You were my favorite." He reached out with a hand, a wounded expression on his face.

"You mean I looked the most like Amelia." Her voice trembled, but Emilie didn't move.

"You know that hurts. I was your friend. I cared about you." He frowned and shot her a hurt expression.

"You just wanted an empty shell that you could lock her inside of."

"Perhaps. But you're so much more than that, Emilie. The power you've got inside you." He closed his eyes and licked his lips. "It's deli-cious. I know you'll never be Amelia. She can go. I don't want her anymore. I want you, Emilie." His voice was soft and warm as it wrapped around her, a thick blanket to guard against cold nights.

She wavered. He tempted her even though she didn't want to be. Vincent had been her friend, and he had cared about her, in his own way. Would it be so terrible to give herself over? She'd still be alive, still have a life, even if it was one in chains. "C'mon, killer. Don't stop fighting now," came Dani's voice, sharp edged and ready to tear at flesh. It brought Emilie back, reminded her in a single instant of everything he'd said, everything he had done.

Spectre lunged at her as she took a step backwards, and the last of the Deveraux talented snapped into place. Their voices echoed around them, a dozen spells all being chanted one on top of the next. He snarled again, and Emilie watched as the shadows began to melt off of him, unable to withstand the force of the spells. Together, they were more than a dozen women all chanting together, all standing together.

"You can't have me." A wind that smelled of decay and thick loam whipped around them. "You can't have any of us," her voice thundered around them. "Not now. Not ever again."

"You can't kill me. Nobody can kill me." He waved his arm and a dark roiling spear of energy exploded from his palm. Three of the murdered Deverauxs chanted louder, and it hit a wall of pale fire, burned away by the luminance.

Spectre snarled and took a step forward, shadows writhing in the folds of his clothing, clinging to his boots, and coming to life at his feet in tentacles of darkness. Marie stepped up, shoulder to shoulder with Emilie, her presence giving her strength. They grasped hands, and Marie's magic flowed into Emilie, filling the reservoir of power she'd need. Around the circle, mediums clasped hands one after another, a circle that burned away the shadows the moment Spectre summoned them forth.

"Maybe that was true once. But without your enchantments, you're mortal as any talented." She exhaled and prepared to dive into herself. She gathered up every scrap of power that existed inside her, preparing her weapon. As she closed her eyes, another spirit broke past the barrier and took her other hand. Grandpa's hand gripped hers, and a reservoir larger and deeper than she'd ever known opened up.

His power rocketed through her, fire to the cold burn of the grave that she knew as her own abilities, and it galvanized her. No time to ask him what he was doing, she was already diving too deep, too fast. The power engulfed her, and the veil in front of her became a blur as she turned into a whirlwind of magic. She grabbed at everything, turned, and then came back to the surface, all of that power moving her too fast.

She slammed all of it at Spectre, watched every spell and enchantment he'd ever cast to protect himself burn away, leaving behind nothing but the shell of an angry man. He snarled, face turned bestial without anything to help him, and threw up both his hands. The light blew away his meager shield, and Emilie saw the force of it hit him and blast his spirit back out of the veil and into his body. The heat of Grandpa's power seared through her, and a lasso roped around her waist, yanking her backwards into her body.

Emilie cried out, barely able to see Marie and Grandpa left behind in the circle. She reached for them, but the power hauling her back into her body was too strong. She was still screaming when she slammed into her body and sat bolt upright in the narrow bed.

In front of her, Dani looked like she'd survived a war zone, oozing burns, and wet blood coating her top to bottom, veilblade glowing in her hands. From downstairs, there was a cacophony of inhuman screams and roars. Something came charging up the stairs. Dani threw herself in front of Emilie, but around her muscular form Emilie saw the hulking mass of Spectre trapped in a body decayed and broken from the many ways he should have died.

Emilie threw her body forward and wrapped her arms around Dani, chanting a protection spell under her breath. The explosion from the fireball still threw them across the room. The pair of them slammed into the wall and fell to the ground in a wet heap. She couldn't breathe, and Dani was bleeding on her, the crackle of fire eating at something on the other side of the room.

Dani came to with a twitch, the blade shining like a star. Emilie took her free hand and funneled what remained of her power back into the blade. There was no time to think about what she was doing, what this might mean. Dani snarled and stabbed up as Spectre threw himself toward them. Dani's blade connected, Emilie's hands still on her wrists, and Spectre screamed as his spirit fled the husk for the last time.

Emilie felt the pull of the spell she'd started and wished there was time to say goodbye. Her spirit chased his as her body went limp and fell to the ground. She hit the veil fast on his trail, saw the border of the river Styx, and stopped. On the far side of the river, she saw the shrouded forms of the Deveraux mediums, and more. Dozens of eyes watched as Spectre was dragged into the river, though he struggled to keep to the shore. The water was too fast, the pull of the grave dragging him away from life.

"Son of shadows, heir of pain, your time has come, you're fighting in vain." As she spoke, the waters rose, washing him farther and farther toward the other shore and what waited. Emilie got close enough that her toes touched the water. "The arbiter of truth follows you too. May your soul find its place. May their judgement be true." A commotion started up behind her, but Emilie ignored it. She ignored the icy feel of the grave as it overtook the equilibrium that gave all things life. She was so cold that speaking the final words was difficult, but after a long moment, she took another step forward, waters cresting past her calves. "May Charon now hear my plea, to ensure his passage I give you—"

"ME!" Grandpa's voice cried out the last word of the spell, his hand on her shoulder throwing her back as his spirit raced into the water and dove under.

Emilie hit the shore and heat suffused her, reminding her she was alive when she'd been prepared to sacrifice everything. The last thing she saw was Grandpa's spirit burning red as he caught Spectre and dragged him across the river, into the mist, to whatever lay beyond.

"NO!" She fell to her knees on the sandy shore and even though she lacked a physical body to be hurt in this place, she felt the pain ricochet through her. In a heartbeat, they were gone. She didn't see him hit the other side. Great walls of fog rolled across the water.

Shock rumbled through her, and Emilie's spirit tumbled back into her body once again, the flesh she'd left behind, the body that she had thought never to inhabit again, back to Dani, back to a world colder and crueler without Grandpa's presence. She didn't want to go back, and all she wanted was to go back. The two thoughts collided as she slipped into her skin.

She'd accounted for the pain of lungs that didn't want to work and a body that had been tossed across her bedroom, but Grandpa's loss was a wound that went soul deep, and it made it hard to breathe. Then she saw Dani's face, eyes frozen in horror before they thawed back to warmth and heat.

"You with me, killer?" Dani's voice was hoarse, her hands rough and wet with blood.

"I...Grandpa..." Emilie collapsed into Dani's arms.

They'd done it. They'd stopped Spectre and his massacres, and the death of so many talented. They had avenged all the people they'd lost. All it cost was Grandpa's life. Grief rolled over her in a wave and carried her under the water. She couldn't catch her breath. She heard her father's shouts as he ran into the house. Dani eased her onto the ground, one hand settled between Emilie's shoulder blades. Each breath hollowed out a piece of her, one she'd somehow never expected to lose. Mom, Dad, Lizzie...but never Grandpa.

And yet, it was over. They'd survived.

31

DANI

Plenty of jobs ended bad. A body count that tipped too high, someone who should have made it out alive left dead on the floor. Bounties that never got paid for one reason or another.

She was used to it.

Not that anyone wanted to get used to it. But that was part of the job, part of the life.

Dani wasn't used to it this time. Watching Emilie die in her arms and then come back cut too deep. She'd thought—hell, she didn't know what she'd thought.

Sitting on a bed in the Lockgrove house with her arm in a sling and gauze wrapped around the burns on her leg, all she did was turn over what had happened, over and over again. None of it made sense, the way everything went down. Emilie didn't have any injuries, so she'd gotten to stay home while they carted Dani off to the hospital.

While they'd put Ephraim's body in a black bag to be brought to the morgue.

She didn't stay long. Apparently, the Lockgrove's had more power in this town than she'd wagered on. Nobody asked any of the normal questions, even though a damn pillar of the community was dead in the house when they'd arrived.

Not like she could tell them what happened, anyway. Yet again, she had plenty of pieces but no answers, just Emilie's face as she sobbed over her grandpa, Phillip's shame as he watched them. Pain and sorrow was nothing new in the life of a hunter, but this one stung more than usual. What she needed was answers, and the only person who'd have them was the one person she didn't want to talk to.

Phillip Lockgrove.

He'd know what happened to Emilie and how Spectre had just disintegrated into nothing in moments after years of terror. She'd seen the look in Emilie's eyes and figured out what the other woman hadn't said. Something had happened inside the veil, where hunters didn't breach.

It would still be another day or two until she could leave. At this rate, Joe would know Spectre was dead before she got back down there, but she'd promised to head back down after this job was done. Still, she needed answers.

How had Spectre gone from the biggest bogeyman on this coast to a pile of dust and ashes on the floor in almost the blink of an eye? What she suspected wasn't... Dani didn't want to consider it, consider that maybe the reason Emilie said goodbye and then looked so horrified when she woke up as Spectre disappeared was that she'd intended to die.

Could she really have intended to sacrifice herself to do what no one else had done? And somehow, someway, Ephraim took the bullet for her. A plan inside a plan inside a plan. What was she supposed to do with that? She was stuck in this big-ass house with a woman who'd she'd come to care for, who had tried to leave without so much as a glance behind her on the way out. Dani didn't want any part of it anymore.

This town and all of its history had reminded her. Emilie had almost seemed like someone Dani wanted to stick around. Then she'd tried to bail. Good reason or not, it didn't matter, not when Dani was so used to death, murder, and mayhem. She needed solid people with her, folks who would lay their lives down if they had to, but only if they had to. Offering up oneself like a sacrificial lamb wasn't okay.

It didn't matter, anyway. Dani's presence here was temporary. Another day and she'd be fit for the drive down to Virginia without any hassle. Emilie had her whole life now, and a rogue hunter sure as hell didn't fit into it. She'd done her job, and the sooner she got out of here, the better for everybody involved.

"Hey." Emilie snuck into the room, her voice so quiet Dani barely heard it at first.

Dani raised an eyebrow and leaned back against the window pane. "Hey yourself, killer."

"I know you're probably headed out soon. But I... Dad thought... You must have questions. About..." Her hands tangled together, and she looked up.

Dani didn't want to meet her eyes. Hidden in those pale blue eyes was the woman she'd come to know over the last few days, come to trust, to care deeply about. Living the hunter life meant roots and relationships weren't an option. Maybe Emilie had made her think that this time would be different, but Dani had watched her die and then come back, and she couldn't do it again.

She'd lost enough people to the monsters. She didn't need one ready to tap.

"Yeah." She tried for levity, but it didn't translate to her voice. "I have my suspicions."

"I did what I had to do. You don't—you weren't there, beyond the veil. I had no choice."

"You had a choice." Dani was weary, bone numb of this place and these people. Talented, always mucking things up. "We could have—"

"It was a curse," Emilie interrupted her, voice thick with tears. "Amelia cursed him so that he couldn't follow her, but it kept him alive. He couldn't enter the veil so long as she was there."

"You're not making any sense."

"Then listen to me. You broke her tether, let the spell that kept her trapped in the veil go, but there was only one way to be sure that Spectre stayed dead. A soul had to ferry him across the Styx, make sure his feet touched the other side and stayed there and—"

"And you what? Volunteered? Emilie, that's not okay."

"I did what it took!" She took a shuffling step toward Dani. "I was ready to sacrifice everything. *Everything!*" She swore under her breath. "Do you know what that takes? Do you have any idea?"

"I do." Dani shook her head. "You got a taste of what hunters look at every time they pick up a job."

"It's not the same."

"You're right. I don't want to die."

"You think I do?" Emilie took another step closer. "I just came back to my life. I fought to stay alive. Why do you think I'd trade that for nothing?"

"Because you almost did."

"I almost traded my life for the lives of everyone who Spectre would have hunted down. Funny that you of all people don't seem to get that."

Dani swore and stepped forward so the two of them were almost nose to nose. "You deserve better than that! Why is that so hard to understand? I can't... I can't do this with someone else." She reached out and took Emilie's shirt in her hands, shook her, tried to shake some sense into her.

Emilie wrapped her hands around Dani's and pried them open, but didn't step back. She licked her lips and looked up. "I thought you'd understand. He killed my mom, my sister. I couldn't... I couldn't let him get away with it. Even if it meant I didn't make it out alive."

Their hands intertwined, so close they'd be embracing if either of them moved a muscle, and Dani didn't know what came next. Canyons of things unsaid lay between them. She didn't have any right to be upset with the medium. She wasn't Dani's friend, wasn't her partner. She was a job, and soon as Dani could pack her gear, she'd be nothing but a memory. No matter what it felt like right now.

Gentle as she could, she untangled herself, heart in her throat, and took a step back. She gave herself enough room that she didn't want to reach out anymore. No point in getting attached now. It was almost time to beat feet and get away from this town and everyone in it. Emilie didn't move, only watched as she stepped back. But hurt echoed through her eyes at the distancing.

Good. Better to make this a clean cut, or as clean as she could when a job ended all tangled up like this.

"I know you're probably leaving soon." Emilie sighed and fidgeted in place. "But you should come to Grandpa's funeral tomorrow. He'd have told me to invite you."

"I don't know about all that. I didn't really know him, you know?"

"Maybe not. But your family did. You're the last Black standing. You should come." Emilie huffed out a sad sound that was supposed to be a laugh. "Is it stupid that I don't want you to leave? I—"

"Look. What we went through, what we did? It's a whole-ass thing. But this town, it ain't my home. No ifs, ands, or buts about it. I got no reason to stick to this town, this place."

Hurt flashed in Emilie's eyes, making her feel like an ass. "It was your home once, you know. You don't—you don't have to leave."

"Yeah, I do." Dani turned away, looked out the window at her truck sitting in the driveway out front. "My job, my life? It's out there on the road. Spectre ain't the only monster chewing on folks."

Emilie didn't answer, but a moment later the door closed. Dani was alone again with her thoughts. Under different circumstances, maybe she'd have stayed. Maybe.

Part of her considered it, staying in this little two-horse town, fixing up the house that was apparently hers, but the rest of her clamored for the next fight. Even without looking, she knew the precise location of the veilblade, though she hadn't touched it since getting discharged from the hospital. As though it vibrated on a frequency that resonated with Dani now, the blade was a part of her.

Packing her things didn't take long, but she'd been dragging her feet. The easy excuse was a throbbing shoulder that was supposed to stay in the sling for another day or two. Even that couldn't really account for it though, not when packing her life into a pair of duffels was second nature. She never used to even need to think about it. Her body just got the job done while she decided over how long to stay before hitting the road. In the end, she figured tomorrow was the day. She'd leave during the funeral. It'd hurt Emilie, but a clean break was the best call.

Dani wasn't sure she believed herself, but she had to try.

EPHRAIM'S FUNERAL was a quiet but complicated affair. Patriarch of the Lockgrove family, he'd been a bigwig in the talented community. People of every shape and color poured into town. In a way, it was an event not to be missed. The service was held at a graveyard in front of an honest to God mausoleum. Dani had broken into enough of them over the years, but she'd never been around for someone being interred into one.

Hunters weren't big on funerals. Irish wakes were as close as they got.

She'd intended to be long gone by now, but there were questions she had for Phillip, questions that Emilie wasn't capable of answering. She kept her distance, unwilling to intrude, invitation or not. These people were here to grieve together, hold on to one another as they worked out what a world without Ephraim Lockgrove looked like.

They deserved their time and space without someone from the outside getting in the way.

But he was the reason Emilie still had a pulse, and for that Dani watched from behind a tree, taking occasional sips from a flask in her pocket. In black jeans, a dark sweater, black leather jacket, and knit cap, she probably looked like a stalker. She was certainly underdressed compared to all the tailored suits and designer dresses.

The echo of eulogies and prayers didn't make it across the grass, but the shake of shoulders as people sobbed and ramrod straight spines of those unwilling to give themselves over to emotion conveyed the sentiment. It was easy enough to pick out Emilie's bowed head next to Phillip, flanked on the other side by Andromeda and Merc.

Half a flask later, the funeral broke up. The crowd dispersed as cold misty rain settled over the cemetery, leaving Phillip alone in a crowd of empty chairs. His eyes found hers, and she realized he'd known she was there the whole time, watching.

She might as well see what he wanted then.

"You didn't have to hide, you know." His voice lacked any bite.

"I didn't want to intrude. Bad enough you and Emilie have let me hang out for a few days while I heal up enough to drive."

"You knew him too, even if just for a few days. I think if there'd been time, he would have liked you. Always was a fan of spunk."

"Yeah?"

"Yeah. He was fond of your mother too. Val. When she was still Val."

Dani nodded and let her eyes drift further away. "I don't… I'm just not sure how to process any of…that. Valkyrie or Valerie, or any of it really." She met Phillip's eyes. "She's been the kind of hunter I emulate since my first job and now…" She gestured helplessly. Dani shook her head and wished she hadn't even come.

"I meant what I said the other night. I have the research on your mother, bladesingers, the corruption that comes with tragedy, all of it." He leveled with her. "If—when—you leave, it's all yours." He waited a beat. "And of course the Black farmhouse is in your name now as well."

"Sell it." Dani rubbed at the back of her neck. "I can give you a bank account or something, but that place doesn't belong to me. Not really."

"It could," Phillip said carefully. "Upkeep is already handled by the council, and it would be easy enough to lay glamours back over it again. That farmhouse has been in your family for a long time, I'd hate to see you get rid of it on a whim." He paused. "Besides, even a veteran hunter needs a place where they can get away sometimes, don't they? A spot to…" He waved his hand in air. "I don't know, heal their wounds and make bombs or something?"

"Ya know, you had me goin' there for a second, hot stuff." Dani laughed and shook her head, tipping her face up to the sky. "Hold on to the house then. For now. Ain't nothin' changing though. This place isn't home." She turned and started walking back to her truck.

She wanted to return to the grill and let Joe wrap her in one of those bear hugs and never let go. But she'd settle for the next job, the next hunt.

32

EMILIE

When Emilie had woken up after Mama's death, it'd felt like dying all over again. A torrent of grief that didn't let up drowned her over and over again. Every breath was a brand, a wound unhealed, that tore deep into her soul and left her incapable of anything resembling healing.

With Grandpa, it was different.

His loss was a wave, the tide washing in and out, bringing grief with it as it poured over her. She'd be almost fine for a few minutes, or an hour or two, and then it'd hit her all over again. He was gone. It was her fault, and the regret was eating her alive. Combined with the look on Dani's face when she'd worked out what Emilie had tried, it was all too much.

The double loss faded everything to gray and muddled the world around her.

She became lost.

For ten years, she'd put off coming home, buoyed by Dad's mercurial attitude, which kept her away. She'd run as far and as fast as possible away from all the things that haunted her, most of all a past she couldn't remember. Coming back, she'd sworn she'd reclaim what the fire stole from her, but it wasn't so simple.

She'd gotten the answers she wanted, and what did she receive in return? Memories enough to give her nightmares for the rest of her life, a legacy of death, and losing Grandpa. It wasn't even like leaving well enough alone would have spared her. She'd been damned if she did, and damned if she didn't, and she just hadn't known it at the time.

There would be a wake back at home for a man who hadn't lived there in decades. If it bore any resemblance to the funeral, Emilie was fine with missing it. There would be hordes of people who'd known him as patriarch of the Lockgrove family, or through the auction house, or a dozen different ways. Emilie wasn't sure any of them had known the real man behind the duty.

She wanted to scream. The world kept on spinning, but she didn't know how she fit into it anymore. It would have been easier in a thousand ways if he'd just been a few minutes late. If the spell had been completed without him and she'd pulled Spectre across the Styx, none of this would be her problem. The thought was cruel. He'd saved her, and she knew it, but she didn't have to like it.

Dawson wasn't a big town, and the roads all intertwined. One neighborhood was built almost on top of the next from one side of town to the other. Ringed by the mountains and crowded by forest and rivers, it was easy to walk in circles. She'd left the cemetery and intended to make for home, but the thought of facing those people was too much.

Instead, she'd found her way across town to Grandpa's rancher. Her whole life, it had been a safe haven from the Lockgrove house, filled with love and laughter and magic. He'd been the foundation of her life post-fire, and in an instant that connection was severed, leaving Emilie to flounder by herself. What she needed right now more than anything was a touchstone, and with Grandpa gone, his house was her best bet.

Coming back to town had been important to try to move on, find closure for what happened to Mama, to the house, to Emilie. But now that it was over with, she didn't feel better. The life she'd lived between the house fire and returning to Dawson was nothing she'd been proud of. She had no job, no freelance clients, and the lease on the cottage was about to be up. It was a life turned to loose ends, and she was unable to grasp the pieces and pull them back together again.

She unlocked the front door and walked in, expecting to see a meticulously kept house, same as it always appeared, whether Grandpa had been sick or well. Except it wasn't. Boxes and boxes filled the living room, each one tagged in boxy letters: Emilie kitchen, Emilie bedroom, Emilie books. All of her things from the cottage had been shipped here. Even after he was gone, he was still watching out for her.

The thought made her eyes water and her breath unsteady. She didn't know what the world looked like without Grandpa, only that it was a quieter, darker place than it had been a few days ago.

One hand traced along the back of the couch as she walked through the house. His presence lingered in everything, the smell of pipe tobacco and cinnamon pressed into the fabric and the walls alike. Even though she knew better, it felt like he was here with her. She reached out with the internal radio, hoping somehow that he had left a piece of himself behind, that he'd speak to her. But there was nothing.

Only the chill of the grave met her like ice in her veins and the static of a radio unable to tune into anything.

On the counter in the kitchen, sat a recorder with a note that said "Play Me" in Grandpa's sharp, elegant script. Emilie stared at it, as though it might grow teeth and bite her if she did as it asked. It only took a moment to give in though. How could she say no?

"Emilie,

If you're listening to this message, then it means I'm gone. One way or another. It was only a matter of time, dear heart, and I hope you're not too terribly angry with me about it. If I'm right, it means that I made sure Spectre crossed the Styx in lieu of anyone else. Trust I had my own reasons.

I wish I could be there for you now, my dear, because you have decisions to make. There is a great wide world out there, and I, for one, think that you should take advantage of everything it has to offer. Don't make yourself small. Decide what you want and chase it.

God knows there is money aplenty in a family like ours. This house is yours now as well. A medium needs a place all their own to escape the voices of the dead. I hope that my home can be that place for you.

There is a bag for you on the kitchen table. It has some of my journals and my personal grimoire. Use them carefully and live bravely, my dear.

Love always,

Grandpa."

The recorder went silent, and wet tears traced their way down Emilie's cheeks. Somehow, he'd known before she did what Spectre's death would cost. Grief frosted over her, a sharp wound that carved out the piece of her that would always belong to Grandpa. Ice crawled its way through her skin, and she watched crystals form over the recorder. It was the last piece of him, held in her hands, suspended in frost.

He'd given her a choice beyond what anyone else ever had. Yet again, Emilie stood at a crossroad, no clue which path would lead her to the future she craved.

But his words had lightened the load. This hadn't been her fault. He wasn't dead because of her, no matter how much it felt that way, no matter how much it hurt. Ice cracked under her fingers as she tightened her grip around the recorder and looked around the room.

Staying in Dawson to try to pick up a life she'd left behind a decade ago was a choice, one that had been choking her. She could make peace with Dad, somehow carve a niche in this town.

It wasn't what she wanted.

She wanted to see the mountains and travel along the waterways. She wanted to spread her wings, whatever that meant. It seemed like her options were wide open for the first time in her life. No longer weighed down by the weight of her mother's death on her shoulders, she could do or be anything she wanted.

Staying in this town would mean none of that. It'd only be a matter of time until small-town life ground her into a creature of bitterness and regret. What Dad had done wasn't something she could forgive so easily. He might have helped in the fight to take Spectre down, but that didn't mean she wanted to see him. Dawson was safe, and on paper it seemed like the right choice, but Emilie could feel in her bones how wrong it was.

She'd lost years to choices made for her. She nearly lost herself as she tried to be the person she'd thought her family wanted her to be. This time, whatever path she chose would be her choice. And she didn't want the safety of a life planned and predicted and insured. She wanted the open road and everything it had to offer.

No, that wasn't true.

She wanted Dani and everything that came with her. Warts and all.

It took twenty minutes to make it from Grandpa's rancher back to the Lockgrove house, even running as fast as her legs would take her. Her thighs burned, her lungs ached, and when she skidded to a stop half a block away, she'd been more than half convinced Dani would be gone.

If she was, Emilie wasn't quite sure what that would mean. How exactly did one hunt down a hunter who lived a literally nomadic existence?

Lucky for her, she didn't need to figure that out. Merc's car was parked across the driveway, blocking Dani from leaving. The two of them were chatting away, but when he noticed Emilie, he flashed her a smile and said goodbye to Dani. He hopped into his car with a two-finger salute and grinned as he pulled out.

Emilie owed him a killer birthday present.

Dani raised an eyebrow and watched her walk up, but didn't say anything. Emilie had a boulder sitting on her chest as she tried to find the right words to explain that what had occurred between the two of them was more than just a job for Dani, or finding out about Emilie's past. It meant more than that.

"So here's the thing," she said as she crossed the distance between them. "There isn't anything here for me. In Dawson, I mean. I can barely look at my dad and this isn't—it's not where I wanna be." She sidled closer, only a few inches between her and Dani, the heat rising between them almost palpable. "I have this money now, and you need someone to, I don't know, take driving shifts with." She sighed and bit her lip. "If you're interested, I wanna be anywhere but here. Normal isn't a thing when you hear dead people and can call ice to your fingers."

"You may have a point." Dani smiled. "This your way of asking me to take you on the road?"

"Yes."

"Ain't an easy road to walk." Dani cocked her head and watched Emilie.

"Yes, because my life has been simple and easy to deal with up until now." Emilie laughed and stepped closer.

"Not for people who wanna give up either."

"I don't wanna give up." She reached out and hooked her fingers through Dani's belt loops. "I wanna live. And I wanna make sure other people do too."

"You could have something close to normal here," Dani protested weakly.

"I don't want it." Dani made a sound low in her throat and reached out, one hand cupping the side of Emilie's cheek as she came down for a kiss. It started slow, gentle, as though she were asking if she'd gotten the signals right. When Emilie moaned into her mouth and wrapped her arms around the taller woman's neck, the whole world slipped away.

It was like all the puzzle pieces that made up her life settled into place for the first time.

By the time they separated, Emilie's heart was beating too fast and her head was spinning, but she didn't feel so lost. It was like Dani slotted herself into the broken places in Emilie. She held onto the other woman and laughed under her breath.

It took the two of them twenty minutes to get Emilie packed away into the truck, a letter on the kitchen table for her father with her phone number at the bottom. She could leave, but disappearing in a puff of smoke would be cruel. She couldn't do it, not even after everything.

She settled into the sway of the truck as Dani gunned it past the town limits, climbing back up and into the mountains. Emilie's directions got them back to the main roads, and unlike the last time she departed Dawson, there was no guilt, no pain at what she left behind. She wasn't leaving forever, but she was closing a chapter.

"What comes next?" Her voice was sleepy, but Dani held onto her hand as low clouds obscured the stars.

"Next comes Virginia, and the next job, killer." Dani laughed, low and throaty and full. "That's the life. Welcome to the road."

As Emilie fell asleep, she almost thought she heard her Grandpa laugh, pleased with the choice she'd made.

Keep reading for the first chapter of Book 2 in Legacy of Shadows *Sins of Survival*

CHAPTER 1

EMILIE

Emilie swallowed and turned to her companion with a wry turn to her lips. "I was hoping that some of the wards would still be intact."

"No dice?" Dani leaned back against the truck and gave Emilie a lingering look. "I mean, I did say this was probably a fool's errand. But did you wanna listen? No." She tsked quietly under her breath, then winked and turned back to grab something from inside the truck.

A year on the road—and in her bed—their lives getting more and more tangled together with every breath, and she still managed to steal Emilie's heart in such small, frenetic ways.

Dani was tall and athletic, with dark wavy hair she only tamed when it was time to fight, whiskey-brown eyes that set Emilie on fire, and a trim frame usually hidden under a leather jacket and jeans. Today was no exception, but she'd added a grey knitted cap to the ensemble, muttering about cold ears. Emilie turned from the moldering building in front of her to watch her girlfriend as she rummaged through the truck.

Emilie looked like a pale shadow next to her. Her own white-blond hair was getting longer, brushing the tops of her shoulders and framing her face. Her plump frame hadn't slimmed down so much as adjusted to hours on her feet as she worked with Dani, one job after the next.

After her dip in the Styx, the cold didn't bother her much these days. It'd been one of many things she'd discovered last winter, her first as a mature talented, the depth and breadth of her magic waking all the way up. She'd wanted nothing more than to ask her Grandpa if it had been the same for him.

November was warmer than it used to be, but the wind was cutting through everything tonight. They'd lost the light, another reminder that winter was still on its way.

"Don't get snotty," Emilie warned, turning back to the decommissioned building, trying to work out the best way to get inside without being spotted.

The Johnstown Municipal Library had been closed, and the stony brick building staring down at her now didn't look particularly friendly. Broken wards tried to flicker and chain together but remained dull and useless where they'd been placed. Time and erosion were doing what magical means couldn't and erasing their protective bearing one tumultuous rainstorm at a time.

At some point, this had been a collective, one of the places where talented gathered to share magic and knowledge, their little games of power and society happening in back rooms filled with texts that required special gloves to open. For safety, of course.

What she needed to know was whether they'd left by themselves and how long ago it had happened. Too many collectives had gone dark lately. There had to be a reason, and she was determined to find it.

"Snotty? What are we, ten?" Dani closed the truck, stepping over to join Emilie, one hand draping around her shoulders.

She leaned into the contact, happy to tuck her head under her girlfriend's while they kept bantering. She might not get cold, but Dani was a solid force, and she appreciated her for what that was.

"No?" Emilie rolled her eyes in response, even though Dani couldn't actually see it, before taking a step back and tucking an errant strand of hair behind one ear.

"So, have you worked out how we get inside?" Dani's lips curled up into a dark smile.

Heat rushed through her, and Emilie shot her a look before shaking her head, trying to ignore the flirtation. Instead, she turned toward the building, taking a few faltering steps closer. They had work to do, and she would not be distracted. She'd probably fail of course, but right now, it was the thought that counted.

"Not entirely?" Her voice was scratchy and higher than it should have been, but she tried to talk through it. That Dani could still do this to her with a look after a year was absolutely unfair.

Emilie wouldn't have had it any other way.

"Mmm." Dani mock frowned and stalked forward a few steps, closing the distance between the two of them. "See, I'd bet there's at least one window around back that's been busted in." Her voice dropped an octave. "You know how it goes with places like this." Slowly, she circled around so that her presence was at Emilie's back.

Her hands draped across Emilie's shoulders, voice barely a whisper as it slipped past her ear. She was so distracted by the sensation of Dani there, she missed her words entirely.

"What?"

From behind her, Dani snickered, but it soon morphed into a full-on belly laugh. She had to pull away from Emilie and brace her hands on her knees as she tried to catch her breath.

"You're terrible!" Emilie laughed and took a shove at Dani while she low-key lost it in the middle of the street.

Without any more thought, she marched away from her erstwhile girlfriend and her truck, bag swinging with her hips. Dani had been dragging her feet about coming out here at all, but Emilie had made it clear she was going. And her overprotective hunter girlfriend—who also just happened to be the holder of a legendary weapon—wasn't willing to just let her wander off and hope nothing happened.

Behind her, she heard the moment that Dani's laughter died off, her boots echoing Emilie's own footsteps. In general, they cased out jobs in advance. Made sure that each was something they were a good fit for. She couldn't speak to the way anyone else worked, but she followed Dani's lead, and after a year, they were both still up and swinging.

No thanks to you, a nasty voice in the back of her head piped up, and she smothered it mercilessly. There was no time for that kind of talk while they were in the field. As if they ever weren't. One job blended into the next, only long stretches of pavement and anonymous rentals to differentiate one from another.

It didn't take long for Dani's long strides to overtake hers, and if Emilie wanted to, she could time them by her heartbeat. She never made it far before her hunter was gliding in front of her in a peculiar sort of predatory way, ensuring there was nothing waiting for them bearing too many teeth.

Around the corner was a window boarded up badly, but nothing else waited for them, and for the briefest moment, Emilie wasn't sure whether she was disappointed or not. Dani kicked in the boards with barely a glance along the alley, as casual as if she was opening it with a key. It was a smooth action, and Emilie was reminded that this was nothing new for the other woman.

This little expedition was supposed to be checking on a hunch. There *had* been a collective here, and now they were gone, and nobody seemed to care too much. She hadn't asked Dani to come, but here she was anyway. Breaking and entering and all.

Ahead of her, she watched as her hunter easily ducked through the window and disappeared into the dim building for a moment before popping her head back out with a charming smile.

"Looks good. I'm guessing it's been empty long enough nobody is using it much anymore."

"If they ever were," Emilie murmured with a look around before following her girlfriend into the dark.

The library sat far enough away from the city center that it was easy to see why it had fallen by the wayside. She might have a certain kind of reverence for libraries, with their rows of books and organization that ensured things were generally in place to be found, but even she could feel the chill of isolation from the rest of town.

She'd grown up surrounded by libraries that went back two

hundred years, with tomes and scrolls and folios. So much information that if she hadn't been introduced early, she might have drowned among the stacks. In a way, the tall rows of books were more familiar to her than the bars and shops that hunters tended to patronize when passing information back and forth.

This was different, though. For no reason she could put her finger on, when Emilie passed through the window into the library, it felt like entering a tomb.

***

Inside the building, the smell of mildew and wet paper permeated everything, a thick floral bouquet of decomposition that was difficult to ignore. As much as she might hear the voices of the dead, avoiding their bodies had stayed near the top of her to-do list.

Dani waited for her at the doorway, both of them flipping on flashlights as they ventured deeper into the building. Emilie stopped short when the hallway spit them out into a wide room that must have been wonderful once. Tall windows allowed the new moon to deliver weak light, showing off the collapsed stacks that had belched stacks of abandoned books onto the floor.

What had she been expecting? The dim academic libraries she'd encountered between childhood and university? This had been a public library, not a magical archive, but something about the broken stacks and the books left to molder picked at her incessantly.

The weak moonlight didn't illuminate much, but every bit helped this time of year when the dark encroached so early. It'd make the expedition a little bit less fraught, even if Dani still thought she was being ludicrous.

"So, what are we looking for in here?" Dani wandered to where a long wooden checkout counter dominated one wall.

"You saw the wards out front," Emilie answered primly, following her before weaving behind the counter. She started opening drawers, looking for something without knowing *exactly* what it was she was looking for.

"The broken wards?" Dani raised an eyebrow. "Yeah, killer, I saw 'em. But they're broken. Anything they were supposed to be hiding has been out in the open for a while now."

"Maybe." Emilie ducked under the drawer she was tugging at where something was stuck. From underneath, she could see the faint flicker of a ward that wasn't entirely broken. *Hide Me.* She traced a finger against the curved shape and felt a key fall into the palm of her hand. "Solitary talented are paranoid all by themselves. That sentiment is only amplified when you get more of them in one place. Groups make them easier to spot." She popped back up and shot Dani a sly smile as she dangled the key from a leather loop.

"You think a collective was working out of this place?"

"At least a small one. But they were being careful, not operating out in the open." She ran her fingers along the underside of the desk and felt the remains of more wards caved into it. "The wards outside were just the easy ones, but they've got spellwork hidden all over the place."

Emilie made her way to the hallway behind the desk, following it farther into the heart of the library. Instead of a locked door, she found the ruins of a doorframe with the remains of wards gouged out of the wood.

"See this?" Dani passed her, gesturing at the wood. "This is what I mean. Just because you found keys up front, just because there was somebody here at one point, doesn't mean anything is left. Doesn't mean anything is *here.*"

"Humor me here. Hunters and talented come at things from different directions, true or false?"

"True." Dani's eyes followed her as Emilie ventured inside.

"And I happen to be talented and was raised around their stupid circuitous bullshit." Emilie's eyes scanned the room, looking for the wards she knew were hiding somewhere.

"True." Dani was frowning at her now, but Emilie refused to look up.

The problem with relying on nothing but gossip and stories, in Emilie's opinion, always came down to how much information she could cram into her skull all at once. People liked to lie or use subterfuge. Books and wards, however...they were much more straightforward, and she'd always appreciated that about them. Books never asked her to explain herself or how her brain made the jumps from one thing to the next. They simply handed over the information she needed to move on with her day.

The point here wasn't about proving that there was a sanctum past this single room. Or at least, it hadn't been initially. There had been a collective here, and if the buzz of magic against her skin was any indicator, something had happened. They hadn't just moved on of their own accord. She could feel it.

To pinpoint the magical residue and know for sure, all she needed to do was let down her shields and take a peek around the room. And there was no way she was about to do that; the murmur of spirits nearby warned her that if she lit up, she would not be alone.

"Then trust me when I say there is something else here. Or was."

She could feel Dani's eyes on her from the doorway, pinned at the base of her neck. This was why she'd initially tried to arrange for this on a day when she could get out on her own for a few hours. It was impossible to ignore the weight of expectation of finding—well, nothing.

Everyone liked to think that talented were people who could operate without fear. Money could only insulate them so well when things went very wrong. And they went wrong more often than any of the more esteemed families ever wanted to admit.

She'd traced Mama's family thoroughly in the first weeks after leaving Dawson. After claiming her life for what it could be instead of what it was. The Deveraux name went back further than plenty, had been known for the clarity of their talent, and they'd still been hunted like rats by Spectre while none of the other families did a thing.

Her control wavered for a moment, shields dropping long enough for spirit radio to surge around her in a deluge of voices. Emilie's magic, her talents, allowed her to hear the dead. To listen and interact with the spirits and things that dwelled on the far side of the veil. As a child, she'd thought of it like tuning a radio. Now, it was more like an entire radio network.

There were at least a dozen voices braided together, so many that she couldn't isolate a single voice, couldn't quite parse out anything they were saying. Her shields snapped back into place, quieting the noise, and Emilie turned back to Dani, who was now facing the way they'd come down the hallway.

"Did you hear that?" Dani turned to Emilie, head cocked a little to the side.

"No, there was a surge." Emilie waved a hand around. "I wasn't hearing what you were hearing."

Dani went quiet for a long moment before prowling the space between the two of them. "Be careful, and don't go wandering." She pressed a long, lingering kiss against Emilie's lips before pulling back and disappearing back into the library silently.

With no one left to watch her, Emilie let her eyes wander over every spare inch of the room again. She could spot the ruined glimmers of wards along the ceiling and the door jamb. The room was crawling with them, and not a single one was still active.

She kicked the rug underfoot out of the way, revealing a spell circle burnt into the middle of the room. Emilie paused, listening for a moment to make sure Dani wasn't causing a ruckus without her, before dragging the rug out of the way entirely so she could see what she was working with.

Old burns and chalk ground into the grooves of the wood waited for her. Emilie pulled a notebook out of her bag and sketched out the circle for later before tucking it away again, unfamiliar with everything she was looking at.

As she did, the pressure from spirit radio began to rise. If she kept her shields closed tight, she'd end up with a migraine by the time they got to the truck, but Emilie generally didn't let them down while they were on a job unless she had to. She'd learned her lesson the hard way last spring, when a spirit had tried to hijack her body for a thrill ride.

She took a deep breath, incrementally lowering her shields. Not enough to give anything access to her, barely more than was necessary for spirit radio's static to start up again. The voices started back up, but the panic that had infected them a few minutes ago was gone.

"We needed to recharge the wards." The voices began to speak, one voice picking up where another left off. Men and women alike, at least seven or eight people in all. *"Nothing crazy or intensive, but Miriam saw the Scions working in the area. It was a safety precaution since some of the wards went down during the storm last summer. They knew. They knew we were here, and they came for us in the night. The Scions came for us."*

Emilie peeled back another layer of shields, blinking as she took in the room, seeing it for the first time properly. Broken wards flickered from nearly every square inch, but the floor was covered in the spectral remains of blood. It pooled on the floors, it spattered the walls, and somewhere out front, she could hear a woman wailing before her voice was cut short. It was an echo that kept repeating every twenty to thirty seconds, a broken record, a memory of her last moments before they'd been cut off.

She turned back to the doorway and saw the echo of a tall blond man grinning before leaving the room. There was a cold cruelty behind his eyes, and he was liberally spattered in blood. When he left the room, he moved to the left in the hallway, not the right. Deeper into the library.

Emilie let out a heaving, shuddering breath and tried to get her wits about her. This wasn't happening because she'd been wrong the whole time. Her skills at pattern recognition had obviously been leading her astray for months because saying out loud that the Scions of Seraph were hunting talented would be too much.

But as she watched the echo of that man leave the room over and over and over again, Emilie knew that was exactly what had happened.

JOIN THE NEWSLETTER

Want to be the first to find out about events, art drops, and get exclusive stories set in the Legacy of Shadows universe you can't find anywhere else?

Sign up for the Crow Coded newsletter!

https://bit.ly/Crow-Coded-Newsletter

ACKNOWLEDGMENTS

All I ever wanted to do was write books and tell stories, and for years I wasn't sure where to start. Then the story of a woman who goes to face her trauma only to find a real monster caught me, and I spent years uncovering all the details waiting for me.

This book is as much a story about trauma and survival, as it is a love letter to the paranormal worlds that got me through my teens and twenties. Without Buffy and Supernatural, Dani and Emilie never would have made it to the page.

Cinders of Yesterday is my first finished novel, the one I planned and wrote, and rewrote, and rewrote. Writing is so often a solitary activity but the community I found in writing spaces made me feel less alone, isolated, and insane. There are too many to thank everyone, but a few people made this path easier to weather.

To all the teachers who told me to keep writing, to friends who let me rant about plot structure at 3am in diners, the larpers who became family, and every person who read my snippets and fanfic over the last 25 years. Thank you for believing in me and my words. I adore you all beyond measure, you are the family I chose.

Ladz, my first "real" writing friend, and my first cheerleader. Your friendship, kindness and notes have saved my bacon at least a thousand times now. Your initial hype way back on draft 3 kept me excited to keep going and going and going. Can. Heck my dude, I did it! You've been my cheerleader for decades and my writing partner for thousands of words. I wouldn't be here without you in a lot of ways. You helped save me from me, and these babes owe a to to your love, friendship, and support over the years.

Thank you to Ian Barnes, Briston Brooks, Jeni Chappelle, Ann Fraistat, Maria Turead, Ashlee, Tera Cuskaden, and everyone I met online. Thank you for welcoming me, supporting me, and loving my disaster babes as much as I do.

Dad, I made it!! You've supported me since I can't remember when, whether it was instilling a love of stories you'd read or spinning me your own yarns. I made a promise a long time ago to never stop writing, and now here I am. I know your stories didn't make it out into the world, but I carry them with me. Thank you for always believing in me, for never making me feel like my stories were small, or silly. Your belief lit me up when I didn't know if I'd ever make it here. I love you so much, this book is your book too.

Mom, you read me amazing books that I still recall, fed my book-a-day habit, and were endlessly willing to trail behind me at the library or bookstores. Thank you for nurturing my love of words and magic. Thank you for showing me that kindness is its own kind of strength, and that small actions matter. Your unabashed delight as I've sent this book into the world has bolstered me in ways that are hard to explain.

Riggs, my partner, my muse, my creature of chaos. I can't ever thank you enough for believing in me. You've been my #1 fan for 15+ years and one of my favorite people ever. You were the first one who knew I was gonna pull this off, backed me up on every hard decision or new curveball, and without your support I'm not sure we'd be here today.

To all the BAMF Discordant Owls. You know who you are, and I'm so glad we found each other. We're stronger together. Onwards and Upwards!

Thank you as well to the Chipped Cup Collective who help made this edition possible. This queer collective of artists and writers made me feel so much less alone, and I'm so glad y'all found me.

Lastly, thank you to everyone who reads my book, tells their friends about it, or loves it.

I wrote this story for me, but also for you.

ABOUT THE AUTHOR

Jen Karner might just be a crow cleverly disguised as a human author. She never attended college, but she did the required reading anyway. A horror nerd, she loves TTRPGS, and talking about her fandoms.

Jen was raised in the Baltimore suburbs, where she devoured as many books as possible, and spent her afternoons running amok in the woods. She lives in Maryland with her partner, their dog, and a very large orange cat.

instagram.com/articulatedream
tiktok.com/@articulatedream

FIND ME ONLINE

Website: www.JenKarner.com
   Instagram: www.instagram.com/articulatedream
   Threads: www.threads.com/@articulatedream
   TikTok: www.tiktok.com/@articulatedream
   Everything else: www.JenKarner.carrd.co

CHIPPED CUP COLLECTIVE

This edition of *Cinders of Yesterday* was made possible with the support of the Chipped Cup Collective. A gathering of queer creators making a home for micro press and self-published speculative works.

The collective spirit of Robot Dinosaur Press reaches beyond its list, with members found throughout the creative world. Look for this stamp on projects by members of the collective who want to acknowledge that spirit.

For an introduction to our work, sign up to our newsletter at robotdinosaurpress.com/newsletter and receive a free anthology of short stories by RDP authors.

ALSO FROM ROBOT DINOSAUR PRESS

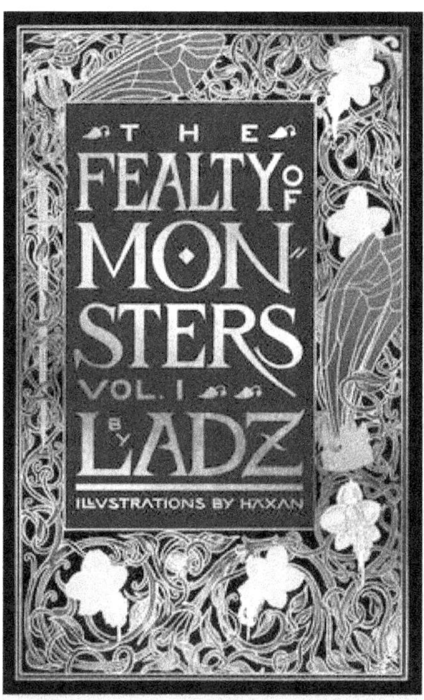

Winter 1917. After years on the run from a dangerous cult, twenty-three-year-old Sasza and his father have established themselves among the Odonic Empire's ruling class. But there's a problem: Sasza is a vampire, and vampires aren't supposed to get involved in human governance. What the aristocracy doesn't know, after all, cannot hurt them.

Unfortunately, Sasza is far more involved than a stealth vampire should be. Not only does he work to quell the rumors of the vampires' responsibility for an unsolved massacre, his lover is also the pro-proletariat Ilya, the Empire's Finance Minister, who tries to recruit Sasza into the same cult hunting him.

Then—the Emperor declares war against the Vampire States. Diplomacy has failed. Sasza quickly learns that he will do anything to preserve peace–including giving in to the monstrosity he spent so many years concealing from even himself.